For Tonya,

a survivor with a great future

HACIENDA BLUES

a novel

by

Wingate Swan

Dinah Swan

Cover Design: copyright © 2013 T.M. Roy www.TERyvisions.com
Book formatting and layout: TERyvisions
Photograph of the Author by Judith Reynolds

ISBN-13: 978-1484115800
ISBN-10: 1484115805

Leaving everything they've known behind, three Southern women embark on a the quest of a lifetime...

"Something else is going on with the locals," Pam said. "It's like they don't see us. They're afraid of something."

"If they never accept us, can you handle that?" Ali asked.

"I don't know," Sarah said.

"Besides bugs, what's most different to you?" Pam asked Ali.

"It's a feeling I never had in Mississippi or anywhere in the south," Ali said. "It feels charged here. Whatever mystical hocus-pocus they're putting out, you want to believe it. Lord, look at the high numbers of nut-nuts in Santa Fe and Taos. They read Tarot like they read *Dear Abby* in Mississippi. The Roto-Rooter man wears crystals and everybody's getting their muscles Rolfed, their colons detoxified, and their chakras balanced. It's health food, recycle, meditate, or leave." Ali smiled. "I kind of like it."

"Shit," Pam said. "I thought you were going to say sweet tea."

Their venture will test their courage, their endurance, their creativity, and their friendships...

...if they survive.

Dinah Swan has written a tale of transformation - three aging Southern belles deal with their personal histories as they create a shared home and community in a vivid New Mexican landscape. Each brings her art and love to the project of restoring an 1850s hacienda at the end of a dusty road. Plenty of challenges, including evil neighbors and a lingering ghost, bring them closer together as friends and allies. Evolving layers of love, commitment, and courage infuse the story with warmth - I really want these ladies to succeed, despite the odds.

~Douglas Walker
Author of *Belly of the Beast*

Books by Dinah Swan

Mary Alice Tate Southern Mysteries
Cana Rising
Now Playing in Cana

Women's Fiction
Hacienda Blues
Romantic Fever

1

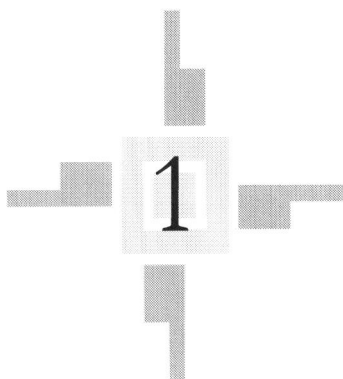

RANDALL CRANE RANG SARAH's doorbell at precisely eight PM. Through the door's beveled glass, Sarah could see him posed with one hand on a Corinthian column looking like Harrison Ford. He smiled as she opened the door and then wrapped her in a tight embrace. She took in his scent, Obsession topped with Scotch.

"You look beautiful; what a pretty gown," he said. He stood at arm's length and appraised her as though she were a Cartier diamond necklace he was considering buying.

Sarah sensed a slight change in Randall and thought likely it had to do with the fact that they recently had become sexually intimate.

I hope he isn't going to get possessive.

"You look pretty swell yourself, Randall. "Would you like a drink before we go?"

"Thanks no. The Governor awaits, milady." He touched his black tie and admired himself in the gilt foyer mirror. Then he slipped her beaded silk shawl over her shoulders.

Sarah felt pretty. The exquisite Paris designer gown, bought by her last husband and hardly worn, wrapped around her curves and made her feel like a slinky. She looked years younger than her age, which, like many Southern women, she rarely divulged. "I'm over fifty and that's more than you need to know," she'd say.

Randall offered his arm and protectively led her out the door, down the steps and across the herringbone brick drive. With mock ceremony he opened the door to his new gray Mercedes.

"You do look good tonight," he said before closing her car door. She smiled her best crocodile smile.

The Mississippi Governor's Mansion, built in 1839 and renovated twice, looked like a perfectly proportioned Greek revival cake, all white columns and Dixie charm icing. Servants abounded, liquor flowed, and the music of southern accents pattered out the open windows and across the manicured lawn.

The party, for a hundred or so special contributors who had helped elect the Governor, was Jackson's premiere spring social event. Sarah knew almost everyone there and glided among old friends, at least her late husband's old friends. Strains of chamber music puttied in the spaces between conversations. The First Lady wanted to show Sarah the improvements to the kitchen.

"You're the only one here who can really appreciate gourmet cooking design. Come look," she purred.

Sarah reverently touched the full set of copper pots and pans suspended above the eight-burner gas range. She itched to put on an apron and take a *Béchamel* sauce out for a spin.

Reluctantly she returned to the ballroom. A couple of state legislators were arguing about funding for education. She bypassed them and was sucked into a throng of wives well into their second juleps.

"Rose Burnam swears she only had her eyes done. She must think we're blind," a banker's wife said.

"Did you see Margaret Ann Dickens? I guess she'll look okay after it settles down, but she's pulled tight as a drum head," a stock broker's wife, herself a lawyer, said.

"Bless her heart. I told her not to go to that surgeon," the widow of a publishing empire CEO said.

"Which surgeon?" Sarah asked.

"Sarah, you don't need any work," the widow said. The other ladies clucked in agreement. Sarah smiled, pleased.

"Sarah, before I forget, Eddy and I want you and Randall to join us next month," the banker's wife said. "We're going to sail around the keys. Make that man take some time off and y'all come."

"Sounds lovely. I'll do what I can."

When she returned to Randall, she could tell several more scotches had passed his lips. He spoke too carefully, as though she were a highway patrol officer who had just pulled him over. He steered her around the salon toward the musicians, who upon seeing him, cut their number short and tooted a flourish as potent as a chamber quartet can muster.

Oh shit. Red alert.

"Ladies and gentlemen, as most of you know I have been courting Sarah Hunter for some months now." He grasped both her hands and faced her.

The room took on an underwater quality. Sarah heard Randall go on and on in slow motion. As Jackson's best trial lawyer, Randall knew how to spin words. The loony smiles on the faces of the listeners told Sarah that the crowd knew what he was leading up to. She saw bubbles rise as he traversed to the question: would she do him the honor of becoming his wife? Possible responses included: A. Say yes and later say no. B. Say yes. C. Swoon. D. None of the above.

Why was she being such a wimp and letting Randall Crane bully her into marriage? She had been a rebel in her youth. Had wealth and three kind husbands lulled her into complacency? She had to take hold of the situation and turn it around fast.

"Darling Randall," she said, gently placing her fingers over his mouth to hush him. "I'd be a fool to say no."

The crowd murmured and licked its chops.

She had to let him save face, the stupid idiot. She put on her best Nancy Reagan eyes. The crowd inhaled.

"But" she paused, "I cannot say yes just yet."

The crowd exhaled.

"I know you men are impatient, but I know you are also a southern gentleman." She smiled up into his face and didn't alter her expression as his hardened to flint.

The musicians, who were experienced in covering embarrassing situations, launched into a sprightly tune as throngs of well-wishers swamped them. Semi-congratulations and best wishes floated through the confused pack. Sarah heard the governor's deaf aunt ask, "Are they getting married or not?" Awkwardness flavored Sarah's next few conversations, and she retreated back to the kitchen to discuss shrimp and grits recipes with the governor's chef.

At ten she feigned a headache and Randall seemed only too happy to leave the party. However, in the parking lot, a partner in his firm, Irving Richardson, plucked the keys from Randall's fist.

"Buddy, you've had too much to drink," Irving said. "I'm gonna carry y'all on home."

Standing on the thick liriope that edged the driveway, Randall swayed.

Sarah was about to remind them that she could drive when Randall said, "Thanks Irv. You're right. Why don't you take Sarah home? She's not feeling well. I'll catch a ride later. Mickey Brewer's here; he lives in Bellhaven too." With that Randall Crane turned smartly and marched back to the party. No goodnight, no kiss my foot, no nothing.

The quiet of the ride back up to Madison ached. It felt to Sarah like being in a moving casket, hushed, soft, and muffled. Irving, pasty in the light of the dashboard, looked like a mortician. He broke the silence only once to ask if the air conditioner were too cold for her.

He told Irving to take me home. It was all planned.

As he escorted her to the door, she had to fight the urge to plead with him to understand that she had not rejected Randall, that she liked him and wanted to go on seeing him, but that Randall had put her in an impossible position with his surprise attack-proposal. Irving could understand that, couldn't he? Later, in the club locker room, he'd defend her, wouldn't he?

Standing in the dim foyer light, she watched him glide down the brick drive to the Mercedes and had an unmistakable sensation that she would never see Irving Richardson again. In fact, that she would never see any of them again.

She felt a strange mixture of fear and relief to be free of "The Randall." That's what her friend Pam called him. The feeling made her remember when she was ten and first dove off the high board: the harrowing climb, the slippery platform, the terrifying fall and the comforting knowledge that even as the chlorine burned her nose, the dive had not killed her.

✦ ✦ ✦

Sarah remembered first meeting Randall Crane. Her husband, Steven Hunter, had hired him for a Madison County real estate deal. Sarah had noticed his movie star good looks, but what impressed her was the way he had looked straight at her and listened when she talked. When Steven died while traveling with her in South America, she had chosen Randall Crane to unravel Steven's snarled estate. Randall Crane had been wonderfully supportive. He had arranged to get Steven's body back to Mississippi and eventually to get Sarah back into Jackson society.

✦ ✦ ✦

"Mrs. Hunter, I have some bad news and I guess I'd better just come out with it," he had said when she visited his office a month after Steven's heart went ka-thunk, and he fell face first into his *feijoada*. "Steven had a lot of expenses: the hunting lodge in Marshall County, the country club, the yacht, all his trips. It's a long list. And as you know he was no stranger to the boats in Vicksburg."

"He has gambling debts, too?" Sarah said. Things kept getting worse. What next, a bastard child in Biloxi?

"He loved poker but didn't know when to fold his cards. I think I know about all the big stuff."

Sarah had imagined herself buried under piles of cancelled checks, wills, codicils, stock certificates and letters testamentary, but with this news, she saw creditors and tax auditors. "What are you saying?" Her voice quavered; she cleared her throat to cover it.

"Probate will clarify everything, but it seems your home is your principle asset. You may want to sell it."

She had never liked the huge eight-bedroom, white-columned monster that Steven had bought, but the thought of being forced to sell it to pay gambling debts felt like saving Green Stamps for years only to find on redemption day that S & H was out of business. Without the faux antebellum mansion on the Deerfield Country Club golf course, could she maintain her charming friends and genteel way of life?

"I'm not selling the house," she said. Tears escaped from her eyes and tracked down her cheeks.

Randall Crane smiled consolingly and nodded. "You don't have to do anything right away. You're still in shock from losing Steven."

"I should never have let him talk me into going to Brazil," she said, taking the silky handkerchief he offered.

"His heart could have given out anywhere. He's at rest now. What's important is to take care of you."

She laid the handkerchief on the edge of the huge desk and wondered when men had stopped carrying real handkerchiefs. This was the first she'd seen in a long time.

"How much money do I have?" she said. "Be straight, Randall. Don't sugar-coat."

"Enough to live on—"

She cut him off with a sigh.

"If you're careful, frugal."

Frugal didn't sound good. It meant prudent, parsimonious, penny-pinching.

"You're not rich. You haven't been for quite some time." He sounded like he was telling her she had a mild but stubborn case of leprosy. "I'm sorry." He looked down at the manicured fingernails that tipped his hands, cradled in starched French cuffs with gold links.

"Can't I sell something other than the house?"

"Well, yes, Ma'am. But a preliminary accounting," he stopped. "The boat is an older motor sailer that will take $50,000 minimum to fix up. Many of the things Steven owned, his real estate for example, weren't paid off."

"He must have had life insurance," Sarah said. Panic leached into her voice.

"He told me he didn't believe in insurance. Carried enough to bury him."

The news whacked Sarah like a tsunami. She felt she'd hyperventilate and throw up at the same time.

"When Bernie Ebbers took WorldCom under, Steven went with him. Of course, there are still some investments and your home is free and clear." He leaned toward her, looking concerned and hopeful at the same time. His expression reminded Sarah of the time she and Steven had been sailing off the west coast of Mexico and their cheerful captain had informed them that their boat had sprung a leak.

-❖- ❖ -❖-

IN THE LIGHT FROM the foyer chandelier, the beads on Sarah's shawl danced playfully in sharp contrast to the paralysis she felt contemplating the fallout from her rejection of Randall. *Gods, why did I sleep with him?*

But she knew why. Only a few weeks ago he'd come by the house with papers for her signature. When he closed his briefcase, she'd invited him for a cocktail. They'd talked about her late husband and after a second drink about her leg.

"An Italian marble pillar from the Hotel Presidente fell on me. Earthquake," she'd said to his question. "Steven escaped without a scratch."

She liked how he asked her directly about the missing half of her right leg. No embarrassment, no awkwardness. He seemed to regard the loss as a battle scar.

"Must have been terrible," Randall said. "You walk so well with your prosthesis I doubt many people even notice."

"I've tried not to be a victim."

"I have a nephew who lost a leg in a car crash," Randall said. "He has a titanium leg," Randall said. "Can run on it."

"Young ones adjust better," Sarah said, finishing her drink. "What nobody ever tells you is that while your body changes constantly, your prosthesis doesn't. It almost never fits quite right. And then your brain creates a phantom leg which hurts, and of course there's a good deal of falling down. I'm sorry. Now I do sound like a victim."

"Not at all." Randall looked fascinated. "I think you're amazing," he said, looking straight into her eyes. "I've never known a woman like you." He reached over and squeezed her hand.

Later, in bed he'd told her that her one leg looked better than most women's two.

-⧯- ❈ -⧯-

Scratching and whining from the sunroom interrupted Sarah's recollections. "Okay, Bernie. I'm coming," she called. But as she took a step backward, she lost balance and sat down hard on the Persian carpet. Her prosthesis swiveled out in front at an impossible angle.

"It isn't fair," she wailed as her whole being gave over to uncontrolled sobs. The intensity of feeling shocked her as much as the fall. She balled up and shook, aware that such an outburst meant something deeper, even if she wasn't sure what it was.

The dog barked louder.

She adjusted the artificial leg. The fall wasn't serious, but when she rose and put weight on the real ankle, it hurt. And the arthritis in her spine, brought on by a decade of unbalanced walking on a prosthesis, began to throb.

Bernie's barks became frantic. His front paws raked the glass door with quick strokes.

Leaning on countertops, chair backs, and walls, Sarah limped to the solarium and opened the door. The russet animal hurtled past her into the kitchen as she quietly slid down the wall to the polished wood floor and wept again.

How could I not marry Randall Crane?

She wished she could still afford her therapist. Dr. Wolff had been so comforting, well worth her huge fees. Sitting on the floor with Bernie licking her tears, rough bits of the therapist's counsel flashed back like dots and dashes of a torn code: "Think about the archetypes of child, prostitute, saboteur, and victim. Do you see any repetition or pattern in your life? What is your understanding of commitment?"

Lately, her friend, Pam, had taken over Dr. Wolff's job.

I should call Pam. Her life is usually a mess, but she has great advice for other people. Sarah limped to the phone and exhumed her address-phone book from a pile of papers on her desk. She dialed Pam's number in New Orleans and as the phone rang, she wistfully traced her finger over Pam's former Jackson number.

2

AM PICKED UP ON the eighth ring, sounding as though she had been unwillingly dragged from a sweet dream.

"My life here is over," Sarah said. "I am now *persona non grata*. I just humiliated Randall Crane at the Governor's Mansion."

"Tell me. Wait. Hold on." Pam returned in seconds. "Don't leave anything out."

After she described Randall's surprise proposal and her ineffective attempt to deflect it, Sarah said, "That jackass set himself up for it, but I'm the one who gets blamed. Pam, nobody would even look me in the eye after— Hell, I didn't even say no. I said I couldn't say yes, yet."

"Why didn't you say 'no, thank you' to his 'Sarah, will you be mine?'"

"Because he surprised me, and I have good manners. It would have been rude to hit him with a flat no in front of the governor. Everybody was looking, grinning, winking and nodding."

"Are you sure you don't want to marry him?"

"It doesn't matter now. He's not going to propose to me again."

"I'm sorry."

"Steven's not dead a year," Sarah said. "I feel I'm just starting to find myself. I couldn't say yes. God, that sounds sappy."

"Pretty sappy."

"I wanted a friend, an escort, not a fourth husband."

"A man with an ego like The Randall's isn't going to want to be your escort." Pam yawned. "What time is it?"

"Close to midnight."

"I doubt he's ever been turned down for anything in his life." Pam started to giggle. "Shit. I so wish I'd been there to see it."

"It's not funny. This is so unfair. I was hanging on by my fingernails, but I was making it. Now the very people I was hanging on for have scratched me off their guest lists."

"Is that what enticing The Randall was all about?"

"I liked The Randall, I mean Randall. I didn't think I'd have to decide about marriage so soon. But you're right. Money, money, money. How am I going to stay in Jackson? Can't you see me reduced to a condominium with all Jackson's finest snickering about Steven Hunter's widow?"

There was another reason for not marrying Randall Crane that Sarah couldn't quite articulate: she had a pattern of marrying strong men who could solve her problems and maybe she needed to stand on her own two feet. She wasn't so clear about this one, but she knew she needed a plan.

"What are you gonna do?" Pam asked.

"I don't know. How the hell did I get myself into this?" Sarah rubbed her right leg to ease the phantom pain. "What would you have done?"

"Try to finesse it just like you did."

"Damn, damn, damn."

"Okay, so you've spurned The Randall, you'll have to get another lawyer, you're poor and everybody's gonna talk about you but not to you. That about cover it?" asked Pam.

"Cover it? No. I won't be invited to parties or for cruises on yachts, or to Ole Miss football weekends."

"Then they really aren't your friends anyway," Pam said. "Why do you care?"

"It's my life, Pam. Was my life." Sarah sighed. "Why didn't I just tell Randall, yes?"

"Listen to yourself," Pam said. "His behavior wasn't okay. This is not a sweet, caring man who is interested in you and your feelings."

"How am I going to get out of this?"

"What about an exotic trip? A couple of months in Paris or Venice?"

Sarah felt a sensation down her spine, a kind of primal recognition of a first-class idea. It felt like when her father suggested a year abroad in Switzerland after the cops had found her and Johnny McMillan half-naked in the back seat of his mother's Pontiac.

"Think that'd work?"

"In a few months it might blow over," Pam said. "Everyone could save face."

Sarah's mind began turning. "I'm sorry I woke you up. I'll let you go back to sleep."

"Call me tomorrow," Pam said.

"Yes."

"Did you talk to Ali today?"

"I left her a message. She's still pretty devastated."

"That bastard."

"I hear he's marrying what's her name," Sarah said.

"Amanda. Is she even of legal age?"

"Wardo is younger than Ali but he's gotta be twenty-five years older than Amanda."

"Poor Ali."

"Pam, why don't you come up tomorrow? We could cook. Maybe Ali would come over."

"I could do that."

"Yeah?"

"Yes," Pam said. "Tomorrow afternoon."

"Thank God."

"It'll be all right, Sarah."

"I don't think so but—thanks, Pam."

"I'll see you tomorrow. Get some sleep. Bye."

"Bye."

⟢ ❋ ⟢

IT WAS ONE O'CLOCK in the morning when Sarah found the snapshots she and Steven had taken in Santa Fe. A second envelope held shots of a rustic old hotel, the Hacienda Angustia.

Sarah had been to Angustia, New Mexico only once, two years ago when Steven had taken her to Santa Fe and then wanted to gamble at the Indian casino just south. She had rented a Jeep, heading north to Ojo Caliente and its famous hot springs, but never made it. The peeling *Hacienda Angustia* sign beckoned like a Dairy Queen marquee in August. She swung off the main road without downshifting, spraying gravel. A large, faded For Sale sign listed to the right: HISTORIC HOTEL ANGUSTIA AND 160 ACRES.

No one was around. Following Steven's advice to do what you want then apologize later if you have to, she took a self-guided tour. Thick adobe walls stood out against the ocean colored sky. Huge cottonwoods draped their branches protectively. Beyond the main gate and courtyard, like sentries, stood a pair of twelve-foot high carved doors. Dilapidated, the hacienda retained a charisma or attitude like a ruined lady who never forgot that no matter what, she had breeding on her side.

Sarah practiced pronouncing Angustia: Ang-GOO-stee-uh, Ang-GOO-stee-uh.

Adobes, kivas, vigas, latigos, ramadas, and fountains. No two rooms were alike and each offered a surprise: a stained glass window, a balcony with a mountain view, an inlaid tile countertop. Most rooms still held old beds, simple tables, chests and a few armoires. It hadn't given its last gasp yet, but it had inhaled and was all set to let go.

The feel was unmistakable to Sarah. Was it the air, the light, the smell? Maybe an energetic vortex, like those she had read about in Sedona, hummed nearby. As the crow flies, Angustia wasn't too far from Georgia O'Keefe's Ghost Ranch. No wonder the artist had moved to New Mexico. Although Sarah wasn't religious, she sensed a reverence about the hacienda through its solidity and age. It bore no resemblance to a Disney hotel or any of the beautiful but soulless hotels Steven had taken her to: the Whistler in British Columbia, the Broadmoor in Colorado, or the Plaza Athenee in New York City. It possessed simultaneously the seriousness of a church, the playfulness of a carnival and the magic of a theatre.

A rusting spiral staircase led to what had once been a rooftop garden. She climbed easily, clutching the twin banisters and hoisting herself up. Dozens of large, weed-choked, terracotta pots dotted the wide terrace. Low, gray mountains in the distance made her wonder where the borders of the hacienda's hundred and sixty acres lay. Across the terrace an arched door led to three rooms, connected to a hall and to one another. Feeling like she was on a treasure hunt, she forged ahead. A leaky roof had damaged the first room of the suite, but the second had a *trompe d'oile* ceiling of sky and clouds and in the third hung a huge gilt mirror. She snapped pictures of everything.

That could be restored she said to herself, gently tracing her finger over the heavy frame. In the mirror's reflection she noticed a built-in window seat looking out over the remains of an orchard. It didn't take much to imagine herself curled up with Bernie and a good mystery. The door banged shut, making her jump. When she tried to open it, it stuck tight. What might have been unnerving in other circumstances excited her. Sarah continued her tour of the timeless, labyrinthine hotel.

"We could restore this with half of what he's poured into his yachts," she said aloud, trying to see in the dimness a glazed tile mural. She made out the word, *Esperanza*. Images of priests or maybe saints looked back at her. But the mural, over twelve feet across, was not religious. Coyotes and jackrabbits were as prominent as holy men. An artist with a sense of humor.

When Sarah went to the jeep for her water bottle, the cell phone bleated. Steven had to fly back to Jackson. She left with her exposed film, but some part of her never left.

-◈- ※ -◈-

SARAH ARRANGED THE PICTURES on the table. As she padded off to bed with Bernie at her side, she hummed *We're Off To See the Wizard*.

I bet it's still for sale.

But as she slid into the huge bed on the silky peach sheets she remembered Dorothy's journey to Oz included the Wicked Witch of the West. New Mexico lay west.

3

WITHOUT KNOCKING, PAM BURST through the back door with half a dozen bulging Piggly Wiggly sacks and another from Hit and Run Liquor. On an upswing in her self-diagnosed manic-depressive cycle, she buzzed like an ion generator. She looked good in her new DK Capri pants and tube top. Her naturally blond hair, newly styled off her shoulders, glistened. Nobody believed Pam was forty-seven. Nobody thought she was even forty.

"Made great time on I-55. I got *osso buco*," Pam said, squaring away the groceries.

"Want a Bloody Mary?" Sarah asked, already pouring two.

Pam wandered over to the heavy antique kitchen table covered with photos. "What's all this?"

Sarah put a Bloody Mary in Pam's hand and began her pitch.

"I'm leaving Jackson. Leaving Mississippi."

"Permanently?" Pam plopped down in a chair at the table.

"I think so. Yes. As soon as you suggested a trip, I knew you were right. You should come with me."

Sarah knew Pam was at a vulnerable stage. She was getting almost too old to attract the kind of men she needed to keep her sense of self-worth intact. Each new man was a tiny bit worse than his predecessor. And there weren't a lot of reasons for Pam to stay in New Orleans.

"To Paris?" Pam asked.

"Not Paris. I spent nine months studying pastry at Cordon Bleu. Didn't like it. New Mexico, near Santa Fe. When Steven and I were in Santa Fe a few years ago, I stumbled on this rustic, old hotel not far from there. I fell in love with it. Arches and courtyards and fountains. Blue, blue sky."

"I went to a wedding in Santa Fe once," Pam said. "It's beautiful, but dry as face powder."

"It's the land of enchantment; says so on all the license plates." Sarah sat at the table, arranging her feet around Bernie who rested beneath it. The red Australian Heeler had been Steven's dog, but he had liked Sarah best. "Look at these pictures."

"What will you do out there?" Pam asked.

"Fix up the hotel."

"This is a hotel?" Pam examined the photos, arranging them like solitaire cards.

"Compared to Madison, Mississippi prices, it's dirt cheap," Sarah said. "I talked to a realtor this morning. It's still for sale. She said it's been on the market awhile with only one low ball offer. The heir refused it."

"Wow. It looks like a mission."

"And Pam, it'd be perfect for your pottery. Santa Fe is close, and you know how art-crazy it is."

Pam sorted through the pictures again, this time more slowly. Sarah paused, letting the beauty of the land work its magic.

"It's beautiful, it's obtainable, and it's completely new to us," Sarah continued. "Whatever emotional baggage we drag out there won't matter. The second half of our lives can be different, better."

"The chance of a lifetime?" Pam asked.

"Exactly." Sarah finished off her drink. "What do you think?"

"Two things. I want to think about it, and I want us to cook. I'm starving."

"And Pam, I want to ask Ali to come too. Just like we talked about doing."

"We talked about retiring together. If all the husbands were dead."

"Okay, it's a little sooner than imagined, but I have a good feeling about this. And there are no husbands to worry about."

"Hold on. First, I'm not sure I can do this and second, I don't know if I can live in a house with Ali. I love her and we go way back, but she can be so obsessive. Did you know that right after she shits, she flushes the toilet? Then she wipes herself and flushes again. Sometimes twice. That's taking hygiene too far, if you ask me."

Sarah smiled, knowing Ali would have similar reservations about living with Pam's fixations. Ali's compulsions seemed based in feelings. Her bathroom habits notwithstanding, she also was super sensitive to sound. Somebody else's throbbing stereo or barking dog turned her into a crazy woman. Pam, however, valued order. Socks and panties had to be lined up in color coordinated rows. Spices needed alphabetizing. Pictures needed squaring up.

"It's not a house, Pam," Sarah persuaded. "It's a hotel on one hundred sixty acres. We can remodel it into separate quarters. There's space for a huge studio, great light. You could make those hand painted tiles."

"How much money are we talking about?" asked Pam.

Sarah detected a shift in Pam's tone after Sarah mentioned a huge studio. "That's why we need Ali. But not just for her money. She's our best friend, and she needs us."

"I think you might be right about Ali," Pam said. "Going out west would be good for her."

"It's not just Wardo dumping her. Ali hasn't had a job in a year," said Sarah.

"Well she's a theatre director," Pam said. "Only three in the entire country work regularly, and they're gay, British and of course, they're men."

"You know what I mean. She needs a change."

"She's vulnerable."

"Are you saying yes?" asked Sarah.

"I'm saying I want to talk about it," Pam said. "Let's get her over here."

The irony of starting a new life down the yellow brick road to New Mexico with a plastic ankle was not lost on Sarah. If Bernie was her Toto and Pam her Scarecrow, that made Ali the heartless Tin Man. Ali needed a new heart, that was certain. They didn't have a lion, but then none of them lacked courage.

The two women launched into a cooking frenzy, Pam whirling around Sarah and the *osso buco* with *risotto alla Milanese* with the ease of a competition skater.

"Did you get a hold of Ali?" Pam asked, as she sautéed garlic and onion.

"I left another message. Considering what her rotten husband just did, I doubt she's up for a fancy meal," said Sarah, poking the veal with her finger to test its doneness. "You think it's done?"

"You're the pro. I'm just a very good cook," Pam said.

"It's done."

"Let's call her again after we eat, Pam said. "We don't have enough for three."

As they dined on the delicate veal with a very nice Cote du Rhone at the twelve foot dining table, Sarah replayed the fiasco with Randall Crane.

"I tried to call him several times," Sarah said. "He won't take my calls."

"His ego's wounded so he has to reject you and make all his friends do likewise so he can feel okay about himself. It's all your fault, bitch." Pam drained her glass. "Classic controlling shit."

Sarah thought about this. All three of her husbands had certainly controlled the relationship, but of course, she had wanted it that way. Hadn't she?

Ali still wasn't home when they phoned her again. Sarah left a message: "Pam is up here spending the night. Call us. We'll be up late. We love you."

After another bottle of wine and a brandy each, the women lounged in Sarah's huge master suite. Pam lay on the Chinese rug and finger-combed its fringe.

"Are you seriously serious about going to New Mexico?" Pam asked.

"Yes. I know it's impulsive but—"

"It's the impulsive part I like best," Pam said.

"Pam, this is deeper than the Randall mess. I need to make a change."

"I could go with you."

"Yeah?"

"Maybe."

"Really?"

"I'd miss you too much if you left." She started on the other edge of the rug's fringe.

"You really think you could come with me?" asked Sarah. She felt excited like a novice tight rope walker stepping out under the big top.

"I am practicing my Spanish right now. *"Donde esta el bedroom-o?"*

"It's New Mexico. They speak English."

"Great, so do I."

Lying in bed, Sarah couldn't sleep. Things were moving fast. It was as if as soon as she announced a wish, it came true.

Now I really have to go. What if it's a mistake and I ruin Pam's life? Maybe Ali's too?

She dozed fitfully, her anxiety sitting on her dream like a sumo wrestler on a lily pad.

4

ELIEVING THAT IF PEOPLE are full of good food, they are far more agreeable, Sarah cooked all the next morning, determined to leave Mississippi with her two best friends. She was excellent with fish and had been trained by one of the best, Chef Claire LeMoyne, who was also the meanest, most intimidating teacher Sarah had ever had or heard of. She remembered the class with LeMoyne and grouper.

"This fish was not caught; it was assassinated," Chef LeMoyne said, nose in the air. "Bury it." Her wrist flicked twice.

The dozen students kept their heads down.

"Madame, it swam this morning," LeMoyne's assistant said with his heavy French accent. "Eet ees fresh," he pleaded.

LeMoyne ignored him and pinched the fresh asparagus which lay on the marble counter. "And the asparagus also swam this morning? Pat them dry immediately."

Always demanding and hyper-critical, Chef LeMoyne knew her haute cuisine. "The flame is too high," she said, wagging a finger in the direction of the wine and tarragon white sauce Sarah was tending.

She was right. Sarah turned it down with a wary eye on the teacher, who was now inspecting the honed edges on the knives.

Years later, Sarah rarely cooked without thinking of the exacting, contentious Chef LeMoyne.

⸙　✳　⸙

THE THREE CLOSE FRIENDS sat on Sarah's glassed-in verandah, attempting to ignore the swan dive of the barometric pressure. The Platters crooned about monogamous true love.

Ali looked thin, but even fifty years and bouts with anorexia hadn't made serious inroads on the good job Mother Nature had done. Her Spanish heritage was securely woven into her appearance even if she denied it. She wore beige linen slacks and a matching top with a Mandarin collar piped in black. On her feet were trendy Jimmy Choo sandals.

Over the phone, Sarah had recounted the story of Randall at the Governor's Mansion, but she saved the New Mexico proposal for lunch.

At two in the afternoon, Sarah served the grouper crusted with pistachios, fresh asparagus crowned with mango sauce, and rice in a white sauce with wine and tarragon. A chocolate torte dripping with raspberry sauce lazed in the refrigerator. Madame LeMoyne would have found little at which to turn up her nose.

"It's a seductive proposition," Ali said after Sarah had detailed her plan. "But I still don't understand the difference between running away and getting a new start." She leafed through the pictures of the hotel as she nibbled her fish.

Sarah could see the nervous jiggle of Pam's foot under the table.

"Why is running away from a dead-end marriage so bad?" asked Pam.

"Pam," Sarah said. Sometimes she hated Pam's bluntness.

Ali stiffened and quashed her tears. "There would be no professional theatre opportunities for me out there. Equity theatre doesn't exist in New Mexico." She poked at the rice, employing a divide and conquer tactic.

Pam changed the music to another oldies CD; the Everly Brothers harmonized *Devoted to You.*

"Aren't you always telling me there aren't any opportunities for a female director, period?" Pam asked. "Then it won't be a change at all." The more Ali resisted the idea, the more Pam seemed to be for it.

"It's a big commitment, Ali," Sarah said. "If you don't want to, we'll look for another partner. It's okay either way," said Sarah, but she didn't mean it. She knew she was manipulating Ali with reverse psychology. The Hacienda Angustia dominated Sarah's thoughts. She felt like a mother who had lost her child, but had one clue as to her whereabouts. The exodus started with a need to escape Randall Crane, but it had developed a life of its own and she couldn't let it go. And now, though Sarah wasn't sure why, the adventure had to include her two friends.

"I didn't say no. I'm not going to let y'all go out to the wilds of New Mexico alone," Ali said. She took a big bite of fish to signify her serious acceptance.

-+- �֍ -+-

ALI, BORN ALEGRIA LOPEZ Calderon, always made it clear that she was not Hispanic and certainly not Mexican. Her mother's family four generations ago had made a desperate flight from northern Spain to the Mississippi coast, and her father was born in Mexico, but they were all American now. She had called herself Ali since second grade.

Years ago, in a theatre interview with a New York newspaper, in an effort to steer the interviewer away from her Spanish roots, Ali brought up the women's movement, crediting it for saving her from anorexia. The reporter had implied that Ali landed her first off-Broadway directing job because she checked the Hispanic box, and the not-for-profit theatre needed to demonstrate cultural diversity in its employment practices. Ali nearly choked on her anger. After the interview the woman had asked her, off the record, if women directors had to fuck producers to get jobs.

"Is that what you think I did?" Ali had said.

"I think you're using feminism, and I don't like it. You're a mess. Look at yourself. You do everything men accuse us of and then want the support of women. I don't know why you hate yourself so much, but I wish you'd leave your sisters out of it," the woman had said and then disappeared into the Spring Street Subway Station.

"You fucking butch dyke," Ali said to the cavernous stairway after the woman was out of sight. But the accusations rattled her, making her feel lonely and making her examine her life in New York.

Not long afterward, she had married Howard Barnes, whom she met on a visit home to Jackson. They married in the Catholic Church, pleasing her estranged family. She moved to Memphis, miscarried twice and divorced. Sarah, using her husband's connections, had gotten Ali a directing job in Atlanta. Ali credited Sarah with saving her life.

-¤- ✵ -¤-

AFTER LUNCH, PAM DIRECTED the loading of the dishwasher. "Plates shouldn't touch the silverware," she said, carefully pointing the knife blades inward, corralling the forks and fronting the bin with short spoons. It looked like a segregated cutlery infantry.

"Why?" asked Ali.

"They'll jiggle and scratch."

Sarah, who at all costs wanted to avoid any kind of argument on this particular day, changed the subject before Ali tried to prove that the forks wouldn't attack the plates or fight with the spoons. She knew Pam would cringe if she saw how Sarah loaded the dishwasher.

"I wish you'd stay, Ali," Sarah said. "We can have a pajama party. You can each have your own bedroom. You can each have two bedrooms."

"I need to go home," Ali said. She sponged the countertops.

"It's going to pour. I-55 is horrible in the rain," said Pam, as she sprayed Windex on the same countertops and wiped with precise, overlapping strokes.

"Come on Ali, Pam's staying another night. If you leave, we'll talk about you," Sarah said, knowing that Ali liked to be coaxed.

"You said I had twenty-four hours to think about this, and I need to go home and think," Ali said. She blotted a spot of water on her slacks.

"The twenty-fours can start tomorrow," Pam said.

"Okay, I'll stay, but I have to pick up Mary Catherine Clark's birthday present at Everyday Gourmet," Ali said. "I ordered her a Gail Pittman lemonade set. Y'all come with me."

"I still feel the effects of two bottles of wine and the same number of brandies," Pam said. "I need a nap, unless you want me to poop out at eight o'clock tonight."

"I'll go. I adore Everyday Gourmet," Sarah said. "Ali, why don't you take the north bedroom, the apricot one?"

"You said I could have two rooms," Ali said.

"I did, didn't I? It has the sewing room. That's two rooms."

"I suppose Pam's in the rose room," Ali said.

"I am and I'm going there right now. Don't go shopping or do anything fun without me," Pam said as she climbed the stairs.

✦ ❈ ✦

"Do you think Pam's jealous of Gail Pittman's success?" Ali asked Sarah as they fought Jackson traffic. "They're both ceramicists from Mississippi, were at Ole Miss together."

"They do completely different stuff. Kilns are about all they have in common," Sarah said.

"I wish Pam would actually produce those tiles she's always talking about," Ali said.

"She made some. I saw them," Sarah said, darting into a parking spot.

"One firing."

"They were beautiful," Sarah said. "I don't think she's jealous of Gail. I think Pam's conflicted. Remind me to stop for some fresh thyme."

"Can we go by Maison Weiss after this?" Ali asked as they entered Everyday Gourmet where inviting homey smells greeted them.

"If you don't tell Pam we did. She'll feel left out," Sarah said.

"She could have come."

"Okay, but don't make it sound like we had any fun."

✦ ❈ ✦

During cocktails the heavens opened, pelting Madison, Mississippi's broad lawns with a sweet, cleansing rain. About seven their dinner ritual began. It was Sarah's kitchen and she

28

was the trained chef, but Ali was used to directing everything and Pam was used to fighting for turf with both of them. They had been making dinner together for over ten years.

"You aren't going to put anchovies in that, are you?" Ali said.

"No, of course not," said Sarah.

"Didn't you just tell Pam you were adding them?"

"Let me worry about the sauce. Go set the table."

"I did. And I put on the music."

The Diamonds were aiiiiii yi yi yi yi-ing through their 1957 hit, *Little Darlin'*.

"Arrange the flowers for the centerpiece. The garden is full of stuff," Sarah told Ali. "It'll be wet. Put on those clogs."

"*Ja whol, mien commandant.*" Ali saluted and goose-stepped out.

Through the window, Sarah watched Ali pick her way among the dripping vines, zinnias, cosmos, and buddleia. Even in the oversized rubber clogs, she looked like the dancer she was. Sarah almost expected a *tour jeté* over the lilies.

The Diamonds reached the spoken part of the song and Sarah and Pam, talking into wooden spoon mics, joined in.

At nine they began the journey through the five courses. Midnight found them sprawled in Sarah's enormous formal living room finishing off their third bottle of wine. They looked cozy among the comfortable antiques tastefully paired with modern art. It had been a long time since they had gotten together like this.

"I don't know why you hate musicals. You are so good at directing them," Sarah said to Ali.

"What was the one you did at New Stage? Wait, I know." Pam parodied Ezio Pinza, singing *Some Enchanted Evening*.

"You cruel bitch," Ali said. "How could you mention that? I will not repeat its name. Pass that bottle over here."

"The reviews were good. I'd remember if they were bad," said Pam.

"Ali never gets bad reviews," said Sarah. She slurred a little and didn't care.

"Because Ali never gets any work," echoed Ali.

"That Latino theatre in D.C. wanted you to direct that Puerto Rican's play. What's his name?" said Sarah.

"They think I'm a Latina or a Chicana or something-a. Eduardo always thought I should push that but—" She stopped at the mention of the never-to-be-mentioned husband who had jilted her.

They were quiet; the air conditioning exhaled around them. Pam and Sarah each fixed their gaze on the heavy crown molding and studied it as though there would be a test in five minutes.

"He moved in with a twenty-two year old girl," Ali said. "I came home from an interview for a job I didn't get, and he was gone," Ali said.

Pam crawled over to the sofa and took Ali's hand. "Don't do this to yourself."

Ali had called both of them after the dynamic, gorgeous Eduardo, called Wardo, dumped her. But now she seemed to have forgotten that her friends already knew the brutal details and she drunkenly trudged through them again, like directions through a swamp, tricky and rife with potential for disaster.

"The big surprise was that I thought all our friends would be disgusted with him and rally around me. She's a baby. She can't even talk yet. But he's invited out, she escorts him, and in another month nobody will remember I was his wife." She covered her face, chewed fingernails pressing her brow.

Sarah tried to imagine the humiliation piled on humiliation that Ali felt. Most painful was that suddenly Wardo wanted children. Ali was well past childbearing and her earlier attempts had ended in miscarriages. All Sarah could do was mentally chant, *"this is earth school, these are lessons, and it's not supposed to be fair."* Wardo wasn't worth all this anguish.

"You'll be in New Mexico and this will seem very silly and far away. You'll say good riddance," Sarah said. She thought but didn't say that Ali had always known Eduardo, three years her junior, satisfied the Latin stereotype. Ali worked six weeks at a time away from home. What did she think was going to happen?

"I called him. I'm so pathetic," Ali said.

Sarah didn't know about this.

"He said he hoped we could be friends." The barely scabbed wound split open.

Sarah wanted to shake Ali and tell her that she couldn't love a man who treated her as he had if she had any self-respect. But that led down the rabbit trail that exposed the truth that Ali probably didn't have much self-respect and it wasn't going to help to say it. It also made Sarah think about Randall Crane and her own vulnerability and blindness.

"New Mexico, the Hacienda Angustia will heal this, Ali. I know you'll feel what I felt there. We're in tune that way. It's a portal, another chance." Sarah grabbed the pictures of the hotel and put them in Ali's hand. "Through this huge arch—look at those beams—is the front courtyard. That's the fountain. There's a chicken sitting in it in the picture, but she'll move. All the rooms open out onto courtyards or balconies. So much light."

"Do you think they have therapists in New Mexico?" Ali asked. She was drunk now, her ideas skating fast and slipping down. "If I buy this hotel I can't afford a face lift."

"Honey, you won't need either there," said Sarah.

Music filled the room. Loud, the stereo pumped out Joe Cocker's *Unchain My Heart.*

"Up, everyone up," Pam said. "Enough of this misery and woe. That South American SOB is not going to ruin our party. First thing we do when we get to Mexico is have a cleansing ritual." Pam danced about the room.

"*New* Mexico," chorused Ali and Sarah.

"We'll freeze his picture in ice, and he'll never get it up again," Pam said. Ali flung herself into the infectious rhythms as though the sound and movement could extinguish her misery.

"Does that work?" asked Ali.

"Yes, but only if you don't care if it works or not," Pam said.

Sarah danced sitting, favoring her sore ankle and honoring her fake one. Before the earthquake that claimed her leg, she had been a superb ballroom dancer. Even Ginger Rogers would have been hampered by a prosthesis.

The cut on the CD changed to *Shelter Me* and they moved deeper into the music, with abandon writhing, shaking, gyrating and laughing. Sarah imagined them dancing like this around the kiva fire in the big hacienda courtyard. Wild women under the stars, coyotes howling in the distance, their boots—no, their bare feet—flying on the hard-packed dirt. Drums would replace Cocker. Later, Ali could play her guitar and they'd sing a sad *corrido* that they learned from Linda Ronstadt's CD. Their creativity would soar. The little town of Angustia would embrace them. The *tres chicas blancas* would triumph.

As Cocker rasped *With a Little Help from My Friends,* and the women danced and sang and drank past two AM, a tiny thought needled Sarah. She had not told Pam or Ali that *angustia* meant woe in Spanish.

5

PAM HAD MET ALI in 1994 through the Mississippi arts matriarch, Charlotte Butterfield.

"We seem to be the only women here without men," Pam had told Ali, after Charlotte introduced them at one of her salons and then was called away to cultivate a major potential donor.

"Yeah, even the men have men here. What do you do, Pam?"

"Whoring mostly, what about you?" Pam said.

"Ditto. I'm a director."

Pam smiled and recognized that Ali was one of those people she liked instantly.

"Movies?" asked Pam.

"I wish. No. MFA in Theatre. Remember plays? You may be too young."

Pam smiled and nabbed two fresh flutes of champagne from a passing waiter. "Want to sit on the terrace?" They had gone on for almost an hour about Pam's teaching at Millsaps and trying to do art, the student who was trying to get her in bed, and the new anti-depressant medicine Pam was trying.

Ali was reporting on her miscarriages and divorce from her first husband, Howard, when an extremely beautiful older woman burst through the French doors and approached as though she had been looking for them.

"I'm hiding from Aunt Charlotte. Can I join you?" She didn't wait for an answer. Pulling a half-smoked Marlboro 100 Light and a box of matches that said OUTRIGGER, WAILEA RESORT from her bag, she said, "Keep on talking. I'll catch up. I'm Sarah Hunter."

In minutes three conversations were arcing over one another with perfect ease. Pam told them about trading boyfriend Tol Tollison for Haley Black, letting Sarah interject how she had remarried after being widowed. Ali told them wild theatre stories that had Pam laughing uncontrollably. When they began to finish each other's sentences, Pam wasn't surprised. Then they discovered that among dozens of common interests, each loved to cook.

"Are y'all free next Friday?" Pam asked. "We ought to cook something together."

-ᵻ- ✻ -ᵻ-

THEY BECAME CLOSE FRIENDS quickly through cooking gourmet meals together. Pam named them the *Chefs de la Lune*, chefs of the moon. Each time they met to cook, one of them filled in more details of her history. At the first meeting Sarah had told them about her amputation.

"The physical therapist told me how phantom limb pain persists making parts that aren't there ache and tingle as though rats were chewing the toes that aren't there. Of course it's all happening in my brain, and the drugs for the pain don't necessarily help and aren't good for me. He warned that the stump changes, but the prosthesis doesn't, so the prosthesis isn't ever very comfortable. But what he didn't tell me was how other people would treat me. That was the biggest challenge."

"Which was?" Ali had asked.

"Repulsion. They say it makes no difference, but you can tell missing parts unsettle most people."

"Isn't there a Dorothy Parker story about a woman with a fake leg?" Pam asked.

"Not Parker," Ali said. "I can't remember. A Southern writer. Doesn't a man steal her leg?"

"Flannery O'Connor," Sarah said. "*Good Country People.* Joy Hopewell tries to seduce a Bible salesman and he steals it. Must be a lesson in there somewhere."

The second week had been Pam's turn. "My history is so dull," Pam said. "I never had anything amputated."

"What about your family?" Ali asked.

"No, I don't think they had any either."

"No, idiot," Sarah said, "tell us about them."

"My parents are dead. I have one brother who lives in California." She stopped. End of story.

"When'd your parents die?" Ali asked.

"I was in high school. They were killed in car wreck," Pam said. She cut herself another sliver of pumpkin cheese cake.

"And?" Sarah asked.

"And I had to raise Timmy. We were supposed to go live with an aunt in Riverside, but I was almost eighteen so we ended up staying in our house. The aunt became our legal guardian, but she didn't really want us living with her." Pam finished off the cheese cake in three rapid bites.

"God, Pam, how'd you do it?" Ali asked. "I can't imagine. You were still a girl."

They peppered her with questions. How had she raised a brother who was in junior high? Did the aunt support them? What did the kids at school think?

"Was anybody else hurt in the car accident?" Sarah asked.

Pam's expression darkened and her whole body seemed to shrink.

"I'm sorry. That was tactless. Don't," Sarah said.

"The car ran off the road. It rolled, and they were dead." She circled her right index finger in the crust crumbs. "My mother shouldn't have been with him. He had to go to San Diego on business. He sold tires, wholesale. At the last minute she decided to go too. There wasn't anybody to stay with us, but she had left us alone before—for a day." Pam started to turn one hand over and over in the other.

"How long were they going to be gone?" Ali asked.

"Four days," Pam said. "Of course it turned out to be much longer." Her expression sardonic, she continued. "She couldn't leave him. They couldn't stand to be apart, so she left us. I always imagined she was kissing him, distracting him, when their Ford left the pavement. She did that a lot."

Pam gave them one of her 'life sucks' shrugs and refolded her napkin.

Ali and Sarah were rapt.

"A few months later Timmy stole a car which was only the first step in a colossal acting-out routine that finally ended him up in a mental institution." She shook out the napkin and folded it again. "Somehow he thought their deaths were his fault. They thought he was retarded." She smiled weakly as though that were the end of the story.

Later, Sarah and Ali talked about Pam. They wondered how much guilt Pam had about her brother, and if he was the reason Pam had not married and hadn't wanted children.

WHEN PAM HAD GOTTEN a good job offer in New Orleans, it was Sarah and Ali that Pam most regretted leaving.

"How long have we been cooking together?" Ali asked at their last dinner before Pam's departure for the Crescent City.

"Six years," Pam said.

"Seven," Sarah said.

"And you're going to break us up after all this time?" Ali asked.

"You'll hate New Orleans," Sarah added. "It's hot, crime-ridden and we're not there."

"And it's below sea level," Ali said without bothering to point out the implications for flooding.

"But I'll have a regular pay check and be able to do my art," Pam said, but she was genuinely touched by their efforts to persuade her to stay.

"This move have anything to do with that guy, T-Bone or Bo-bo or Bo-Peep?" Ali asked.

"'t Beau. It stands for petite Beauregard. A Cajun affectation. Yes. He wants me to live with him," said Pam. She stirred the risotto intently, not looking at Sarah or Ali.

"Did you put white pepper in that?" asked Sarah.

Pam shook her head, no. She knew that Ali and Sarah were both thinking that if Pam wanted to shack up with yet another boyfriend, it wasn't their business.

Frank Sinatra's *Come Fly with Me* wrapped them in surround sound and Pam sang along.

"Pammy, you don't know him well enough for that. He might be another Gary or Dale," said Ali. "Was Gary the one who stole your car?"

Pam ignored the question. "You're feeling smug because your Latin lover, Eduardo finally proposed," Pam said.

Ali waved a heavy diamond ring.

"Greg, not Gary took the green Chevrolet," Pam said. "t'Beau might turn out to be Jack the Ripper. There are no guarantees; I remind you, little miss fiancée of Mr. Señor Macho."

"Let's eat," said Sarah.

One minute into the pear and almond salad, Ali said, "Wardo was born in Argentina, but his mother is American and he's lived most of his adult life right here in the ole USA. He no more has that wife-whore value than I do," said Ali, jabbing the air with fresh baked foccacia to defend her man.

"My point is that nobody knows. You hope, make promises and things change. Dr. Jekyll becomes Mr. Hyde," said Pam.

"If that's true, being careful isn't going to help," said Ali.

Talking with her mouth half full of new potatoes, Pam said, "No. That's why you have to be extra careful. Stereotypes about Latin lovers exist for a reason."

"What about petite Cajun stereotypes?" Ali shot back.

"Or maybe he doesn't change at all," said Sarah, tugging the topic back into the main channel. "My first husband, Arnold, never did. I wanted him to, and he resented that I married him and then wanted him to become somebody else."

"Right away?" asked Ali.

"We were married twenty years," Sarah said. "No, not right away. I was twenty-one and he was twenty-five. I assumed we'd grow up, grow together, even grow old, but at least grow. He got richer, but not broader."

"Pam, we want you to be happy and we're going to miss you. That's all," said Ali.

"God Almighty, Ali, New Orleans isn't very far away. Pass me the salt. He has this great apartment in the French Quarter ten minutes from the institute, and he's a powerhouse in the sack. I'm over forty. What else is there to say?"

"That doesn't need salt," Ali said, passing the shaker.

"A powerhouse? Really? How?" asked Sarah.

Pam couldn't remember when the three had started sharing bits of intimacies about men. Over the years the different stories with different men had created a mosaic. The details were out of order, but the collage taken as a whole formed an accurate synthesis for each of them.

"He reads erotic stuff from back issues of *Yellow Silk*," Pam answered.

"For ideas?" asked Sarah.

"No. Out loud. He likes themes too," said Pam, finishing her tenderloin and thinking how much she'd miss Sarah's cooking.

A murmur slid through the group. "Hummmmm?"

"Themes, like cops? Does he wear costumes?" asked Ali.

"Howard didn't even want lights on for sex," said Sarah.

"Eduardo might go for a fantasy scene if he thought it was his idea," said Ali.

"No cops yet, but I was Jungle Girl last weekend," Pam said.

"I take it that jungle girl and boy don't need much in the way of costumes," said Sarah. She laughed.

"It's hard to imagine the Amazon Basin around the corner from St. Louis Cathedral," said Ali.

"Not if it's hot and you leave the windows open," Pam said. "'t-Beau is fun. He makes me laugh. He could have younger and prettier women, but he wants me. And he has a big dick."

They laughed and pushed back from the table. Pam hoped the part about t'Beau choosing her over other women was true.

"You aren't ever going to get married?" Sarah asked Pam as they cleared the table. She had asked this question before.

"I've been married," Pam said.

"For a week when you were seventeen," Ali said.

"Please. Five months. It was my trainer marriage."

"Well when are you going to have the one you've trained for?" Sarah asked.

"Frankly, I don't see that it makes lots of people—women—very happy. A fat NEA grant or a McKnight is a better bet."

Pam hoped Ali wouldn't start in about children. Pam didn't particularly like children, but knew that saying so was impossible. Women who chose not to have children were selfish bitches, especially to women who couldn't have them.

"You can't cuddle a fellowship," said Sarah.

"So far, I have plenty of cuddles. But, but," she said,

"I think that when we're old we three should live together in a big house in the country. The husbands and boyfriends will all be dead by then. We'll hire younger women to do the heavy work. I'll throw pots, you can cook, and Ali can write a book about our lives."

"An opera," Ali said.

"I'm older than you are. You'll have to wheel me around," Sarah had said.

"Older doesn't mean squat," Ali said. "I could have a stroke and you'd have to ladle oatmeal down my throat."

"The younger women we're going to hire can do that," said Sarah.

"Ladling and wheeling—both job requirements," Ali said.

"*Tempus fugit.* That's the point," Pam said.

"*Carpe Diem,*" Sarah said.

Ali paused, struggling to think of an appropriate Latin rejoinder. "*Veni, Vedi, Vince?* Wait, I know." She raised her half full wine glass. "*Amor, salud y pesetas y el tiempo para gosarlos.* Love, health, and money—and the time to enjoy them."

They toasted.

"The boys used to say, *Amor, salud y pesetas, y mujeres de grandes tetes,*" Ali said. "Love, health, money, and women with big tits."

"That's boys for you," Sarah said. "Always in the moment."

⚊⚌⚊ ✳ ⚊⚌⚊

PAM MISSED SARAH AND Ali so much that she called and visited constantly. After ten years, they were still best friends. The National Endowment for the Arts smiled on Pam, but boyfriend number fifty-or-so left, chucking her into a murky depression. Ali arranged to direct a show in New Orleans so that she could stay with Pam. When Sarah was widowed for the third time, Pam moved in for a month. When Ali married the sexy Argentine who knew she was too old to have babies and three years later decided he wanted a family, Sarah and Pam were there to catch her. Now there were no men in their lives and they were going to drive to New Mexico, fix up an old hacienda and live together.

What could possibly go wrong? Pam wondered.

6

"SARAH, I CAN'T GO," Ali said. "There's a job at the Kennedy Center. The artistic director called this morning."

Sarah's stomach bottomed out. She was going to lose the hacienda if she didn't move fast. Who else could she ask?

"Great, Ali. Directing what?"

"Staging an American musical revival—three shows. Sarah, I'm sorry. This is a big break for me. I'll get my foot in the door. Any work at the Kennedy is going to pay off," Ali said.

"It's okay, Ali. It's my dream, not necessarily yours. You can visit."

"You're still going?" asked Ali.

"My gut tells me to have faith and go. So, yes, I'm moving to New Mexico, as soon as possible. *Carpe Diem*, remember?"

Ali talked on and on explaining, but Sarah cut her off. "You didn't really commit, so it's just not meant to be. I have to go. I'll call you later." But after she hung up, the idea of going without Ali depressed her. The vision of the trio facing the Wild West together had manifested, and it was difficult for Sarah to release it.

She called Pam, but she didn't answer.

The Madison Real Estate Agency promised to send over a rep that afternoon. The broker was firm about her six percent commission. Sarah didn't have much liquid cash. Completely inexperienced in budgeting, it was hard for her to tell how much money she'd need, how much the hacienda would suck up.

Pam called back just as Gail Fletcher-Porter arrived to appraise the house. "You still in?" Sarah asked Pam.

"Yes, but I'm having trouble getting out of my lease."

"You said it was up next month," Sarah said. Her tone betrayed her frustration.

"Well, I was wrong," Pam said. "I forgot I signed up for another year when they announced the rent was going up $150. If you signed another contract, you got the old rent. Shit. I'm sorry Sarah. I don't know what to do."

"I'll call you back. A realtor is here."

"Sarah. Maybe we should slow down. Let's do this, but not be in such a rush," said Pam.

"Somebody else will buy it. This man, Ortega, low-balled and was refused. He's going to make a better offer."

"You don't know that for sure."

"I do too. The realtor, Judy Grace told me," Sarah said.

"Well duh. Of course she did. She wants you to make an offer. She's a saleswoman on commission," Pam said.

Sarah watched Gail Fletcher-Porter purse her lips and twist her hands in impatience. When she saw Sarah watching her, she flashed a Dinah Shore grin and waddled her hands in the air in a way that said he knew how demanding people on the telephone could be.

"I've talked to her several times," Sarah said. "She thinks this Mr. Ortega won't care about the historical value or the natural beauty and will do something to ruin it. She knows him. She even tried to tell me how much he offered so I would have some idea of what to offer."

"Which is illegal. Why do you trust her?" asked Pam.

"She said we could stay with her in Santa Fe if we need to, and she raises yellow labs."

"Dogs are credentials? Never mind."

"Pam, sometimes you have to leap. I think this is one of those times," Sarah said. "I'll call you back." She hung up and turned to the realtor.

"Thanks for coming out so quickly, Ms. Porter," Sarah said, holding her hand out to shake. Her accent spun her words like pink cotton candy.

"My pleasure. It's Fletcher-Porter, but please call me Gail." She was a tall, Joan Crawford sort of woman about Sarah's age whose shampoo and set never budged. Her overly convivial manner was more like that of a Cadillac sales person than a realtor. Enameled bracelets clanked between the clacks of her high heels on the tile floor.

"Shall we take a tour?" Sarah asked.

Gail blazed through the eight bedrooms and bathrooms, across the deep verandas, into the gardens and back to the huge kitchen. "As you must know, high-end properties take some time to sell. I'd like to get a brochure made right away while the flowers are blooming." Then she looked as if she caught a whiff of something dead. "Such a large kitchen." She touched her cemented hair.

"I'm a chef. We like lots of space," Sarah said, mystified why any woman would criticize her kitchen's size.

"Do you cater?" Gail asked.

Suppressing her growing irritation, Sarah said, "No. I'm a Culinary Institute trained professional chef. We're not comfortable in small kitchens. Spoiled rotten, I guess."

Gail gave her a you-should-have-known-better look.

"Unless you sell to a chef, you're not going to get your money out of all this." She flourished a hand toward the hanging rack of stainless and copper pots, the six-burner gas stove with pasta faucet, and the oversized Sub-Zero fridge. "The master bath is a little small too, but it's a very nice home." She grinned again. "I'll call tomorrow with a figure I think we should ask for it," she said. "And of course, you'll need to sign a contract."

Small? You could dance in that bathroom.

"Your agency sold it to my late husband just a few years ago." Soon as she had spoken Sarah wondered why she had. So the agent would know Steven had bought it without Sarah's approval or so she would know Sarah was being loyal to the same agency?

Why am I sucking up like this? She doesn't like my house and has done zero to make me feel comfortable. Sarah thought of Randall's proposal and recognized a similarity with the present situation.

"I'll check in the computer and see if there's anything useful. You'll be re-painting the porch, I suppose," the agent said.

"No. I won't be doing anything. I'm moving to New Mexico. You'll have to get what you can as is."

"New Mexico," she repeated as though it were one of those small countries near Russia that nobody could ever remember.

"Family out there?" she asked, trying to look sincere. Leaving the south was intrinsically repugnant to Gail Fletcher-Porter.

"Yes. Family out there," Sarah answered.

The family I'll create is already there waiting for me. I have faith.

The agent's shiny new Japanese car purred away, and Sarah's faith turned to pudding. She called Pam, but there was still no answer. She tried to decide on prices for the furniture, most of which was practically new from better Jackson and New Orleans furniture stores, but couldn't. She tried to whip up a soufflé for dinner, but contaminated the frothy eggs with an oily spoon. Cooking wine was the only liquor in the house. Without Pam and Ali, Sarah felt as deflated as her soufflé.

"When I'm crazy I cook and if that doesn't work, I meditate," she told Bernie, who looked dubious. "Meditate, meditate, meditate."

Bernie rolled, turning his back to her.

"A few *ohms* wouldn't hurt you either, devil-dog."

* ❋ *

AFTER THE EARTHQUAKE, DURING the months of hospitals and doctors, Sarah had acupuncture for pain management. Dr. Lee had advised her to learn self-hypnosis or some kind of meditation. His theory was that her spirit needed healing as much as her leg.

"Tension in the body directly translates itself to tension in the mind and vise versa. You must free your mind as we work to heal your leg," Lee had said in his lilting accent.

She had compounded into a practice a mélange of techniques that worked for her, however unorthodox. It centered on sitting in a meditative posture and talking to ancestors, angels or the Virgin Mary. She added spirit guides when she found out about them. The meditations included all the trappings: candles, incense, bells, crystals, talismans, a six inch tall plastic Virgin of Guadalupe and a celadon Quan Yin. She had no deep affinity for traditional religion. The earthquake that took her right limb had given her spirituality, or at least the quest for it. She questioned if it were a good trade.

"Beautiful bright angels, guides and powers of the universe of which I am part, help me. I need a sign that this move is right. Ali can't go and maybe Pam can't go until next year. You know all that. My heart says go, but my head says caution. Truth is, I'm about to give it up. I don't think I can do it alone. If you'd give me a sign, a synchronicity, three butterflies, three any things. Please." She tried to clear her mind and stop all thought.

The thoughts didn't stop, but they calmed, and behind her closed eyes an early western movie played. In it she walked in slow motion through the labyrinthine old hotel, touching special treasures, an eagle feather, a kiva ladder, an Indian rug. A guitar played. She wore a long pleated skirt and a soft leather shirt cinched with a silver concho studded belt. She was strong, independent, an aging cowgirl earth mother connected to the land. Outside the hacienda, she wandered through abundant gardens with six-foot high tomato plants that talked to her as a blood red sunset did a full gainer over the horizon. In the vision she had two good feet.

She stood up. The meditation pose had numbed her leg, and she stumbled, sending a sheaf of newspapers to the floor. HACIENDA REALTY (HABLAMOS ESPANOL) jumped out from the open paper. A trio of happy red parrots, the company's spokespersons, decorated the ad. It was too late to call, past seven, but impulsively, she dialed anyway.

"Hacienda Realty, Margarita Sanchez," said a voice with a Mexican flavor rich as chocolate and cinnamon.

"You're still there. Good. I have a house I want to sell," said Sarah.

MARGARITA SANCHEZ COULDN'T HAVE been more unlike Gail Fletcher-Porter. She arrived the next morning in a lemon VW Bug. Swathed in an embroidered dress that made her look like a *piñata*, she barely reached Sarah's shoulder. And *Señora* Sanchez had a contract in her hand.

"I can sell the furniture too, if you want." She adjusted her green mini-reading glasses. "Who referred you to my agency?" she asked, tucking the signed contract into her tooled leather bag.

"No referral. I had a feeling," Sarah said, afraid to explain that she had asked for a sign and the powers of the universe had immediately popped Hacienda Realty's ad in front of her. She was trying to buy Hacienda Angustia. If that wasn't a sign, they didn't exist. And to top it off, the logo consisted of three parrots. She had requested a synchronicity of three. *Voila.*

The realtor nodded, her lids half closed as though she were reading Sarah's mind.

"Would you like something to drink?" Sarah asked.

"I'd love some iced tea. With mint if you have it."

"I have fresh mint." Another sign. This woman asked for mint; Sarah's herb garden was legendary.

While Sarah made the tea, Margarita wandered about the kitchen, caressing objects and praising Sarah's antique patent medicine bottle collection. As they drank, Bernie sat under the voluminous skirt of the realtor, who seemed to have a solution for every problem.

"My nephew, Manny, has a used furniture and moving business. You mark what you want shipped to New Mexico, and he'll take care of it. He'll sell what you leave behind. You'll get much more than if you auction it." She pulled out a cell phone and after a brief consultation in Spanish with Manny, it was settled. "He can come tomorrow morning."

Sarah knew all her old friends, really Steven's old friends, were going to think she was insane to leave Mississippi, and she didn't want them pawing over her possessions, picking up Limoges and Waterford for a song while they were thinking it.

It hardly surprised Sarah when Margarita told her that she had grown up in New Mexico. "My father grew chilies in the south, near Hatch, but we visited *Tia* Gonzales in the north at Rancho Milagro. You will love it there." Margarita scratched Bernie's leathery ears exactly the way he liked it. The furry dog rolled on his back, exposing his speckled belly. Another sign.

Surely the gods sent this mentor to me, this helper who will deliver me.

They were finishing their tea when a car bearing Gail Fletcher-Porter and a young male photographer drove up the circular drive. The realtor, who wore a crisp pink suit bounced across the front verandah like a tennis ball. Her co-worker, in baggy khakis and a wrinkled Oxford cloth shirt, dragged ten paces behind.

"I was going to call you as soon as—I'm sorry, I've engaged Ms. Sanchez instead," Sarah said, ineffectively deflecting the awkward result of her impetuous decision. The situation felt strained, like wearing a favorite dress that mysteriously had become too tight.

Gail Fletcher-Porter's mouth pruned-up and the cords in her neck tensed. She argued that her agency and Sarah had a verbal agreement, a contract, whereupon Margarita produced the signed contract with Hacienda Realty.

"You should have called first before you drove all the way up here," Sarah said. "I'm sorry."

Margarita waggled her head in agreement, her eyes bobbling in and out of focus behind the green glasses.

"May I speak to you alone?" Gail Fletcher-Porter asked Sarah.

The photographer, a sallow, pimply skinned young man, rolled his eyes toward the ceiling and shuffled away to the car. Margarita used the powder room just down the hall.

Alone in the kitchen, Gail Fletcher-Porter said in a voice like scalding grease, "That woman is thoroughly unprofessional. She has been before the Board of Realtors for dozens of violations. She has no contacts. She's never sold a house in Madison. She can't get you a good price." Her volume dropped. "She sells trailers, for God's sake." Her eyebrows and forehead lifted a good two inches and stayed up.

"But yesterday you said you didn't like the kitchen and the porch was peeling and ten other things. I think someone who likes the house can sell it better."

Bereft of further arguments, the realtor spit, "She's the Mexican Realtor; she's not our kind. Surely you can see that."

"I've signed a contract. I don't think the Mississippi Board of Realtors would take kindly to your trying to break it," Sarah said. She smiled sweetly and opened the door for Ms. Fletcher-Porter.

⚜ ❈ ⚜

IN TWO DAYS A colorful Hacienda Realty sign with three red parrots graced Sarah's front lawn. Manny made a deal to sell everything Sarah didn't want to keep. He'd ship to New Mexico everything she couldn't part with.

"You put the red parrot sticker on everything you want sent to you. I don't know what it will cost until I weigh it," he said.

It sounded vague and uncertain. Faith, she had to have faith.

Late at night, she sat nestled in the window seat in her bedroom, running the numbers. If the Madison house sold quickly, it would be easier. But high priced real estate didn't usually turn over fast. She created scenarios with Ali in and with her out. She juggled it every way, but without cash from the sale of her house, she needed Pam and Ali's money or a miracle. *Un milagro.*

"It's a test," she told Bernie. The Heeler leaned against her. "All tests require letting go, choosing the unknown path. I know I'm meant to buy this Hacienda." She closed her tired eyes and prayed for strength from the Virgin de Guadalupe whose picture Sarah had discovered marking a page in a cookbook she was packing. She had taken it as another sign.

The phone rang. She caught it on the seventh ring.

"I found two guys to sub-let the rest of my contract," Pam said. "They're both named Paul. I have to get the manager to agree to let them paint the living room with Sherwin Williams' Apricot Lily. They'll charge me, but I'm free."

"*Gracias*, Virgin," Sarah said.

But when Pam found out that Ali was directing musicals in Washington and not investing in New Mexico, she backed away.

"I figured it out, and we can do it without Ali," Sarah cajoled. "It'll take longer, that's all."

"We can't afford it, can we?" Pam asked.

"Things are not so expensive there and labor is cheap," Sarah said. "With Ali it'd be easier, but Pam, we can do it. I'm going alone if I have to, but I really want you to come. I have such a strong feeling. This will change us, make us grow, give our spoiled, complacent lives meaning."

"That's not like the Chinese curse, 'may you live in interesting times,' is it?" Pam asked. "Interesting usually means war, famine, strife or disease."

They discussed it to death, Sarah wearing down Pam's fears, corralling her arguments and packing them away. It was going to be a lark Pam didn't want to miss.

In the back of her mind Sarah dimly recognized that most of her obsession with the hacienda resulted from the fact that the move was the first major decision she had ever made without a man either approving or directing her choice. But she believed in theory that 'you are what you do, not what you say.' If she wanted independence from ideas and traditions that no longer served her, she had to act like it.

"Worst case scenario, we can sell it and leave," Sarah wooed. "It's real estate, not bonds. Worst, worst case, we'll lose a few thousand, the price of taking a chance."

They agreed to drive in caravan to Angustia on May 1. At seven New Mexico time, Sarah called the Santa Fe realtor and made an offer. By noon a signed contract had been faxed back and earnest money wired. She was terrified and had never been so hopeful in her life.

7

ALI REALIZED THAT SHE was a last minute replacement for a big name director who had wiggled out of his contract. But being second choice at The Kennedy Center for the Performing Arts was like being given a vintage convertible in perfect condition except that the top wouldn't go down. Not bad.

The Kennedy Center paid her expenses, but the hotel room was so small and dark, that she paid to upgrade. She didn't know anyone in D.C. The Kennedy staff for the Festival of the American Musical was efficient but brusque, and they had lives that didn't include her. She bought a bottle of Johnny Walker Black and was slightly hung over for the first rehearsal of *West Side Story*.

Ali and the artistic director had agreed on a classical interpretation of Bernstein's work. No modern-day gang warfare. The Sharks and the Jets would fight their ancient battle with chains and switchblades. The other fights in the production were subtler, but just as lethal.

Three days into rehearsal emotions were running high, swamping the tidal basin of egos.

"No puedo endurar la boca de Juan," the actress playing Maria said to Ali. Juan had bad breath.

"I beg your pardon?" Ali said.

The actress looked shocked. "You don't speak Spanish? I thought you were Puerto Rican. I'm Puerto Rican."

"Sorry. I'm American." Ali wasn't about to go into an *I'm Spain-Spanish on my mother's side and Mexican on my father's.* She was a professional director and the play was in English. The actress, Constansa Cantillano, however, seemed to believe the management had guaranteed her a Hispanic sister, someone who would understand her character from a Latina point of view. From then on, anything Ali did that Constansa didn't like became a skirmish in the larger landscape of racial war. In comparison, Juan's halitosis didn't amount to a hill of *frijoles.*

Other factions quickly formed along sexual preference and ethnic or racial lines. The dance captain for the Jets was a muscled black named Jamal. Ali thought his effeminate flourishes were a joke until they persisted, and she felt compelled to say something to him. After all, her name was going to be on the program. She couldn't have a nellie Jet flirting with the Shark boys. Jamal pretended not to understand what she was talking about and asked her to specify each move that offended her and direct a substitute move.

At the end of week one, the Arab-Americans were harassing the Jews. The less attractive women hated the pretty ones, with a sub group of heavier ones hating the thin ones. Older gays were threatened by younger gays. It was *Lord of the Flies*, not *West Side Story*. Professional on stage, the off stage acrimony brimmed, always threatening to spill over. And it was always Ali's fault.

She first responded to the tension with a bout of anorexia. Then insomnia and sinusitis joined anorexia, triplets designed to make anyone crazy.

I am a professional and I am coping.

Ali thought the choreographer, a balding old jazz dance man with the unlikely name of Tony Perkins, had done a smash job with the dance. The scene of the high school hop at the gym seamlessly pulsed with dramatic tension as the lovers from two worlds met and fell in love.

If only the disparate worlds of the actors could likewise meld.

"You have me so far upstage that no one will even see me. I'm Maria. I'm the star," said Constansa in a barely subdued shriek. Her burning eyes and contorted fists made Ali suspect that Constansa was on some kind of uppers. Ali reached for her psychologist hat and tried to reassure the insecure actress that she was indeed visible and that special lighting was going to pick her out of the crowd anyway.

"Not only that, but the dress you wear in the scene is made of a shimmery organdy. The other girls are in flat, non-reflective fabrics," Ali cajoled.

"It makes me look fat. That shimmery crap bunches around my waist like a tornado. My agent says I don't have to wear it."

Ali looked at the classy rehearsal hall of the Kennedy. Everything you needed to create the best theatre art in the world. How had she drawn the cast from hell? Was everybody in the big time so lacking in confidence, so apprehensive? She knew she had blown it by being nice, by being considerate of these egomaniacs' unrelenting and competing needs. She wanted to shake Constansa, let her have it; to tell her that she had a major role in a top-level production that was going to give her national exposure. She should be helping the process, not sabotaging it. Sabotage. Ali thought that maybe she was the saboteur. She had little ability to discriminate between the time to kick ass and the time to kiss it.

Ali smiled and pulled Constance aside a step. *"Tu eres una hija de puta que chingas todo esto. Una ladrona. Una consentida, chipilona, quien siempre estas llamando la atención y nunca das nada a cambiar.* Get your fat ass in place or you're fired. *Por favor."*

It was unclear whether Constansa was more surprised that Ali did indeed speak Spanish or that she had called Constansa a talentless bitch who fucked the whole process, a thief, a screaming spoiled brat who took without giving.

Constansa snapped and dove on top of Ali, sending both beneath the director's desk. Twisting, pinching and pulling they writhed, Constansa getting the better of Ali until Constansa raised her head fast and slammed it into the desk. She was out cold.

A catfight such as this was unprecedented at the Kennedy and the artistic director was only interested in damage control. He offered to pay Ali her full contract if she would resign and disappear.

"She was completely insubordinate, refused my direction and attempted to disrupt the process with her insane demands every day. She attacked me. And you want to fire *me?"* Ali asked the artistic head honcho.

"What's new?" he replied. "She has a better contract than you do. Ali, you can see you can't go back to that cast."

"I could sue both of you." Ali couldn't believe she was coming out as the bad guy.

"Yes, but that would cost you for a lawyer, and it's not a sure thing. And if you did that, I couldn't pay you immediately. This is a sure thing," he said. "Take the deal, with my apologies. I'll keep my eye open for something else for you."

Yes, I'll bet you will. Summer stock in Montana directing Moon Over Buffalo *or a tour of* Oklahoma *in Zaire.*

"This is murder. My career is over after this, surely you can see that is a sure thing," Ali mimicked.

"I chose you for this job," he said. "I'm sorry, Ali."

Ali knew further argument would be fruitless. Better to grab some dignity and exit. She wasn't a saboteur; she was a sell-out, a prostitute. She was about to break out in sobs.

"Thanks," she said, opening the heavy office door. The dense carpet hushed her footsteps. She felt insignificant and thought that if she passed a mirror, likely her image wouldn't even reflect. She walked the twelve blocks to her hotel, filled the tub, and got in with Johnny Walker.

✦ ❉ ✦

SARAH PACKED NIGHT AND day. Pam called every eight hours for reassurance until she was packed, and cutting bait seemed less of an option. Manny's bright red parrot stickers dotted the house. Sarah walked among them, using her cane to save her overworked leg, and appraised the value of her life thus far based on the objects she'd elected to keep: the comfortable furniture, extra right legs, sterling flatware for twenty-four, photographs, oldies music and every gourmet cooking implement imaginable.

She dressed slowly that evening, almost ritualistically, for a small *bon voyage* party being held in her honor at Charlotte Butterfield's grand home in Woodland Hills. She suspected it had more to do with her deceased husband than with her departure. She slipped on the muted chartreuse linen sheath, careful not to wrinkle it. Pair after pair of earrings were tried and rejected. Amethysts ringed with gold won.

But the coming evening made her anxious. It was so final. Once Charlotte Butterfield had bid you goodbye, you couldn't stay.

At the party she did her best to stay sober and explain to those who seemed interested why she was leaving Mississippi for New Mexico. She knew that to most of them, regardless of the cause, it was a little like leaving the Garden of Eden for the ninth circle of hell. The shock of losing Steven and therefore needing a new landscape would have worked except that everyone knew about her and Randall Crane. No one mentioned him. In a fit of paranoia, she imagined him down at Bravo's on a Friday afternoon saying nasty things about her in retaliation for her refusal to marry him. And of course she couldn't talk about the deeper urge to move on and change her life.

"But Sarah, don't you need your people around you?" asked Belle Toulme, an octogenarian who somehow missed that Sarah was no longer in Jackson high society.

"I'm scared, Belle, but I'm more scared to stay here. I'll end up watching soap operas and drinking a bottle of wine every day."

"Well, that's not so bad," said Belle.

"My family is gone. This world will just get narrower and narrower for me."

"But doesn't that happen everywhere when you get old?" Belle set aside her plate, leaving a half-eaten stuffed artichoke heart.

"I don't think it does in New Mexico, but don't ask me how I know that." Sarah smiled, trying to look like she was game for anything. She thought of tough and talented Annie Oakley.

"And I won't be alone," she added. But Sarah knew that to Belle and everyone present, women outside the protection of kith and kin were definitely alone. Then she remembered that Annie-get-your-gun-Oakley mostly wanted to be with Frank Butler.

Charlotte interrupted with a speech that eulogized the philanthropy of Steven Hunter and by association of Sarah and announced how Sarah would be missed in Jackson.

"Y'all know there's not a better cook in Hinds or Madison County," Charlotte oozed. "I am going to miss your shrimp remoulade." Like confetti, others flung the names of dishes Sarah was known for: barbequed lamb, Saltimbocca, Key Lime pie, Coq au Vin. She felt she was at her own culinary wake. When the waiter passed with chilled champagne, she snatched one and downed it.

If Ali or Pam had been there it would have been tolerable, but she was alone among acquaintances who had already written her off. No one even mentioned visiting. Slowly it occurred to her that stay or go, she'd never again see most of the people in the room.

Shit. If this is a disaster, I can't come back.

Sarah was too drunk to drive home. Charlotte had her man, Lawrence, chauffer her. No sooner had she entered the house than she ran into the glass coffee table, barely escaping a fall.

"You hate me because I'm not staying," she shouted to the quiet house. "I'm selling you." The house mocked her with a sinister silence not unlike movie haunted houses just before poltergeists catapulted the china. "You're trying to kill me. But I'm getting out." She sank into the sofa and leaned back. Her twisted prosthesis poked out at a forty-five degree angle. Everything hurt. "Bernie? Here, Bernie." The dog ambled in, winking with sleep. "Bernie, we're leaving, going to the Promised Land," she slurred badly. "I always hated you, house. Steven bought you, not me. You have bruised me, tripped me, burned me and sucked me dry, but I'm escaping." She hiccupped. The red parrots grinned at her in the yellow glare from the porch. They looked happy but not especially trustworthy. Bernie sat beside her and was there when she awoke with first light, hung over and sick with doubt.

"What have I done?" she whimpered to Bernie. He whimpered back, but he mostly wanted his kibble.

⊹ �֍ ⊹

MANNY SANCHEZ'S RED AND yellow truck with a rainforest of cheerful parrots on the sides could hardly have been more incongruous in Sarah's upper crust driveway. His crew lacked English, and she suspected they lacked green cards too. When they began loading her boxes of whisks, knives and graters she interrupted them, "No, I'll take those with me in the car. I may need them."

If this is a catastrophe, I can always get a job at a nice truck stop, and it'll be easier if I have my Wusthof knives.

A worker replied in Spanish, but ignored her request. He took the box of kitchen tools, placing it in the van.

Protests or finding Manny to translate seemed like more trouble than simply removing the box. When the men moved into the library to dolly out the cartons of books, Sarah climbed the truck's ramp. As she lifted the carton of kitchen implements, a shriek came from behind an armoire. She had surprised one of the movers, who scrambled over furniture and boxes to escape her. He quickly disappeared into the house muttering in Spanish what sounded like an invocation—lots of *Nuestra Senoras*.

"Joaquin is from a village that holds a superstition about *cojos*—people with one leg," Manny said. "He thinks the missing part is looking for its body, like a ghost, and he don't want to be around when the leg shows up. I'm sorry, Mrs. Hunter."

"Maybe he's right. I'll stay out of the way," she said, clumping behind Manny, who removed her box of expensive knives from his van. "I'll be in the sun room if you need me," she said.

She pushed open the solarium door and froze. In the dazzling light an apparition rose before her sun-shocked eyes. Brilliant rays glared, fanning out behind a female figure dressed all in white. Was it the Virgin Mary or maybe Joaquin's limb-hunting ghost? It spoke.

"Sarah, I drove all night. Can I still come with y'all?"

Dumbfounded, Sarah blinked and the apparition turned into Ali.

Alarmed by Sarah's silence, Ali added, "I can speak Spanish. That might come in handy in New Mexico."

"That might be useful in the living room," Sarah said. She hugged Ali's boney shoulders and knew she must have been fighting anorexia again. Wounded, dumped, childless and absolutely wonderful Ali. Sarah knew Ali would bloom in Angustia. They all would.

We are so lucky to have this chance. Seriously, what could go wrong?

8

ALTHOUGH THEY DECIDED TO drive in caravan in case someone had car trouble, Pam zoomed ahead, her green Miata convertible vanishing across the Mississippi River and into the Louisiana haze. Sarah hoped Pam's change in plan wasn't a sign of rebellion.

Sarah's Toyota and Ali's Honda caught up with her at a truck stop near Monroe. A sexy but worn Texan, bound for wherever Pam was headed, had just about wormed his way into the shotgun seat.

"Are you out of your mind? You can't pick up hitchhikers, Pam. It's not the sixties," Sarah told her, glaring at the man who had skulked away when Sarah and Ali pulled up.

"He's not a hitcher. We had lunch together at the counter," Pam said. "Why are y'all driving so slow?"

"You're not Thelma or Louise and anyway you know what happened to them," said Ali.

"And you're not my mothers," said Pam, slamming the car door.

"Please come inside with us while we tee-tee. We need to stay together," Ali said.

Sarah pulled her car into the shade and rolled all the windows down. Bernie wouldn't leave and it was unlikely anyone would risk getting in the car with him. She caught up with Pam and Ali, and as they passed Pam's lanky, would-be passenger, he touched his hat and said, "Ma'am." It wasn't hard to see why Pam had been attracted. Tanned skin covered sinewy muscles. His hips were narrow, eyes deep blue. All he needed was a hot shower.

Ali got a veggie sandwich on whole wheat and Sarah, pastrami with extra cheese. Pam, who had already eaten, watched in silence, circling a napkin through a puddle of water on the table.

"It looks like it's going to be hard to stay together all the way so why don't we pick towns on the map for stops," Sarah said, sounding like a schoolyard peacekeeper. She couldn't imagine what was pushing Pam, but she didn't want to risk a confrontation when going back was still an easy option.

"Let's meet tonight outside Dallas at the motel you booked," Pam said. "If you're not there by seven, I'll be in the restaurant."

Ali started to protest, but Sarah cut her off. "Fine. Call one of us on your cell phone if anything changes. You have the directions to the motel?"

Pam nodded. She was tearing another napkin into strips and then rolling each length into a ball. They looked like miniature cannon balls.

"Pam, is everything okay?" Sarah asked. She forced Pam to look her in the eye.

Taken by surprise at the question, tears filled Pam's eyes and slopped over the rims. "Leaving was harder that I thought it was going to be. And every mile I drive it seems crazier to be doing this." She started organizing the paper balls into rank and file.

"I thought you wanted to do this. I was the doubter," said Ali, who was picking the vegetables out of her sandwich with her long fingernails and eating the green things in small bites. The untouched bread looked forlorn as if it knew it was already garbage.

"I did. But that was before I sold my bed and left my cat with two queers from Plaquemine Parrish."

"Pam, I bought the place on your commitment—"

"I know, and I'm going. You asked me if everything was okay. I told you," said Pam. The scrawny napkin she was using to swab her face dissolved, leaving white gauzy bits plastered to her cheeks.

"Let's get there first and look it over before you fall apart," said Ali. Without a mirror, she touched up her lipstick.

"Okay. See you in Dallas." Pam found her sandals under the table and slipped into them.

"Wait," said Ali, catching her arm. "You look like a paper mache project that went very wrong." She cleaned Pam's face of napkin debris and then hugged her.

"See you tonight." Pam squeezed out of the tight gray booth. A few heads turned as she slipped through the crowded truck stop and out into the bright daylight.

When Ali and Sarah pulled back onto Interstate 20 heading for Dallas, neither Pam nor the sexy drifter were in sight.

━┼━ ✳ ━┼━

PAM PULLED HER EYES left to check out the man sitting behind the steering wheel of her car who said his name was Kenny Hatch. He had volunteered to drive. He did look a little like

Brad Pitt from the *Thelma and Louise* film. She eased her tongue over her teeth and wondered what it would be like to have sex with him.

"What do you suppose your friends were so worried about? Do I look like a serial killer?"

"What do serial killers look like?" asked Pam.

"You know what I mean."

"You haven't heard that picking up men in truck stops is potentially dangerous?" asked Pam, pulling hard on the straw in her empty thirty-two ounce Dr. Pepper.

"Sure, but didn't you say y'all were on an adventure? Starting over in the Promised Land? Fear and adventure don't go together to me."

"Land of Enchantment, not necessarily of promise. And fear is fundamental to adventure."

"You got no reason to be scared of me. In case you're rethinking this."

"I'm not, but you gotta know that I'm not going to be able to take you past Dallas," Pam said. "It's not worth it to me to upset them that much."

"That's okay." He smiled at her, looking for a moment like a young Paul Newman.

She wondered again what he was like in bed and imagined her hands sliding down his muscled back as he lay on top of her. He looked like he'd be a good kisser.

Pam had thought his companionship would make her less nervous and less sad. She had barely managed to get out of New Orleans without hysterics. Leaving felt like giving up, not like moving on. A dozen failed relationships and a job that never turned into a career haunted her. Leaving Mr. Bingle, her cat, with Paul and Paul had seemed like a good idea a week ago. Now she felt like Judas. Tears welled in her eyes, and she clapped on her sunglasses to hide them.

"It's okay," he said, pulling the Miata off the interstate at the next exit. A Dairy Queen loomed beside a gas station, a perky red contrast to the dusty countryside. A hand-lettered sign in front read, DRIVE THRU WINDOW CLOSED. COME ON IN WHERE IT'S KOOL. He left her in the car with the motor and AC running and returned a few minutes later with a milkshake too thick to drink. "Drink this. It's called a Blizzard. You'll feel better," he said.

Tears continued to leak from Pam's eyes but she took the Blizzard.

"I stopped at a Dairy Queen in Shuqualak, Mississippi one time," Kenny said. "I had no idea how to pronounce Shuqualak. After I got my chocolate sundae, I asked the girl at the counter, 'How do you say the name of this place?' She looked at me careful and then said real slow, 'Day-ree Kuh-ween.'"

Pam choked on the shake as she made the fiddly transition from tears to laughter. Ten miles later when he asked, she told him some of her life story. He was a good listener, looking over at her every few minutes like he was getting ready to sketch her.

"You want my childhood, the ten minute marriage or the story of how I had the bad judgment to move in with a man named t'Beau, who after a month sold my jewelry to buy Saints' season football tickets?"

"Tell me about your parents."

"They're both dead."

"No, tell me one story that you remember that tells about them."

Pam felt dual compulsions. She wanted to tell this stranger some secret, to share a confidence, but talking about her mother and father frightened her.

"When I was about twelve my little brother, Timmy and my parents and I went on a vacation to a lake somewhere in Arkansas. Timmy is mentally challenged. He's not a retard, but he's slow. He's also very sweet and irritating. He thinks aliens live among us and that he wrote some of Bob Dylan's later songs. He's planning to sue Bob." Pam circled the straw around and around the bottom of her DQ cup summoning the courage to go on.

"When we got to the lake my parents put us in one cabin, and they took another. We ate meals in a dining hall, and we played baseball a lot. At the end of the week my parents came and picked us up. I think we saw them twice all week. Once they were necking on the porch of their cabin and another time they were swimming. Mama waved at us as if we were neighbors. I guess we were."

"At least they picked you up," Kenny said.

"They didn't dislike us, but they didn't know what to do with us. They were totally devoted to one another. Children must have been an upsetting surprise to them."

"Maybe I should have picked the ten minute marriage story," Kenny said.

"You can have it for dessert." Pam felt relieved to leave stories about her parents. "I married at the tender age of eighteen an equally vacuous teenager who said he wanted to make me happy. He had no means of doing so, but the parties and wedding presents distracted me. It lasted five months. Interestingly, he turned out to be a kleptomaniac, and I felt compelled to return the crap he stole."

"What'd he take?" Kenny accelerated to pass a Swift truck.

"A pink neon surf's-up sign, a bullwhip, 800 golf balls. I think returning a fake coat-of-arms from a country club pushed me over the edge."

"Why'd you take the stuff back?"

"Then, I thought it was because I didn't want him to get arrested. Now, I think it was an attempt to control him."

"You never got married again?" He didn't look at her when he asked.

"No." Her answer came easily; she knew he wouldn't quiz her about kids.

"See, from my way of thinking, you were smart not to marry. You knew in your gut they wouldn't work out. Me, I always got married. Did it three times. Wore me out," he said.

Kenny, who had worked jobs from trucker to cement finisher in every state in the South, had a shy sweetness about him. Pam could see how people could take advantage of him. He only looked like Hud. He'd been a real cowboy as a youth until busting broncs caused a disk to herniate. Back on the highway with Pam behind the wheel, he told her one story about himself.

"You were a model?" Pam asked.

"I had a tiny role in a movie in Texas. Somebody saw me and decided they could make money on me."

"Fashion? What kind?"

"Lord 'a mercy, they wanted me for photos, advertising. But by the time they got through shaping my eyebrows and chiseling my cheekbones, I didn't look like what they'd picked me for in the first place."

"What'd you look like?"

"A girl with muscles."

"I bet you were very popular," said Pam. She could imagine a spiffed up Kenny Hatch selling Calvin Klein underwear, sagey-tough men's cologne or almost anything leather.

"Do you know how you look? To women, at least?" she asked.

"Women come on to me pretty often. I 'spect I know the message I must be giving off. Lots of them want to take me home and put me in the shower, in their bed, and under their thumb."

"In that order?"

"Pretty much. Sometimes the shower's last," he said.

Pam thought his story was sounding more and more like a country and western ballad and that probably half of what he said wasn't true. But she couldn't deny the feeling he elicited from her. Sidelong glances at his chest through his tight shirt with a missing button gave her a familiar itch.

"I got a place in west Texas," he said. "I have to evict the current resident, but it's mine long as I pay the taxes." He changed the radio station like a local that knew what was where.

She wondered why he was telling her this. Was he obliquely pointing to a future rendezvous? And if he was doing some unconscious projecting, what was the subtext of her part of the conversation? She accordion pleated her DQ cup.

"That's where you're headed?" she asked.

"Near Lubbock," he said. "To get my property, I need to pay a lawyer a retainer. I had the money but, well, that's another story. I don't have it anymore." He shrugged in the boyish way of those not particularly bothered by adversity.

Aw shucks, Pam thought, forcing herself not to think about his nest in the west where likely ex-wife number three was squatting. She focused on the hair on Kenny's muscled forearms.

"What are your girlfriends like?" he asked. "Did I see one had a missing leg?" They were talking easily, like airline seatmates on a long flight with little to lose by telling the truth.

"That would be Sarah. They're my best friends. I just hope we can all live together in one hotel."

"A hotel?"

"We bought one outside Santa Fe. Or near Santa Fe. Somewhere. We don't plan to run it. We're going to live in it."

He smiled and raised his eyebrows slightly in an approving glance. "How'd Sarah lose her leg?"

"Earthquake in Mexico. Her last husband, Steven, was doing some kind of business deal and part of their hotel collapsed. He was probably off with one of his girlfriends while marble columns were squashing his wife," Pam said.

"You never trusted him," Kenny said, playing mind-reader.

"You're right. He was always hitting on her friends too."

"But she wouldn't leave him," he said.

"I don't think she ever knew about the women," Pam said. "He loved her too. Don't get me wrong. He was good to her. Steven needed more than most people."

"He said that?"

"Yes. The one time he came onto me. Sarah thinks it's better for women to be married to men who can take care of them. It's weird because when she was young, she was a hell-raiser according to her own report."

"What do you expect tamed her down?"

"She's a chef. Bona fide and certified. Thirty years ago nobody would hire a woman, so she got married. She's been married three times."

"Three marriages can tucker you out," Kenny said.

"She just narrowly escaped doing it again. It's one of the reasons for this move."

"Why didn't you tell her about her husband running around on her?" he asked.

"I never could decide if it would help more than it hurt."

"It's not good to be the one with the bad news," he said.

"I think they used to kill the messengers if the news was bad," said Pam.

"Then I bet a lot of them changed the news."

The sun bore through the windshield as they smiled in unison. A hundred miles later the traffic thickened and the vaporous cloud of pollution and dust that sheathed the Big D metro area came into view. She didn't want Ali and Sarah to know that she had picked up Kenny, but she didn't want him to leave yet either.

"There's a big truck stop 'bout a mile up ahead. That'll do," he said, wiping out the dilemma in two easy sentences.

As she pulled in, the same gloomy feeling she had leaving New Orleans took over. Kenny had become an interesting person in the last three hundred miles. Even in his seedy condition he was a better man than t'Beau or her last beau had been.

"Come in and I'll buy you a cup of coffee," he said, pressing his thigh against the car.

Gigantic trucks hissed and crawled about the tarmac, a feedlot for semis.

"I better not. Better get on," she said, thinking how much she was starting to sound like him.

"Maybe I'll see you on down the road," he said.

She knew he meant the road of life, but she couldn't help thinking in more concrete terms.

He touched her hand, held it, gently pressing his thumb into her palm. She looked up at him and knew if he told her there was a motel close by, she'd get them there before rush hour started. But he tipped his hat, said, "Thank you, Pam," or "Ma'am"; she wasn't sure which, and sauntered away between the steaming monster trucks.

She felt sick as she blazed onto the crowded freeway. *Shit, in less time than it takes to say James Dean, he'll be with some babe in a red Mercedes headed for the nearest Best Western. And I let him walk off because I have to meet two girlfriends.*

9

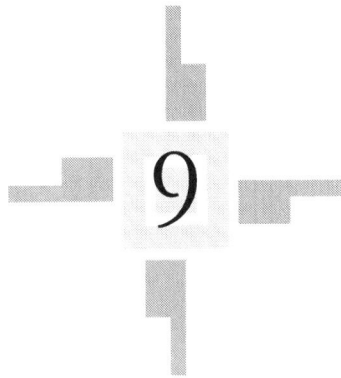

SARAH AND ALI SCANNED the packed Texas Steakhouse, but couldn't locate Pam. They checked again at the motel desk and returned to their room. "I'm not waiting all night," Ali told Sarah. "I'm starving. Let's go eat."

Ali helped Sarah over the uneven pavement back to the restaurant. "She'll waltz in hours late and explain, 'Heavens, I had no idea it was so late,'" Ali imitated Pam's voice. "I was fucking loser number three hundred's brains out and lost track." Ali let the Steakhouse door bang shut behind her.

Sarah laughed and struggled up on to a bar stool to wait for a table. Ali ordered two white wines, and the bartender began an elaborate explanation of the county liquor laws.

"I have to join a club to get a drink?" Ali asked the bartender, who looked like Mr. Dillon's sidekick, Chester.

"They's funny liquor laws in this county, I guess. Liquor's not legal by the drink 'cept in a club." He wiped the counter that didn't need wiping and surveyed Ali's cleavage.

"How do we join?" asked Sarah.

"Sign up right here." He pushed a register at them and extracted a blank membership card. He smiled a Texas-sized smile and then stroked his sparse moustache and goatee.

"How much?" asked Ali.

"This is extortion," said Sarah. "We're passing through. We want a glass of wine, not a membership."

"It don't cost nothin'. Free," he said, filling in Ali's official Texas Steakhouse Membership Card. "Tonight's special is Texas Two-Steps," he said. "Double shot of tequila with a sangria chaser."

Forty minutes later, two plates heaped with chicken fried steak and mashed potatoes smothered in white gravy, barbeque beans, slaw, and Texas toast arrived on the arm of an overly cheerful waitress who said her name was Corley Beth and to holler if they needed anything else. Sarah couldn't quite imagine yelling across the cavernous room, *"Corley Beth, more beans!"*

"You aren't worried about Pam?" asked Ali between bites.

"I think she'd call if there was trouble. She's over forty, and she's late, not AWOL," said Sarah. She swirled the house red in its thick, oversized glass and wondered if everything in Texas was big.

Ali took another bite of mashed potatoes. "I think she's with that guy—the one that was at the truck stop."

"That guy or another guy. It doesn't matter, at least not to her," Sarah said. She felt weary from the long ride and the heat. The air conditioner in her car refused to deliver really cold air. It was worrisome. Bernie panted constantly. She doubted there was a Toyota dealer between Dallas and Wichita Falls. Second to this worry was Judy Grace's unanswered phone. Sarah repeatedly pressed the redial button on the cell phone, but the realtor was out of the zone.

She watched Ali forking down beans and chasing them with Texas toast drenched in butter. "Hungry?"

"I don't usually like this kind of food, but this is good. Is this a real steak?"

"Chicken fried steak, I believe, is an inferior cut of beef that is tenderized, breaded, and deep fat fried," Sarah answered. "The gravy is mostly hydrogenated grease and white flour." Sarah feared for cooks whose only culinary experience involved food such as she was eating. Being a chef was elating. She expected slinging hash was debilitating.

"I knew it wasn't chicken," Ali said, chewing contentedly.

Sarah was relieved to see Ali eating. Being dumped by her husband had cost her ten pounds and the disastrous directing job, another five.

When they got back to the motel there was a message from Pam that she was in her room asleep and would see them in the morning.

"Was she alone?" Ali asked the bland young man at the desk.

Dressed like a Mormon missionary, he gazed dully back. "I couldn't say, ma'am."

"Come on," Sarah hissed to Ali, pulling her arm and nearly knocking herself off balance.

Back in their room, Ali considered telephoning Pam. "Did she tell you she was going to get a separate room?" she asked Sarah.

"Pam is like this with men. You know this about her, and you better get used to having strange men around that you think aren't good enough for her," Sarah said.

Ali pulled off her slacks and dug around in her suitcase, exhuming multiple plastic bags stuffed with cosmetics.

"I'm going to take a shower. Want the TV on?" She touched the power button as she passed the set.

Sarah's eye traced Ali's slim figure: high breasts, flat stomach, and taut thighs.

"I don't want the TV," Sarah said as Ali closed the bathroom door and an earnest CNN reporter tried to sound enthusiastic about a so-so news day. A minute later Sarah thought she heard vomiting followed by multiple flushes.

Gods. One is a bulimic and the other's a nymphomaniac. I think we'd better call it the Hotel California. She could hear the Eagles singing about being able to check out but not being able to leave.

⸙ ✻ ⸙

WHEN SARAH AND ALI walked into the motel lobby the next morning for their complimentary breakfast, Pam was munching Cheerios and watching morning talk TV. Sarah felt Ali stiffen and prepare for an inquisition.

"The coffee machine is weird," Pam said, oblivious to any tension. "Let me show you how to work it." She punched the buttons on the dispensing machine that spit out five ounces of coffee. She gave neither explanation nor apology for the previous night.

"He's not here," Sarah whispered to Ali as Pam expertly guided the machine to give up its coffee. "We can't change yesterday, but we can sure screw up today. Don't say anything."

"I say we stop in Wichita Falls for a rest and meet in Albuquerque tonight," Sarah said. "We have a reservation at the Howard Johnson on I-40 East. That okay?"

Ali and Sarah looked at Pam for her consent. She nodded. Sarah suspected Ali was suppressing asking Pam if she would again require her own room.

It was hot for early May and Sarah started worrying as soon as she was back on the road. Fifty miles out, her car air conditioner breathed its last breath.

"It's hotter than hell, and it's not the hot part of the day yet," she yelled into the cell phone at Ali. "What? I can't hear you." The highway noise was deafening, but with the windows closed the heat was unbearable. "I'm going to have to get it fixed in Wichita Falls."

Sarah pulled over at the next public rest area and called Pam. "Where are you?" she asked.

"Almost in Springtown. Where are you?"

Sarah didn't need to look at the map to know that Pam was not on Texas Highway 287. "You're on the wrong road. There's no Springtown on 287."

"I'm on 281. It goes the same place," Pam said.

Sarah, who was dripping with sweat, had a hard time not swearing. Here was capricious, creative Pam choosing the road less traveled and inconveniencing everybody.

"I have to stop in Wichita Falls and get the AC fixed."

"How long will that take?" asked Pam.

"I have no idea. Find the Toyota Dealer and meet me and Ali there." She clicked off before she told Pam to go to hell. Sweltering and worried about the heat's effect on Bernie, she was in no mood to tolerate Pam's whims. "Just a little farther, Bernie."

The Toyota steamed into the garage. Pam, Ali and Bernie waited in the parking lot wedged under the shade of a lone elm.

"Mrs. Hunter, I can work your car in, but I know it won't be ready today. You say you're headed to Albuquerque?" The Toyota service manager, dwarfed by his high counter, peered earnestly at her. His cap read, "Aggies" and Sarah fantacized about reporting him to Toyota for being out of uniform.

"We're going to find a motel. I'll call you with my number, and you can call me when it's fixed," Sarah said. She strained to sound no-nonsense, like an FBI agent.

Already, Sarah was imagining the things that could go wrong. They'd forget her, the AC would need a part they didn't have, they'd fix it and lose her number, and when she called them, she'd never get through the multiple levels of the answering machine.

"Hal, we're going to our mother's funeral," Pam said in a voice like melting pralines. "We can't wait." Pam had walked up behind Sarah. "My sister here can't drive in the heat without air, and I'm afraid we're going to miss Mama's burial." Pam's eyes were watering. She dug out her wallet and pressed a couple of twenties on the stunned manager. "If you could help us. Fix this car now?" Her gaze lassoed him and never slackened.

The man with Hal embroidered on his pocket seemed terrified and unable to distinguish between a tip and a bribe. He opened and closed his mouth repeatedly and blinked like a newborn. Sarah, irritated by Pam's transparent ploy, was about to pull the money back and tell Pam to go away when five oily fingers grasped and pocketed the two bills.

"I understand. My Mama died last November," he said.

At lunch over burgers, Sarah described the scene for Ali. "You should get her to be in one of your plays. She was weeping for our departed mother," Sarah said.

"I'm just mad that he took my money," Pam said finishing off the French fries. "If I'd been really good, he'd have given the money back and fixed the car for free."

Sarah's Camry was ready by three and before dark they were in Amarillo where they picked up I-40. They decided to continue and drive the 286 miles to Albuquerque so that they could keep their appointment the next morning with Judy Grace, the Santa Fe Realtor.

Even with the delay and the heat, Sarah's enthusiasm about the old hotel was infectious.

"I'm sure we can live there. At first, it'll be like camping out. There's water and electricity and I ordered a port-a-potty just in case," Sarah said, as they lay in their HoJo beds late that night. Ali and Pam shared a queen bed, giving the other to Sarah. Getting up in the middle of the night to go to the bathroom on one leg was a challenge, so Sarah kept a female urinal bedside. It was really a plastic two-quart pitcher, which didn't work particularly well. Nothing did. Unbalanced by the missing limb and dopey with sleep, often as not she spilled.

"Just in case what? The toilet doesn't work?" asked Ali.

"No, Ali," Pam said. "If the roof leaks, we can all live in it."

"We'll get a plumber out there immediately. There's one in Angustia. I checked," said Sarah. She didn't tell them that in spite of several calls, Juan Jaramillo, the plumber, had not called her back.

"I have to have a toilet. That's not negotiable," Ali said.

Sarah couldn't sleep for thinking about taking possession of the old hotel. She could see Manny's truck pulling up with her things, the kitchen stove warming a thick soup, the plums on the trees ripening. Like ants, workers would come and go, reviving the place while she scrubbed and planted and schemed.

At six she was up making coffee in the room's diminutive Mr. Coffee. Hotel Angustia, shrouded in pink mystery, waited only a few hours away.

10

NTENSE TRAFFIC ON I-25 and an accident at the Montgomery exit choked the route to Santa Fe. Then road work squeezed the highway down to two lanes. Sarah drove carefully in convoy behind Ali with Pam in the lead. Sarah noticed when an old model VW Bug took advantage of a gap and passed Pam, dangerously swinging in front of her. She heard Pam lay on the Miata's horn.

The Bug slowed; its driver, a man, gestured wildly at Pam. He swerved sharply to the right and drove on the paved shoulder, slowing, coming even, and keeping pace with Pam. Pam sped up and Sarah could see the man hanging out of his car, yelling and shaking his fist. Road rage.

Ali braked and the VW pulled in front of her, behind Pam. Sarah grabbed her cell phone, but felt it ringing in her palm before she could dial.

Ali yelled, "He's crazy."

"Stay back, don't crowd him," Sarah shouted. The word *crowd* coincided with a crunch as the bug rammed Pam's Miata, which just missed colliding with the Jeep in front of it.

Two signs came into view: the green New Mexico 550, Cuba and Placitas exit sign and a white End Construction Zone. Like a clogged drain suddenly cleared, the traffic sluiced out into four lanes. Sarah watched the outrageous VW Bug driver blaze into the newly opened left lane and cut in front of Pam.

Sarah could see Pam's right turn blinker winking. Mr. Crazy slowed. The exit was just ahead. For a pursuer, he had gotten himself into a stupid bind. He was in front of the prey he tracked. He exited. Pam didn't. Half way up the exit ramp he stopped. Sarah imagined he was testing to see if he could drive down the steep embankment to follow Pam. Wisely, he chose not to risk a roll over. Sarah watched him in her rear view mirror standing beside his car shaking his fist. She was pretty sure he was yelling, "I'll get you."

Ali and Sarah followed Pam to Santa Fe where she pulled off into a restaurant parking lot.

"He cut me off, and I honked at him. I swear I didn't even glare at the son of a bitch," Pam said. She fought to control her shaking.

"Probably on drugs," Ali said.

"Well he needs more of them if you ask me," said Pam.

They went inside and ordered coffee while they waited for the Highway Patrol. Sarah repeatedly dialed Judy Grace, the realtor, to let her know they'd be late. She got the same cheerful recording each time.

Officer Powell methodically took down the information. Sarah had the license plate of the VW and of a United Van Lines truck that certainly saw the chase.

"Why'd you wait so long to call the police? You say this happened 50 miles south?" He scratched circles with his pen on a napkin to make the ink flow.

"If some maniac had rammed your car and clearly was trying to hurt you, would you pull over at the next exit so he could catch up with you?" Pam looked pissed off, tired, and ten years older.

"You think he's still following you?" the officer asked, looking around like a dazed bear as though the lunatic driver would walk through the door of the pancake house any second. "You sure you didn't know him from some place?"

"Like where? We are driving across country. Moving to northern New Mexico. We don't know anybody." Pam was gripping a fork, almost screaming. "Are you going to do something before he kills somebody else?"

Patrolman Powell's shoulders drew up like a rooster's feathers. However, the possibility of harm coming to another driver when the authorities had been formally notified of the road rager's presence refocused his attention.

They followed the officer outside and watched him amble to his patrol car. Sarah wondered again why law enforcement people wore such tight uniforms. She thought of over-stuffed sausage casings.

"I'll never see a dime," Pam said, rubbing the dents in the rear end of her car as though she could massage away the damage.

"Wow. Welcome to New Mexico," said Ali.

"I think we should go on to Angustia," Sarah said. "Judy may be waiting. Even if she's not, the place is ours, and we need to go see it. Are you okay to drive, Pam?"

"Yes," Pam said. It's the Wild West." She spit on the asphalt. "Bring it on."

"Pam, I gotta say, you were very cool faking out that crazy bastard like you did—making him think you were going to turn off," Ali said.

"I was lucky, Ali. I was scared shitless."

"Sometimes when we let it, intuition takes over," said Sarah.

Pam just looked at her, her blank stare a substitute for the sarcastic comeback that Sarah knew was brewing.

"It's got to be uphill from here," Ali muttered.

"You mean downhill," Sarah said.

"Yeah," Ali said, sliding into her car.

As the three cars tamely motored out of Santa Fe toward Espanola and the Highway 285 turnoff to Angustia, Sarah thought about Officer Powell's response. Was he so unhelpful because they were women, three white women, or was there some cryptic form of communication they had failed to use and to understand? She looked at the blazing blue sky and inhaled deeply three times. "It's a test, not a bad omen," she told Bernie, who lazed on the back seat. "Heroes are always tested. They don't just waltz in a snatch the holy grail." Bernie had no comment.

⸎

SARAH LED THEM OFF 285, but missed the turnoff for the hotel and had to ask directions in the tiny town of Angustia. A young man at the gas station-grocery store said he didn't know and an old man sitting in front of the cantina only spoke Spanish. Then from nowhere, an old crone appeared who knew exactly where the Hotel Angustia was. In a mixture of English and Spanish she gave them directions as though she had been expecting them. As she drove away, Sarah saw the old woman who said her name was Maria Idelphonso de Cantu draw open a violet umbrella against the broad, indifferent sky.

Sarah realized that she had missed the turn because someone had torn down the ageing Hotel Angustia sign by the road.

But as soon as she turned in she recognized the feeling she had two years ago when she visited. She stopped the car. Ali and Pam pulled up behind her.

"What's wrong?" Pam asked, getting out of her car.

"Nothing. I just wanted to feel this before we get to the hotel," Sarah said.

"We own all this?" asked Ali. She finished touching up her lipstick in the visor mirror and joined them.

Sarah nodded. "The hotel's down there. This is our driveway," she said. Her face took on an enraptured look, like a saint in a sentimental religious painting. "Look out there. That's our barn." She turned. "And over there is our pond."

"And over there is our RV?" asked Pam, pointing to an ancient Winnebago at the end of the driveway.

"That's not supposed to be there. Unless Judy drove it." Already Sarah was marching toward the vehicle, warming up her "you're trespassing" speech. She peeked in the dusty windows. It was empty. Bernie, who dogged her heels, pricked his ears.

"Maybe someone just parked it here. Thinks the place is vacant and nobody will care," Ali said.

Sarah's joy at arriving was eroding fast.

"Come on Sarah, give us a tour of the hotel," Ali said. "We'll call the sheriff if we have to."

Sarah gave the rusting RV another glare and walked toward the hotel. Beyond a broad stand of oaks, the gravel road split into a circular drive leading to the old hotel's main entrance. The forlorn gate sat open, like the mouth of a dental patient who was going to need a lot of work. But when she blurred her vision, the peach adobe edifice crowned with terracotta tiles looked majestic. It was what Disney copied when it wanted an authentic Southwest look. From a distance, she could feel that whatever was wrong could be fixed.

Chanting broke the quiet and swelled alarmingly across the scrubby ground. There were cries, maybe sobs.

Bernie barked; a ridge of fur stood up along his backbone.

"Somebody's in there," said Ali, stating the obvious.

Sarah started forward, ready to rout the intruders, but Pam grabbed her arm.

"Wait. They may not know the place has been sold."

"Well they sure as hell know it isn't theirs," Sarah said.

"They're doing some kind of ceremony, I think. How long has this place been vacant?" Pam asked. "It isn't going to make anything better if you bust in on them and order them out."

Sarah scuffed the gravel, hesitating. Bernie waited for a signal.

"Besides, from the sounds of them, they outnumber us about ten to one," said Pam.

Minutes later, the trespassers emerged from the hotel. They looked like extras from a Good Friday pageant, bloody, sweaty and euphoric. Some wore monk's robes, most were clothed in white, but all carried short leather whips. One man dragged a crude eight foot wooden cross, cutting a groove in sandy dirt. Shuffling quietly, they ignored the three women. A few went to the RV, others toward two Army surplus tents camouflaged by the scrub.

"This is so creepy," Ali whispered.

"Excuse me. Hello. Excuse me," Sarah called out, hoping to sound assertive when she felt frightened.

No one even looked at her.

"Which one do you think is the leader?" asked Pam, as the bedraggled creatures passed. "The one with the cross?"

"I have no idea," Sarah said, furiously dialing Judy Grace.

"I think they're *Penitentes*," Pam said. "I've read about them, but I thought they did this shit around Easter."

"Well they're a little late," Sarah said.

"Or very early," said Pam.

"They beat themselves to atone for sin, to suffer what Christ suffered, to do penance," Ali said.

Again, Judy Grace did not answer her phone.

"*Perdón Señores. El hotel es nuestra propertidad ahora. Lo siento mucho, pero es la verdad*," Ali called out to a group of men, telling them they were on private property. The men looked insolent. No one acknowledged her. "Maybe they're deaf."

"Maybe they're aliens," Pam said.

"Come on," Sarah said, heading for the hotel. She whistled and Bernie followed, bolstering her courage.

Walking over the blood speckled-tracks of the worshipers, the three women entered the once-grand adobe structure. A faded sign by the door ironically welcomed them, Bienvenidos a la Hacienda Angustia.

Ali stopped. "Before I go any further, I have to tee-tee, and I am not doing it in the bushes with those guys in bloody robes watching. And I did not see any Porta-Potty." She looked expectantly at Sarah.

"Let's check the bathrooms," Sarah said. "Judy said she'd try to get the plumber. Maybe he's been here."

Pam laughed. The eerie caustic sound echoed in the cavernous lobby. "I'm sure he just popped right on out. Christ, Sarah, plumbers want credit card numbers before they even schedule you," Pam said.

Bathroom after bathroom was dry. However, lime stains indicated that water had run in the recent past.

"Here. Pee in this." Pam handed Ali a chipped enamel pan. "Toss it outside when you're finished."

Ali looked disgusted, but took the pan and disappeared behind a bathroom door. "Hand me some Kleenex from my purse," she called out.

An hour later the realtor from Santa Fe had still not called. In addition to no running water, they discovered that there was no electricity and no one was answering the phone at the electric company.

"Maybe they close for a siesta," said Ali. They sat under a huge cottonwood tree getting more depressed by the minute. The *Penitentes* hunkered down just in sight.

"They look like they were waiting for someone to show up and tell them what to do," Ali said.

"Maybe a movie director," Pam said. "Cut. That's a wrap," she called, but none of the robed visitors acknowledged her.

"This is too weird," Ali said.

Even Sarah had to admit during the tour of the place that it looked less magical than she remembered. "The power was on when I was here. I turned on a light in the kitchen," she said, trying feebly to defend herself. *What made me buy this albatross?* She poured Bernie a pan of water from her last Ozarka Springs gallon.

When she dialed the electric company for the fifth time, a female voice answered. After Sarah's lengthy description of the location of her property, the voice that belonged to Helen Montoya told her that Sarah was not in the region served by the company. She was given another number to call. The second company was at a loss as to why she was calling; it supplied liquid propane. Back with the brisk Ms. Montoya, she was told that the supervisor would have to call back. Sarah missed the solicitous treatment she would have received in

Mississippi where people apologized for inconveniences even if they weren't to blame. In contrast, Ms. Montoya had not one, 'I'm so sorry, Ma'am,' and she sounded irritated.

"You think I'm getting the run around?" Sarah asked.

"The question," Pam answered, "is why are they running you around?"

"Before you go getting paranoid, let's go to the company's office," Ali said.

"I have a bad feeling about this," Pam said.

"It's a minor setback, Sarah said. "Look around. If it were fixed up, this place would be spectacular. We're wallowing. We need a plan."

"First we have to get rid of those religious freaks. They're using that big room behind the lobby for a sanctuary," Ali said. She finished the last of her bottled water.

Sarah had an image of the coming nightfall with the ghostly men wandering around. She didn't like it.

"They won't talk to us. You want to burn them out?" asked Pam.

Sarah jerked to attention at Pam's sarcasm. "Not burn, something better." She ran as fast as her leg could travel to the car, popped the trunk, and rummaged.

She returned with a stuffed plastic bag. "Not burn, fumigate. I brought insecticide bombs."

Following the instructions on the fumigation devices that Manny had recommended, they sealed the main part of the hotel as well as they could with plastic and masking tape and marked the doors with the yellow 'Caution' tape that came in the kit. Sarah ignited the bombs, which emitted a disappointing phitt.

A half dozen of the *Penitentes* stood near the hacienda's front gate, watching the women. Sarah could feel their eyes cut right and left. An hour later, she heard the RV's engine rasping and coughing. The engine caught finally and the Winnebago lumbered away like an injured dinosaur. As though signaled, other groups packed their tents and goods and walked away in different directions as though they were leaving a ball game.

"That's weird," Pam said. "They ought to be, well I don't know what they ought to be doing, but they ought to be doing it together."

"We got rid of them," Ali said.

"Thank God. They were scaring me," Pam admitted.

"But we can't go in either," Ali said. "Not for twelve hours. What are we going to do?"

"You could visit Española, and Taos isn't that far. Maybe there's something in that little town we went through. Not Angustia, the other one, Rico? I'm staying here," Sarah said. "Bernie too."

"For God's sake, Sarah. You're not a homesteader. Nobody's going to jump your claim," said Ali.

"I have a feeling. It's crazy but somebody needs to stay. I'm not sure why. It'll slip away if I don't."

"Where would we sleep?" asked Pam.

"I have Steven's camping gear. There's a tent. It's a big one."

Ten minutes into the set up of the high-tech tent, a car crackled the road's gravel. It was a new Chevrolet Tahoe, all black with tinted windows.

The women stood together, the nylon tent billowing around them like one huge blue dress they didn't quite know how to slip on or off.

"Damn. It's the Darth Vader mobile," said Pam.

After a long pause, the door opened and a man got out. Dark, Hispanic, middle aged and tall, he strode toward them, a smile breaking as he moved. His teeth, like Chiclets, shown white. His suit was as dark and spotless as the Tahoe.

"I am sorry to intrude. I'm Jami Ortega." He shook hands with each of them as they recited their names and assured him he was not intruding. "So you're the new owners. When do you open for business?" His Spanish accent was heavy, but someone had taught him to enunciate, to sound final consonants. The effect was that he sounded like Count Dracula.

"We're not going to run the hotel," Pam said.

"We're going to live here," Ali said.

"We do live here," said Sarah. She noticed his manicured fingernails, the tips long for a man and very white.

"I own the land to the northeast. We share a border for maybe two hundred yards," he said. He smiled.

The more cordial Ortega became, the more nervous Sarah was.

"Oh, I forgot," he said, turning to his car. "I brought some wine to welcome you." He crossed the courtyard, his honey Italian leather shoes daring any dust to settle.

"A case. How nice," Ali said. "Say, you don't know anybody who we could hire to do some of the work for us, do you?"

"In the country it's very hard to get labor. If you find someone, send him to me when you finish." He laughed.

Sarah heard the flinty patronizing edges of his chuckle.

"We're not picky," Pam added.

"I'll keep my eyes open for you. But now, I won't keep you from your work," he said, turning to leave. "Do you need some help with the tent?"

Sarah suppressed Ali's "yes" with her "no."

"We'll manage. Thank you."

"If anything comes up—here take my card. Give me a call," he said.

Sarah read, "Jami Ortega" and realized that, in Spanish, Jami was pronounced Hi-me.

"Well, actually," Ali said, "do you know anything about the water here?"

Ortega looked alarmed for an instant before his smooth manner closed over the rip. "The water?"

"And the electricity. It's turned off." Pam said.

"I don't know about the water, but as for the power, part of your land is in one district and part in another. It can be very confusing," he said.

"I'm sure we can straighten it out," Sarah said. She wanted him to go.

"And I'll give you a tip," he said, pronouncing tip as *teep*. "When you have pest control come out to spray, call Southwest Insect Control. They won't cheat you. Or at least not as much." The patronizing laugh again. Then he pointed at the sealed doors. "But I see you do your own pest control."

Sarah was getting more upset with every *teep*. She heard him sowing mistrust and fear. He was the man who had made an offer on the property and been beaten out. What was he after?

"You're the Mr. Ortega who wanted to buy this property, aren't you?" asked Sarah. There, the cards were on the table; the cat was out of the bag. She felt a sting of adrenalin at her brashness. In Mississippi she would never have been so blunt.

"Yes. I always try to buy land adjacent to my land, if the price is good. I wasn't fast enough this time." Another smile. "And the town, Angustia, I like it. In English *Angustia* means anguish, you know."

"What?" Pam said. "Anguish? I thought it was a last name. Did you know that?" Pam asked Sarah and Ali.

"I knew," Sarah said.

"I never thought about it," Ali said. "Angustia means woe. We can change it, the hotel's name, not the town, of course."

"No. Nothing ever changes in Angustia," he said.

Sarah wasn't sure what Ortega meant by that, but she knew it was another subtle discouraging word.

"If you decide it isn't right for you and want to sell, call me, please." He glided away and slid into the vehicle like a hand into a glove.

The dark Tahoe whispered away down the drive, barely stirring the dust.

"We bought the hacienda of woe?" Pam asked.

"Angustia can mean sadness, misery, wretchedness, angst, torment, pain, despair," Ali listed the synonyms. "A flexible noun."

Pam toyed with the words, "House of Misery, Hotel of Torment?"

Ali added, "Heartbreak Hotel?"

Pam pointed to Ortega's business card in Sarah's hand and said, "Better hang on to that."

Sarah stuck the card in her bag as though it were a tropical man-eating plant. So innocent looking, but when you turned your back, you were dinner.

11

A T DUSK, THE WOMEN sat around a campfire in the old kiva fire pit of the large front courtyard of the hotel. The voluminous, lightweight tent quivered in the evening breeze. Bread, cheese, wine, and canned chicken noodle soup made up supper. Sarah's cell phone's battery was dead, but Steven's flashlights worked. After the last of the *Penitentes* had wandered away, Pam had found the rented Porta-Potty. The worshipers apparently had moved it.

"If it's not too full, maybe we can drag it back with one of the cars," Sarah said.

Ali shook her head and looked up in a gesture that meant, *my God, what have we come to?* "I may just stick to my slop jar."

The twilight closed out with a brilliant sunset. Purple and gold shot from the orange ball as it dipped behind the gray hills. The arresting beauty lightened the tension of Ortega's visit. Like Girl Scouts, they watched the stars appear and soothed themselves with retelling stories that they had told one another years ago. Stories about their men dominated.

"You told me you lost your virginity to Bobby Ray Gorenflo in his car," Ali said to Pam.

"I told you I lost it by degrees to Bobby Ray. We started in the car. Complete penetration was achieved in his cousin's hunting cabin," Pam said.

"My first, Ronnie Fitts, must have been retarded," Ali said. "We were necking in the dark end of the veranda, and he'd only feel up my top." Ali smiled into the fire as the remembrance took over. "I was practically straddling him, but he didn't take the hint."

"I remember this story. You put your hand down his pants and—" Sarah interrupted.

"No, no. *I* shoved *his* hand down inside my pants, threw back my head like a movie queen and said, 'I can't stop you, Ronnie.' "

"What'd he do then," asked Pam.

"He fiddled around awhile. I think all that wet, foreign tissue scared him. Then I had an orgasm, and he went on home."

"Ain't love grand," Sarah said.

"Your turn, Sarah," Pam said, refilling their wine.

She thought about telling them a story they'd never heard—about sex with Randall Crane. How early on the morning after they'd slept together, she'd dressed, putting on the prosthesis with a red T-strap shoe and how Randall had pulled her back into bed. Randall was her first lover since her husband Steven had died. It had felt so good to be held, and Randall had proved the night before to be competent in bed. But the night before it had been dark, and she hadn't worn her prosthesis.

She thought about telling them how as Randall was thrusting toward *Oh-baby-oh-baby*, she was transfixed by the sight over his shoulder of her red T-strap bouncing on the bed. She had considered wrapping her legs around him, hugging his thrusts, but held back, thinking the shoe might rub. She had rarely had sex with the prosthesis on and never when it wore a shoe. His orgasm had precluded a decision. But she decided not to talk about Randall. It was too fresh, and she hadn't yet forgiven herself for her mistake with him.

"When I was a senior in high school, my History teacher kissed me," Sarah said. "I think it was my first French kiss.

"How old was he or she?" Pam asked.

"Mr. Byron was probably over forty."

"Ick. You let him?" Ali asked.

"He told me he was writing a book and the main character fell in love with a young woman. Of course as writer, he, Mr. Byron, didn't know what that felt like."

"And he wanted you to help him feel," Pam said. "What a sick prick. I hope you reported his ass."

"No. He only did it a few times, and he never pushed for more than kisses. Well, he did touch my breast a little once when he got carried away."

"He'd be put in jail today," Pam said.

"No, you don't understand. I wouldn't have ever reported him. His kiss was the most important thing that happened my senior year."

"He was using you, Sarah," Ali said. "A person in a position of trust—"

"That's hindsight. Maybe I used him too. He made me feel special, desirable. Suddenly I was experienced. I had knowledge. My girlfriends felt it without ever knowing about Mr. Byron."

"I would never let my History teacher kiss me," Ali said. "You're lucky he didn't talk you into doing more."

"True," Sarah said. "Growing up stinks."

They sat for some minutes in silence, breathing the clear, dry air, perfumed with mesquite and sage.

Sarah looked at her two best friends in the fire's glow. Perspiration and dust had taken away the Southern gloss, but they looked alive in a new primitive way. Sarah thought they looked gorgeous. L. L. Bean should be photographing them.

Pam broke the stillness. "Ali, you have to sing us a song. Get your guitar." She delicately stirred the fire that needed no stirring.

Ali warmed up with a Joan Baez rendition of *The Night They Drove Ole Dixie Down* and segued into *El Paso.* Pam and Sarah joined her whenever they remembered the words to the Marty Robbins ballad of star-crossed lovers and racial tension in Texas.

Then her fingers found older melodies on the guitar, songs in Spanish, and later her voice remembered the words. She sang about *la llorona,* the weeping woman, about lovers who left never to return, and about a woman from Malaga whom the singer could never obtain.

Sarah and Pam sat as quiet and still as the stars above. Ali had a strong, dramatic voice with a broad range. Her falsetto, *y decirte, niña hermosa,* cut chills. The music raced across the night like wild fire and when she stopped to drink, the quiet ached.

"You never sang Spanish songs before. For us. They're beautiful, bewitching," Sarah said.

"They're not a part of my past I particularly embrace. I don't know why I started playing all that old stuff. It just came out," Ali said.

"Of course it's no match for your show tunes, but it's a nice change," Pam said, stretching her legs away from the flames.

"Let me guess," Ali said. "You want *Happy Talk* from *South Pacific* or Get Me to the *Church on Time* from *My Fair Lady*?"

"I want to be Nurse Nellie Forbush." Pam, looking a lot like Mitzi Gaynor, scrambled to her feet to sing and dance about washing a man out of her hair.

More show tunes and wine took the women into the late hours. Ali sang a final song in Spanish about a dove until her fingers became raw from the steel strings.

Something snapped.

"What was that?" Sarah asked. Fear coated her voice. If someone were going to attack them, she wouldn't be able to get up quickly. It was dead quiet and then far off a muffled thunk. Sarah put her hand on Bernie to calm him.

"Could be animals," Pam said, sweeping the powerful flashlight like an airport beacon. The light zigzagged crazily, turning trees into monsters. "What kind, I can't guess."

"Let's get in the car and lock the doors," Ali said. She was up and moving toward her Honda, the guitar under her arm.

"No. It's okay," said Sarah. "It's gone, whatever it was."

"Gone?" Ali stopped. "How the hell do you know it's gone? Your mystical voices say so?"

The Camp Fire Girl mood evaporated, killed as only fear can kill.

Sarah thought about telling Ali that yes, she had been told, but it was more correct to say that she had a feeling, not a message in English. It was more like radar. She had always had clear intuition, and removed from electricity and distractions, it was stronger. "There are all kinds of animals that see us that we can't see," Sarah said. "Some make noise. I was paranoid for a minute."

The muffled pop and hiss of the fire sounded.

"Well don't do it again." Setting down the guitar, Ali grabbed the enamel pan and walked just out of the firelight's reach.

"You don't need a pan, Ali." Pam said. "You're outside."

"Don't tell me what I need."

"Pam, if you'll help me up, I'm going to bed," Sarah said.

"Let's all go to bed," Pam said.

They waited for Ali. Bernie followed them into the tent.

When they were settled and the light extinguished, Sarah lay on her cot listening. Someone had been out there. Had they been eavesdropping on their stories of adolescent sex or something more sinister? She lowered her hand over the cot's side and felt for Bernie.

12

SARAH WAS AWAKENED BY a clank, outside, probably by the fire pit. She poked Pam.

"Maybe a wild dog smelled the soup pot," Sarah whispered. "Did you leave out any food?"

Bernie was sleeping soundly, wedged between Ali and Sarah.

"Damnit, we ate all the food," Pam said. "Move. I am not cowering in a nylon tent waiting for whatever it is to come and get me." Pam zipped the shorts she had pulled on with the tee shirt she had slept in and pushed out of the tent.

"Who's there?" Pam barked.

"*Buenos días,*" *Señora* Cantu said. The woman from Angustia who had given them directions sat crouched in front of a small fire. Her smile roused a web of lines in her face which seemed to float above her tiny body. Swathed in an indeterminate number of layers of dark cloth, she looked like a raven against the mauve morning sky. Her speckled enamel coffee pot again raked across the rusty grill. "You gringas like coffee, no?"

Pam smiled. Even a run down hotel in the middle of nowhere looked better when there was hot coffee.

"We gringas like coffee, *si*," Pam said.

As the old woman pulled bundles from beneath her layers, Ali and Sarah tumbled out of the tent and crowded around the fire. The bundles turned out to be an assortment of *pan dulce* and *empanadas*, likely homemade. As they munched and drank the strong coffee, Pam told *Señora* Cantu about the squatters they had found when they first arrived.

"What do you mean they weren't real *Penitentes*?" Pam asked *Señora* Cantu.

The old woman brewed a second pot of coffee. "*Penitentes* don't walk this time of year, and they wouldn't go inside a hotel and whip themselves," she said.

"There's blood on the floor," Ali said. "Come look."

Like a team of forensic specialists, they marched to the hotel and pulled away the rest of the tape and plastic.

Sarah had the feeling that *Señora* Cantu knew a lot she wasn't telling them. Sarah also felt that this holding back, whether a matter of culture or of personal style, would dissolve in its own good time. But Sarah, always impatient, could never willingly wait for a story even when the effect would have been more intense with delay.

"See? Blood," Pam said, pointing to the dark specks.

The woman crouched, swiped a finger through the drops and smelled them. "Maybe blood."

"The men are gone. Why does it matter?" asked Ali.

"Because if it was fake blood, they were fake, and we have to wonder why they were here," said Sarah.

"Blood, but not human. Chicken's blood, I think," the woman said after all but tasting the dark liquid.

"How do you know?" asked Pam.

"I've chopped a lot of necks," the *Señora* said flatly. She smacked the edge of her right hand into the palm of her left, then rose and ambled back to the fire pit and the coffee. The women followed.

"Why were they here?" asked Sarah. She feared the answer, knowing it wasn't going to portend good things even if the intruders had left. And of course, they could come back.

The old woman laughed. "Fumigation, whose idea was that?" she asked, changing the subject. Apparently she wasn't going to reveal her theory so easily.

"Mine. If they send a plague, we'll be ready," Sarah said.

"Very good." She clapped her hands. "Like the coyote. You know about the coyote, the trickster?" she asked.

"I know all about the coyote," Ali said.

"Don't tell them. I'll tell them a coyote story the next time I come," *Señora* Cantu said. "Why do you think these men, these *Penitentes* were here?" she asked, turning Sarah's question back to her.

"I think they tried to scare us away," Sarah said. "Maybe they think of this land as theirs. We're intruders."

"We're white, we're women, and we don't have men with us. That's scary to them," said Pam.

"What do you think?" the woman asked Ali.

"Conspiracy."

The strange woman raised her thick eyebrows and looked like a startled owl. When she said *"who"*, she appeared to be imitating one. "Who, who is making this *conspiración*?" she asked.

"Who knows? We don't know anybody here," Pam said, hesitantly pouring *Señora* Cantu's goat's milk into her coffee.

"It might have something to do with our realtor," Ali said. "She was supposed to meet us here and hasn't even called. Maybe we don't own the place after all." She looked like she didn't necessarily think that was a bad thing.

"It's the man who made the first offer," Sarah said. "He's connected." She looked to *Señora* Cantu for confirmation, but the old woman sat poker-faced. "I think he knew we were coming. He stopped by to welcome us right after they left."

The *Señora* slurped her coffee and said, "Maybe it's nothing serious. Things move differently out here. You know, *mañana*."

"*Mañana*? Tomorrow? Hell, I doubt we'll have power before Christmas," Pam said.

"What are you going to do?" the *Señora* asked.

"We're not leaving, if that's what you mean," Sarah said. "Help us get water and electricity. What do we have to do? Pay off somebody? What?"

"It never hurts to grease the wheels," *Señora* Cantu shrugged.

"Wait a damn minute. Are we talking about paying off the electric company so they'll connect the power?" Pam asked.

"Oh no," *Señora* Cantu said. She shook her head.

"Oh. Well good," Pam said.

"If only it were that easy," *Señora* Cantu said, brushing the breadcrumbs from her lap.

"What? What the hell does that mean?" Pam was almost shouting. "And who are you? Do you work for them, whoever they are?"

"Stop, Pam. *Señora* Cantu brought us breakfast," said Sarah.

"And a Trojan horse too? Excuse me." Pam stomped away from the fire circle.

Pam's outburst shocked Sarah, and she wondered if it was connected to Pam's learning what the word, angustia meant.

"We went out on a limb to buy this place," Sarah said. "It was my idea. Pam and Ali had never seen it before yesterday." Sarah tried to lose the whine in her voice. "Things aren't going well. We can't find our realtor, the place is decrepit, there's no water or electricity, on the way here Pam was almost killed by some guy with a bad case of road rage, and of course, the *Penitentes*. What else? Oh, Jami Ortega came by with a case of wine and an offer to buy the place."

"That doesn't necessarily come under the heading of 'Things That Aren't Going Well'," Ali said.

"Do you know him?" Sarah asked *Señora* Cantu.

"I know him."

"You think he's okay?" Sarah asked.

Ali added, "Would he try to con us?"

"Jami Ortega grew up near here. Now he's a *patrón*," the *Señora* said. The old woman rose painfully. "You will survive and keep your land if you can see things differently. Your old ways won't work well here in Angustia." She scratched Bernie's head.

Sarah wanted to grab the woman and shake her. This was no time for obscure, mystical prognostications. Next, she considered offering to buy her help. It had worked with Hal at the Toyota Dealership in Texas. Then she stopped. What would be a new way of dealing with these people? She'd start with the *Señora*.

"Thank you for the food," Sarah said. "You have helped us so much. Come visit again; we'll be here."

The old woman gathered her things.

"I'm putting in an herb garden," Sarah said. "Maybe you could advise me on what grows best in this soil?"

Señora Cantu rewarded Sarah's shift in attitude with a Jack o' lantern smile and slight nod. She started off across the road heading for a field, but turned back and waved. She yelled something about the coyote, but Sarah couldn't understand her. As she started off again she began to sing in Spanish. Her cracked voice matched her gait

"Shit," Ali said, staring after her. "She was here last night watching us."

"What?"

"I sang that song last night. The last song I sang. She's telling us she was here."

"She's telling us more than that," Sarah said. "I think she means to help us, but she can't tell us outright what to do. It's some weird code."

"Maybe she wasn't the only one watching us," Ali said, heading toward the main road. "Let's look around."

Sarah followed. Pam was reorganizing her car's contents again and ignored them as they passed.

"Maybe the *Señora*'s being watched too," Ali said.

"What are we looking for?" asked Sarah, trailing.

"I don't know. Tire tracks, clues."

"The impostor *Penitentes*?" Sarah asked.

"Or whoever sent them. Little towns out here can have very closed societies. You can move in, but in a hundred years you'll never be accepted."

"Hell, we're probably making way too much of all this," Sarah said. As she turned to look for whatever clues might be present, she missed a lump of granite, stumbled and landed flat on the ground. "I'm okay. I'm okay. Help me up," she said, trying to make the fall seem harmless. She didn't want Ali and Pam to see her as a liability.

As Ali hoisted her up, Sarah's eye caught something red in the brush along side of the road. It was an oily red plastic two-gallon gasoline container.

"Maybe they planned something else," Ali said, poking the can to hear the gas slosh.

"Don't tell Pam about this. She'll think it's the New Mexico Ku Klux Klan. We don't know what it is," Sarah said. "Someone's trying to scare us."

"They're succeeding," Ali said.

"Only because we're playing into the fears they're generating in our own minds. Let's try what *Señora* Cantu said. Look at things from a different perspective. If someone were trying to hurt us, she'd have told us," Sarah said. "We don't even know if it's gasoline."

Ali unscrewed the lid and sniffed. "Kerosene, I think."

"If they were going to burn us out, they would have done it," Sarah said.

Sarah felt panicky at the thought that Ali and Pam might abandon ship. Every hour it became clearer to her that she needed them. Now, she knew she needed something positive. Something that worked. "I'm going to Judy Grace's office in Santa Fe and see what the hell's going on. And then I'm going to buy a generator."

"Better buy some gas there too. I'll bet the ole station in Angustia just sold its last gallon," Ali said.

"I will. Ali, this sounds silly, but I think we're being tested. Maybe they want to drive us off or maybe they want to see what we're made of. Maybe the kerosene, no electricity and the rest are simple screw ups not even directed at us. I know we can make it here. We have to break the code; that's all."

"You sure you aren't trying to prove something to yourself?" asked Ali.

"I'm not sure of anything except that driving back to Mississippi is not a good choice for any of us. *Señora* Cantu knows things she's not telling us. She wants us to figure them out," Sarah said. "Don't panic."

"God, don't tell Pam that theory."

"Ali—"

"Okay, let's go find the realtor-bitch and get a generator. And I forgot to ask you, did you know there was a water purification system in Steven's camping stuff?" Ali asked.

"I'm not surprised. My dear late husband had every piece of gear you could buy. Think it'll work?"

"I think so. There's water on the property, probably a spring."

"Good. Great." Sarah smiled and looked relieved.

"Sarah? I need to tell you that I'm only good for a little while at this. I always hated camping. If locusts arrive, I'm gone," Ali said.

Sarah jounced along to the car, her shaky gait reflecting her inner discord. All her dreams could evaporate or go up in smoke so easily.

13

AT DUSK THAT DAY, the trio sat by the campfire, eating the food Sarah had bought in Santa Fe. They had removed all of the fumigation warnings and opened up the hotel. A shiny yellow gasoline generator sat under the ramada. The loaded Toyota held still more survival supplies.

"We have to adjust our thinking," Sarah said. "Whatever we used to do, we have to question and see if there is a more indirect, subtle way. *Señora* Cantu was trying to show us by example. We have to be patient." She wiped chipotle sauce from her chin.

"As former Southern Belles, that shouldn't be too hard— the indirect part. Patience is something else," Pam said.

"Subtle and indirect isn't so easy either," Ali said, munching black bean chips and salsa. They were practicing eating what they thought was Southwestern food. They agreed that they missed cheese grits.

"We could count our blessings," Sarah said, spitting out a jalapeño. "On the good side is the weather, the sun, the sky. I never felt better."

"We have electricity as long as the generator works," Ali added. "And pure water."

"Purified one gallon at a time with a hand pump," Pam said.

"And the tent. It's a great tent," Sarah said.

"No mosquitoes," Ali said.

On the negative side, it was clear that the hotel and grounds were in far more serious decay than Sarah had known or admitted. Many of the old adobe bricks were reverting to dirt, the roof would likely leak when it rained and in spite of a small spring, there was no running water in the pipes.

But more important to Sarah than climate, electricity or adobes was that she could feel the energy and power of the land and she suspected Ali and Pam felt it too. It was more than the mere beauty of the place, which was impressive. It was like being high on morphine. No wonder somebody had tried to drive them away.

"Okay, so this reverse thinking goes like how?" Pam asked. "If they send in snakes, we make pets out of them?"

"I think it's more than making the best of a bad situation," Sarah said. "We anticipate the snakes and are ready with traps."

Pam finished off her taco and reached for the bag of chips.

"They certainly think differently here," Pam said. "Last year, in Jackson my car battery died in the post office parking lot. Every man and woman that walked by asked me if I needed a jump or a ride. Here, we can't even get people to give us directions."

"We need water. I know the system used to work," Sarah said. "So why doesn't the well or the spring or whatever work? What is our *old* way of thinking about this problem?"

"We call a man, and he comes and fixes it," Ali said.

"Two points for you, Ali," Sarah said. And a new approach?"

"We stop bathing and only drink Bourbon?" asked Pam.

"We harvest the marijuana that's growing three pastures over and pay to have water trucked in," Ali said.

"What?" Pam said.

"What?" Sarah said.

"Hells bells, don't you two ever walk around here?" Ali said.

"Maybe that's why they want to get rid of us," Pam said.

"It's only about ten plants. I couldn't find any more."

"It might be a set up. Some DEA hot shots wing in on an anonymous tip and bust us," Sarah said.

"I thought of that. It's not growing any more," Ali said.

"Ali if somebody was watching you harvest it, they might have seen where you put it," Pam said.

"Where did you put it?" Sarah asked. "And when did you find it?"

"This afternoon. I was just taking a walk. But I didn't cut it down. I found it cut, stacked and ready for transport. But whoever planted it will be back to get it soon, and I think we should be watching for them when they do," Ali said.

"Oh boy," Pam said. "This is a different approach. Will we need jumpsuits and night goggles?"

"But we don't shine lights on them and catch them," Sarah said.

"We don't?" asked Ali.

"We find out who they are. We need information we can barter with. We don't need to catch the local doper," Sarah said.

"I think we need to be very cool around this Judy Grace when she gets here," Ali said. "If she ever comes. Something's up with her."

Sarah had finally gotten through to Judy Grace, who said she had thought they were coming in next week. She had been on a four-day cruise off Mexico, and her cell phone had not functioned. Judy apologized and would drive up the next day.

"I think she's on the level," Sarah said. "She really wanted us to get the property. She doesn't like this Ortega guy."

"We have to find out more about him," Ali said. "He seemed okay."

"What is it we want to know?" Pam said, packing up the leftovers.

"Why he wants the land," said Sarah.

"Maybe for the same reason you did," Ali said.

"I don't think so," Sarah said. "Not if he was behind the fake *Penitentes*."

"Who said he was?" Ali asked.

"I know," Pam said. "There's buried treasure here. Spanish conquistadors or rich, corrupt priests came through here and had to dump their booty. They never got back to it."

"You might be right," Sarah said. "We have to go to the courthouse in Santa Fe and check the records. Everything pertaining to the land as far back as possible."

"Sarah, I was kidding. I don't think there's buried bullion."

"I don't expect a trunk of doubloons, but there's something here," Sarah said. "Maybe it's some mineral, or Anasazi artifacts or a glory hole," Sarah said.

"If we go pawing in public records, Ortega—if he is the bad guy—is going to find out," Pam said.

"So?" Ali asked.

"Maybe it's better if thinks we're three dumb broads."

"You said the adobes were made from the mud right here," Sarah said.

"It's obvious," Pam said.

"And aren't you are a ceramicist who might want to know about the earth on your property?" Sarah said. "Let them know you're researching geologic stuff—soils, minerals, rocks. Part of the restoration of the Hotel Angustia."

"Okay, but I think you ought to work on *Señora* Cantu," said Pam.

"I am."

"How?"

"By planting my herb garden, cleaning my kitchen and digging in. She's not going to tell me anything until she knows I'm worth it," Sarah said.

"Hey, it's nearly dark. We need to talk about the stake-out at the marijuana patch. There's a quarter moon tonight," Ali said.

"I am not squatting in chiggers to watch some hippie steal weeds," Pam said. "How do you know anybody will show up tonight?"

"They'll need to dry it after harvesting it," Ali said. "It'll rot sitting in a pile on the ground."

"How do you know so much about growing pot?" Sarah asked.

"I thought everybody knew that," Ali said. "Forget about that part. There are three good places to hide. At least one of us should be able to see him clearly."

"It could take hours," Pam said.

"It will take hours. We have to be there before he is. We have to be patient," said Ali. "Spray yourself with DEET. Watching moonrise is a very contemplative thing to do. We can meditate."

"You don't know for sure he or she is going to show," whined Pam. "And DEET is toxic."

"Wait a minute. Shouldn't somebody stay here and create the illusion that we're all here?" said Sarah. "Pam can do that. We'd better get going. I can't walk fast across open fields."

"You can't walk fast period," Ali said. "You should be the one to stay here. It's going to be crazy getting you back here in the dark."

"Okay, okay damn it. I'll go," said Pam. "I still don't see how it's going to help us to know who some small time dope grower is."

"Maybe he's related to somebody who can help us. It's leverage. Maybe he's kin to Ortega," said Ali.

"You're so focused on Ortega being the bad guy, you're going to miss the real enemy, if there really is one," said Pam.

"He gives me the creeps. What can I say?" said Sarah.

"It's getting dark," Ali said.

"Go on. Get going," Sarah said.

As the two left the courtyard, Sarah could hear their voices float back through the shadowy brush.

"Did Sarah say a glory hole might be here?" Pam asked. "What the hell is that?"

"I don't even want to guess," Ali answered.

Fifteen minutes after Ali and Pam had disappeared into the trees, Sarah began to worry. What if the drug guy had a gun? What if there were guys not guy? What if they had a dog?

She feverishly tried to keep the camp looking and sounding like more than one person was around. An AM radio station played and she asked questions aloud that were not answered and answered ones that were not asked. Bernie looked very confused. The moon rose at nine, a fat fingernail in an inky sky. Sarah smelled the sage, rough and sweet, and listened for Ali and Pam's return. Only a distant coyote's heartbreaking yowl creased the night.

14

"I GOT A GOOD LOOK at him, and I am telling you he wasn't more than six years old."

Sarah could hear Pam's voice arguing with Ali as the two smashed through the brush. The moon was low, and their flashlight beams arced wildly, illuminating sprays of fine dust.

Sarah turned off the Albuquerque radio station, silencing the country twangs of a brokenhearted lover.

"You saw somebody? Did you get a picture?" Sarah asked.

"Pam didn't take off the lens cap," Ali said, dumping her spy gear.

"I didn't need a picture. I saw him clear as day," Pam said.

"Did he take the marijuana?" asked Sarah. The nervous feeling she got when Pam and Ali fought rose and lodged in her solar plexus. Why couldn't they work together and put aside petty crap for the greater good?

"Ali attacked him so he dropped it and ran," Pam said.

"I did not."

"You did too. And what was with making all that noise?"

"I hardly made any—"

"Sounded like a rhino thrashing around," Pam said.

"You didn't want to go in the first place so you sabotaged it. I had the lens cap off and you put it back on."

"Stop it. Stop. What happened?" Sarah said.

Pam pulled a cold Dos Equis from the cooler. "You tell her," she said to Ali.

"We waited; he came, a child if Pam's right. He's gathering up the plants so I sneak closer. He hears something and bolts—runs smack into me." Ali acted out the scene.

"What he heard was you scrambling in the ditch. If I heard it, he heard it," Pam said. She expertly slid a sliver of lime inside the neck of the beer bottle.

"He surprised me. I thought he'd leave the way he came in. Shit fire. If it's a kid, he's not much of a threat."

"That depends on who his daddy is," Pam said.

Sarah interrupted, "A child that young probably isn't growing pot, so he's working for somebody. Would you recognize him if you saw him again?"

Pam shrugged. "He looked Mexican and little, like all the kids around here. But his hair was in a bob."

"A bob?" repeated Ali.

"Like a Dutch boy. Bangs and straight at the sides," Pam said.

Sarah thought that perhaps the child was female or Native American, but she didn't want to confuse things more than they were. It wasn't certain there was a child. "So where's the dope?" she asked.

"We put it in the ditch near the little shed. I'll burn it tomorrow," Ali said.

"I'm going to bed," Pam said. She shot Ali a parting *you-screwed-up-the-mission* look.

When Pam turned away, Ali mouthed, "Bitch."

Bernie followed Pam to the tent and settled down just outside.

Sarah and Ali didn't speak until long after they heard the hiss of the tent zipper. The fire had burnt out and only the mesmerizing coals winked back at them. The breeze kicked up the scent of pinon, mesquite, and the ubiquitous sage and eased the toxic friction.

"Sorry I got so pissy, but she did screw it up," Ali said.

"It could be so wonderful here for us," Sarah said.

"I'm trying, Sarah," Ali said. "Pam just needs to get laid."

"It's more than that. Maybe she's homesick."

"Maybe, but not for New Orleans," Ali said. "Don't ever say I said this, but I think she's homesick for her family."

"Her family was so dysfunctional that—"

"That's why she needs them. So she can fix them."

"They're dead," Sarah said.

"Yeah. So it's going to be hard." Ali poked at the fire, creating mini tornadoes of ash.

The nightlife had vibrancy unlike that of Mississippi darkness that twitched with millions of creatures swinging on the food chain. Sarah thought about humid southern nights and remembered the snakes. People said that no matter where you were in the south, you were never more than a few feet from a viper den just below the soil. The northern New Mexico night seemed comparatively void of life. No mosquitoes whined. A moth made a desultory effort to flutter near the battery camp light. The desiccated air pulled at every living thing, sucking its moisture.

"What are you thinking?" Sarah asked Ali.

"The difference water makes. Water is the most important substance on earth."

"I'm trying to do Cantu-think, but it's not working," Sarah said.

"Can-do think?"

"Tu not do, like *Señora* Cantu told me to try. She'd know which skinny little kid had a hair cut like that and who he was related to, but I can't ask her directly," Sarah said.

"She's coming back tomorrow?"

"We're the most interesting thing to pop up in this county in a long time. I predict daily visits," said Sarah.

"She looks like one of those *curanderas,* folk healers, in the country in Mexico," Ali said. "Clothes like black bandages. Lord knows what might be stored underneath."

"She wears Nikes."

"Maybe it's as you said. She'll confide in you when she sees she can trust you," Ali said. "So don't ask her to tell you about the boy; make her trust you."

"Trust needs time, and I don't have that much," Sarah said. She was keenly aware that if things didn't look up soon, certainly Pam and probably Ali would insist they sell the place to the highest bidder. A sinister picture of the obsequious Mr. Ortega formed in her mind—part Pancho Villa and part Godfather.

"Not only time," Ali said. "Tell her some of your secrets. Indebt her."

"I don't have any secrets she'd be interested in. I can't tell her I fucked Randall Crane."

"You *idiota-Americana*. You're a professional chef. Lay a little kitchen magic on her," Ali said. "You used to drive Pam and me crazy with your folk wisdom: fluffier omelets with cornstarch, fluffier whipped cream with confectioner's sugar. Or is it the other way around?"

"I told her I was planting herbs. I hope I can get her to help me."

They sat in quiet, tasting the strange New Mexico sensations. Sarah's mind spiraled around the plan to win over the old lady. It was better than thinking what would happen if Judy Grace didn't show up the next day.

"Don't forget it might all be a tempest in a teapot," Ali said, scrambling to her feet.

Ali disappeared into the dark, ostensibly to use the bathroom, but when she returned, she held her guitar. She played softly the familiar melodies of her childhood, looking like an amnesia patient emerging from confusion.

Sarah watched Ali's left hand flex to form the chords. Like quicksilver her fingers passed fret to fret. She looked beatific in the light of the embers, her thick dark hair curling around her face. Sarah smiled at the contradictions she saw in Ali. Always an artist underneath, she could flip in a blink into a street brawler fighting for a parking place, or into an electrifying seductress winning the man of the hour. Sarah wondered where Ali's odyssey into Latino music and the sounds of her past would take her.

"They used to make me play whenever company came. I hated it, but I'd practice for hours so I wouldn't screw up," Ali said, as though she were reading Sarah's mind.

"It got you a lot of attention; didn't it?" Sarah asked.

"They never asked me if I wanted to. And I had to learn the Spanish guitar. I wanted to play like Emmy Lou Harris."

Sarah mumbled, "Umm," giving Ali space.

"Do you know that play, *The House of Bernarda Alba,* by Garcia Lorca?"

"No. What's it about?"

"My family. The widowed matriarch, Bernarda Alba, has a bunch of unmarried daughters, and there's only one eligible bachelor around, Pepe."

"I thought your sisters were married," Sarah said.

"Don't be so literal. The play is about domination and control. So Pepe and the youngest daughter are in love, but Mama Bernarda says the eldest must marry first, and Bernarda rules with a heart of corroded pig iron. They're all terrified of her, and hateful to each other. In the end the young girl commits suicide, and Bernarda takes a shot at Pepe. We never know if she hits him or not, but the daughter is certainly dead. I didn't want to be that girl."

What? Was there no middle ground? Sarah wondered why Ali couldn't have kept some of her Spanishness without being what her mother wanted her to be, but she said, "Whatever Pepe was, he wasn't worth dying for."

"Pepe meant escape," Ali said. Her fingers executed an insanely difficult passage in the music.

"Well, you're not that girl," Sarah said. She pulled herself up to her knees, readying herself for the tricky balancing act of standing up. "Your Mama can't hear you, and I'm not going to tell on you. It's your music too, Ali. Claim it if you want to."

Sarah teetered toward the tent, unzipped it and disappeared inside while Ali played *La Paloma*, the first song she had ever learned to play on the guitar. She sang softly the Spanish words and the cooing sounds of the *paloma*, the dove.

Sarah let the music lull her. *Maybe nothing bad will happen.*

15

GREATLY RELIVED, SARAH WAVED enthusiastically when Judy Grace's new Ford Bronco pulled into view on the dusty road. Pam and Ali stood beside Sarah just inside the arched gate.

"Jesus Christ, Sarah," Pam said. "That woman has put us through hell with her stupid mistakes. Quit being so friendly."

"Shut up. You're mean enough for both of us," Sarah said, holding onto her smile.

"I am so glad to meet you in person," Judy said, jumping out as soon as the Bronco stopped. Her boundless enthusiasm sounded almost southern. "This is Miles Tutor. I hope you don't mind that I brought him along. If he can't fix your water, nobody can," Judy said, pointing to the short, pudgy man who was sliding out of the vehicle.

"So much for new approaches to old problems," Pam murmured.

Miles looked glum and hot, but briefly pumped each outstretched hand.

Sarah felt insanely cheerful as though she could inject, if not some goodwill, some good luck into the situation.

"I'll take a look around," he said, and without waiting for directions, shuffled through the courtyard into the hotel.

"You certainly sound like you're from the South. I love southern accents. They're so—" Judy Grace said, waving her flared fingers that said, *sexy-sultry-seductive.*

In her most overdone Delta molasses voice, Pam said, "How could you let us come out here with these conditions? And I'm not just talking about the lack of water and electricity." The accent shifted out of southern and into pissed off. "Some of the locals have harassed us. What if things had gotten out of hand? What if the country *caballeros* or *vaqueros* or what ever the hell they call themselves had gotten a little tanked up and come on out here for a little fun? Hmmmm?"

Judy Grace was unable to speak for a moment. It was impossible to tell if it was fear of a lawsuit or the image of three ravaged women that silenced her. Sarah took over.

"It hasn't been very pleasant here, Judy. We're upset. We depended on you. You said there was water and power and instead we had *Penitentes* and prowlers. And there's more."

"More?" Judy squeaked.

"Like marijuana growing on the property. That little fact wasn't disclosed," Pam said.

Concern hardened the realtor. In spite of liberal foundation makeup and lipstick, she paled.

"Tell me everything you know about this Jami Ortega," Sarah said. "I think most of our problems are linked to him."

"He wants to intimidate us and buy the place when we run away," Ali said.

"And if he isn't behind this, who is?" Pam asked.

Sarah imagined that Judy Grace would think their suppositions ridiculous. She'd say they were tired, stressed and over-reacting.

Judy Grace paused.

Sarah knew they looked sunburned, dirty and rumpled. Bernie looked more like a white magnolia than any of them did. But she hoped they looked determined.

"Jami Ortega lives south of Ojo Caliente, but owns land all over the state," Judy began. "He's a predator. When someone gets into trouble, Ortega sweeps in and buys their place before they know what happened. Half the county is related to him or beholden to him. He's capable of harassment, but…" Her voice faded.

"But?" Ali said.

"He does everything legally." Judy said. "What he did to my friends was get their place condemned by the county. Later on he bought it from the county because the county didn't need it after all. Surprise. But *Penitentes* sound too theatrical for Jami Ortega—too much room for things to get out of his control."

"Does somebody else want it?" Pam asked.

"No one's made an offer," Judy said, her color warming a bit. "Look, you can sell this place to him. He'll probably give you what you paid. I'm sure he's furious that somebody outsmarted him. But—" Again she stopped.

This time Pam said, "But what?"

"It's a terrific property, cheap even by rural New Mexico standards. It has water, views; it's close to Santa Fe. The hotel is historic. You could buy a trailer to live in short term."

"Three trailers," Ali said.

"Think about it," the realtor continued. "In a few more years, you won't be able to touch this much land, and certainly not for this price."

"Why do you think Ortega wants this piece so much?" asked Sarah.

"Two reasons. You know about macho? *Machismo*?" Judy asked.

Pam and Sarah simultaneously looked at Ali.

"That's why he wants it now," Judy said. "He didn't want to lose it, especially to outsiders, to women. He has problems with women."

"What kind?" Pam asked.

"He beat his wife, and she left him. I think that pushed him over the edge."

"Beat her?" Ali asked.

"Broke her jaw and detached a retina. Maybe other things," Judy said.

"Why isn't he in jail?" asked Sarah.

"They made a deal. She got a divorce and some money in exchange for not pressing charges."

"I bet she moved away, and I know she's never stopped worrying about when he'll turn up again," Ali said.

"Nobody knows where she is," Judy said.

"If saving face is one reason, what's the other?" Sarah asked.

"I can't tell you why he wants it, but I know him. There's something valuable here that he knows about," Judy said.

Sarah felt a thrill. This was the second confirmation that there was something valuable on the land over and above the place itself. *Lagniappe.*

"I brought something to eat and drink. Can we sit down while Miles pokes around?" Judy asked, pulling a huge tote bag from her Bronco. When no one objected, she pushed past them and marched into the kitchen where she poured lemonade and set out fresh fruit and croissant.

"You think its something like the government is putting a highway through here and the owner stands to profit?" asked

Sarah. She swirled the lemonade in the blue plastic cup, her eye following the miniature maelstrom to the bottom.

Ali picked up a slice of green apple and sucked it. Inside they heard Miles Tudor bang something and swear.

"Or right-of-way for a gas or oil pipeline," Pam said.

"Of course it is," Judy said. "But what? Could be minerals or buried treasure. It could be something sentimental. They say there's a ghost here, but they say that about every old hotel."

Before they could react to the idea of a ghost-roommate, Miles Tutor emerged from the main hall. "The government might want it for dumping nuclear waste or something secret, like that Area 51 near Roswell," he said, wiping his wet fingers on his pants. "Anyway, you got water."

They cheered and ran about like sugared-up kids, turning on faucets and splashing. Ali hugged Miles. Sarah thanked Judy for finding the water engineer and thought that whatever he was charging them, it was worth it.

"It's hard to say if anybody tampered with the system or not," he said. "It's mostly the original hotel water system. There's a small natural spring, an aqueduct, a cistern, and all manner of pumps and gizmos." He chugged his lemonade. "I'll try to show you how it works. It's old and has been remuddled lots of times. You probably ought to think about getting a new system."

"How much will that cost?" Pam asked.

Sarah looked away to avoid the accusation in Pam's eyes.

"Don't ask," the engineer said.

They had water. Judy Grace offered to meet Pam at the records office in Santa Fe to help research the hotel's history, geology, tax records, even the ghost, who Judy remembered was supposed to be a young woman. When the two left early that afternoon, the mood at the hacienda had greatly improved.

"Electricity and hiring workers hold the highest priorities," Pam said. They were back to their endless listing.

"What do they expect us to do?" Sarah mused.

"Who's they?" asked Pam.

"The enemy. Probably Ortega. The electric company. Who knows?" Sarah said. They sat on the shaded veranda in the new Wal-Mart chairs Sarah had purchased. The ancient, asthmatic fountain gurgled in the courtyard as the spring forced its waters through mineral-encrusted portals.

"Unless we owe it money, the electric company can't deny us power," Pam said. "Eventually it'll turn on the juice, but it's taking its time because—"

Ali cut Pam off. "Because of Ortega or whoever controls the electric company. I say we get a lawyer and—"

"That's what they expect us to do," Sarah said. "Why up the ante and give them the excuse they need to be nastier to us? I say we use the generator another week and see what happens. They have our request for service in writing."

"Okay. What about getting workers?" Pam asked. She finished off the last of Judy Grace's papaya.

"Maybe we can get people to work if we pay more," Sarah said. "I'll ask *Señora* Cantu." Already the escalating costs were starting to worry Sarah. "What we can do now is make a list of everything that has to be done before winter."

"Winter?" Ali said.

"In four months it'll be cold at night. Fall rains may come," Sarah said.

They agreed that the core of the hotel that included the lobby, kitchen and prime hotel rooms had to be made habitable and that roof had to be patched. The rest of the place would have to wait. What they didn't agree on was who got what room or rooms to convert to private quarters.

They walked through again, stopping in a large room that might once have been an office.

"My pottery studio has to be on the ground level. It makes sense for my room to be near it," Pam said.

"I thought you wanted the view of the mountains," Sarah said.

"I do. So if I had the two rooms next to this one, that'd be perfect."

"Pam, I can climb the steps a few times a day, but I have only one good leg. I have to be on the ground floor," Sarah said.

"I want the three rooms on the back, second floor," Ali said. "Any problem with that?"

"No, but it's going to cost more to do all three and the balcony outside," Sarah said. "That's a disproportionate share."

They wandered room to patio to room. With enough money each space offered endless possibilities. Without it, they were dreary and worn. Most walls sported cracked plaster and curling paint and whole sections of adobe walls and Saltillo tile floors were reverting to dirt. The carved wood doors refused to fit into their jambs, preferring to laze ajar. The windows, however, were perpetually frozen by old paint and time. One room smelled damp, though no water was nearby.

"Let's have a lottery. We can draw for the contested spaces," Pam said.

"Okay, but I have to be on the ground floor," Sarah said.

"Fine, but there are several ground floor locations," Pam said, "including that huge dining room that we'll never need."

They turned into the dining room and stepped onto a floor of long, wide planks of heart oak. At one end of the room was a massive fireplace, the kind in which a caldron of stew or a whole hog could cook. Scattered about the dining hall were old chairs, their stretchers broken, seats split, and heavy tables big as doors. A row of seven tall windows pierced the long southern wall, each with a deep sill. Outside the remnants of a garden poked up in the tangled vegetation.

"Not very cozy for a bedroom," said Sarah, imagining her bed floating in the middle of the huge room as in some Marc Chagall painting. But it would make a great restaurant.

"Think of all of it as raw space. Like lofts in New York City. Don't be so traditional," Ali said.

Leaving the huge dining room, they crossed into the lobby.

"I found and bought a hotel," Sarah said, a little more forcefully than she intended. "That's not traditional."

"Then why are you trying to decorate it like your Aunt Charlotte would?" Ali said. "I'm going to burn those marijuana plants. I vote for Pam's lottery idea, but in the meantime I'm going to camp out in the room at the top of the stairs." Ali left them in the lobby under its wagon wheel lighting fixture. Shreds of cobwebs drooped from its heavy chain.

Sarah crossed behind the old reception desk. "This could still work as a hotel," she said.

"Can you imagine how much work that would be?" Pam asked.

Sarah ignored Pam comment. "Try to find out about the social history of this place when you research it. I keep thinking of the *Wizard of Oz.*"

"There's no place like home?" Pam said and clicked her heels together three times.

"Exactly. Dorothy went on a quest for what was right under her nose. Damnit, we're not seeing the real value of this property, and Ortega does," Sarah said.

"You think he wants to make it into a hotel again? Its value is in what it really is?" Pam asked.

Before Sarah could answer, the heavy double doors leading into the cavernous room behind the lobby burst open. Startled, they screamed. Sarah stumbled backward, barely avoiding a fall. A breeze rode through the room and out.

"The ghost," Pam said, and started into the room the ersatz *Penitentes* had used for a sanctuary.

"Wait, Pam. Somebody might be in there," Sarah whispered.

Pam didn't hesitate. Inside, the only light came from a series of a dozen, fixed windows thirty feet up. Sarah crept in behind Pam.

"No wonder they picked this room. It feels like a church," Pam said.

"It must have had some special purpose. It's too big for a storage room. Look," Sarah said. She pointed to an iron slot in the floor into which a bolt on the door fitted. "Somebody had to have pulled this up for the doors to open."

"Well, they're gone now," Pam said. Clearly the room was empty.

"Don't tell Ali about this. At least don't say it was a ghost."

"Sarah, it wasn't a ghost. I was kidding. Get a grip. Doors pop open sometimes without the aid of the supernatural."

"What are y'all doing in here?" Ali asked. Her voice reverberated around the room. This time it was Pam who nearly toppled over.

"Shit, you scared me. What's wrong?" Pam said.

"Wow. The reverb in here is terrific," Ali said. "Like a shower."

"Is something wrong?" Sarah said.

"No. I want you to look at something I found," Ali said.

"Heroine or illegal arms?" asked Pam.

"Come see."

"Dead bodies?"

Letting Sarah set the pace, they headed out of the hotel, through the courtyard toward the dilapidated hot house, near a warren of old sheds. "I think Ali's right. We should move into the hacienda today. Find temporary quarters," Sarah said.

"Is it okay with you if my temporary place is the room I want for the studio?" Pam asked.

Sarah flinched at Pam's pushiness. Was Pam always going to be so difficult? "Sure, Pam."

"Ali, where are we going?" Pam said. She pulled stickers from her pants legs.

"Quit bitching."

"Did you burn the marijuana?" Sarah asked Ali.

"I was about to when I found this thing." They stood before some sort of overgrown mound.

Pam pulled back the weeds and vines that covered the hive shaped structure. The discovery of a small door rewarded her considerable tugging and sweating. It looked like an opening that would entice Alice in Wonderland.

"Holy Mother, it's a kiln." Pam crawled inside.

"Get out of there, Pam. Snakes might live in there," Sarah said. Structures like this needed exploration, but it was better to have some man go in first.

"The inside isn't damaged. I can't believe it." Her entombed voice thumped out.

Ali poked her head inside the clay tile-lined pod. "What's that?" She pointed to a fabric wad.

"A pillow. Somebody was napping out here. There were no other signs of bedclothes, but the oven now had the disquieting feel of former occupation, like abandoned miners' cabins or Anasazi cliff dwellings.

Still outside, Sarah called in, "Can you use it? Would it fire pots?"

"I guess so. Look around. Whatever they made, pieces aren't far," Pam said.

Like anthropologists, they poked through the dense undergrowth looking for clutter the past always left strewn about. Ali found a pile of red dirt that resembled an anthill.

"Adobes?" Ali asked.

"Tiles," Pam said. "You don't fire adobe bricks. This is so cool." She walked around and around the kiln as though it were a shiny new Chevy in need of some tire kicking. More decayed tiles were discovered. "They fired the floor tile here."

"Like Saltillo tile in Mexico," Ali said.

"Think it still works?" Sarah asked, poking at a pile of red dirt that did turn out to be an anthill.

"It used to," Pam said. "One way to find out."

"I'm going back to the house," Sarah said. "Manny Sanchez is supposed to deliver my stuff this afternoon, and I'm going to pick out a bedroom."

"Watch out for the ghost," Pam said. "Just kidding."

"Oh my God, what's that? A spider?" Sarah asked, pointing to the kiln above Pam's head.

"Where?" Pam screamed, wiggling away.

"Just kidding."

As Sarah trudged back to the hacienda, she took time to admire every tree, hill, and blade of grass. Her eye traced the soft curve of the courtyard wall. The hacienda was becoming familiar; becoming hers. Slipping her hand into her pocket, she squeezed her lucky charm, a carved raven with one wing that opened and folded back to reveal a tiny hiding place.

Give us peace.

She moved her personal things into a small room with large windows and then sat outside to look for Manny Sanchez's moving van. Patiently she rested in the shade of a tree whose name she didn't know and watched a line of ants march out of sight. When she rose to start dinner, Manny had still not arrived.

He's run off with my furniture. Thank God I didn't let him take the pots and knives.

16

MANNY SANCHEZ AND HIS parrot-splashed truck did not arrive that day or the next or the next. When Sarah finally got through to Margarita Sanchez in Jackson, she said she didn't know the whereabouts of her nephew.

"But he's a good boy. He's probably helping someone who had trouble," Margarita said. "Don't worry. And I showed your house twice last week."

"And?"

"No offers yet, but don't worry."

Sarah felt a bad taste gather at the back of her tongue. It tasted like worry.

✳

SARAH SAT ON THE large open patio, alternating between scratching Bernie and trying to manifest Manny Sanchez's truck. Pam was in Santa Fe, digging through public records. Stacked like cordwood in the courthouse basement, most hadn't been looked at in decades Pam had said when she called. Judy Grace was hosting Pam for a few days. Sarah felt jealous of hot showers and modern kitchen appliances.

"Just going through the newspapers will take forever," Pam said. "Judy located the tax records. She's making copies. Are you going to go shake down the electric company and get our power turned on?"

Sarah had begged Ali to deal with the electric company. "I'll find some laborers, if you'll take care of the utilities," Sarah said.

Ali agreed.

They needed someone for heavy cleaning and painting, someone else to fix the roof and patch the walls, another to cut back brush and clean out the courtyards and fountains. Maybe in a month they'd be ready for a carpenter to refit their individual quarters. They were still negotiating among themselves for personal space. The competition fostered shifting alliances, but so far, open conflict hadn't erupted. And Sarah knew that by the time they got to remodeling and decorating, all the money might be spent.

Ali wouldn't be back from the electric company for at least an hour. Sarah tried to imagine what it would be like to laze about the terrace with nothing more to do than plan the next meal. She didn't want to go into town and scrounge for help. *Señora* Cantu had told her what to do.

"Ask around and put up a note on the board," she had said. Sarah almost laughed. She knew her inquiries would draw vague looks that said *quien sabe?* or *no hablo Ingles*.

Señora Cantu visited often. The first few times she had invented an excuse for her presence. Now she turned up daily to monitor progress and offer oblique advice. She seemed to appear without ever arriving and disappear just as mysteriously. After three weeks in New Mexico, the strange old lady remained their only acquaintance.

"In Mississippi," Sarah told Bernie, "we'd have been to three church socials by now and I'd have invitations to join the garden club, the country club and the DAR."

Sarah fanned herself with her printed notice that offered to pay well over minimum wage for work on the Hotel Angustia. Ali had typed it in both English and Spanish—clear and simple on white paper. Then her vision refocused over the paper's edge to a corner of the patio ten feet away from her.

The huge rattlesnake sat coiled; only the tongue moved. Sarah felt the adrenaline sting her muscles, but her only movement was to gently slip her fingers beneath Bernie's collar.

The rattler watched her coolly. Its colorless jaws were ornamented as though embossed by a tiny diamond-patterned waffle iron. The skin was flawless; no blotch, scar or mark intruded on the waxy surface.

It's almost impossible for a poisonous snake to look anything but menacing. This one, however, looked confident. It didn't want to fight. Not yet at least. Sarah slowly edged off the plastic chaise, pulling Bernie along. Her eyes never left the snake. A thin black whip of a tongue flicked, in-out, in-out. Safely inside, she watched it through a window only a few feet away from the resting reptile. She felt it watch her too.

"Snakes are good," she told Bernie, who was beginning a new nap on a Mexican blanket. "They're symbols of regeneration. They shed their skins and begin again. They're good omens," she said. She thought she sounded convincing, but the chill that ran up her back and shoulders said differently.

-❖- ✳ -❖-

"THE POWER AIN'T ON out there?" Juan Tornillo asked Ali. She couldn't determine his position with the rural New Mexico electric company, but she recognized the runaround when she saw it.

The stuffy office never made it out of the late sixties. Orange plastic chairs with duct tape repairs lined a wall of filthy windows. Paint drips clogged the cracks in the institutional brown vinyl tiles. Two window air conditioners bravely puffed away. On one, the broken plastic letters of the brand name that had once spelled Westinghouse now read stinghouse.

Ali knew Tornillo wasn't worth too much effort. It was clear that somebody else would make the decision to turn on the power, but Ali wanted to exercise her persuasive skills. Mentally, she ran through her list of tactics and chose food and cleavage from the bottom of the file. She was holding in abeyance Spanish heritage, lawyers, and bribes.

I'll draw the line at sex with this pendejo.

She casually set the chocolate cake with a missing slice on the counter near Tornillo. The fudge icing's odor reached him before he saw the three-layer confection. Ali ignored him and pretended to search her purse for her deposit receipt.

Tornillo may have been low in the power company pecking order, but he knew who Ali was. He repeated that he thought the electricity was on. As he talked to her, his eyes never left the cake. A pair of lace panties or a hundred dollar bill would not have riveted him more.

"No sir," she said letting her Southern accent rip across the sticky counter. "I have my deposit receipt here someplace. Wait a sec." Without explanation she removed her light cotton jacket and sat in one of the orange chairs. The tight top with a built in bra and spaghetti straps was the same color as the cake. Further rooting in her bag produced the receipt and she returned to the counter. Tornillo examined as though it were a Dead Sea Scroll. His eyes repeatedly darted: receipt-cake-cleavage.

She smiled the smile she had used when she played Sally Bowles in *Cabaret*: innocent, but seductive. "Can you help me, please?"

He licked his lips.

She adjusted one strap, which had the effect of lifting her left breast an inch. As the soft flesh of her chest undulated, Tornillo rose slightly on his toes.

He dropped the receipt.

"It'd sure be nice to get the power turned on. I know you'll do your best. Thanks." Ali took back the receipt.

"Is that a cake?" Tornillo asked. His voice squeaked the absurd question.

"Chocolate fudge. I didn't want to leave it out in the hot car. Say, would you like a piece?"

Tornillo rubbed his fingers on the fake wood counter top and then on the dull white shirt that covered his protruding belly, buying time to decide if he could eat the cake and not get caught by his boss.

"Maybe just one little piece." He sounded like a child.

Inexplicably ready with a knife, Ali carved a five inch chunk of cake and delicately placed it in front of him on a brown paper towel.

"We made it last night."

"How? You ain't got propane," he said, munching so greedily that he didn't notice the information he involuntarily revealed.

The propane company had been hemming and hawing about the need for a new tank. Ali's theory was that they didn't want to put a new LP gas tank out in the sticks only to have the new owners leave in a few months. Ali wondered what else Tornillo knew about the hacienda.

"My friend is a professional chef. She made it in a Dutch oven in the coals of the fire. I made the icing. Do you like it?"

Tornillo rhapsodized about the icing, his favorite, and was angling to get another piece when the office door opened.

"You know you're not supposed to eat out here, Tony," a tall man, clearly Tornillo's superior, said. His rebuke was edged with threats of harsh punishment. He sounded like the kind of guy who could lock someone in a dark closet for a weekend.

Tornillo, his teeth black with chocolate fudge, choked and gulped, bits of cake flying out of his mouth onto the counter. Where Tornillo looked soft and Santa-like, this new man was hard as steel with the warmth of the Terminator. He wasn't going to have any cake. His eyes crept over Ali's shoulders and seemed to slip between her breasts and dive down into her underpants.

"Ma'am, this is the County Inspector, Mr. Tyrone." Tornillo looked like he had just stepped in dog shit. "Maybe he can help you." He retreated to the back room with the rest of his cake.

Tyrone returned his dark gaze to Ali, who by now had pulled on her jacket. "What's the problem, Miss?" If Ortega was the real boss, Tyrone was his boy, and he wasn't going to be seduced with peeps and sweets.

Ali explained again the lack of electricity and his office's failure to call her back.

"I did try, but your cell phone was either off or you were out of range. Out here in the country, we don't have that many towers. Cell phones can be a problem." He squeezed a Camel from its pack, his eyes never leaving her.

Ali tried not to look at the bottlecap-sized lump over Tyrone's left eyebrow. It unbalanced his face, making it more sinister.

"I don't think the company can refuse to sell us electric power," Ali said. Her implication hung in the air like a rancid fart. She didn't know who Tyrone's legal boss was, but of course he had one. Surely, Ortega didn't have the whole state in his pocket.

His eyes narrowed. "I inspected that old hotel six months ago. It's a wreck. Until the infrastructure is upgraded, it's not safe. You can get power, but you can't live in it."

"What?" She didn't want to tell him that they had just moved in.

"I'll inspect again after you correct the problems," he said. He looked like he enjoyed making her uncomfortable.

Judy Grace had said nothing about this, but if Tyrone were right, Sarah, Pam, and she could probably get out of the deal. The sale would be void. Just what Ortega wanted.

We need a lawyer, Ali thought.

"Can you be specific about what we have to do?" Ali asked.

"Sure." Tyrone gave her a sick smile that showed his stained teeth. "I'll get you a punch list. Maybe the end of next week."

She imagined that Tyrone knew some archaic regulation and was twisting it to use it against her. Ultimately in a court of law it wouldn't stand up, but right now it could delay renovation and altogether halt occupancy. Ali collected her cake, feeling like a rube.

Tyrone waved goodbye, his eyes filled with victory.

Bumping down the dusty road she regretted offering tits and ass for electricity. Pam would have said *it's okay to be a prostitute if you know that's what you're doing. You're selling out for something bigger you need.* Ali felt slimy.

On the way back to Angustia, Ali spotted *Señora* Cantu at the grocery-gas station. She pulled the Honda over. She knew the *Señora* would understand any informal method of getting business done.

The place had a convenience store look in front, but appended behind was a long, low building. Shelves ran straight back without aisles piercing them so it was necessary to walk all the way to the back or the front to get to the next aisle. As she walked deep into the cavernous store looking for *Señora* Cantu, she had the feeling she was walking back in time. Fewer and fewer items were on the shelves. She passed bottles of hot sauce spaced six inches apart, two lonely boxes of oatmeal, a dusty package of Faultless starch. A fluorescent light with a faulty ballast buzzed overhead, casting the naked shelves in a sulpherous glow. She felt dizzy.

Something ran past, brushing her. She screamed and whirled around sending a bottle of Karo to the floor. The syrup rolled, zigzagging down the aisle toward the front of the store. Running just ahead of it was a small child in ragged jeans and a red T-shirt.

The boy harvesting the marijuana.

A voice at her side said, "He's one of the *huerfanos.*" It was *Señora* Cantu.

Ali looked around trying to determine how the old woman had crept up on her. Had she been tucked into a shelf with the emergency candles and rat poison?

"The orphans?" Ali asked. There's an orphanage in Angustia?"

Cantu laughed. "No, *Señora, gaminos.*

"Homeless children?" Ali asked. She forgot about asking the woman about the subtleties of county permits.

"*Como se llama el chico?*" Ali said, asking in Spanish the name of the ragamuffin who had just disappeared out the front door.

"Gabriel. *Simplemente* Gabriel."

Risking directness again, Ali asked in Spanish, who does he work for?" *Por quien trabaja?*

Señora Cantu smiled. "He's Lukey's boy, for now. Helper, not son. Sleeps in his garage. He's maybe eight."

Ali started to ask more, but *Señora* Cantu put a hand on Ali's arm. "Could you give me a ride out to my brother's?"

Ali helped the old woman into the car and followed her directions.

"Pay attention so you can get home," *Señora* Cantu warned. "Here on it's all private dirt roads."

Cantu denied any important knowledge of Ortega, but did tell Ali that Lukey was Ortega's cousin. Lukey had done time in prison on a drug conviction, but was back with his wife, Amelia. They lived out in the country.

"This Gabriel doesn't have any relatives?" Ali asked.

"Yes and no. He and his Papa came through with some migrant workers on their way to Colorado. The boy was sick and stayed at the clinic one night. The workers left."

Ali interrupted, "The father left his son here?"

The *Señora* nodded and waved a boney finger toward the left fork of the road. "He came back at the end of the season and got a job doing auto repair. Gabriel was living with *Señora* Lopez by then." *Señora* Cantu rolled a cigarette; the tobacco covered her lap and drifted down to the floor mats. "After the *Señora* died, he moved around."

"Why didn't Gabriel live with his father? He moved here, right?" Ali asked, turning sharply to avoid a pothole.

"His father is a drunk who gives him nothing but beatings."

"What's the father's name?" Ali asked.

"Enrique Cardenas. You'll see him. He's around."

Ali wondered how the boy had survived. Where was his mother? Ali had to force herself to squelch the tide of maternal feeling that rose, threatening to engulf her and pull her out to sea.

"Listen, forget about Gabriel for a second and tell me about getting permits in this county," Ali said.

In a tangle of Spanish and English, the *Señora* told Ali how things worked in Angustia. By the time they approached the house, Ali understood that laws and regulations were largely at the discretion of the enforcer unless one wanted to make a stink. Making a big stink, however, could be dangerous.

"I want to file for the temporary permit today," she said. *Señora* Cantu had explained how people somehow got around inspectors and regulations by obtaining a temporary permit to occupy, to irrigate, to blast, to just about anything.

"You can do anything in this county for ninety days," Cantu had said.

"After the ninety days they can close you down, but usually they don't bother. My cousin slaughters his livestock and all his neighbors'. He got a temporary permit in 1989," Cantu had told her. The shrug that followed said the cousin was still in business.

Ali let *Señora* Cantu off at her brother's rambling farm house whose dilapidated condition was effectively concealed by bowers of climbing roses and expansive beds of flowers and vegetables. Ali refused the invitation to come in.

"Next time. I have to get this permit."

Ali turned left when she shouldn't have, and it took her ten minutes to realize she was lost. When she turned the car around, she saw a dark truck kicking up a tail of dust, coming on fast. She sped up, but in seconds it was riding her bumper. Ditches and fences hemmed her on both sides. Pulling off wasn't an option. In her rear view mirror she could see a big man in a cowboy hat.

Her cell phone informed her that she was not in a zone. She drove faster, looking ahead for a driveway leading to a house. There was no house, but there was a large white and black cow in the road ahead.

I'm not going to kill a cow.

Slowing, Ali honked at the languid bovine that had escaped her pasture. The same ditch and fence that held Ali on the road prevented the cow from doing more that trotting ahead in front of the car. The menacing truck, pistons throbbing, followed. Ali tried her cell phone again. Nothing. When she looked up from dialing, the truck's driver was at her window walking at the speed of the cow and her car.

"Stop," he said.

The car doors were locked, but getting past the cow, that had now stopped to graze on ditch grass, was still impossible. She stopped and turned her toughest look on him.

"What? Why are you following me?" she yelled through the tinted pane.

"What were you doing coming up to my place?" he said.

"I got lost. I let *Señora* Cantu off at her brother's," she shouted.

Ali knew the dangers of wandering up country hollows where you weren't known or invited. Years ago it had been illegal distilleries, now it was meth-amphetamine labs. They had them in Mississippi, but she had read that New Mexico led the nation in meth production.

"Who?" he asked.

"Cantu. None of your goddamn business. I just got lost." Ali read in this man a distaste for weakness, a man who paradoxically elicited fear, but hated it when he found it. She continued her aggressive tone, "Get that damn cow out of the road and leave me alone," she yelled through the window. The glass fogged, but she could see the meanness ebb from his eyes.

It worked.

He pointed his finger at her and then backed away. His whistle and yip caught the cow's attention, and it hurried its crooked gait to the end of the fence and scooted into a hidden opening. Ali couldn't help being impressed with the man's authority and power with the animal. She had to admit, he'd gotten her attention too.

Ali didn't wait for good-byes. She left him behind in a blur of white dust, and this time found the route back to town.

Both Tornillo and Tyrone were gone by the time Ali got back to the utility office in Angustia. The clerk glanced at the special ninety-day permit Ali had just gotten from the county office and promised the power would be on the next day.

It can't be this easy, Ali thought. *Maybe you get a break every now and then.* She had the distinct feeling that if Tyrone had been there, things wouldn't have gone so well. The whole process seemed reminiscent of voter registration practices in the south prior to civil rights legislation.

At least I got it. I'm not totally useless, she thought as she carefully tucked the permit into her purse.

"You have to post it. Put it in a clear plastic bag so the rain doesn't fade it out," the clerk said. "Course there hasn't been any rain in months, but still—"

"I'll put it on the front door."

The clerk looked over her shoulder and then whispered to Ali, "The County will make us shut it off in ninety days unless it passes inspection."

"Mr. Tyrone is sending me a list of things we have to do," Ali said.

The clerk pressed her lips together tightly and looked down at the scratched counter. "By then, maybe some more things will have to be done."

"I see," Ali said. "Thanks."

She drove toward the hacienda more confused. What new tricks would Tyrone and Ortega pull? And she wondered why the clerk seemed to be warning her.

17

IN THE SANTA FE's record repository, Pam churned through reams of information on the Hacienda Angustia. She organized the disparate facts and took a book of notes.

Judy Grace's connections in Santa Fe smoothed the way to get a lot done fast. Moreover, Judy was gathering all the information from tax records that the hotel had generated in a century. She said she felt she owed the women some help.

Pam read that the Cordova family had built the hotel in 1851. As the winds of the economy had blown, so had the prosperity of the hotel. It had been bought and sold three times and expanded four times. In spite of being slightly off the beaten track, it had managed to be a going concern for many years. The Great Depression sounded the death knell for the aging property, and it had not been run as a hotel since WWII.

Alone in the records vault for hours, Pam looked at her watch. It was almost four. Everything closed at five. She had gathered a stack of volumes to reshelve, when the windowless room plunged into complete darkness.

Then she heard footsteps, very quietly coming toward her. Easing out of her chair, Pam felt for the wall and thought of

Wait until Dark, the movie in which blind Audrey Hepburn was pursued by bad guys. Pam, like Audrey, realized that if it was dark for her, it was dark for the other person too. Pam stifled the urge to call for help. Better the stalker didn't know where she was. Easing down on all fours, she crawled under the heavy oak library table. Carefully she pulled her purse in beside her and let one hand rummage. The footsteps had stopped and the only sound was Pam's breathing. Her hand crept over her car keys, a pen, wallet, checkbook and a travel-sized dental floss.

She felt for the space between the chairs and hurled the floss container to a far corner of the room. It smacked the wall and skittered to the floor. The intruder stepped only one step, but betrayed his position. He or she was standing beside Pam's table.

Pam's fingers curled around the small pair of scissors at the bottom of her bag. Slowly she extracted them, ready to stab anything that presented itself such as a shin or foot. It was too black to see. She froze. She was still waiting when an entire section of bookcases packed with heavy volumes crashed around her.

She sat beneath the table in the dark. She was unharmed but had to fight to keep back tears. She thought the prowler had left, but waited for what seemed like ten minutes, listening for any sounds. Then in the blackness, she dug her way out from beneath the table, found the door and alerted the desk clerk.

"We're going to have to close this room until someone can reshelve this stuff," the clerk said, looking at the mess.

"How long will that take?" Pam asked, retrieving her scissors and stowing them in her bag.

"I can put in a work order tomorrow. Not too many people go through this older material," she said. "It won't be a high priority."

Pam stepped over the volumes and around the fallen bookcase, appreciating that she had been protected by the heavy table.

"I really need to finish going through these. I was just getting to the stuff I need," Pam said.

"I can call you when it's done, but it's not safe like this. You said the case just fell over?"

"Yes," Pam said. "See, they're all joined together by those metal strips? I think this one was top heavy anyway and the strip broke and down it went."

"Yeah, looks like. Good thing you weren't under it. It could have killed you."

Pam gave the clerk her cell phone number, collected her notebook and left. Pulling out of the parking lot, she watched for a tail, but didn't see anybody.

⚬ ❉ ⚬

PAM RECLINED IN THE pricy, lush blue leather chair in Judy Grace's den, and sipped an expensive California Pinot Grigio. Judy had offered her hospitality for as long as Pam needed it. She had decided not to tell Judy about the bookcase avalanche. She didn't want to spook her, and she needed her help. All Judy could do was call the police which wasn't going to help.

"I wonder why they built the hotel where they did?" she asked Judy.

"In the west they build everything with availability of water in mind. You have a spring," Judy said. She was painting her toenails an intense red-violet that matched the sunset shaping up beyond her patio.

Her home, bought by Judy and her former husband for $150,000 before Santa Fe became a destination for the rich and spoiled, was both beautiful and comfortable. Completely southwest in its design and décor, it blended with the sandy hills and ravines. In spite of the harmonious digs, Pam felt anything but calm.

"Weren't there Indians around here?" Pam asked Judy, who was drying her toes with a three-inch battery-powered fan.

"God, yes. Everywhere. Still are. Jicarilla, Zuni, Navajo, bunches of Pueblo tribes. Why?"

"I don't know. Just an idea that maybe the hotel had something to do with Indians," Pam said.

"Nineteenth century Indians wouldn't have been allowed to set foot in a hotel. When it closed in 1940, they still wouldn't have been given a room," Judy said.

"Not rooms. Trails, trading posts, things like that. A crossroads of some kind."

"The University has a terrific Native American Studies program, and I just happen to be friends with Wanda Begay," Judy said. She rose to get her phone book, walking on her heels, her still-damp toenails raised.

"She's the director?" Pam asked.

"Better. The museum curator. Thinks everything of historical value in New Mexico is her personal concern. God help you if Wanda catches you trying to make off with some Anasazi artifact."

Pam returned to labeling and alphabetizing her file folders. It felt good to organize something, to have a little control. She was safe here.

Judy returned from her phone conversation with Wanda Begay a half hour later.

147

"She's dying to meet you," Judy said. "We can have lunch with her at the university tomorrow if you want."

Pam nodded yes to lunch. "Did she know anything about the hotel?"

"Not much, but she said that was only because she's never investigated it. But she knows somebody who saw the ghost," Judy said.

"What ghost?"

"Your ghost. The hotel ghost. I told you." Judy said.

"Who?"

"A woman who died there. A suicide. Her appearances are written up in several accounts of psychic phenomena," Judy said.

"No, who saw the ghost, my ghost?" Pam said.

"Oh. Alex Tso. He worked out there when he was a boy—hired by the people who leased it to pasture cattle and horses. Wanda said he said he saw Lorena McCragg lots of times."

"She has a name?" Pam gaped at Judy. Now there was a fourth woman at the hotel. She had an identity. She'd probably want a ground floor room with a view.

"And get this: he said she changed her clothes. One time he'd see her in a blue robe, the next a white dress."

"Did she have different hairdos too?"

"He made Wanda a believer. She's bringing him to lunch if he's free," Judy said. "After I feed the dogs, I'm getting in the hot tub. Join me?"

"Right behind you."

-⟐- ❊ -⟐-

AFTER MIDNIGHT, WHEN PAM'S files were ordered in folders and boxes and her body soaked in seaming water, she wandered out onto the balcony that spanned a rocky arroyo. She never slept very well and tonight was no exception. Looking over the heavy iron railing, she felt the earth fall away. Santa Fe's lights flickered in the distance through the warm summer breeze. It felt so different from the south.

Why do they call it the land of enchantment?

In answer, a shooting star arced through the seamless black. She made a wish, and imagined Kenny holding her and easing her loneliness.

I wonder whose arms he hitchhiked into.

-◈- ✳ -◈-

THE NIGHT BEFORE PAM had departed for Santa Fe to research the hotel, she, Ali, and Sarah had sat under the stars contrasting Mississippi and New Mexico. She noted the absence of moisture, and Ali the absence of biting insects. For Sarah, people created the chief disparity.

"They're not rude here, but they're brusque. At home people say hello when they pass by even if they don't know you. They wave to you from their cars. In stores, they actually want to help you."

"It's the wild west," Pam had said. "The spirit of independence, make it on your own, it's what you can do, not who you're kin to."

"I'm sure they have good hearts, but most of them don't have squat for manners," Sarah said.

"They're not very friendly," Pam said.

"You mean the locals?" asked Ali.

"Especially them," Sarah said, moving so that Bernie could join her on the plastic chaise.

"Something else is going on with the locals," Pam said. "It's like they don't see us. They're afraid of something."

"If they never accept us, can you handle that?" Ali asked.

"I don't know," Sarah said.

"Besides bugs, what's most different to you?" Pam asked Ali.

"It's a feeling I never had in Mississippi or anywhere in the south," Ali said. "It feels charged here. Whatever mystical hocus-pocus they're putting out, you want to believe it. Lord, look at the high numbers of nut-nuts in Santa Fe and Taos. They read Tarot like they read Dear Abby in Mississippi. The Roto-Rooter man wears crystals and everybody's getting their muscles Rolfed, their colons detoxified, and their chakras balanced. It's health food, recycle, meditate, or leave." Ali smiled. "I kind of like it."

"Shit," Pam said. "I thought you were going to say sweet tea.

— ⁜ —

WHILE PAM DUG INTO the hacienda's history, Sarah dug into the soil of its long neglected gardens. She could hear Ali's music pulsing from the central courtyard, and she knew Ali was doing her sound and movement exercises. She'd dance wildly, chanting vowel sounds for an hour until she reached some elevated emotional state. Then she'd cry or talk to people who weren't there. Ali said she found it healing. Sarah found it puzzling.

Pam often said Ali ought to teach her technique in Santa Fe. "In Santa Fe there's a workshop for everything," Pam had said as the three finished the last of Ortega's wine. "I read an ad in some free newspaper that a woman, who doesn't even pretend to have credentials, charges $150 an hour for people to tell her their problems."

"Maybe she listens well," Sarah laughed.

"You could call yourself Dr. Charlatina."

Ali looked irritated. "It wouldn't hurt you to develop some technique for—"

"For what?" Pam asked. "Healing my inner child, creating a spiritual space? What a load of horseshit."

"Pam, we're human beings. We have histories we need to deal with," Sarah said. "Biography becomes biology."

"I meditated in the seventies, did therapy in the eighties and swallowed Prozac in the nineties," Pam said. "I'm sticking to art these days."

"You wouldn't be the first to work things out through art," Ali said.

"What do you think I need to work out?" Pam asked.

"Nothing. It's none of my business."

"What? Tell me," Pam said.

"Cynicism, for starters," Ali said. "You make fun of what I do to vent my frustrations, my grief. I'm sorry I said anything."

Pam looked as if she was going to attack, but then clapped her mouth closed. Sarah thought of a lid being held down on a pot of boiling water.

"Sorry if I hurt your feelings," Pam said. "I still think Dr. Charlatina could make a fortune in Santa Fe."

18

RANK AND FILE OF new seeds and seedlings spread before Sarah on the back of the forgotten garden. Increasingly anxious about her furniture, she looked up again to the south, hoping to see Manny Sanchez's truck, but only *Señora* Cantu appeared.

The *Señora* wanted to know what Sarah had planted and what she planned to do with her harvest.

"I'm a cook, a chef. I use lots of things that most people don't use or know about." She pointed to her verbena. "That's good in so many soups. I have to have fresh, so I grow my own," Sarah said.

Dirt caked her fingernails, as she tenderly tamped around her transplants. She touched them like they were pieces of fine jewelry.

The old lady was poking in a row of seedlings. "What are these?" she asked, petting the leaves with her stick.

"Medicinal stuff for tinctures and teas," Sarah said. "Do cone flowers do well here?" she changed the subject. "They thrive in the South." She pointed to the site where seeds of cosmos, impatiens, Johnny jump-ups, and cone flowers were buried.

The old woman remained by the medicinal plants, but Sarah deliberately refused to say more about them. All Sarah felt she had to offer was knowledge of growing and preparing food. She couldn't really whip up a magic tonic, but *Señora* Cantu didn't have to know that. Also, Sarah was pretty sure that *Señora* Cantu had some cronies who were monitoring Sarah. There was a community out there if Sarah could prove herself. The purposely mysterious garden was the first step.

"Garlic do well in this climate?" Sarah asked.

"Si. Ajo, muy bueno." She hobbled away from the interesting plants. Her gait, the result of advanced age and likely arthritis, matched Sarah's. "You planted all this by yourself?"

"Yes. Isn't there some other way to hire workers? Nobody has called or come by."

The old woman stopped, turned and ambled back to the rows of thin plants. "I don't recognize these," she said.

Sarah caught the meaning of the obvious non-sequiture: tell me what I want to know, and I'll tell you what you want to know.

"That one is Oregon graperoot, *mahonia aquifolium.* Good for diarrhea."

"Diarrhea. Ah, now I remember Ricky Gomez has three sons who do odd jobs." She looked back at the plants.

"That's a special astragalus, Huang qi. I don't know if it will grow here, but it's the best immune booster there is. The Chinese use it on cancer patients."

"Ask for Pedro Gomez. He's the best.

"You think Ortega put out the word that nobody should work for me?"

"*Quien sabe?* Who knows? But he could do that." She crouched over another clump of seedlings. "The Gomez brothers don't get along with Jami Ortega."

"But the Gomez's must have seen our notices."

"Maybe they're on vacation," she said and laughed a long, unbroken riff of gurglings.

Or maybe the Gomez trio was waiting for a word from you, Sarah thought.

"Oh, I forgot. Your Help Wanted signs disappeared last night. You have some more to put up. In case the Gomez boys don't want to work."

Before she could query the *Señora*, a shriek from the courtyard burst over Ali's music. A series of unintelligible commands followed. Sarah and *Señora* Cantu loped toward the noise.

When Sarah pushed open the ancient, hand-carved gate, she saw Ali with a strangle hold on a tiny, dark-skinned child. He or she was struggling and yelling in Spanish, but Ali held fast.

"Who are you? *Como te llamas?*" Ali yelled right back at him. Why are you spying on me?"

The child kicked at her, and she grabbed a handful of its hair. "You little urchin, I'll snatch you bald. Talk."

"Ali, don't hurt her," Sarah called.

"It's a him," *Señora* Cantu said.

The child yelled that he didn't speak English. Ali released his hair and spun him around to look at his face.

"You were the one in the store. The same one who came for the marijuana plants. Who are you?" Ali asked.

The boy looked down at his dirty bare feet.

"Gabriel. He's Gabriel," *Señora* Cantu said. "Enrique Cardenas's boy," she whispered to Sarah.

When the boy looked up and saw the *Señora*, he bolted for her and grabbed her tight around the waist. From within the black expanse of her skirt, he explained in Spanish his presence in the courtyard. It had nothing to do with pot or stealing or spying. He had heard the music and then saw Ali dance.

"He likes your dancing. He says—Tell her yourself. You speak English," *Señora* Cantu said, shoving the boy toward Ali.

Mute, he stared and sucked a fingernail.

"Okay. Go away, liar." Ali said and turned the music on again.

Surprised, Gabriel, turned to *Señora* Cantu, but she only shrugged.

"I want to dance. *Señorita, enséñame bailar.*"

"What? I didn't hear you," Ali said, feigning indifference.

"I want to dance, too," he said. "Please."

"You can't just dance. You have to learn steps," Ali said.

She turned down the music and slowly turned to him. "What will you do for me if I teach you? If you even have talent to learn," she said. Her hands were on her hips and she wore her I-don't-take-shit-from-anybody expression.

"What do you want?" he asked.

"I'll think about it. Come back tomorrow morning at nine. If you're late, don't come at all." She turned away, lifted her thick hair off her neck and closed a bone barrette over it.

Gabriel scuttled out the gate. Ali watched him go.

Señora Cantu and Sarah helped one another walk the bumpy turf back to the garden where they found a man with a grizzled white beard. He studied the ground and poked it with his cane. *Señora* Cantu launched into an animated conversation with him in Spanish while Sarah tried to decide if he was the *Señora*'s husband or father. He was neither.

"I told him you needed help," *Señora* Cantu said, "but I'm surprised he came."

Sarah looked at the old man and wondered what help he could possibly offer.

155

"Dominguez grew up right over there," the *Señora* pointed north. "He'll work in the yard for thirty dollars. He needs to pay off his storage unit bill."

Sarah didn't have any idea how much work she'd get for that amount, but she agreed and asked the *Señora* to tell him in Spanish what needed to be done.

⁂

WHEN SARAH GOT UP the next morning, three men stood by a truck in front of the main gate. They pointed at the roof and overlapped their Spanish sentences.

Her questions, "Are you the Gomez brothers?" and "Did *Señora* Cantu send you?" confused them. She called Ali to translate.

"I don't know what roofers usually get in New Mexico, but these guys are cheap," Ali said, after she struck a deal and the men were tearing off shingles.

Pam called later, saying that she had planned to come back, but instead was having lunch with a man who knew about their hotel ghost. Did Sarah mind?

"No, that's fine," Sarah said. "Some roofers showed up and took off all the rotten shingles. We have an open-air lobby now." She didn't mention Dominguez. She'd paid him fifteen dollars. Who knew if he'd come back.

"Are they insured? Bonded? Licensed? Like a real company?" Pam asked.

"It was all in Spanish. Hell, Pam, we have to take a chance. I've done everything but give blood to get somebody to work out here," Sarah said. However, she thought, if you can do better, get your ass here and do it.

Sarah felt glad for the break; things were quieter without Pam stirring them up. Sarah worked long hours on the garden with the ancient man who not only had returned, but it seemed had his own ideas about what work was important. He moved at a snail's pace, but cleverly redesigned her irrigation system so the garden had an even supply of water from the spring. He said, in Spanglish, that there was another spring on the property, a big one. But he couldn't find it and later decided maybe it was on another ranchito. He said he had often played at the hacienda as a child.

At seven the next morning, when Sarah went out to her garden carrying her third cup of coffee in one hand and dragging a litter loaded with garden tools, she found a group of young children in her courtyard. Gabriel stood but wouldn't look at her.

"It's okay. Don't be afraid," Sarah said. The children froze, all eyes on the dirt. "You're a little early for your dance lesson, aren't you?"

"They want to dance too," he said. An avalanche of Spanish followed.

"Hold on. I'll get Ali. Uh, *la teacher, instructor-o.* Wait." She headed for the kitchen but turned back. "Hey, did you have any breakfast?" As soon as the words were out of her mouth, she knew she had shamed them. They were painfully poor. Breakfast wasn't a sure thing.

"I mean, since you got up so early for dance class, and it doesn't start until nine o'clock."

They looked at one another. Sarah beckoned, turned her back and walked into the kitchen. Better not to beg them or make them feel more self-conscious.

One by one the twelve trickled into the huge kitchen. A few apparently had been there before.

"It's a real house again," one whispered.

Sarah drew up long benches and the youngsters filed in, reminding her of a scene from Oliver Twist. They were having Sarah Hunter's special organic oat cereal instead of gruel, but they looked as small and vulnerable as any of Charles Dickens' waifs.

Thirty minutes later, Ali strolled in seeking coffee.

"What's going on?" she said to Sarah through clenched teeth. Gabriel slipped from the table and ran over to her.

"They want to dance, too," he repeated. His Mexican accent was thick, but his voice had lost its childish quality.

He was so small. Today he was considerably cleaned up, as were all of them. Ragged but clean. A patch on the side of his head where someone had cut out a tangle of hair gave him a lopsided look. The eleven at the table sat frozen as though they were one eleven-headed child. *Surely they have homes,* Sarah thought.

"I'll teach all of you, but I must have my breakfast, *mi desayuno,*" Ali said. "Sweep the patio. Not a grain of sand. We begin at nine," she said and clapped her hands. They scattered like starlings.

"Ali, I couldn't send them away," Sarah said. "They had so much hope in their little brown eyes. And I could tell they were hungry," Sarah said.

"I know what I'm doing, Sarah," she said. "Come help me."

In her bedroom, Ali pulled her red dress on over her head. "Did you ever watch Sally Struthers on television?"

"Gloria, from *All in the Family?*"

"Late night TV infomercials. Pleas for dollars for starving children?" Ali said.

"These aren't actors. They're real." Sarah smoothed Ali's dress. She guessed it was a theatre costume from some play

Ali had been in. It was tight through the hips and flared at the hem, reminiscent of flamenco dancers. It was perfect.

"I know. What I don't know is why they're here. Who sent them?" Ali said.

"Oh my God. I didn't think of that. Ortega's spies?"

"Whoever. Worm their way in, look around, take or leave something. And don't forget the marijuana." Ali brushed her hair out and let the static electricity fluff it nearly into an Afro. Then she wound it into a tight bun and slid red lipstick over her mouth. "And it's also possible that they only want to dance. Let's go."

At precisely nine, Ali walked out onto the large shaded patio and gave a signal to Sarah. The CD player filled the courtyard with *El Jarabe Tapatio.*

"You will all learn the hat dance today and if you do well, you may come back next week. I expect you to do these simple steps perfectly. Get a partner."

Sarah watched, rapt. Some of the children learned fast and even the younger, less coordinated ones, faked it and ended up at the right place at the end. They were heartbreakingly cute. She thought they should film a commercial, maybe for Jell-O.

Ali worked them hard and tolerated no playing around. Frantically, Gabriel pushed and tugged at his little friends, helping *la maestra*, who said everything in both English and Spanish.

"Toe, toe, heel, heel," Ali said. "This is not difficult. How are you going to learn a *Paso Doble* if you can't do this baby stuff?" She stood in the shade of the overhang, snapping her fan in her palm.

It was all Sarah could do to keep her mouth shut. How could Ali be so stern?

"It's almost ten. We'll dance *El Tapatio* one final time. Places," Ali commanded and clapped once.

Sarah hit the CD play button. Eight bars of introduction drove the dancers to a peak of anticipation. Then they exploded into a furious flurry of toeing and heeling. Sarah could see that Ali was obviously charmed in spite of her aloof mask. They danced well for youngsters with no technique to back them up. Most had a dramatic flair and tossed their heads, looked at their partners flirtatiously and beat up a cloud of dust with their tiny bare feet.

Sarah let them out the front gate, slipping a granola bar to each child as though it were Halloween. "*Adios, hasta* next time," she called.

Ali met Sarah in the kitchen. Ali had changed into her painting clothes, and looked ready to tackle the first room of her suite. "What'd you think about the children?" Ali asked.

"I don't care if they are spies," Sarah said. "I don't care if they're aliens. Their energy is so good. They filled the house with it. Do you think they'll come back?"

"Them and more. Every bored kid in the county is going to show up next week. Better stock up on oatmeal," Ali said.

"You can have auditions. A dance company. Ali, think about it. It wouldn't take much time. I'll help," Sarah said.

"And we'll get a barn, Mickey. Or was that Judy Garland's line?"

Ali couldn't deflate Sarah's enthusiasm. "We already have a barn, but I think the courtyard would work better. It's more Spanish."

"It occurred to me that putting on a little performance for the parents might be a good thing, for us. Of course, we'd be using innocent children to make inroads into the community.

160

For our own gain, as it were," Ali said. She poured a bowl of Sarah's gazpacho and swirled the spoon in lazy S's.

"I'm not above that," Sarah said. "Besides, it'd be their gain too." Sarah clapped on her worn garden hat. "Bernie and I are going to garden until it gets too hot."

"Dominguez coming back?" Ali asked.

"I think he's done until he's back in debt," Sarah said.

"What?"

"Never mind. Are you going to paint your suite?"

"Doesn't seem like anybody else is."

Sarah stopped in the doorway. "Ali, don't you know anybody who could scrounge up some dance shoes for the children?" Sarah asked.

"Free shoes?"

"Donated shoes." Sarah cinched the bolo of her hat.

"Maybe."

"Get them some pants and skirts, too."

Outside, the roofing crew shoveled the last of the old shingles into the truck bed. In the excitement of the dance lesson Sarah had forgotten about them. Carefully, she approached.

"Tomorrow is Sunday. Work tomorrow or come Monday?" Sarah said, a little louder than she intended. "*Lunes? Cuando* you return?" Her pigeon Spanish elicited multiple nods and *Sí, Señora*s.

As they piled in their truck, she heard the confusing word *mañana* that could mean literally tomorrow or merely later.

"Have faith," she said to herself and Bernie, who trailed. "We've made progress, and we're not out of money yet." She smiled, imagining the refurbished hacienda glowing against a wild New Mexico sky.

19

Lorena McCragg was only nineteen when she died. Pam made a note on a page titled, Hotel Ghost. Lorena had come west to marry Abram McCragg, but he had died shortly after her arrival. Destitute, she went to work in the Hacienda Angustia's kitchen. Fifteen months later, her body was found in a cave; her death ruled a suicide. Without family to clamor for retribution or even an explanation, she was buried and forgotten.

Alex Tso, however, didn't buy the suicide rap.

"I saw her all the time," he said at lunch with Pam and Wanda Begay of the Native American Museum. "When I was real little, I thought she was real. Then my brother told me she was a ghost. Navajos aren't supposed to interact with spirits."

"Your brother saw her too?" Pam had asked.

"Lots of us Indian boys did," he said, reaching for another cheese biscuit.

"But you did interact with Lorena McCragg?" Pam asked.

"She never talked," he said, speaking around the biscuit, "but I thought she wanted me to see her, to know her somehow. That's why I don't think she killed herself."

Pam put down her fork. "What was she like?"

"She was mad at something or somebody."

Wanda asked, "What'd she do to make you think that?"

"Like, there were always problems in the kitchen," Alex said. "I think she caused them. I think she could make things fall off shelves."

"Could she really move things?" Wanda asked. "You saw her knock things down?"

"I never saw that, but I know she could stop up the sink and make the stove fire go out. That happened all the time. Oh, and a big mirror fell off the wall and smashed."

"Did she stop appearing?" Pam asked.

"No, in fact on my last day of work before I went to boarding school in Albuquerque, I found her and told her I was leaving. I said goodbye. I was still a kid."

"What happened?" Wanda asked.

"I'll never forget it. She was on the back staircase. She hung out there a lot. She looked so sad when I told her. I felt bad. I told her I'd come back after I graduated." Alex said.

"Did you?" Pam asked.

"No. I meant to but by then it seemed silly."

Pam didn't say anything to Alex, but she thought it was time for Alex to come back to the hacienda. If Lorena had ever been around, chances were she still was.

The waitress brought coffee.

"My favorite hotel ghost story is in southwest Texas," Wanda said. "They reopen an old hotel and a tourist sees a woman on the balcony. She's in Victorian clothing so the guest asks about her. But the hotel manager says he doesn't know anything about a lady in a costume and, get this, there isn't any balcony on the hotel. The tourist goes back and sees he's right. The balcony, however, is in many of the old photos of the hotel and in one there's a woman who looks like the lady the tourist saw. Isn't that cool?"

⁌ ✳ ⁍

PAM PACKED THE CAR with her research on the property—boxes and boxes of photocopied records and pictures—unsure if any of it would be useful. She had called about the re-opening of records storage room, but no one knew when it would be reopened to the public. She had a feeling that she had been deliberately interrupted and frightened because some important clue lay hidden in the volumes. She also had a promise from Wanda that she would come up and examine the adobes. A potter herself, Wanda was something of an expert on old abode bricks. And Alex Tso, she thought, could be counted on to come up and look for Lorena McCragg when the time was right. Pam felt good; she had done her job well. She headed her car into the summer sun, bound for the Hacienda Angustia—for home.

As Pam turned into the hacienda's drive, she saw Ortega's black hearse-like SUV. She felt slightly nauseated and thought she'd better get inside fast before Sarah bought some snake oil. She found them in the hotel lobby that now, with its roof missing, looked like a scene from Guernica.

"Buenos días, Señorita," Ortega said. The amusement in his voice made it clear that Pam was much too old to be called a *Señorita.*

Ali and Sarah sat under the open roof in the plastic chairs while the *Señor* paced, fully in control of the scene. Ortega gestured to the third chair.

"I'll stand," Pam said. "Been driving for hours." She waved dismissively, a gesture she'd seen him use.

"You have been away on a trip?" he said.

164

Treep? Pam felt sure he knew she'd been away and probably what she had been doing. It had to be one of his men who frightened her in the courthouse basement. Maybe that was why he was here. He wouldn't know she hadn't unearthed anything useful. And unless Lorena McCragg shook loose a file, Pam doubted the documents in the Miata's trunk would help them.

"Just some paperwork with our realtor. It's nice to be home again," Pam said.

The New Mexico sky blazed a dazzling blue, but the hacienda looked as though it might collapse. Cruelly exposed by the intense light, the cracked, unpainted walls and layers of dust created an overwhelmingly oppressive sensation.

Ortega smoothed the knife crease in his dark tailored trousers. Expensive, pristine cowboy boots with menacing pointed toes peeked out beneath the hems.

"I'll get to the point," Ortega said. "I am prepared to make you a better offer for this land. I want to move my horse farm here." He went on about the fallow fields and access to the highway for transport. Pam could see him trying to read each of them, searching for a chink.

"How much are you offering?" Ali finally interrupted.

"Five percent more than you paid, and I'll give you whatever time you need to vacate." He smiled as though he had just offered them *Let's Make a Deal's* grand prize.

A long pause buzzed in the afternoon sun.

"The hacienda is more work than I expected," Sarah finally said.

"And it's impossible to get anybody to work," Ali said. "You wouldn't believe what I went through at the electric company." She looked straight at Ortega, but he only gave her a sympathetic shake of his head.

Ortega pointed to the posted 90-day occupancy permit. "Ninety days won't be enough. Then what will you do?" he asked.

Pam couldn't believe they were about to sell out to this opportunist who was now oiling his way around their patio. Sarah caught her eye when Ortega's back was to Sarah. Sarah's expression was unmistakable—*play along with us.*

"It's hard to make friends here," Pam said, joining in.

"Of course, not like in the south where you lived," Ortega said. "The old ways persist in these small villages. Closed societies."

"I don't like the idea of having a ghost here. I never felt okay with that," Ali said.

"You have seen the ghost?" Ortega asked.

Pam wondered if there was anything he didn't know about the hacienda.

"She's here," Ali lied.

Ortega frowned and pursed his lips, wrinkling his moustache into a caterpillar. He didn't seem to like hearing the ghost was back.

"And there are rattlesnakes. One nearly killed Bernie," Sarah lied.

Pam thought their complaints were getting ridiculous, but couldn't resist commenting on the dryness. "My skin is turning to alligator hide. In Jackson, I look ten years younger."

"I am sure you exaggerate, but Northern New Mexico has been in a serious drought for three years now. They say there's no sign of a break." Ortega said.

"How many horses do you have?" Pam asked.

"Maybe three hundred, but don't tell anybody," he smiled conspiratorially.

"How are you going to water three hundred animals here? Our little spring barely takes care of the household needs." Pam said.

For the briefest moment Ortega looked like he had just seen the ghost. Then he recovered. "Oh yes, but it is worse where they are pastured now. The spring is something at least. I can truck in the extra water," he finished.

Pretty good recovery. "Double what we paid, and we're gone tomorrow," Pam said.

Sarah almost came up out of her chair, but Ali grabbed her arm.

"You can't be serious. It's not worth even the five percent more. I am trying to be a gentleman but—"

"Mr. Ortega, you wouldn't be here if it wasn't worth double and maybe more," Pam said. "I'm trying to be a lady, so I'm going to ask you politely to leave. We own this place and for another seventy something days we can even live in it. If we decide to sell, you'll read about it in the multiple listings."

Ortega's eyes swept over Sarah and Ali for confirmation of Pam's opinion. Wide-eyed, they nodded.

"You were playing with me, hmm? So many problems, *Señor*. I think you will regret your fun. I know some games too. Adios *Señoritas*," he said and turned. Again the sarcastic tone in *Señoritas*.

Pam wanted to throw something at his departing back, but it was Sarah who stopped him.

"Don't be mad because you couldn't cheat us. You had your chance to buy the hacienda and you failed. It's ours, and we intend to make it our home."

Bernie's ears stood up.

"Ustedes están tres viejitas secas sin idea de los problemas que estén posible," Ortega spat back.

It must have been his tone of voice that riled Bernie. Barking furiously, he tore out after Ortega, who turned at the last moment and delivered a sharp kick to Bernie's jaw. The dog wheeled and cried.

"Bernie," Sarah yelled. "Come." The dog obeyed. Before Sarah could tell if he was injured, the black vehicle spit gravel and Ortega was gone.

Only Bernie's pride was hurt.

"What'd he say in Spanish?" she asked Ali when calm had returned.

"We're three dried up old ladies who have no idea of the problems that are possible. I think that's what he said."

"Shit," Sarah said. "I don't believe it."

"Yes. Usually they throw in at least one *puta*, whore," Ali said.

"We're too dried up to be whores," Pam said, and they laughed. The tension released.

Sarah turned to Pam. "What did you find out in Santa Fe? Come on Pam, I need to hear some good news."

"Nothing to report except the stuff about the ghost," Pam said. "We have a hundred jillion files to go through. Judy and I photocopied everything to do with the property."

"What are we looking for?" asked Ali.

"Anything unusual, like if there was an Indian burial mound here," Pam said.

"Or buried treasure?" Ali asked.

"Affirmative."

"Judy said to watch for gaps in sequences. An important record could be lost," Pam said.

"Or stolen?" Sarah said.

"Missing," Pam said. "Wanda Begay directs the Native American Museum. Judy introduced me to her. She's going to look through some of the museum's records when she has time."

"Tell us about our ghost," Sarah said.

"Alex Tso says she was murdered, and she's plenty pissed about it."

"Is she violent?" asked Ali.

"She broke a mirror once. Who knows." Pam thought of telling them about the bookcase assault, but decided to wait. What could they do but become more paranoid?

Around the fire that night, the women theorized about the presence of Lorena McCragg. If she was nearby listening, she didn't let on.

"That Ortega scares me more than any ghost," Pam said. "Maybe it wasn't such a good idea to humiliate him." Even though she had participated, she thought it was stupid of Sarah and Ali to unnecessarily provoke Ortega. But she didn't say that. Nor did she say anything about the boy they called Gabriel, who seemed to have moved in while she was away.

"I know his kind, and Pam, it would only be a matter of time before it would come to this anyway," Sarah said. "He would push and intimidate until he got what he wanted."

"All we did was tease him a little, and it wasn't in front of his *caballero* buddies," Ali said. "Who's gonna know he lost face to three little dried up old ladies? Mean, dog-kicking son of a bitch."

"Look, we got a permit for ninety days," Sarah said. "My garden is a foot high, the roof is getting fixed, we have water and Ali has a dance troupe. Things are looking up."

"And there are no mosquitoes," Ali said.

"I think we're catching on to how things work here," Sarah said. "Breaking the code."

In silence they considered this possibility and how, if it were true, they might have changed to make it so.

Pam cut the quiet. "Do you really think we look ten years older here than in Mississippi?"

"I expect the dames of Mississippi would think so," Sarah said, "but I think we look better. Like women who have something better to do than apply makeup."

"My eyeliner was starting to creep before I stopped wearing it," Pam said.

Sarah pushed up the brim of her straw cowboy hat. "We wear hats because we need them, not because of the way they look."

"So you think we look okay?" Pam said.

"We look good, real good," Sarah said.

Pam wanted to catch Sarah's positive attitude, but Ortega had rattled her. She thought about how he looked and about how he had treated his wife. *He's smart and he's dangerous. We're out of our league.*

20

FOUR DAYS LATER, THE roofers had not returned. Sarah anxiously scanned the horizon for them, for Manny, and for anyone who could help. Her gaze traced the flank of a distant hill and caught what she thought was a wounded animal. It looked like a coyote, circling and stumbling. She headed toward it, but didn't have to get too close to see it was Bernie and that he was half-dead. Then she ran.

Without a thought for her one leg and its attendant difficulties, she lifted his forty pounds, carried him to the hacienda and into her bed. A veterinarian was over an hour away. She was tearing through Rodale's Herbal Guide when *Señora* Cantu arrived.

"Charcoal," was all the old woman said as she went to work preparing a mixture to force down the dog's throat.

THAT NIGHT SARAH LAY in her bed beside her poisoned dog crooning songs she had made up for him, or rather remade. Words extolling the cunning, craft, and beauty of Bernie-the-Mighty were inserted into opera arias, oldies, and even advertising jingles.

Señora Cantu said that if he hadn't ingested too much of the poison, he might make it. Sarah held him like a sick child and petted him when he moaned in pain. She wanted to kill Ortega, something slow and painful. She dozed off and awoke when a wind banged shut a window. Thunder clamored across the sky followed by intense rain.

"It hasn't rained since we got here," she said aloud, fastening the old window.

Bernie lay still, struggling for breath.

"Oh, shit. The roof."

Sarah tottered as fast as she could to the lobby. The storm had knocked out the electricity, but in the rapid flashes of lightning she could see Pam draping plastic over the vulnerable, exposed adobe walls. Ali was sweeping muddy water out the front door, but it was rushing in faster than she could get it out.

"Get a flashlight," Pam screamed over the roar.

Sarah fumbled in the dark behind the desk and found the flashlight. She jiggled the switch.

"The battery's dead," she shouted into a clap of thunder. Sarah could see Pam, standing on a table, struggling with the wet plastic. In the next lightning flash, Pam was gone. Water sloshed around Sarah's ankles and the possibility of slipping down was edging toward probability.

"Pam," Sarah called over and over. What if Pam had hit her head and was now drowning on the lobby floor? In the next brilliant zap of light, she saw Pam rising through a plastic shroud, surrounded by the wind-ripped sheets. She looked like a figure in a snow globe—maybe a hurricane disaster scene. Before Sarah could move to help her, a crash came from the room behind the lobby. Instinctively, Sarah and Ali slogged toward it.

"Don't go in there," Pam screamed into the wind's roar.

Ali opened the door.

The row of twelve high windows in room the *Penitentes* had used for their phony ritual had simultaneously imploded.

Before Ali could push the door shut, a small shard grazed her temple. Blood joined the rainwater rivulets down her neck.

"We can't do anything. Get out of here. Go to Ali's room," Pam shouted.

"No. Bernie's in my room. Go there," Sarah shouted back.

Pam grabbed Sarah's hand to help her through the muck as the three struggled out.

In the dark, Sarah found dry towels and passed them out. The storm's fury had diminished, but the rain was still heavy. She found her battery powered camp light and turned it on.

Sarah and Pam screamed.

"Son of a bitch, Ali you're bleeding," Sarah said. The rain had spread the blood down the entire front of Ali's nightgown. Sarah thought of vampires.

Pam held the light to Ali's face while Sarah gently blotted the wound.

"It's not too big. Hold still," Sarah said.

"Let me see," Ali said.

"Apply pressure," Pam said. "You have to stop the bleeding."

Ali hoisted the light near a small mirror to examine the damage. "I think it needs to be stitched," she said. The way she said it indicated she knew a trip to St. Vincent's Hospital in Santa Fe was not in the offing. Cementing that decision was another whack outside the hotel. A massive tree branch fell, and it sounded as if it landed on something metal.

✦ ✤ ✦

ALI WOKE WITH FIRST light. The ire of the storm was spent; its damage was far-reaching. She woke Pam and Sarah and the trio crept into the lobby to survey the ruin. Three inches of mud covered everything. Old stucco had washed away exposing more fragile adobes. Already, exposed adobe bricks now resembled ant hills. Outside, half of Sarah's garden was washed out and a mudslide covered the kiln. An oak branch rode the top of Ali's car.

Stupefied, they sat in the dank air, watching the sun turn the wet to steam.

"There's no power," Ali said.

"My cell phone won't work," Sarah said.

"Probably everything's out all over. How's Bernie?" Pam asked.

"The same. Cramps are pretty bad still," Sarah said.

"Sarah, if you want me to take him to the vet, I will," Ali said. She touched her cheek. Dried blood edged the Band-Aid on her cut.

"You mean to put him down?" Sarah asked and dissolved into tears. "I can't lose my Bernie." Sobbing, she left to return to her dog.

"I guess it's a good thing ole Manny never showed up with the furniture," Pam said. Then she started laughing.

Ali watched Pam's hysterics, lost in her own thoughts, jolted to reality by the arrival of an official looking truck.

"Fuck a duck," Ali said.

Pam, whose laughter had metamorphosed into tears said, "What? What's the matter?"

"It's the inspector guy. This is not good."

The man slowly got out of his truck and ambled over to Ali's Honda.

"Ladies," Tyrone said, nodding. "Looks like you sustained some damage." With one shove, he flipped the heavy branch off the top of Ali's car. It looked like a giant ax had slammed down on the roof.

"Not so much. Can I help you?" Ali asked.

Tyrone sauntered over to the two women.

"It's bad all over the county and more thunderstorms are predicted." He pulled a red tag and a form from his jacket. "I'm going to have to red tag the place. You got a roof falling in, ancient wiring. Is your water still running?" he said.

"What does a red tag mean?" asked Pam. She still wore her bathrobe and muddy garden clogs.

"You can't use the place until it passes a full inspection. You girls could get killed in there." He looked at Ali's bandaged cut as though he were going to touch it.

"We're not girls," Pam said.

Tyrone smirked.

"We have a temporary permit. You can't kick us out before that," Ali said. She pointed to the permit, still dry as baby powder in its Ziploc bag.

"Can and am. You have twenty-four hours to get out of the building, but if I were you, I'd leave now. It's not safe here." He slid his hands into his pants pockets and let the double meaning sink in. "When you get it all fixed up, I'll come out to inspect."

"You've got to be kidding," Pam said.

Looking like the bad man in a western film, he sauntered to the door and wired the tag to its handle. "Sorry, ladies." He turned toward his truck and walking away added, "I'm not kidding about more rain."

✛ ❊ ✛

Sᴀʀᴀʜ ᴇʏᴇᴅ ᴛʜᴇ ᴄʀɪsᴘ red tag that had forced a meeting of the three women. They sipped their instant Maxwell House in silence. Water from the storm sat in pools reflecting their misery.

Ali chewed her cuticle, spitting bits on the sodden floor while Pam's fingers roved through the hairs on her forearms, snatching out the irregulars.

"Want more coffee?" Sarah asked. Numb with exhaustion, she felt the brunt of her impetuous decision to pull up stakes and boogie to New Mexico. It seemed to be over and there weren't many pieces to pick up. And the mud was starting to stink.

Ali shook her head. She mumbled something Sarah couldn't understand, but Pam stood and held out her cup.

"I'd love some coffee," Pam said, deliberately slopping the remains from her cup on the floor. "Real coffee and a hot shower, a toilet that flushes, a phone that rings, a lamp that lights, and a roof that does what roofs are supposed to do." With each phrase her volume lowered. Almost whispering she said, "I want to accept Ortega's offer, on bended knees if necessary, and get the hell out of here."

Ali looked up. "I'm with Pam." Her left foot smacked the old Saltillo tile floor and a slow cucaracha had eaten his last meal at the Hacienda Angustia.

Pam glared at Sarah, challenging her.

"His offer will stink," Sarah said. "Under the circumstances, he won't give us what we paid. *Señora* Cantu says there's a treasure here. Something valuable. We just have to find—"

Pam cut her off. "The babblings of a crazy old lady, the only person in town who will talk to us, is no reason to stay. Sometimes you should cut bait."

"And sometimes you need to fight," Sarah said.

"Let me review for you the reality of this nightmare and then you tell me how we can refuse Ortega," Pam said. "One, he wants the land, who gives a shit why, and he controls the building inspector, the bank, the hardware store, and the butcher, the baker, and the goddamn candlestick maker." She was pacing now, blazing through the kitchen by the blackened mouth of the fireplace, past the ten-foot doors and under the soggy, dried herbs that some long-dead cook had hung from the solid fir beam.

Sarah tried to interrupt. "But—"

"And two, we can't get materials, an occupancy permit, or workers who will show up, but we do have a red tag that won't go away."

"Sarah, I don't think the electricity is going to come back on anytime soon," Ali said. Compared to Pam, she sounded gentle. "They have all the power. They can wear us down. Anyway, it's like we're on Mars. We don't fit in here." She nailed another roach.

Sarah knew they were right. The situation was impossible. It was easier to leave and leaving was a response she knew well. Also there was no man to step in and take charge. They were helpless. She felt like a one-legged, ageing *Doña* Quixote, dreaming impossible dreams. Maybe Ortega would take pity on them if they kissed his tight ass really well.

And yet the feel of the kitchen, a place that begged for care, the wacky garden that promised everything for a drink of water, and the New Mexico light, the shifting indescribable light gave her hope.

Quietly Sarah said, "Go if you want. I'm staying." Holding back tears, she continued. "That son of a bitch Ortega knows something, but even if he didn't, I'm not running. I'll find a way to buy you out." The sob in her throat blocked more words, and it took all her will to stuff it back.

Pam lightened up a little at Sarah's emotional display. "It's not the Alamo, Sarah. We can go somewhere else. There are lots of ranches."

"I planted a garden and half of it's still out there. I'm going to eat those onions and carrots and radishes. That bastard may win, but he's going to remember Sarah Weddington Hunter."

"Sarah, how can we fight him?" Ali asked.

Sarah took strength from the consideration that resistance was even a possibility for Ali. "I don't know. But we have to find a way. Maybe we'll buy what we need from eBay; we'll live on less and get tougher. I don't know, but we've got to fight. We've got to stay."

"That's a great Scarlett O'Hara speech. I'm sorry Sarah. I'm out of here," Pam said. "I'm going back to New Orleans." Pam walked out into the morning that had decided to be clear and dry, and drove off in the convertible.

Ali and Sarah sat in silence as the sounds of the car faded.

"When did she pack?" Ali asked.

Sarah didn't answer and their silence metastasized into despair.

Ali ran her index finger around the perimeter of her Band-Aid. "Think it'll scar? I don't think it'll scar," she said.

Sarah thought about captains on sinking ships and replayed the scene from the movie *Titanic*. She was feeling the icy water of the north Atlantic strike her in the chest when a soft whining topped the ocean's fury. Bernie, wobbly but very alive, was licking her fingers.

21

WITH NO PARTICULAR ROUTE in mind, Pam headed south. In Madrid, pronounced Mad'-drid by the locals, she ate lunch. Sitting at the bar, barely able to get down the hamburger she ordered, she attracted the attention of hippie-looking guy about her age. He had a sweet, sad appearance—a little chewed up by life and surprised that things hadn't been easier. He admired her sun hat, then her smile. After she paid and slid off the stool, he asked her if she wanted to get high.

"That's not a question I hear very much anymore," she said.

"In Madrid it is. I'm Wade. My pickup's in the parking lot."

The smoke hit the windshield and blossomed like an atomic bomb cloud, filling the cab. It was good weed. Pam could feel herself relaxing into a honey-sweet high. Wade talked incessantly, something about a job he used to have at a foundry where they made bells. He also used to have a family. Half listening to him, Pam thought that most of Wade was in the past and the energy he used to fuel his past robbed him of much of a present. She identified with the malady.

She got back on the highway about three that afternoon, surprised that Wade hadn't invited her to spend the night.

"I could live in a place like Madrid," she said aloud to her reflection in the rear view mirror. A bit of the marijuana high lingered, curling around her senses. "A cute little outpost locked away in a hippie time warp could work for me. Make those hand-painted tiles, hang out, get stoned and get by. Why not?"

When she bumped into Interstate 40, she turned and headed east, but had gone only ten miles before she started looking for another less-traveled state road. Since Madrid she had felt pretty sure that going straight back to New Orleans wasn't such a great idea. A less direct route would permit time to think. A right turn out of Moriarty headed her in the direction of Roswell, the town that had built a reputation on UFOs.

Why would extraterrestrials have crash landed in Roswell? Mere chance or were they scoping out the New Mexican desert for some reason? She looked out the window and imagined a Puebloan alien colony hovering in the haze. Maybe Ortega had come from there.

The mindless advertisements for cars, ice cream and upholstery on a Tucumcari radio station segued into a religious program. Pastor Jimmy Rathborn was preaching the gospel of prosperity. His high-pitched voice revved like a drill, now yelling and then whispering.

"God wants you to have all the SUVs, speedboats, and fifth-wheelers you want. Manna from heaven will come down unto you if you have faith." Luxurious trips to theme parks were promised.

She was familiar with Rathborn's southern counterparts, and listened for him to get to the part about how this rush of riches would begin with an offering paid to Rathborn. The bigger the donation, the bigger the reward.

She hit the off button.

With speed control set on seventy, she took off her hat and let the sun warm her blond streaks. The sun visor drooped and she caught her reflection in the mirror.

"Shit, I look old."

Aridity was the enemy. She traced the deepening lines from the side of her nose to the corner of her mouth. Ali said theatre make-up people called them naso-labial folds, and they were a big deal in making younger actors look older and vice versa. In addition, faint lines ringed her mouth and eyes—arroyos on their way to becoming grand canyons.

One good thing about New Orleans was its humidity. It had a high crime rate, notoriously crooked government, vice, poverty, and all the problems poverty spawned, but by God it was wet, and you didn't look so old there. She slammed the visor back up in place.

Sooner or later, road trips always made her think of the hours she had spent in the backseat of her parent's car with her brother.

"Timmy, Timmy," she said, continuing to talk aloud. "I need to visit you more often." However, the doctor at the home in which her brother lived wasn't sure, on balance, that Pam's visits were positive.

Timmy lived in northern California in a place for people who couldn't quite make it on the outside. As a child he was tagged mildly retarded, but Pam believed it was environment not heredity that did Timmy in. The only sane thing her eccentric parents did was to provide in their wills for half-assed care for their son.

Like slipping into a wet raincoat, the well-known, crippling sadness enveloped her. The worse she felt, the slower she drove. "How could they not love their children? We looked just like them. What was it?" she asked for the millionth time.

The parade of psychotherapists Pam had seen had always asked if she and Timmy were physically abused by their parents. No, never that. Pam wondered which kind of abuse was worse.

Her latest therapist had told her that her parents were obsessed with one another in a toxic, co-dependent relationship. Their apparent rejection of her wasn't really about her at all, but developed only as a side effect of their psychosis. The therapist had then suggested Pam get off anti-depressants, stop being a victim and move on.

Pam had tried suicide instead, and it hadn't worked either.

By the time the lights of Roswell were visible, Pam was depressed enough pull into a truck stop and seduce the first loser that looked her way. She needed to do something spectacularly destructive.

"Maybe if I really bottom out on men I can break the cycle," she said. "Find one who is cruel and not especially attractive with lots of bad habits. One who hates animals and of course, hates me." She had to smile at her own morbidity and penchant for drama.

She pulled into the giant parking lot, the tiny Miata dwarfed by the throbbing tractor-trailer rigs. She swiped lipstick across her mouth and ran a finger over her front teeth. When she opened the glove box to stow her cell phone, a blue scrap of paper sailed to the floor. Bold black numbers, a telephone number not in her handwriting, were scrawled on it.

"Maybe it's from one of the sons of bitches in Angustia," she said. "One of the AWOL roofers or Ortega himself." But the area codes in New Mexico were 505 and 575. This one was 210.

"What the hell." She punched the numbers on the cell phone and listened to the rings. Pressing the receiver hard to her ear so she could hear, she counted nine and hung up. She checked Information. Area 210 was San Antonio. Then it hit her. Kenny Hatch, the hitchhiker, had left her his number.

Foregoing the chance to bottom out for the present, she went in the truck stop's restroom and washed her face using the liquid coconut soap in the dispenser. Drying with stiff paper towels, she tried to imagine how somebody else would describe her. "She probably used to be real cute," they'd say. "Eyes are kind of sunken and her neck is starting to go." She waved the magic mascara wand over her lashes and put on more lipstick, but the combination of exhaustion and bad lighting made her look like a picture she had seen of a used-up Appalachian woman.

She fled the fluorescent gloom, stepping around a yellow sign that warned, CUIDADO! PISO MOJADO—CAREFUL! WET FLOOR! and headed for the food counter. She ordered a sandwich to go.

"It's $6.95," the young woman whose name tag identified her as Nonabah said.

Pam dug into her purse and opened her wallet. She felt for the bills three times before she recognized there weren't any.

I had over $200 cash. Oh shit.

Wade, the sweet, hippie doper, had lifted the money as he flattered her in the smoky cab of his Dodge Ram.

Could I be stupider?

"You take MasterCard?" she asked. She supposed that Wade hadn't stolen the credit card because he didn't have the energy to forge her signature and worry about the paper trail.

Outside a light rain was wetting the car's seats. She struggled to put up the top, swearing at Wade and her own foolishness. In the next thirty miles she ate half the sandwich, chewed two fingernails to the quick, and made a good start on the inside of her left cheek. She thought about the radio preacher, Jimmy Rathborn, and what she had in common with his sheep.

Heading south on 285, she made Fort Stockton while almost falling asleep at the wheel. The Lamplighter Motel promised "klean rooms," but Pam hardly saw the bed before she was asleep. San Antonio waited two hundred miles down the road.

It wasn't until the next morning when she had dressed in the tiny bathroom that she began to worry about what she would say to Kenny if she found him. She peered into the spotty mirror, trying out perky, carefree smiles and searching for her lost youth.

Thirty miles nearer San Antonio, with an untouched McDonald's breakfast that was turning into a pool of grease in its protective carton, her worry bred panic.

"I can't say I was just passing through. Hell, he probably won't answer anyway." She rolled the blue paper between her fingers as though contact would tell her why he had left it for her. She thought about Wade and wondered why she thought Kenny was any different.

But the phone number had been left weeks ago. Maybe he changed his mind by now. And what if he didn't answer? Was she going to hang around San Antonio calling every few hours? How pathetic was that? She could see herself wandering through the Alamo, punching redial every fifteen minutes.

By the time she caught up with the inbound morning rush traffic, her anxiety level topped out, and she pulled off at the next exit determined to just dial and see what would happen.

Her hand shook as she punched in the numbers.

"Rapid Release Bail Bonds," a man's voice twanged.

She read the numbers on the phone. A five should have been an eight. Dialing again in slow motion she prayed Kenny would remember her, meet her for coffee and let her move in with him. Two rings. Rejection by a hitchhiker she hardly knew would be hard. Four rings.

"Animal Rescue League, Joan speaking."

Pam checked the numbers on the cell phone. This time they were correct.

Shit, who put an animal rescue number in my car? Where's the people rescue number?

"Uh, sorry I must have the wrong number."

A second from pressing the disconnect button, the woman named Joan said, "Hang on a sec. I can't hear you." Then she yelled, "Kenny, turn off that vacuum. I can't hear the phone."

Kenny.

"Is Kenny Hatch there?" Pam asked. She held her breath, ignoring the sting of adrenalin.

The moaning vacuum quieted. "I'll get him. Hold on."

"I'm holding, I'm holding," she murmured.

"Hello," he said.

The familiar voice was sunshine after fog, Robert Redford's smile, and hot buttered biscuits.

"Kenny, it's Pam. I don't know if you remember—"

"Hold on. One of them's getting loose," Kenny said.

She held on, digging her fingernails into her palms for sounding like a junior high girl trying to get lucky with a tenth grader.

"Oliver nearly escaped, sorry. Pam. Pam, where are you?" he asked.

"West of San Antonio."

"Don't go into San Antonio."

"No?"

"You're on I-10 right?"

"Right."

"Seen Leon Springs yet?"

"No."

"Pull off at that exit. If you beat me there, wait," he said and hung up.

Pam rocked herself in the bucket seat of the sports car. He was coming to get her. Even if he turned out to be the worst man in her life, and there had been some doozies, for this moment she felt wanted. Speeding toward the Leon Springs exit, she turned off her internal critic by reminding herself that Kenny Hatch was good looking, funny and now it appeared that he liked animals. And what was more, it appeared he liked her too.

She exited as directed. The blacktop immediately turned to dirt and gravel. She barely had time to see if her mascara had run or her lipstick had faded before she saw the blue van. It circled her car, kicking up a swirl of white dust.

"Follow me," Kenny shouted out the window, heading back down the road.

The back of the van said: ANIMAL ALLIES: ANIMAL RESCUE TEAM OF SAN ANTONIO. A NO KILL FACILITY.

Good, at least I won't die out here.

She followed him through an open gate and then through another he had to open and close behind them. A house and a dozen outbuildings lay ahead.

"Pull up behind the house," he said. Two yellow labs tore down the driveway toward them.

"Oh, God, now we're here and I have to get through awkward moment number two hundred," she said aloud. It occurred to her that she could choose to say nothing. She could be cool. Or she could say, "Hey Kenny. Wow, look, animals." She wished she could, but forty plus years of low self-esteem wasn't about to allow that.

The imaginary critic's voice at her shoulder sneered, "He's being nice, but face it, you're chasing boys and that is never cool. Try not to humiliate your pathetic self too much."

22

KENNY OPENED PAM'S CAR door, took her hand and pulled her out.

"Gosh you look good," he said. He grinned, waited for a second and then grabbed her in a bear hug. "I'm real glad to see you. I kicked myself for not doing better with my phone number. I was sure it got thrown out or you never saw it." He looked at her again like he wasn't sure who she was. "I'm going to shut up now. Come on inside and meet my sister."

All the awkward replies and lies weren't needed. She was being herded toward the door of a house that seemed to go on forever. Added onto several times, it looked like what the Disney studios might cook up for a movie that celebrated a zany family of non-conformists.

"I hope I'm not interrupting anything," Pam said and immediately wished she'd just kept quiet. Quiet had been working.

"Heck yes you are and thank God." He casually put his arm around her shoulders as though they walked together into his sister's house every day.

"Joan? Come out here. I want you to meet somebody," he called.

Kenny's sister looked like a pink marshmallow encased in cutoff gray sweats. Her tee shirt pictured a confident Siamese cat above a caption: Chaos, Panic and Disorder. My work here is done.

After introductions, Joan insisted she had to finish scooping the cat litter boxes, and that Kenny could vacuum later, even tomorrow. "You have to keep up with the litter boxes when you have sixty cats," Joan said and made her exit.

Pam looked around and saw only the two long-haired cats, one on top of the refrigerator and the other on its back in a cat hammock slung in front of a window.

"Where are all the cats?" Pam asked.

"Outbuildings," Kenny said. "The big one that used to be a caretaker's house we divided into enclosures. That many cats can't live all together in one room. The pig has the old pump house, and the dogs live on the porch except when it's too cold or too hot and then they come in here. The horses have a barn, the rabbits have a hutch, and the ferret has a cage.

"Where'd they all come from?" Pam asked. Kenny handed her an iced tea and guided her toward the kitchen table.

"Joan finds them or they find her," Kenny said. "Twenty of the cats came from a crazy man who was stealing other people's cats. He'd been collecting for years so it was impossible to find the owners. The guy left to go to his brother's funeral, and the neighbor who watered them called Saint Joan. She rescued them."

"Just took them?" Pam asked, glad to have something easy to talk about. She sipped the cold tea, strong and double sweet.

"His place was a nightmare. Some of them died, but she saved twenty."

"She does this all by herself?" Pam asked. Pam wished she had the guts to do something like Joan did—rescue something or at least take charge of something.

"About six people volunteer. And now I'm lucky seven. For a while anyway."

Pam was dying to ask about his plans. It was hard to tell if she might be in them if she didn't know what they were. The critic voice came on her internal PA. *You don't even know this guy and you're plotting a future with him? How pitiful is that? Shame on you.*

"Want to see Nguyen?" Kenny asked. He pushed back from the table and stretched.

"What's a nguyen?"

"The new potbelly."

"Pig?"

"Oink, oink."

Kenny gave Pam the deluxe tour, ending in the cat house.

"This is Cheerio, the white one is Sunshine, that's Oliver," Kenny said, pointing out cats. As he petted Oliver, three black cats, triplets, emerged from a cat condo. "Bella, Monroe, Ben," he greeted them.

"How do you know who's who?" Pam asked. The three black cats looked at her with scorn.

"Ben's a little bigger, Monroe has an overbite and Bella's toes are all pink." Kenny sat on a low stool near the fan that cooled the felines. All of the cats swarmed about him. Ben jumped into his lap.

Everything was geared for the once miserable, abandoned occupants. Pam felt right at home.

A man with a sister who takes in orphaned animals couldn't possibly be a bad man, could he? She watched Kenny stroke and baby-talk Bella.

They visited the rabbits and then headed over to barn. In the silence she was about to start the inevitable explanation of why she'd come, when Kenny asked if she'd like to ride the horses over to Choke Springs for a picnic.

"A picnic?" she repeated.

"Yes. Blankets on the ground, fried chicken, a few ants? Any of that sound familiar?"

"Yes to the picnic, but I'm not much of a rider."

"Neither are these horses. You can wear what you got on. I'll get us some food," he said, leaving her in the barn to be scrutinized by Frieda and Diego, the horses.

The last time Pam had ridden a horse was when her father had very briefly managed a dude ranch in Alabama. She and Timmy had worn tan riding pants and dark blue shirts with snaps. Their mother regretted they couldn't learn English saddle. They had two lessons before their father was fired, dashing Pam's vision of herself as a modern day Annie Oakley.

They left just after noon. It took an hour to get to the tiny hot springs hidden in the granite outcrop. Kenny tied up the horses and laid out old saddle blankets near the shallow pool.

"Put your feet in the water," he said. "It'll feel good. I'll get the grub."

On a flat rock overhanging the pool, Pam inhaled the mineral scent. Bubbles ejected from the pebbled bottom.

After cold fried chicken, cold biscuits, tangerines, and chocolate chip cookies, they sat listening to the spring gurgle. Pam's urge to get it over with, to 'fess up and let him know she was headed nowhere, welled again. She played the leading sentences in her head: *Well, I guess you're wondering why I'm here, and Things didn't work out so well in New Mexico so I thought I'd move back to New Orleans.*

Kenny, his eyes half-closed, lay on a rock ledge over the pool. Pam chewed the raw corner of her mouth.

"I don't care why you're here, and I want you to stay as long as you want to," he said before she could speak. His voice bounced off the rocks, taking on a reverberated, sexy quality. "I hope that whatever happened, it wasn't too bad and you're okay."

"Thanks. I'm okay. Now I feel like I've fallen down Alice's rabbit hole."

"Sounds painful."

"No. Feels like time has stopped here." She wished he would take her in his arms and let her cry on his shoulder. She'd cry for Timmy, her crazy brother, her mama and daddy, for the friends she'd abandoned in Angustia, for the stolen $200 and for all her fuck ups. There were too many to count. Her hot tears would slide into the steamy pool and her sins would wash away. It would be like having her soul steam-cleaned.

But he didn't touch her, and he didn't tell her about any of his troubles.

When Pam woke up, dusk had fallen and taken the temperature with it. Kenny was eating a piece of chicken.

"Hey, Sleeping Beauty. I saved you a piece. You slept over an hour," he said.

She felt dizzy. He tossed her a water bottle, and she drained it.

"Want to take a dip? It'll warm you right up if you're chilly." He stood beside the pool and unceremoniously began taking off his clothes.

Pam, who thought she'd seen every kind of naked male body, was in awe. In the half-light, the muscles she'd admired and fanaticized about glistened. He was gorgeous. Completely at home in his skin, he moved into the pool as naturally as one of the ducks on his sister's ranch.

"Feels good. Take off your clothes behind that rock over there if you're shy," he said.

Oh, great. Now I have to either strip my middle-aged body bare in front of him or admit I'm embarrassed about it.

Beyond the low hills, Mother Nature was choreographing a Georgia O'Keefe sunset, but it would be an hour before it was dark.

What the hell, Pam thought, and sitting on the rock ledge, she wiggled out of her white Capri pants and unbuttoned her shirt. Her skin looked blanched and vulnerable against the granite.

I don't need to look twenty-five. A healthy forty would be fine. Shit. I hate this. At least my pubic hair isn't gray.

She hoped the steam was restoring the years that Angustia had put on her in only a few weeks.

She took off the shirt, slipped in the pool and gasped from the shock of the heat. For a moment, neither of them moved as the searing mineral water caressed their bodies. Then, taking the same chance at the same moment, they stepped together, locking in an embrace. His mouth found hers and kissed it like he would never stop. Kisses toppled over kisses, hungry hard ones and tender-as-kitten-whiskers ones. With Herculean effort, she pushed away her thoughts and only reacted to his touch. The critic, who knew that her breasts were too small, that her stomach pooched out too much, and that her buttocks were dimpled, hunkered down and waited.

She felt his hands slither down her wet back. Kneeling in the water, he pressed his face to her belly and then nuzzled her breasts. They spoke no words. There was only their breathing until he put his hand between her thighs, and she let escape a deep, low sound. Her knees gave way, and she slid chest deep into the water, wrapping her legs around his waist.

Later, when in each other's arms they lay exhausted on the rock ledge and Pam had the lucidity to think, she realized that no man before had ever made love to her for so long. Thirty minutes had been absolute tops start to finish; ten was normal. She smiled knowing that she probably resembled a cooked crustacean with bad hair. She didn't care. Or at least she didn't care much.

Maybe the steam softened my naso-labial folds and I look younger.

Kenny rubbed her neck and the desire flamed again, hot and urgent. She kissed him and felt his erection on her thigh.

"We'll get hurt doing this on these rocks," he said.

"Sit up," she said. When he did, Pam lowered herself onto his lap and filled herself with him. She rocked him and this time he groaned. When he came, the horses answered his cry with guttural trills. They remained entwined, feeling the energy undulate round them. The mythic Tantric snake was loose.

He told her he wanted her, but before she could relax into the idea, her internal censor was back with blue, pursed lips asking, *but what about tomorrow?*

They rode home in the moonlight and spent the night in a behemoth old travel trailer on Joan's land. She told him about the past three weeks in New Mexico, including the attack in the record storage room in Santa Fe.

"So you figure this Ortega guy is trying to grab the place?" he asked. Kenny wrapped around her on the bed that took up one whole end of the vehicle.

She could smell the spring's water mixed with his masculine scent.

"I figure. It's hopeless. I just left. I couldn't take one more dead end," she said. The truth was that she missed Sarah and Ali. Her hostile departure, bred of blame and guilt, had cut her off from her two best friends.

"Did the dog die?"

"I don't know." She had almost forgotten poor Bernie. "You hate me now?" she asked.

"Yes. And you're going to have to pay for being so bad," he said. He was pulling off her night shirt. "After I get through with you here, you're going to have to eat one of Joan's breakfasts and if you survive that, we're going to call your friends in, where'd you say it was?"

Pam was giggling too hard from the tickles to answer, "Angustia."

At breakfast, Joan's tee shirt said, Proud to be a crazy cat lady. She set a stack of pancakes, two eggs over easy, hashbrowns, and two sausage patties in front of each of them.

"Got molasses, honey, homemade fruit conserve, and syrup—natural or chemical," Joan said. "Somebody's coming at ten to look at Cheerio and Sherwood. I have to hurry. They need fluffing bad."

After Joan departed to groom the felines, Pam and Kenny, too full to move, sat on the screened porch.

"I think I'll call them. You really think I should call them?" she asked Kenny.

"Hell, yes. First they might be worried about you. Second you might want to mend a few fences."

"They'll be so pissed off—"

He cut her off. "Then apologize. Third, you got some money tied up in the hotel. You can't just walk off."

"They'll send me my part when it sells," she said. "And why are you being so nice about them? They didn't like you one bit."

"I'm talking about you, not me."

"Oh."

"Look, you like the place. You light up when you bitch about it. You gonna let someone bully you out of it because it's not easy to keep?" He paused and took a long look at Pam. "What do you have that you value that you didn't have to fight for?"

"I'm not a fighter," Pam said with some of the old creepy feeling returning. Implied was that she didn't have anything of value, period.

Kenny shifted his tack. "Everything y'all did to make it work sounds like what I would have done except one thing."

Pam looked up, waiting.

"You didn't call for help."

"The only help's been bought off. I don't think the Federal Government would come to our rescue."

"Maybe, maybe not. And maybe there wasn't anybody to call then, but there is now," he said. He took her hand. "I haven't been to Santa Fe in months."

"Kenny, you can't take this on. We'd still lose and trying to hold on could be dangerous," Pam said. The emotion in her voice caught in her throat. Tears misted her eyes. His kindness was unbearable. She was pretty sure she didn't deserve it.

"Think about it. Take some time. I'll be here."

"Okay."

"I hope you'll be here too." He kissed the backs of her hands, and said softly, "I need help cleaning the cat cages this afternoon."

23

PAM TRIED TO CONTACT Sarah and Ali, but their cell phones weren't working. Two days later there was still no connection. The officious computer-generated voice repeated, "I'm sorry, the customer you are calling is out of the area. Please try your call again."

What if something had happened? She was the only one who knew exactly where her friends were.

"This stuff was in the trunk of your car. You want it inside?" Kenny stood holding three cardboard file boxes.

"Damn. I forgot about those. It's information about the hacienda," she said.

"Interesting?" he asked.

"I have no idea. The flood and the red tag arrived before I had time to look."

"Still no answer?" he asked, opening the first carton.

She shook her head no.

"I asked a friend of Joan's who lives near Santa Fe to drive out there and—"

"What?" Pam said.

197

"Joan knows everybody in the animal rescue business. There's a big shelter near there. She said it has a tiger."

"Kenny, what'd they say?" Pam asked.

"Couldn't see anybody around, but there was a big blue tent. And a bull dozer was blocking the road. Was anybody talking about paving the road?"

"Nothing will ever be paved out there."

"He said there weren't any people or cars." Kenny pawed through the Hacienda files as though he were looking for something—a birth certificate or proof of immunizations.

Pam dialed Sarah and Ali's numbers but got the computerman again. "Maybe I'd better go back and check on them." Earth moving equipment sounded ominous.

"And do what? Report them missing to the sheriff who certainly knows all about them?" he asked.

"Maybe they're all right."

"Then you don't need to do anything. They're fine."

"I need to know. They're my friends. I abandoned them when it got tough and—" Pam suddenly stopped. She didn't finish her sentence, but thought, just as my parents abandoned me when it got tough. But what had gotten tough for them? She had no clue.

Kenny was quiet for a moment then said quietly. "We'll leave at first light."

Later Pam thought how cleverly he had brought her around to the idea of going back to Angustia. He had a way. She'd have to watch him.

About midnight, Kenny's climbing into bed woke Pam. When she'd gone to bed, he was still reading the files on the hacienda.

"Go back to sleep. You have to get up in a few hours," he whispered into the back of her neck.

She slipped her arm around his shoulder and pulled him to her, his cool skin meeting her warmth. She couldn't remember when she had gladly let a man awaken her in the middle of the night. Before when some hot, throbbing member had insinuated itself, she had feigned sleep. This was new.

"You wanton hussy. Put that down," he said, pushing closer.

"You put it down. You put it up," she said.

He smelled woodsy good. He couldn't be a bad guy if he smelled so good, could he? She didn't want to examine that notion too much.

"Did I ever tell you about the time my Uncle Leo and I went to hunt for a couple of missing calves?" he said.

"No. I'm dying to hear." She began a series of kisses that started at his throat and roamed down and down. She watched him struggle to continue.

"Oh mercy. I'll tell you tomorrow," he said.

⸻ ❋ ⸻

THEY WERE OUT OF Texas and into New Mexico by mid-morning. Just over the state line, Kenny pulled into a Mexican restaurant with a hand lettered 'closed' sign in the window.

"Want some breakfast? I need some breakfast," he said.

"Is it open?"

"Manuel?" Kenny called. It sounded like Mahn-oo-well.

His call was answered by a woman's voice, her words in Spanish. The door opened. "Kenny, Kenny. Come in. *Ven, vente aquí.*"

Manuel, who looked like the revolutionary, Emiliano Zapata, appeared beside her.

They traded good-natured insults: Kenny was too skinny, Manuel too fat and he was also lazy.

"Let me introduce my girlfriend, Pamela," Kenny said. He smiled like a kid.

Pam shook hands with Manuel and Rosa.

He said girlfriend. Damn.

Rosa's Restaurante y Cantina was open only to them. Rosa brought out huevos rancheros and a mountain of homemade tortillas. In the deluge of Spanish, Pam thought she understood that Kenny and Manuel used to hunt together, and that between the two of them, there wasn't anything worth knowing that they didn't know.

An hour later they were blazing up Highway 285 with the top down. It was late May, but still a mantle of wildflowers, teased by the recent rains, blanketed the roadside. Pam wondered if the dogwood, azaleas, and redbud were spent in Mississippi. Instead of the ubiquitous Kudzu vine that laced and choked the land, here were rocky hills and stands of fir and squatty pinion. Without the wildflowers, Pam thought it would have looked like the moon.

"Tell me about the natural spring at the hacienda," Kenny said. "Is it bigger than the spring on Joan's land?"

Pam had taken over driving. "It's a pump house, not a swimming pool."

"That's it? Just the one spring?"

"Yes, but we have plenty of water," she answered. "There's a geothermal report in the file box. Did you see it?"

"Yes, but it's not complete."

"Pages are missing?" Pam asked.

"No, but the report is still incomplete," he said.

"How do you know?"

"I worked my way through school in the oil fields. Geologists run oil fields," he said.

"You're a geologist?" she asked.

"Would you like me better if I was?" he asked.

"No. Well, maybe."

"Sorry. I know a lot of them though," he said.

Pam was dying to ask about school. What school? College? Major? When? Her image of the sexy hitchhiker she had only wanted to bed was shifting rapidly. Next he'll say he majored in Elementary Ed or pledged Sigma Chi. However, she decided to keep quiet. He'd tell her before it mattered.

It was late when they neared Santa Fe and found a motel. Kenny took her to an Italian restaurant, and they pretended they were in Italy. The food was mediocre, but it had a miniature replica of the Trevi Fountain. They tossed quarters into the artificially blue water.

"What'd you wish?" she asked.

"If I tell, it won't come true," he said.

She wished he would never leave her.

✢ ❈ ✢

EARLY THE NEXT MORNING, they took a circuitous route: driving around Angustia, cutting through a field on an old tractor path and entering the hacienda from the back. Kenny's theory was that if you didn't know what you were going to encounter, it was better to sneak up on it. They parked. Pushing through a hedge, Pam flushed a covey of quail. Cautiously, they walked toward the hotel. Beyond the potting shed, Pam saw Sarah kneeling over a row of robust garlic.

"Sarah?"

"Pam!" Sarah said. "God, you scared me." Her gaze cooled when she recognized Kenny.

"Sarah, are you okay? Where's Ali?" Pam asked.

Sarah let Pam pull her to her feet. Awkwardness hung between them like notes out of tune.

"I'm sorry I left like I did," Pam said, lunging forward to embrace Sarah.

"Where'd you find him?" Sarah whispered. "Isn't he the guy from the Slidell truck stop?" Her tone said *the no account bum from the truck stop.*

"Monroe. Things are never what they seem to be. Aren't you always saying that?" Pam whispered back. She smiled. "Kenny, I'd like you to meet Sarah Hunter."

"How do, ma'am. Nice place you got." He looked ready to shake hands, but didn't make a move.

Sarah nodded. "I've done better," Sarah said. She tucked her straggling hair under her hat with her right hand.

Pam had trouble absorbing Sarah's coldness. Sarah was always warm, cheerful, and optimistic.

"Mind if I take a look around? Need a little stretch," he said and ambled away before anyone could answer.

"Why did you bring him here? Hell, how'd you find him?" Sarah asked as soon as Kenny was out of sight.

"He's not what you think, and I like him," Pam said.

"You like them all," Sarah said. "Are you staying or just passing through?"

"I had to make sure you two were okay and bring back the records I photocopied. I took them with me by mistake," Pam said. This was not shaping up to be the homecoming Pam had wanted.

"So you're staying?"

"Yes," Pam said. "How are you?"

"We are dandy. The county's blocked the road, it said, to repair a culvert, but no one's come back. It's impossible to get in or out. Ali's dance lessons have ceased. According to

Gabriel, the children and their mothers have been forbidden to come here because it's dangerous. Of course the roofers, who according to *Señora* Cantu's cousin are pals of Ortega, haven't returned. Dominguez and *Señora* Cantu come and go; presumably their ages make the enemy think they're no threat. Ortega offered $10,000 less than what we paid, and Mr. Tyrone comes by to make certain no one's living in the hotel. Oh, and the rattlesnake came back. That about covers it. Lots of coming and going. And now you've come back with what's his name." She dug mud from beneath a fingernail and flipped it to the ground.

"Kenny," Pam said.

"Pam, I hate to say this but your men are always such losers."

"Why do you care?"

"Because if he's here, I have to live with him too," Sarah said.

It irritated Pam that she had to justify Kenny to Sarah. "And all your men were winners? And I'm not just taking about Randall Crane, the shyster you almost married." Pam stopped, wishing she hadn't gone so far.

Sarah looked stunned.

A horn blast in the road drew their attention and halted the escalating argument. A UPS delivery driver, just visible behind the yellow tractor, was waving. "How do I get in? I have five boxes."

Kenny, who had returned from his walk, helped the driver ferry the load to the courtyard beside Sarah's tent.

"Nobody could tell me where you were," the driver said. "I thought I'd never find you." His unflattering brown uniform pants slumped in the seat and pooled about his ankles.

"Who'd you ask?" Sarah said.

"Folks in town, guy parked up the road a piece," he said, taking back his clipboard after Sarah signed for the delivery.

"Guy on the road?" Pam asked.

"Said he was watching migratory birds. I didn't have the heart to tell him it was too late," he said, heading back into the UPS truck.

"I'm going to clean up," Sarah said. "Ali's in Taos buying groceries. She'll be back in any minute. Are you staying?"

"Yes. Kenny too," Pam said.

"Keep out of the hotel. They'd love to catch us occupying it. They'd probably march us barefoot to Fort Sumner," Sarah said. She dried her muddy hands on her pants and pulled off her straw hat. Pam could see Sarah hadn't washed her hair in days.

"Judy's looking for another buyer, did I tell you that? Meanwhile, I'm growing my garden," Sarah said and ducked into the blue tent.

Pam looked at the garden site where Sarah's seedlings and transplants had nearly doubled in size. Regiments of lettuce, radishes and spinach defined the rows with their emergent leaves. She couldn't help admiring her friend's tenacity—growing a garden on land you were likely to have to give up.

"What's in the boxes?" Kenny asked.

"Let's see," Pam said.

The UPS boxes contained the shoes Ali had dunned from two dance groups in New York. In addition there were black boys' pants, yards of miscellaneous fabric, and an assortment of hats. They were closing the boxes when Ali's dented Honda pulled up beside the backhoe. Ali jumped out and ran to Pam.

"I was so worried about you," Ali said, hugging Pam. In a whisper she added, "Why'd you bring him here?"

"He's okay. You'll see," Pam said.

Pam introduced Ali to Kenny, who immediately excused himself and sauntered past the tractor and down the road.

"Sarah met him?" Ali asked.

"Yes. She hates him too."

"I don't think Sarah's feeling very well," Ali said. Probably too much cortisol from stress. She won't talk about it."

"She's probably depressed," Pam said, relieved that Ali wasn't going to eviscerate Kenny.

"Or exhausted from mucking out the hotel," Ali said.

"God, I forgot. What happened to Bernie?"

"He survived. Doesn't seem quite the same to me, but he's alive."

"I opened your boxes," Pam said. "I knew you wouldn't care."

Ali reopened a box and examined the Capezio shoes.

"What are you going to do with all this dance stuff?" Pam asked. "Sarah said the dance troupe died."

"It was murdered. Where'd Kenny go?" she said, changing the subject. "That his name?"

"Yes. Out front looking masculine in case the enemy shows up," Pam said. "You didn't answer my question. What about all this dance costume stuff?" Pam repeated.

"I don't know. Ortega's goons told the children and their parents that it wasn't safe here. The implied threat in 'safe' seemed obvious."

"They're fucking terrorists," Pam said.

"Fuckin' A."

"Sarah has no intention of giving up," Ali said. "You know that. We might have to force her to sell. I had a free introductory chat with a lawyer in Taos today. Don't tell her."

"Isn't there any good news?" Pam asked.

"Gabriel says the children's mothers liked the Folklorico class and don't like being intimidated by Ortega. They're giving their husbands a hard time about it," Ali said.

"That's not going to be enough," Pam said. "What's that play where the women withhold sex until the men stop the war?"

"*Lysistrata?*"

"Maybe they should try that," Pam said.

"I think they are," Ali said.

"What are you going to do when winter comes?" Pam asked.

"Sarah's ordering a yurt. If you and Kenny stay, we could get a good price on two," Ali said.

"Sounds like something you eat. What's a yurt?"

"Sort of a hogan," Ali said. "Think of a flat-topped, straight sided teepee."

"You're going to camp out all winter?" Pam asked, amazed. "Won't your Ferragamo's get muddy?"

"Oh prodigal daughter, go to hell," Ali said and laughed.

Sarah emerged from the tent. "Ali has a new Orvis Catalog," Sarah said, joining them. She had made a serious effort to clean up, but she still looked dulled, like a gold coin too long buried under ocean mud. "She's our expert on living in the wild."

"It's not Orvis," Ali said.

"Did you tell her about Gabriel?" Sarah asked.

Ali gave her open mouthed innocent look that said there's nothing to tell.

"He's staying here now," Sarah said.

"I don't believe it. I leave for four days and Ali takes in a child?" Pam asked. "What about his father? You told me he had a father."

"His father could care less," Ali said.

Here it was again. Pam the child-hater. Only heartless bitches didn't love children and take them in.

"I didn't sign on to raise kids," Pam said.

"One boy is not kids," Ali said.

"And when or if we sell the place? Is he going with you?" Pam asked.

Sarah took over. "The father won't let Ali adopt Gabriel. She can't legally take him anywhere."

Pam felt astonished by the speed at which the boy had wormed his way into the hacienda and into Ali's heart.

Shit, if we lose the place, she'll have to leave him. That or she'll take him and become a fugitive.

"You're not one to talk, Missy," Ali said. She sounded angry. "You skulk back here all dewy eyed with a Louisiana truck stop bum. I'd say Gabriel is a better risk."

"Could we talk about this later?" Pam turned away. "No, on second thought let's don't talk about it at all." Walking away to find Kenny, she wasn't sure why she had such a negative reaction to Gabriel. He was just a kid. She wasn't crazy about children, but she didn't hate them either.

I was a kid once.

❖ ❖ ❖

PAM SHOWED KENNY THE hacienda. The kiln was still partially covered in mud, but someone had scrubbed out her studio. Everything looked run down, but still it felt good to be home. She wished she hadn't been so bitchy to Ali.

At two, the dong, dong of a brass bell floated from the hotel announcing *comida*, the main meal. Even under stress, Sarah prepared meals, good ones. Made in her improvised outdoor kitchen, she laid out salad from the garden, chicken cacciatore, fried green tomatoes, homemade bread, and wild berries. Gabriel sat close beside Ali; Kenny and Pam held down the other end of the long table. Made of a huge mahogany door over sawhorses, the table was covered by a rough linen cloth. Juice glasses filled with wild flowers nestled among the platters. Mismatched chairs surrounded it. A light breeze cooled the afternoon sunshine. But before *postre*, fresh berries in cream, Pam found herself embroiled in another argument.

"I'm not living in a yurt," Pam said. "A yurt is a tent. It snows here."

"We'll have the hotel fixed by then," Sarah said, ducking her chin to her chest and digging in.

"How? You going to climb on the roof and nail shingles?" Pam asked. She ripped off a chunk of bread.

"We'll have to fix the walls first," Ali said. "At least the real bad one. You could do that, Pam."

Pam ignored Ali's suggestion.

"I can't believe you're going to stay out here, Ali," Pam said. "Ali, of the three showers a day who has cans of air freshener in her car, who won't eat leftovers, or sleep on polyester sheets. Where'd she go?"

"We have lots of running spring water," Ali said.

Pam was about to redouble her attack when she noticed Ali smoothing Gabriel's hair. The boy was looking lots cleaner and several pounds heavier in his new clothes.

Oh my God. She's fallen for this kid. She'll live in a yurt in the snow for him. Pam looked over at Kenny who sat quietly spooning down berries.

"So you're going to outwait Ortega?" Pam asked.

"He can't keep this up forever," Sarah said.

"What makes you think he doesn't have another plan to get rid of us?" Pam asked. "Maybe get the place condemned. Torch it. I don't know what all's possible."

"Goddamn it, Pam. You leave us and then waltz back and have the gall to say our ideas aren't good enough. I think it's clear you want out." Sarah rose and stood unsteadily on her good leg. "I know you think it would take a miracle, but I have faith in hanging on as long as I can." She was crying. Bernie moved beside her.

It struck Pam, watching Sarah weep and stroke Bernie, that Sarah had turned their adventure into her last hurrah. There was no going back. Sarah would prove herself an independent woman who could make her own decisions or she would die trying. Her death might be figurative, but if Sarah failed with Angustia, the Sarah that was left over would be only a shell.

And in that moment, Pam knew that she didn't want out. She was scared to be in, but she desperately wanted them to convince her that it would work. She had hoped that Kenny would make it seem okay, but he wasn't enough.

She felt her own tears sting. "I'm sorry. I'm just scared." She made her way around the table to Sarah and stood close to her. "Not of Ortega. I'm afraid to make a home and to lose it. It's better if you never make it."

"Then you'll never have a home," Sarah said. "All we need to make this work is to stick together." Sarah sat on the oak bench. "This is my first home. This one is all mine and not my daddy's or my husband's. Help me if you can, and if you can't, stay out of the way."

Pam sat beside Sarah, wiping tears with the back of her hand. *I do want this. I want it to work.*

As she was about to tell this to Sarah, the quiet was slowly taken over by an engine's whine. When Pam looked up at

Sarah her misery had tuned to surprise. Sarah was smiling, waving and on her way to greet the approaching truck. It was Manny Sanchez's moving van, red parrots and all.

The two men in the cab with Manny stayed put while he lumbered toward Sarah.

"Sorry I'm so late, Mrs. Hunter," Manny said. "I can explain. Maybe first you should see about moving the 'dozer so I can get my truck close to the door?"

"I expected you over a week ago," Sarah said.

"Y'all need something to eat?" Ali said, joining them. "We have plenty. Call your friends."

"The bulldozer?" Manny repeated.

"Is my furniture all right?" Sarah asked.

"It's fine, and I got a real good price for the stuff you didn't want," Manny said. "That big mirror alone—it's all written down, all legal." He smiled broadly, pulling out a sheaf of folded papers.

Ali took the papers from him and sorted through them.

"The tractor-thing belongs to the county," Sarah said. "Could you get your truck in the back way?"

"Maybe. If the ground's not too soft," Manny said, looking at the table with more interest.

"Sure y'all don't want something to eat?" Ali asked.

"After we get unloaded," Manny said.

In her Toyota, Sarah led Manny's van to the old farm road. The truck made it within fifty yards of the courtyard before bogging down to its axles.

Manny and his two compatriots swore a lot in Spanish and walked around the truck like they were thinking about blowing it up, but were unsure of where to set the dynamite. Then they shrugged and opened the back. Sitting on Sarah's sofa and chairs were two men, two women and three small children.

Stunned by the bright sunlight, they blinked like blind puppies. Then they froze like rabbits.

Manny didn't rush into an explanation of who his passengers were. They got out of the truck, but stayed close, ready to dive back in.

"Sarah," Ali said. "They sold the furniture you didn't want in Mexico." She waved the papers Manny had given her.

"They've been in Mexico?" Sarah said.

"Maybe they better all have something to eat," Ali said.

"Maybe they better do some explaining," Pam said. She didn't say it, but she thought how like Sarah it was to ship her stuff off with someone she hardly knew and have him show up late with illegals hiding between her armoire and étagère.

"Algo de comer? Comida?" Ali invited the group to the table. She didn't have to ask twice.

As the group finished off Sarah's *comida*, Manny introduced the four men, two women, and three children.

"They ain't got green cards," he said, chewing. "I thought it'd be better if you didn't know about them." He plucked a third piece of bread from the basket.

They ain't got English either, Pam thought.

"*Somos* wet backs," the youngest child baby-talked.

His mother clapped a hand over his mouth.

I was wrong, Pam thought. *They know two words.*

"Where are you taking them?" asked Kenny. It was the first thing he had said since "pass the butter."

"They have construction jobs waiting in Texas," Manny said. "They're skilled workers. The boss in Texas ain't gonna want to turn them in. It'll take maybe a year for them to get caught and sent back." Manny didn't seem upset by any of it. "They live in the Morelos Mountains, in a little village. Somebody destroyed the marijuana crop. Now they're starving."

Pam doubted much of Manny's story, but she couldn't help feel sorry for these people.

"I don't understand," Sarah said. "You sold my stuff in Mexico. Why?"

"I knew I could get a good price from some *gringos*. Americans who want American things. I didn't know I was going to run into them at the border." He pointed at the Mexicans who were silently moving though the *comida* like Biblical locusts. "They're family. Anyway I have a cashier's check made to you, Mrs. Hunter." He handed Sarah the check.

"Wow," Sarah said. It was twice what she expected.

"Again, I apologize for not getting in touch with you," he said. "Once I had them in the truck, I didn't want to run any risks."

"When are you leaving?" Ali asked. She looked over at the refugees. The men were in their early thirties, strong and dark-skinned. The women looked more Indian than Mexican, squat with hip-length black hair.

"Right away." Manny said something in Spanish and the four men headed for the truck to unload Sarah's possessions.

"I hope you won't say nothing about this to any authorities," Manny said.

"We're not on real good terms with the authorities around here," Sarah said. "Don't worry."

"I'll pack some food for you to take," Ali said.

"Wait," Pam said. "Do you have to leave today? What if we hired you to do some work here?" As she spoke, she felt her words sealing a commitment. She hoped Sarah and Ali heard commitment in them.

Sarah instantly began a routine of enthusiastic 'yes' gestures. "Can you stay? We'll pay the same as in Texas," Sarah said.

Manny waved his relatives over and translated pieces of the discussion.

"If the law comes out here, they'll ask for their ID, which they don't have," Manny said. "The sheriff would want to know how they got here, and I'd be in trouble. Probably you too."

"We need a roof and some other little stuff," Sarah said. "Stay and put on the roof. It won't take long. Do you know how to roof?" she asked.

"Sure, that's no problem, but—"

"I'll not only pay you, but if you get caught, I'll give you all of this." Sarah held up the cashier's check. "I'll put it in a money order for you as a guarantee," Sarah said.

The Mexicans didn't understand Sarah's words, but they understood the gesture with the check.

"If we hide the truck, no one will know you're here," Pam said. "They can only spy on coming and going by the main road."

"Put the truck in the barn," Sarah said.

"You understand that knowingly harboring, not to mention hiring, illegal aliens is illegal, don't you?" Kenny asked Sarah.

"Yes, and I also know that knowingly turning away opportunity that knocks only once is stupid," Sarah said.

The truck, rid of its load, labored out of the ruts and into the old barn. While Kenny filled and raked over the tire tracks, Sarah set about finding bedding for the women and children. Ali cautioned Gabriel about saying anything to anyone about the arrival of the visitors.

"We better go into Santa Fe and buy some shingles," Kenny said to Pam. "Three cars ought to be enough."

"Too bad we can't take the moving van," Pam said.

"That's the last thing we want to do."

"Do you think they know how to put on a roof?" she asked. Even though it had been her idea, it seemed questionable now. She mentally ticked off problems including no liability insurance, no green cards, no credentials.

"Probably," Kenny said. "But if they don't, I do."

Pam looked at Kenny and felt her doubt dissolve. *Here's a man who can do something beside complain, and he wants to live with me. Unbelievable.*

24

ALI PROVED VITAL TO the renovation. She translated everything from "where are the nails," to "can we have tortillas?" She found she liked speaking Spanish—Mexican Spanish loaded with idioms and slang. She also liked having a purpose. Without her, the work would have been slowed by half.

It turned out the four Mexican men knew how to build or rebuild most anything. Three days later and nearly finished with the roof, two of them shifted to repairing doors, painting walls and teaching Pam to make adobe bricks, the old Mexican way.

"He says you're putting in too much water," Ali said to Pam, translating, as Pam struggled to mix a batch of mud for the large adobes.

"Last time he said I didn't put in enough," Pam said. She was sunburned and filthy. "If we work around the clock, we'll have enough bricks by Christmas."

One of the men, Jorge, took the wood paddle from Pam and stirred the muddy mess.

"Christmas is okay," Ali said. "We only have to fix the wall by the front door. Kenny says the rest is cosmetic and won't bear on getting the permit."

"Kenny says?"

"Look, he knows a shitload more about building than we do. He's rewiring the lobby right now—"

Pam interrupted, "No, he's gone to Albuquerque, but that's not the point. It's just that you say 'Kenny says' every other breath. I thought you didn't like him."

"We need him." Ali said. "I think he's like most of the men you attract—nice but irresponsible. He'll leave one day with some bullshit and never come back. I won't be the one who's hurt if he goes."

"I thought we weren't going to talk about this," Pam said, working another paddle into the mud soup.

"Why'd he go to Albuquerque?" Ali asked.

"To get a circuit—" she broke off. "Why do you care?"

Ali stomped away to the two Mexican women, Lourdes and Maria, who she had been supervising. She didn't trust Kenny, the good looking drifter who for some reason reminded her of her ex-husband, Wardo. She wasn't sure how many more emotional thumps Pam could survive. And there was another thing; she thought she heard jealousy in Pam's voice. *Caramba, does Pam think I'm trying to steal her man?*

When Ali found Lourdes and Maria, she showed them how to scrape and clean the plaster walls in preparation for painting. Ali asked them to begin in the hall at the top of the stairs.

Minutes later there were screams, a loud crash, and more screams. Lourdes and Maria came barreling down the stairs. Terrified, they spoke in fits and bits, invoking the Holy Mother's protection. Maria hid under her *serape*.

The huge round mirror, whose silver had blackened, lay in a thousand slivers on the floor. Everyone ran into the hotel lobby. Amidst wailing, shaking, and praying, Maria finally got out that a ghost had pushed the mirror off the wall.

Un espíritu.

The three children started to cry.

Ali translated. First the women had seen the ghost reflected in the mirror. Then the ghost had somehow heaved it onto the floor.

"They don't think we'll believe them, and we'll make them pay for the mirror," Ali said.

"Ask them what she looked like," Pam said.

Ali tried to calm the women and assure them that they didn't have to pay for anything.

The figure the women saw looked exactly as Alex Tso had described Lorena McCragg except they insisted that the ghost's hair and clothes were wet.

"I doubt it'll make them feel any better, but you can tell them it really is a ghost," Pam said. "And they'll probably see her again."

"And they'll probably be getting the men to get the hell out of here," Sarah said.

"Ask them to work in the garden," Pam said. "They can sleep in the tent if they feel safer."

Ali translated and the women scuttled outside. The men returned to their work, but their expressions were wary and they had *adios* in their eyes.

Pam and Ali cleaned up the broken glass. Ali held up a large shard and looked for Lorena in it.

"You think Manny told the men that we weren't on good terms with the local law? Or that Ortega could get his buddies to round them up and send them back?" Pam asked.

"Who knows?" Ali said. "If Lorena shows up again, it's moot anyway. They'll be gone." She thought how fragile the whole operation was. All they had accomplished at the hacienda which supported her new sense of home and family could shatter like glass.

"Maybe you should have told them that Lorena McCragg was the Holy Virgin Mary," Pam said.

"Or the Holy Ghost?"

⚜ ✳ ⚜

THE LATE AFTERNOON SKY worked itself into a typical New Mexico spectacle with blue violets and red oranges chasing one another toward the horizon. Ali sat on the patio watching the three men on the roof hurrying to finish. They wanted to leave the next day, and Ali couldn't blame them. She wasn't sure how she would feel if Lorena McCragg confronted her on the staircase. It was easy to say you weren't afraid of ghosts when one wasn't staring at you. She rose to find Gabriel and then to help Sarah to make a light supper for everyone, when men's voices, harsh and from several directions broke the serenity.

"Get your hands up. You are under arrest."

The men on the roof dropped to their bellies and froze. The Mexican women and children were being herded into the front courtyard by a heavy man in a white cowboy hat. The admonition to raise hands continued. A dozen men, all armed, closed in.

Ali ran to Sarah. "Have you seen Gabriel?"

"Not since *comida*."

"No talking," a man barked.

To Ali they looked mean and like they meant business, but they didn't look like sheriffs and deputies. *Oh shit,* Ali thought, *they're immigration or border patrol. Someone tipped them about Manny's illegal relatives.*

The men from the roof were now cowering in a corner of the courtyard with the other Mexicans. One had been hit in the face and was bleeding. The two Mexican women were practically hysterical, quieted only by grim threats from the man who seemed to be in charge. Well over six feet tall, he wore a gray long sleeved shirt. His neck looked uncomfortably squeezed by his collar and a turquoise bolo tie.

"Do you have a warrant?" Sarah asked. She sounded tough, but Ali knew she was bluffing.

Like a television redneck sheriff, the big guy sauntered over. "Are you Sarah Hunter?"

"Yes. Who are you?"

He looked to Ali like he was going to smack Sarah as he moved within inches of her face.

"You're harboring people who have no right to be in this country," he snarled as though it were a personal insult to him.

Ali could hear the Mexicans being interrogated in Spanish. Terrified, they offered no resistance. She looked for Gabriel but didn't see him. Then she realized Manny wasn't among them either.

Manny had been glad to hand over his friends as paid workers, but he personally had yet to so much as pick up a staple. Usually, each afternoon, he napped in the cab of the van hidden in the barn.

Sarah was pleading with two men to put their guns away.

"If they're illegal, they'll be sent back over the border. They don't deserve to die over this," she said.

"I'll decide that after I decide what I'm going to do with you," the big man said, his tone of voice like taut barbed wire. Enjoying the power, he pointed his gun straight at her. "You're in violation of a dozen laws. These stinking wetbacks steal jobs and then get on welfare—"

"It's my fault, not theirs," Sarah said. "I asked them to stay."

"No, it was my idea," Pam said. She was being guarded by a short, fat man who occasionally jabbed her with his rifle.

Oh hell, Ali thought. *They're all admitting guilt. Idiots.* "I asked them," Ali said. "We needed them to fix the roof. No one else would work for us."

"You ladies don't seem to be too popular around here," the big man said. He turned and spat on the patio bricks.

A woman screamed. A slap sounded. Sobs. One of the lawmen was pushing himself against one of the Mexican women. His gnarled hand was working up under her skirt.

From the first *"Get your hands up"* Ali had worried about what might happen to the illegals. The enforcement men might decide to have some fun. The women were certainly in danger, and probably the men were too. An accident could be arranged; bad things could happen and they could all end up dead or wishing they were.

Ali felt her blood stop. What could she do? Was he going to rape this woman right here in front of them? And if he was, who might be next?

"Martin," the boss grunted.

The man took his hand away and backed off a step. He eyed his boss, smiled and nodded. Then in one quick move, he snatched down the woman's loose peasant blouse, exposing her breasts. "Peek-a-boo," he said, his voice dirty and shaming.

The men laughed, nasty and loud.

Humiliated, the woman yanked her torn blouse up and squeezed her eyelids tight to shut off her screams.

The Mexicans were panicked. Ali could tell from their frightened glances back and forth that they were planning to run for it, waiting for the right moment.

That's probably what the SOBs want. Moving targets. But it was getting dark. Maybe they had a chance. Maybe Kenny or Manny would come back and— And what?

Ali was trying to think what to do if bedlam erupted. What could she do to help them get away? Where were her car keys? She was poised, ready to run when a man's voice over a bullhorn flooded the yard.

Methodically, over and over he instructed everyone not to move, to throw all weapons aside and lay face down face on the ground with hands out front. Men in uniforms with bigger guns rushed in from all directions. Their search lights seared the hacienda. Before she dove for the dirt, Ali saw the man who had been guarding her lying face down, his gun thrown aside. A new army had arrived.

The Mexicans, who didn't speak English, were totally confused. They sank to their knees, epithets and prayers in Spanish flying.

Ali yelled in Spanish, telling them to lie down, hands out in front. *Abrazos enfrente.*

A uniformed man passed close to pick up a gun, and Ali read NEW MEXICO DRUG ENFORCEMENT ADMINISTRATION on his insignia.

For the next two hours everyone waited on their bellies as the DEA scoured the hotel. The eerie glow of their lights gave everything a surreal look. Ali forced herself to spell difficult words: *eleemosynary, Kosciusko, Yoknapatapha,* to ward off her rising panic.

At first, the search focused upstairs in the hotel, but when no drugs were found, it moved out. Frustrated in their attempts, the DEA men tried to punch holes in the ancient solid walls. Sarah's newly delivered furniture was ripped and scrutinized, as was every crevice, crack and chink of the hotel. Drawers were dumped, contents of boxes scattered, pictures torn off walls, rugs pulled up. The cars were all but turned inside out.

Ali felt sick to see their hard work decimated, but at the same time she realized these men had stopped the first group, whoever they were. She prayed there weren't any drugs to be found.

Two hours is a lot of time to lie and think and after the initial panic wore off, Ali realized that someone had obviously told the DEA there were drugs at the hacienda. Whoever had planted the marijuana that she had burned, likely had tried to plant other drugs and then tipped the authorities. But they weren't finding any marijuana, crystal meth or other illegal drugs.

What they had found, they finally decided, was a bunch of white men with illegal guns, a bunch of illegals with nothing, and three women with funny accents.

"Cuff the boys with guns and put them in the van," the big man in gray shouted. A man approached the boss and whispered something.

"Leave the fucking wetbacks here. That's somebody else's job," the boss said.

A white van rolled into the courtyard.

"Be sure you get all the weapons," the boss ordered. "Most of them are illegal."

In minutes, the faction that had been harassing the Mexican workers was being shuffled into the van. Then they were gone, and it was totally quiet except for the muffled crying of the three children and their mothers.

Ali tried to explain to the Mexicans that they weren't going to be arrested after all. They didn't act like they believed her. Sarah found battery-powered lights, and Pam started a fire in the fire pit. The tent was in shreds and everything was turned over, broken or scattered.

Out of nowhere Manny sauntered in.

"I heard all the noise so I just laid low," he said. "They didn't come out to the barn or the sheds. Too dark, I guess. Maybe they'll come back tomorrow," he said.

"Happy thought," Sarah said.

"No. Somebody told them what to look for and where to find it," Ali said.

Sarah thought of the boy, Gabriel. Hadn't he been in charge of the marijuana?

Manny's *compadres* gathered about him and spoke in hushed, agitated Spanish. Ali couldn't hear it all, but it was clear that a ghost and not one, but two separate groups of *Federales* were too much for them.

They were packing up when the lights of an approaching car bounced on the rough road. The Mexicans ran to the moving van in the barn. Ali made a mental note they had to buy a shotgun, maybe three of them. But it was only Kenny returning from Albuquerque where he had gone to buy a circuit breaker panel.

"Wait a minute," Kenny said, after they described the fracas. "Men with guns, not the local law enforcement, came to get Manny's people and then the DEA came and took those guys away?" He looked at Pam. "That makes no sense."

"That's what happened," Pam said.

Ali knew Kenny was right, but there was no other explanation she could think of, and she hated men like Kenny who always thought they knew everything. She hated being dependent on him. Where had he been three hours ago when they needed him?

It didn't take much to decide that Manny and his crew should leave immediately.

"The DEA might have called border patrol," Kenny said.

Ali and Pam packed what food could be found in the debris, Sarah paid Manny what they owed him, and Kenny drew a map that included a stop at Rosa's Mexican Restaurant just shy of the Texas border. The four of them waved goodbye as the moving van stole away into the darkness.

Stunned, they sat by the fire, too exhausted to survey the DEA's damage.

"What was the first bunch wearing?" Kenny asked. "They must have had uniforms."

Ali was annoyed that he continued to quiz them.

"No, they had attitudes. Attitudes and guns," Sarah said.

"They probably weren't lawmen at all," he said. He sat close to Pam, one arm around her. "What's his name, Ortega, probably his goons sent to frighten off your help."

"No, no. Ortega sent the drug guys," Ali said. "He planted some marijuana out here. I found it the first day." She stood up fast, her face clouding with fear. "Oh, shit. Where's Gabriel?"

Ali grabbed one of the fluorescent camp lights and tore out toward the kiln. Gabriel wasn't in it. "Gabriel, Gabriel," shot through the dark, but found no target.

"I can't look for him," Sarah said. "My leg hurts too much."

"Stay here. He might come back to the fire," Pam said, taking off to help Ali. "Somebody needs to be here."

"Wait, Pam," Kenny said. "I'll go. You look inside. Take a light with you."

Ali stumbled from shed to shed, calling, "Gabriel."

I'd be a terrible mother. I can't even take care of one little boy. As Ali berated herself, the knowledge that Gabriel might have had something to do with the night's events wound its way into her consciousness. Had he planted the drugs and the DEA just couldn't find them? Or was he supposed to plant them and didn't? If that were true, then he'd be in danger from Ortega. Hoarseness already abrading her voice, she called the name of the child who was probably in trouble, the child who had stolen her heart.

25

THE PHANTOM PAIN KEPT Sarah awake much of that night. Zinging sensations hurt toes that were no longer there. Bernie lay pressed close to her sleeping bag. Everyone had slept outside by the fire. The tent lay in a heap and although the hotel was intact, the red tag still hung by the door like a bloody abscess. Following the letter of the law seemed prudent.

Ali fed the fire all night and watched for Gabriel. Only Kenny could muster the energy to make coffee when light finally came. Ali grabbed a cup and took off across the field to comb the ranch for Gabriel. Pam headed in the opposite direction to search.

Morning revealed that the damage caused by the DEA wasn't as bad as Sarah had thought. Much of her furniture would need reupholstering, but the solid old hotel had not yielded. When she went to check for damage to her car, she saw *Señora* Cantu coming down the road at a pace faster than usual. She looked intent, like a raven focused on a morsel.

An uneasy feeling gripped Sarah.

"They fixed the tower. Your cellular phones should work now," *Señora* Cantu said, settling by the small cookfire. She didn't comment on the ruined tent.

"Good," Sarah said, waiting to be told the importance of this information or the reason for the visit.

"Going to be hot today."

"Yeah. It's the first of June, isn't it?" Sarah said. "Summertime." She heard the lyrics in her head about the living being easy. No, not so easy here.

Kenny said hello to each of them and got up, stretching his stiff legs. "Excuse me, ladies," he said.

"Tell the girls the boy is not out there," the *Señora* said.

Kenny looked at her and then without another word headed for the fields.

"Where's Gabriel?" Sarah asked.

Sarah thought that *Señora* Cantu probably had the scoop on all of last evening's events at the Hacienda Angustia. Usually she took about thirty minutes before getting around to whatever gossip or instruction she had. This morning was different.

"Some of Ortega's men didn't come home last night," Cantu said. "A few are in a little trouble over guns. Nothing too big, I hear, but Jami Ortega isn't very happy."

"What the hell happened?" Sarah asked. "First one bunch rough up Manny's guys, then another bunch cart the first bunch off in a van."

"That's not important now," Cantu said, leaning toward Sarah. "Ortega couldn't know for sure when the DEA would come or even if it would. Bad timing for him."

"You're saying it was a coincidence?"

"*Mi sobrino,* Juan, told me Ortega's men are pretty mad at him. Juan says Jami Ortega got anxious about you fixing the roof so fast, getting your permit, maybe. You know." She took a long draw of hot, black coffee. "So he sent in his boys to scare away your workers."

"And the DEA boys came when—"

"*Que coincidencia,*" *Señora* Cantu said.

Sarah thought the *Señora* looked like she knew more than she was telling.

"So the whole town's against us now," Sarah said.

"No, no. *Contrario.* Jami Ortega has bullied them all for years. They're watching you. There're no bets on you yet, but no one ever came this close to keeping him from what he wants."

"We just want to be left alone," Sarah said. She rubbed her aching knee, working her fingers under the prosthesis' cuff. "Gabriel's connected to this, isn't he?"

"We have to do something about Gabriel," the old woman said.

"Where is he?"

The *Señora* ignored Sarah's question. "He was supposed to hide contraband in the hotel for the authorities to find," she said. "They didn't find it, so he must still have it."

"I knew Ortega was trying to set us up," Sarah said. She couldn't imagine how *Señora* Cantu knew all this. "When did you find out about the drugs?"

"The drugs aren't the important problem," Cantu said. She wiped her mouth on her sleeve. "Gabriel betrayed Jami Ortega. Made him look like a fool. Angustia is small. Everyone knows most everything by now." She painfully bent to retie her shoelace.

"Where's the boy?" Sarah repeated. She felt confused about not only what had happened, but about whom she could trust.

"At Lukey's. Before the boy moved in here, he slept in Lukey's garage."

"He's a child. They won't hurt a child," Sarah said. Even as she said the words she knew that Jami Ortega was more than capable of hurting Gabriel.

The *Señora* explained the situation. "Jami Ortega can't let anyone embarrass him. He has to do something to punish Gabriel for helping you. Maybe he'll only dump him over the border."

"Leave him? In Mexico?"

"But I don't think he'll do that," Cantu said.

Sarah breathed an audible sigh. "Good," she said. "Why's he at Lukey's?"

"My cousin used to work for Ortega. My cousin would get drunk and brag about how smart he and Ortega were. He claimed Jami Ortega was running guns, drugs, whores, and generally stealing anything he could."

"Does your cousin still work for him?"

"No. Julio is dead. His wife thinks Ortega killed Julio. You must listen, *chica*," Cantu said. But when he was alive, *mi sobrino* said that Ortega accidentally discovered that he could sell children. He sold a *puta's* baby to a white couple for a lot of money. Later he got connected with some Asians, not Chinese or Japanese, I don't remember. But Julio said they could get a lot of money in the black market. Homeless *niños*, runaways, it didn't matter."

Sarah felt a sticky, gray sickness rise in her throat. She considered vomiting. "Child slavery. The sex trade. Oh my God, you think he'll try to sell Gabriel to some male sex—" She couldn't finish.

"He may give Gabriel to them. Ortega will do something with him. I'm sure of that." The *Señora* spat into the fire's ashes sending up a small whirlwind.

Sarah squinted at the low gray hills in the distance. They looked as unfriendly and unyielding as death. The blooming flowers she had planted smelled funereal. A column of ants marched toward her.

When Ali, Kenny and Pam returned, *Señora* Cantu retold the story. Sarah watched Ali harden to flint.

"Where does Lukey live?" Ali said.

"Wait," Kenny said. "Please. You go drive up there and demand him, you might get shot for trespassing," Kenny said. "You don't really have any rights to him anyway."

Sarah waited for Ali to either flip out or melt down.

"Where does Lukey live?" Ali repeated, her emotions thoroughly repressed, her voice even.

"Ali, let's make a plan," Pam said. "We can do something, but let's get the odds on our side. Kenny's right."

Ali's eye twitched and her lips rose into a scowl. "We don't have much time. I'm going to get a shotgun and go get him."

Señora Cantu, who had dropped out of the conversation, sat back in the plastic chair. Sarah knew from experience that the woman was biding her time. *Señora* Cantu knew more.

"We can go tonight and look the place over," Pam said. "Gabriel's smart. He'll know we're coming for him."

"He'll be gone by tonight. I've read about this shit," Ali said. "He'll be hogtied with duct tape in the back of a truck headed for a boat to Thailand."

"You don't know that," Kenny said.

"Talk all you want. I'm going," Ali said.

Only when Ali headed for her car did *Señora* Cantu speak. "My son's sister-in-law, Esmeralda sold Lukey's wife's some eggs this morning. He's hung over. *Muy borrachado.* He was too drunk to beat her up last night."

Ali slowly walked back and stood in front of the *Señora*. "Tell me what to do," she said, her voice choked with hatred and fear.

"Lukey won't do anything until Ortega tells him, and Ortega is real busy this morning," she said. "I'll go. Carlotta will go with me. She sells honey. Lukey's not going to bother with old women selling honey."

"How will you get him?" Sarah asked.

"I don't know yet. He's probably locked in the garage," she said. "But there's another problem."

"What?" Ali asked.

"What do you do with him after you get him? He can't stay here," Cantu said.

Sarah could see that it would only be a matter of time before Gabriel was abducted by Ortega or met with some arranged accident.

Pam touched Kenny's arm. "What about Joan's place? Just for a week, until we find something safe?"

Kenny shrugged. "I could ask. She likes to rescue things."

"Will you call her?" Pam asked.

Sarah looked at Kenny and realized that he would do anything for Pam. *He's in love.*

"Where is this place?" *Señora* Cantu asked.

"His sister's cat ranch in Texas," Pam said.

"*Un rancho de gatos?*" *Señora* asked. "Who's ranching cats?"

"Long story," Kenny said. "I'll call Joan." He walked off to find Pam's cell phone.

"Unless somebody has a better idea, I'll go get Carlotta and some honey," *Señora* Cantu said.

"Who's Carlotta?" Sarah asked.

"*La viuda de Julio.* Cousin Julio's widow."

26

PAM TUGGED ON THE leather fringe of her belt. They were all nervous, but Pam could see that Ali was about to jump out of her skin. It had taken over an hour to hustle up Carlotta and the honey and get her and *Señora* Cantu over to Lukey's house. Carlotta, the widow of *Señora* Cantu's cousin, Julio who had worked for Ortega and according to Carlotta, been murdered by him, was thrilled for the chance to get back at Ortega.

On a rise overlooking Lukey's place a half mile away, Pam, Ali and Kenny waited in Sarah's car, ready for the rescue. Sarah, shotgun in reach, waited at the hacienda.

Lukey Alejandro and his wife Amelia lived in the gray sand hills east of Angustia. The house's porch sagged and the siding cried for paint. Clearly, maintenance scored low on Lukey's list of priorities. The yard was full of broken auto parts; the house looked full of broken dreams.

The plan was for *Señora* Cantu and Carlotta to grab Gabriel if Lukey was passed out. If not, on a signal, the others would blast in, counting on strength in numbers. Through her binoculars, Pam could see Carlotta's old Ford station wagon jerk to a stop in front of the dilapidated house.

"Come on," Ali murmured. "Hurry up."

Carlotta, maybe seventy and built like a Saguaro cactus, plodded to the front door beside *Señora* Cantu. Pam could see the box of honey jars. No one answered. Carlotta banged again.

"Maybe they've already left," Ali said.

Pam could also see Ali was struggling to hold it together. She was chewing the inside of her lower lip and pressing her long fingernails into her fingertips. Pam understood that Ali was upset; they all were. But she also thought she saw something essentially different in Ali. Gabriel's disappearance had shifted something in her; she now possessed a firmness, a sense of purpose. She even looked different.

"She's setting the honey down on the porch," Kenny said.

"Where are they going?" Ali asked.

The women disappeared around the side of the house.

"She said Gabriel might be in the garage," Pam said. "Can you see another building?"

"No."

"Let's go," Ali said.

"Give them a chance," Kenny said. "Wait two minutes."

"Wait two minutes," Pam said a beat behind Kenny. She smiled. She liked the closeness simultaneity bred. It was foreign to her and utterly delicious. She valued Kenny's strength, but even more, she appreciated how he made her an equal partner in whatever they did. Nabbing kidnapped children was no exception.

But they didn't have to wait two minutes. Carlotta shot from around the side of the house running as fast as she could, which wasn't very fast. She mounted the steps, jerked the blue scarf from the box of honey and waved it frantically. The sign to come fast. *Rápido.*

"That's it. Go, go, go," Ali screamed, shoving to get in the car.

Pam banged her shin hard on the car door, but hardly felt the blow. As the car picked up speed, she questioned their hastily drawn plan. What if Lukey, shotgun in hand, waited inside?

"Keep watching her. See where she wants us to go," Kenny said. The Toyota slid around a curve kicking up a gray swirl.

"She went back around the side," Pam said, choking. She was leaning out of the car window, balancing the field glasses.

Pam felt Kenny pull the car out of a skid as they sped into the gravel driveway. "I'm going to turn the car around to face out toward the road," Kenny shouted above the noise. "Pam, you stay with the car. Keep it running. If it gets weird, go for help."

"Okay," Pam said, unfastening her seat belt. If it gets weird? She wondered briefly where help might come from.

"Ali, come with me," Kenny said. "He trusts you." As crazy and dangerous as it was, Pam was exhilarated. She looked at Kenny and wondered why he was doing all this for them. And she knew she was falling in love with him.

Kenny drove in beside the house near a ramshackle garage-shop, did a 180 turn and leapt out of the car with Ali behind. Pam clamored into the driver's seat. *Señora* Cantu stood beside the shop door holding a trowel. Shattered glass from the pane in the door lay at her feet. There was no sign of Lukey.

"The boy, he's in there," the *Señora* said. "Not conscious."

"He's too heavy for us," Carlotta said.

Pam could see Ali push past Kenny into the garage. She emerged holding the slack body of Gabriel. Kenny took him from her and laid him on the back seat. *Señora* Cantu and

Carlotta humped along to the station wagon and got in. Their tires spun in the dirt and the station wagon lurched forward.

Pam hit the accelerator before the Toyota's doors were closed. The car cleared the front gate. In the rear view mirror Pam saw a woman sitting on the front porch swing petting a black cat. Pam thought the woman must be Lukey's wife, Amelia.

"He's breathing and his heart's steady," Ali said.

"That's good, because there's no doctor we can trust," Pam said.

Near the main highway, behind an abandoned Diamond Shamrock station the two cars made their prearranged rendezvous. Ali's car waited where they had left it. Carlotta stayed in her station wagon, the motor running. *Señora* Cantu struggled out and opened the back door of the Toyota. She examined the child, pulling up his eyelids, feeling his pulse and smelling him. "A barbiturate maybe," the old woman said.

"I have to take him," Ali said. "He doesn't know you, Kenny. He might think you're going to do something bad to him."

Pam thought Kenny would have a better chance getting Gabriel safely to Joan's ranch near San Antonio, but she knew Ali was determined.

"Okay. Directions are easy." Kenny said. "I'll call Joan; she'll be looking for you."

"Don't get stopped," Pam said. "Ortega might own the Highway Patrol."

"I better take Sarah's car," Ali said. "With the dent in the roof, mine's too conspicuous."

"Call us when you—" she stopped and wrapped her arms around Ali. "Please be careful."

Pam watched Ali drive away in Sarah's car with Gabriel wrapped in Carlotta's scarlet rebozo. Pam knew it was possible that she'd never see Ali again.

"She doesn't have any clothes with her," Pam said as Ali's car dipped below a hill and out of sight.

"Joan will lend her a cat tee shirt," Kenny said. He put his arm around her shoulder. "Joan understands rescue. If Ali makes it to San Antonio, she'll be fine."

As they drove back to the hacienda, in Ali's car, Pam replayed the rescue mission in her head. She broke the silence. "What do you think about Lukey's wife on the porch?" she asked.

"She'll tell him she didn't see anything," he said.

"She could have stopped us."

"Maybe he'll kill her," Kenny said, taking her hand in his.

Pam sank into the warmth of his touch. In the burn off of the adrenalin rush, she felt closer to him than ever. She wanted to pull off the road and have sex, the hard, urgent sex of *desperados*. The kind of sex that might keep the idea of falling in love at bay. Her feeling for him was way past affection, but she prayed neither passion nor reason would loosen declarations. Be in love. Don't talk about it.

They pulled into the hacienda's drive and parked by a truck.

"Shit, that's Tyrone's truck."

"Who?"

"The red tag man."

"Well, we're just in time," Kenny said.

Pam could see Sarah in front of the hacienda's door, arguing with Tyrone. Tyrone squinted in the sunlight; the bulbous knot over his eyebrow seemed to throb. He didn't look happy to see her and Kenny.

Pam and Kenny walked slowly as though a trap door might open beneath them.

"He says he can't remove the red tag," Sarah said. She turned back to Tyrone. "We've done everything you said we had to." Sarah waved the list of required upgrades and repairs.

Pam could see that stress was taking a toll on Sarah. She looked bone tired.

"Why not?" Kenny asked. He turned his head, jutting his chin forward and looked straight at Tyrone.

Pam could almost smell the testosterone in the air.

"Because of the storm, I'm booked up. And I'll need some help with this inspection. It's a big place," Tyrone said.

Pam wanted to call him a liar. "When can you do it?" she asked.

"I'll have to get back to you," Tyrone said. "Shouldn't be too long." He looked at Kenny. "I didn't get your name."

"No, you didn't," Kenny said. He never took his eyes off Tyrone.

Pam looked at the two of them. Tyrone was bigger and meaner-looking, but Kenny could probably take care of himself in a fight.

"Except for repairs, stay out of the hotel," Tyrone said looking at Pam. He moved his hips in a way that was at once menacing and sexual.

He's a bully's bully, Pam thought. *Would probably cry like a little girl if he ever got busted.* Bullies fed on fear and weakness in an opponent. She pulled her shoulders back.

"You work for Ortega, Tyrone?" Pam asked. "You another of his lackeys, frightening women, trying to scare them from their home?" She forced her voice to hold steady.

Tyrone's eyes flashed. He took a step closer to Pam and looked down at her as if she were a termite.

Kenny stepped between them.

"Having him here won't make any difference in the long run," he said, cutting his eyes to Kenny.

Pam could see that Kenny thought differently.

"You're a coward, Tyrone," Sarah said. "We aren't leaving."

Tyrone smiled. "Well, I am. For now. I can have you put in jail if you violate the order and occupy this dump." He turned and walked with deliberate slowness to his truck. He backed up and spun the rear wheels, throwing a cloud of dust into the air.

"Shit, is he scary or what?" Pam said. Her heart pounded.

"He's a mean dude," Kenny said. "Got that ugly knot on his forehead in a fight, I'd bet."

"He's going to delay forever," Sarah said. "He'll finally inspect and find ten new things we have to fix. Look at this place. We'll never pass."

"I think he thinks you'll give up before he has to inspect," Kenny said. "If they tried to plant drugs and that didn't work, they must have another plan. I don't mean to scare you."

Sarah twisted her ring on her finger. "I'm grateful you were here," she said.

Pam agreed. Independence and self-reliance were important, but sometimes brute force back-up was necessary.

"Look, Kenny, I'm sorry I was rude to you," Sarah said. "I thought you were—" she broke off. "Thanks for all your help."

Kenny nodded.

"Hell, I didn't even ask about the boy," Sarah said. "And why are you here? Where's my car? What happened?"

Pam explained Gabriel's rescue and Ali's trip to Texas.

"They'll come here looking for him," Sarah said.

"I expect so," Kenny said.

"This is about to get dangerous, isn't it?" Sarah said.

"No. It's already dangerous," Pam said. "We can sit around and worry or we can do some work."

Pam could hear the change in her own voice. She didn't want to run from Tyrone and Ortega. Her adobes were in the hotel, she had the makings of a pottery studio, and Kenny was with her—for now anyway. But more than that, there was some new voice that had been added to her internal chorus. It didn't tell her she was pathetic, unlovable, and stupid. It told her not to let others push her around and not to let them decide her worth. Maybe her parents were wrong. Maybe she was okay, or at least she wasn't not okay.

"Kenny, will you help me with the windows in the room behind the lobby?" Pam asked.

"What are we going to do to them?"

"They blew out in the storm. I'm going to put stained glass in them."

"Like in a church?" he asked.

"Yes," Pam said. Years ago she had learned to make stained glass lamp shades and window panes to sell with her pottery at craft shows. "It looks like a chapel. I'm going to make it one."

"It used to be one," he said.

"How do you know?" Sarah asked.

"What?" Pam asked.

"That historical material you copied. A priest used to come and say Mass. There wasn't a church fifty miles of here back then," Kenny said. He gently pinched Pam's shoulder. "You ought to read your own homework."

There were no pictures of the original hotel chapel, but there were several old newspaper accounts of ceremonies held there. A Catholic priest had ridden over from Albuquerque to marry three couples at the same service in June, 1889.

Pam took the photocopied clippings from Kenny and went into the chapel. Knowing it had been a church made it feel different. She squinted, searching for clues about its past. If a cross had been mounted, the uniformly dirty walls weren't telling its location. Then she saw them: two rectangular depressions in the floor. Kneeling, she felt the old saltillo tiles. Something had once fit into them.

"Sarah, Kenny," she shouted. "I know where the altar used to be."

It wasn't religious zeal, but some equally passionate force threw Pam into a frenzy after she discovered the old footings for the altar. The chapel called to her to be restored the way an orphaned puppy cries for help. The idea of restoring it touched the deepest core of her creativity, and creativity had always been the one reliable thing that gave her life meaning. With her negative internal voice at least temporarily silenced, Pam felt she was on the verge of doing her greatest creative work ever, a work so stunning it could save her.

The next day, leaving Sarah at the hacienda with Carlotta and *Señora* Cantu, Pam took Kenny to Santa Fe to search for stained glass. An antique dealer told her about an artist near Tesuque who salvaged architectural features from old buildings. They found him in a rambling house and studio combination that backed up to the foothills of the Sangre de Cristos. Stacks of old windows, boxes of brass door knobs and bins of carved molding filled every available space. The artist had left stained glass and moved to welding metal sculptures and gladly sold Pam a huge wooden crate filled with pieces of glass that looked like shaved jewels.

She chattered ceaselessly to Kenny on the long drive home in order to drown out any internal voices that might try to shake her courage. *I'm building a chapel. That's a good thing. Right?*

JOAN CALLED THE HACIENDA to let them know Ali and Gabriel had arrived. Ali was sleeping and would call later.

Ali called the next day. "Gabriel seems okay. He loves the animals."

"The pig?" Pam asked.

"Yes, Roy and Trigger too," Ali said. "I haven't told him I'm leaving yet."

"Joan's okay with him being there?" Pam asked.

"She adores him. Not sure she'll let him leave."

"No one's come looking for him here," Pam said.

"I doubt that son of a bitch Ortega needs to. He knows."

"*Señora* Cantu says Ortega hasn't been seen in Angustia since the night of the raid on the hacienda," Pam said.

"He's planning something."

Pam felt the tug of fear. She had been so involved in restoring the chapel that she had forgotten the toll fear exacted.

"I'll be back next week," Ali said. "Joan says Gabriel can stay as long as we need him to, but I need to get back. I can't let you two do everything."

"Be careful, Ali," Pam said.

A WEEK LATER, THE June sunlight through the twelve small windows made glorious colored patterns on the chapel walls. A patchwork of shell pink, citrine, and amethyst hues spread over the simple altar that Kenny had made. Sarah, Pam, and Kenny stood by the door admiring their creation. They had worked almost non-stop as though making a chapel would keep them safe.

"I could make some pews or benches," he said. "Of course, way back, people stood in church."

"It looks beautiful, Pam," Sarah said. "You're such an artist."

"I didn't do this alone," Pam said. She felt good in the chapel, calm, like she thought church craftsmen centuries ago had felt, building a monument to God's glory. She ran her hand down the smooth plaster wall and imagined the hand-painted tiles she planned to set. It would be an abstract mosaic of the New Mexico landscape covering the entire wall behind the altar.

Below each of the windows she had written the name of one of Jesus' apostles. Lettered over the door was 'Chapel of the Apostles,' the same name it had borne a hundred years ago.

"When did Father Gallegos say he'd get here?" Sarah asked.

"You've asked that three times," Pam said. "Four. He said four o'clock." Pam repeatedly pressed the tiny creases in her skirt and adjusted the concho belt Kenny had bought for her in Tesuque.

"I'll wait out front," Kenny said. "Make sure he doesn't miss us." His steps echoed, and then faded.

"You think the candles are okay?" Sarah asked. "I've had a hundred dinner parties, but I've never decorated a chapel."

"I think they usually have white, but this in New Mexico, the Land of Enchantment. Maybe chartreuse is better," Pam said.

She brushed her fingertips over the altar, admiring its simplicity and grace. She and Kenny had designed it together. He had built it from fallen trees on the property and hand rubbed it with tung oil for hours. She looked out the door and could see Kenny standing in the sun looking west for the priest as though he would arrive on horseback.

For the Mass, Kenny was wearing his one good shirt, a white, long-sleeved one stuffed into almost-new pressed jeans. Pam remembered the first time she saw him at the truck stop in Louisiana and felt the same stirring inside. He exuded sexual energy. He looked like a bad boy, but he wasn't acting like one. It worried her.

"Do you think the diocese would help us outfit the place?" Sarah asked. "Somebody must sell those racks for candles— the ones people light and then say prayers." She rearranged the blossoms in one of the five vases.

"That'd be good," Pam said. She pinched her skirt's creases more frenetically.

"What's going on?" Sarah said. "I know you. You're not telling me something."

Pam marveled at how Sarah could tell when something was up with her and Ali, but had never suspected her own husband, Steven of cheating on her.

"I invited a few people to the service. I hope you don't mind," Pam said.

"Who?"

"Everybody," Pam said. "The whole town. I put up a notice at the grocery."

"Why didn't you tell me?" Sarah asked.

"Because I know it's a good idea, but I know how paranoid you are right now," Pam said. You're tired, your leg hurts all the time, all this stress is making you crazy."

"And it's not affecting you?"

"I should have told you."

"Does Kenny know?" Sarah asked.

"I told him this morning." Pam hurried to assuage Sarah's feelings by explaining her idea. "You agreed to have the chapel reconsecrated—"

"I did not," Sarah interrupted. "It was never deconsecrated."

"Okay. I acted without consulting you or Ali," Pam said. "I'm sorry. I'm asking you now. I want to hear Mass, and I want others to hear it too. And not just to manipulate them into accepting us. The chapel wants it. Can't you feel it? Things want to be what they are. A forgotten storage room is a chapel again. It matters."

Sarah shrugged. "Okay. It's something we can give back to the people. Some of their ancestors worshiped here."

"Thank you," Pam said. She wasn't sure Sarah understood her need, but Sarah's acceptance was enough.

"And I like that they're going to have a harder time helping that SOB Ortega run us off if we give them back a church," Sarah said.

"I don't think you should say SOB in church," Pam said.

"How many do you expect?" Sarah asked.

"I think a few of the women will come," Pam said. "*Señora* Cantu is bringing Carlotta and Dominguez. Maybe the parents of some of Ali's dancers will show up. It's about God, not about us."

"It's a good idea. Just next time trust me enough to tell me," Sarah said.

"Okay. Did I tell you I saw the ghost?"

"Lorena McCragg?" Sarah said. "Damn it, Pam. When?"

"The back stairs where Alex said he always saw her. I'm going to try to get him to come up here. I told her I'd met Alex, but she wasn't impressed."

"Did you invite her to Mass today?"

"No, but I could. She's probably still around," Pam said.

AFTER FATHER GALLEGOS HAD drunk a glass of cold sweet tea and looked over the photocopied material on the chapel that Pam had put together, he toured the hacienda chapel.

"You've done a beautiful job," he said. "We can't determine from any records that the chapel was ever deconsecrated. The place simply fell into disuse and was forgotten." He unpacked a leather case with the things he would use to say Mass.

As Pam watched him place the chalice, ciborium, cruets, and host box on the white chasuble, two then four people entered quietly and stood together at the back. Then more came. By the time Father Gallegos had placed the Corpus Cross on the altar, about thirty people stood in the chapel.

"You didn't tell me we'd have a crowd," the priest whispered to Sarah.

She smiled and shrugged. "They probably heard it was you who was coming."

"I hadn't planned a sermon, but I could give the one I said last Sunday," he said.

"Would you?" Sarah said.

"In Spanish, if they'd like. They are probably mostly Spanish speakers."

"Father, you do what you think is best," Sarah said.

"But I thought a Mass in Latin. The last time one was said here, undoubtedly it was in Latin," he said. He was fussing with his surplice, which refused to lie down.

"Whatever you think," Sarah said, retreating to the side of the chapel to stand with Pam and Kenny.

"He's going to say Mass in Latin and a sermon in Spanish," Sarah said to Pam.

"A linguist," Pam whispered. "Maybe he could talk to the ghost."

"*In nomine Patris, et Filii, et Spiritus Sancti. Amen*"

A boy from the group went forward at his mother's push and lighted the green tapers on the altar. Clothed in worn jeans and a shirt two sizes too large, he stood by to assist the priest. A dozen more people came in.

"*Gratia Domini nostri Jesu Christi, et caritas Dei, et communicatio Sancti Spiritus—*"

The delicate amethyst, celadon, and rose from the stained glass windows played over the worshipers. For whatever reasons, they might have shunned the hotel's new owners, but they weren't going to shun the new occupant of the chapel, God Almighty.

"*Sit cum omnibus vobis,*" the priest said.

"*Et cum spiritu tuo,*" replied the congregation.

Because they had to stand, Father Gallegos gave a brief sermon. Neither Pam, Sarah, nor Kenny understood much but as Pam watched the people, she witnessed a gradual settling, a relaxation among them.

"Look at them," Pam whispered to Sarah. "Do you think the priest is telling them to chill out?"

"I think he's talking about St. Paul's letters," Sarah said.

"They look like they never stopped coming here," Pam said. Her eyes misted and she reached for Kenny's hand.

A few men leaned against the back wall; children sat on the floor. An ancient lady swathed in a coarse cotton *serape* knelt, alternating her attention between her rosary and Father Gallegos.

When the benediction finished, the crowd shuffled out. Sarah and Pam went to thank the priest, but Kenny followed the worshipers outside.

"It was beautiful," Pam said. She was still wiping tears from her eyes. "I hope you'll come again."

"Yes," Sarah said.

Kenny came back in. "Excuse me. I think you better come outside."

The low angle of the late afternoon sun lent a vibrancy to the tableau in front of the hotel. The light intensified the pinky-brown adobe walls that backed the orange, blue, fuchsia, white and purple of the people's clothing. Pam thought it was too bad that one of New Mexico's many artists wasn't around to paint it.

A child came forward and handed Sarah and Pam bouquets of roses, the stems wrapped in wet paper covered with tin foil. Then everyone nervously looked at an old woman whose iron gray hair wound into a bun secured by a turquoise barrette. She wore an apron over her cotton dress; men's corduroy slippers covered her feet.

She approached Sarah and Pam and said in careful English, "Thank you for what you have done." She paused and looked first at Sarah then at Pam, taking them in slowly as if she would take a part of each with her. When she turned, the others came forward one at a time and shook Pam and Sarah's hands. They grasped and held for only a second before releasing and moving away, but in that moment conveyed their appreciation and more importantly, their acceptance.

Pam let her tears go in a rush of emotion. *Nobody is going to take this chapel away from us.*

27

ALI'S TRIP TO SAN Antonio from Angustia had been 880 miles of terror. Thinking she was being followed by a green minivan, she detoured and got lost in a maze of country roads. Afraid to ask directions, she tried to backtrack, finally dead-ending at a rusty trailer. The old Indian woman inside didn't speak much English. She pointed to what she called "town."

Back on the highway, Ali's eyes darted between the unconscious boy on the back seat and the rear view mirror. Every car seemed to be tailing her. When Gabriel woke up nauseated, she had to stop for him to vomit. Twenty miles later he needed to stop again. Later, in a deserted rest area, two men pulled in, sending her into hysterical paranoia. By the time they reached Joan's shelter, Gabriel was in better shape than Ali.

That was late Wednesday, June second. Ali's nerves were shot and she couldn't stop crying, so Joan gave her a sedative and put her to bed. Ali woke up on early Friday with Gabriel sleeping beside her and a potbellied pig on the floor.

Fear was her waking emotion. Had they made it? Were they followed? But her anxiety melted as she watched Gabriel sleep. She closed her eyes and breathed deeply as though she could inhale his essence and protect him within her body. She petted his head with one finger and let her thick dark hair caress his neck.

When and how had this powerful feeling gathered? Perhaps, like an ancient seed pod, it had just been waiting for the right conditions to blossom.

He opened his eyes and reached for her. She thought she'd die.

✦ ❈ ✦

"The boy's taken to the place all right," Joan said, setting down a platter of hot pancakes. "Yesterday, while you were asleep, he helped me treat the animals for fleas and ticks, brushed half the cats and put a spell on Nguyen. That potbelly won't leave his side."

"Thanks for taking care of him, of us," Ali said. She sat facing Joan's ample breakfasts. "It was an emergency."

"Kenny said y'all were having a little trouble. Why don't you just call the police?" Joan asked. She eased another pancake on Ali's plate.

"There are no police. The sheriff works for the bad guys, and no one's done anything illegal that we can prove," Ali said.

"Ortega is the one wants to get the place?" Joan asked. She ran her fingers through her springy salt and pepper hair.

"By sheer accident, we bought it out from under him," Ali said. "We can't figure out why he wants it so bad." She shifted so that she could get a better view of Gabriel outside playing Frisbee with the two Labrador retrievers.

"You have other children?" Joan asked.

The words, 'other children' struck Ali. It implied Gabriel was her child. If he was, then she wasn't childless after all.

249

"No. Two miscarriages," she said. Ali wasn't sure why she had told Joan that painful fact. Maybe it had to do with the setting. According to Joan, over a hundred animals had been given another chance here.

"That's hard. You still married?"

"I lost the babies with my first husband. We divorced. That was probably why. My second husband recently left me, and my biological clock wound down some time ago so—" She didn't finish.

"You going to adopt the Mexican boy?" Joan had finished her breakfast and was stacking cans of pet food in a cupboard.

"If it's possible. He has a father." Ali nudged back a pancake.

"Who doesn't want him but won't let you have him?"

Outside, Gabriel smiled and waved, and Joan saw Ali's eyes fill with tears.

"Yes."

"You love him?" Joan said.

There was the question. And if she did love the boy, was it because she was so desperate for any child? Why the panic to mother? Pam didn't have it, and if Sarah ever had, she'd lost it easily enough. But Ali did love him, blindly and without foundation. Excruciating, all-consuming desire.

"Yes. I'm so scared—if I take him, if I don't. What if he doesn't want me to?"

"You're all he talked about yesterday. Wouldn't sleep anywhere but with you last night," Joan said. She flopped down in one of the many comfortable chairs and fanned herself.

"He's vulnerable, horribly needy," Ali said.

"You might make a good pair. Course you're going to have to adopt Nguyen and a couple of dogs too," Joan said, watching Gabriel rolling with Trigger and Roy.

After breakfast, Ali, who managed to get down half a pancake, helped Joan clean up the kitchen.

"He can stay here as long as you need him to," Joan said, picking up a ball of cat fur from the chair.

Ali opened her mouth to protest, but stopped. She didn't have many alternatives. "You're sure?"

"He's no trouble," Joan said. "I've saved hundreds of animals. Never saved a little boy."

"I need to go back to Angustia," Ali said. She squirted detergent onto a hot, wet sponge.

"I know," Joan said. "Kenny said as much. Gabriel will be okay here."

With dripping, soapy fingers, Ali squeezed Joan's hand.

⊹ ❀ ⊹

"I'M NOT LEAVING YOU for long," she told Gabriel. They had been at the cat ranch a week. "You're staying with Joan until it's safe. I'll be back in a week."

"Okay," he said, dry-eyed, tight-lipped.

"I'll call you every day so we won't worry about each other."

"Okay."

Waves of emotion almost knocked her over. In spite of being forced to survive nearly on his own, he was sweet-natured and loving. Ali could see him force himself not to cry, not to make things harder on her. She touched his shoulder.

"Gabriel, you want to tell me anything about something Lukey or Ortega gave you to put in the hacienda? Drugs, maybe?"

"No."

"If they did give you something and you still have it or know where it is, it would be good for me to know," she said.

251

Gabriel looked at his bare feet.

He's trying to protect me, she thought. *He knows.*

The boy said nothing.

"I know you're scared, but I need to know. Those men were DEA, Drug Enforcement Administration. They didn't find anything so maybe you still have it. It's dangerous for you." Ali couldn't find the right words to explain the consequences to Gabriel. The illegal drugs themselves were problem enough, but Ortega wanting to recover them and further, to punish Gabriel created and overwhelming conundrum. "You think about it. You can trust me."

Gabriel looked up at her and nodded. He looked as old and wise as a Zen Master, and it made Ali shudder to think of his stolen childhood.

She explained again how he was going to stay on the ranch with Joan and help her. Then she gave him a tight hug and a kiss on his cheek and got into Sarah's Toyota. She started the engine and eased forward, waving back to Gabriel and Joan, standing on the porch. At the gate she looked in the mirror to see the boy charging down the gravel drive toward her. She slammed on the brake and had him in her arms as the cloud of dust kicked up by the car backwashed over them.

"I love you. I'll be back," she said. Her voice was husky, and it wasn't because of the dust.

-⚙- ❈ -⚙-

DRIVING NORTH TOWARD ANGUSTIA, the tension of the past weeks returned to Ali, but with it came the relief that she had committed to taking care of Gabriel. She planned to adopt him or simply make him her own in some other way if his father or the law wouldn't cooperate. She could hear him call her "Mama-Ali," and felt her perspective shift in synch with this new commitment.

But commitment to Gabriel meant commitment to the hacienda. She had met with Enrique Cardenas, Gabriel's father, and straight out asked for the boy. She thought the father would want money, but in the end, he refused to give him up, though he was happy for Ali to pay the boy's way.

She watched the speedometer, careful not to give anyone a chance to pull her over.

Life for Gabriel would be better in Angustia where he knew people and was liked, Ali thought. Even if she could snatch him away to Mississippi, he'd look different and feel alien there. She had to make it safe for him to live at the hacienda.

She stopped only for gas and bathrooms and figured she'd make it into Angustia before dark on Wednesday.

The late afternoon sun's rays refracted sharply giving the northern New Mexico landscape its characteristic enchanted guise. The low hills in the distance turned mauve as the eastern sky went thalo blue. Fifteen miles from Angustia, she spotted the jet black Chevrolet Tahoe behind her.

She knew it was Ortega, and she sensed that he knew that she knew. His car pulled alongside her, edging her over to the shoulder. Braking hard, she tried to slip in behind him, but he was too quick. The Tahoe cut her off, forced her to the side of the road and to a stop. He parked tight in front at an angle, making escape impossible.

She checked the locks on the doors.

He took his time getting out of the heavy, dark vehicle and sauntering over to her window. He wore a suit, this time dark blue. His hands were empty.

It's still light. We're on a public road. He won't kill me.

But she thought how he might be able to get her into his car and take her somewhere else. He could do things that would make her tell him where Gabriel was. She was shaking when he leaned on the Toyota.

"It must be warm in there. Please come out. I only want to talk," he said. His accent sounded like Ricardo Montalban, Mr. Rourke from the *Fantasy Island* TV series.

"I won't tell you where he is. You can kill me, but I won't tell you," she shouted, fogging the window with her breath. She was barely in control.

"The boy is a minor issue. But I have an offer you might be interested in."

"Move your car," she shouted.

"Listen to me first, and I will," he said. "I promise." He took out a cigarette and ceremoniously lighted it.

Ali tried to control her breathing: four counts in, four out.

"I'll leave you and the boy alone if you help me," he said.

Ali knew she couldn't trust Ortega and that certainly his offer would be duplicitous. However, desperate for assurance that Gabriel wouldn't be harmed, she snapped the lock and slowly opened the door.

He backed off, giving her space.

"What?" she asked.

"I want the land the hotel is on. I am willing to pay you to persuade the others it would be best to find another place. In fact, I have a place in mind you can show them," he said.

"Why would I betray my friends for you?" she spat.

"You don't know how much I'm offering," he said, sailing the cigarette onto the pavement.

A truck blasted by, kicking up the smoking cigarette and sending a shower of sparks back to the blacktop.

Ali thought it might be worth playing along with him. When he mover closer to her, she didn't back off. The smell of his bold cologne mixed with the tobacco made her want to heave.

"How much?"

"A hundred thousand. You could take the boy back to the south. I can persuade his father to let him go. He'd be all yours." He smiled.

In spite of a thin trail of acne scars, Ali could see that Ortega had been handsome in his youth. He still looked good in spite of the hardness that suggested he enjoyed others' suffering. Up close she could see his long eyelashes, and she imagined that once long ago he had a mother who loved to admire them.

"I'd have to think about that," she said.

"Of course. Don't think too long. I have a good idea the boy is in Texas."

Ali felt sick. She knew Ortega was right. Gabriel would have to go to school—maybe Ortega had a picture of him. The thought of Ortega hurting Gabriel sent a bubble of anger through her. When it burst, she lunged, slapping Ortega's face and screaming curses at him.

In a move so fast and hard it knocked the breath out of her, Ortega slammed her against the car, jamming his knee between her legs and holding both of her wrists in one of his hands. She never saw him take out the knife, but she felt him deftly cut a thick lock of her hair. She couldn't breathe and screaming for help wouldn't do any good anyway.

"I'm quite serious, *Señora*. You think very carefully," he said in a hoarse whisper. "Don't underestimate me." Slowly, like a lover, he ran his thumb down the side of her face. Then he jerked up his knee, hitting her pubic bone hard. The lock of hair and the knife disappeared into his coat. He was driving away before she could control the pain between her legs and squeak, "Help."

As she fell back into the driver's seat she heard his overly articulated accent echo, *"I have a good idea the boy is in Texas."*

Ali seized the steering wheel to control her shaking. A car whooshed past. She wanted to race back to San Antonio, grab Gabriel and run. Slowly, her paralyzed brain relaxed. The more she thought of Pam, Sarah, and Kenny, the more the fear abated. She wasn't alone. She picked up the cell phone.

28

"**P**AM, KENNY, THE POWER'S back on," Sarah shouted. She started gathering dirty clothes and barely beat Pam to the washer. There had been no electricity, except from the generator, since the storm.

"It may not last. Tell Kenny the juice is on," Sarah said.

Pam looked smug. "God works in mysterious ways," she said, looking toward the chapel. "Let me know when the washer's free."

But the power stayed on and about two in the afternoon Sarah heard the tractor in front of the hacienda come to life. She walked out to the road to see a scruffy man with a bald head and red face drive the machine away. A county road maintenance truck crawled behind. Shortly after that a woman from Tyrone's office came by and removed the red tag from the front door.

"Guess you got it all fixed, huh?" the young woman said, looking around bug-eyed. She was plump and wore scuffed high heels.

Sarah wanted to quiz her about the suddenly unnecessary inspection, but she didn't want to trigger one. Nor did she want to be tricked by Tyrone. She smiled.

The young woman edged into the lobby, curiously tacking about the room like a sailboat with a drunken captain. "It's going to be nice when you get it all painted, huh?"

"We hope so." Sarah had just poured a glass of pineapple juice and wasn't sure if she should offer the visitor some. The woman seemed reluctant to leave. Sarah couldn't decide if she wanted a tip or a tour. She was examining the lobby counter that Kenny had refinished when Pam came in to measure again for the chapel tiles.

"Hi, I'm Maria Herrera," the woman said.

"She took off the red tag. I guess we can move back in," Sarah said.

"Really?" Pam asked, looking inquisitive, but doubtful.

Sarah answered Pam's look with a shrug.

When Pam opened the chapel door, Maria followed close on her heels and genuflected just inside.

"I heard it was beautiful," Maria said, studying each of the twelve high windows as though she were going to buy one. "Are you going to open up the hotel again?"

"No," Pam said firmly. "It's a private residence now."

Maria licked her bacon-colored lips. Sarah could see her working to form her words carefully.

"My sister, Guadalupe, we call her Lupe, is getting married. It's kind of short notice. Well, uh, I wondered if—well, it's a Catholic Church, isn't it?"

"Yes. Since 1850," Sarah said.

"1851," Pam corrected.

"Would you let us have the wedding here?" Maria said. Her gaze didn't meet Sarah's or Pam's.

Pam looked at Sarah. "Okay with me," Sarah said.

Sarah thought this was just the kind of thing Pam must have had in mind when she invited the people of Angustia to Mass.

"On one condition," Sarah said.

Maria looked at her, tense, ready for "no."

"You hire me to make the wedding banquet," Sarah said.

Maria's smiled and clasped her hands in front of her chest.

"Yes, yes. My mother can tell you what we'd like and my aunts will decorate the chapel, if you say okay."

"Okay. Okay." Sarah said. "How many do you think there'll be?"

"Not too many. Maybe only fifty. It needs to be soon. Can we have it a week from Sunday?"

Sarah guessed that Lupe was pregnant and needed a husband fast. Sarah remembered how in Jackson she had received an invitation to a friend's daughter's wedding at which the girl planned to wear a designer maternity bridal gown.

"Sunday?" Sarah repeated. Could she be ready in just ten days?

"That'd be June twentieth," Maria said.

While Sarah went into mental culinary overload, Pam took Maria over to the wall behind the altar.

"I'm making these hand-painted tiles for the chapel," Pam said.

Maria nodded and delivered another smile.

"For the lobby too, but the chapel is first," Pam continued.

"If you have some brothers or uncles I could hire for a few days, I could have it ready for Lupe's wedding."

Sarah watched Pam's arms fly about as she described her design to Maria—a mosaic of hand-painted tiles that would fill the chapel with the same dynamic earth and sky that stood outside. Pam still bitched about New Mexico and all their problems, but the tile project had given her a purpose. Sarah wondered what Pam would do when the chapel was finished. Maybe she'd tile the whole hacienda until it looked like the Alhambra.

"I can paint them pretty fast, but I need someone to help me make them, bisque them, fire them after I glaze them and stick them up on the wall."

Maria looked reverently around the curved walls. "I can just see it. Lupe's fiancé, Juan, will come and bring others. Juan will work all night if Lupe tells him to."

"She'll need wedding music," Sarah said. "Maybe her mother should visit the chapel tomorrow."

"Yes. And *mis tías,* too," Maria said.

Sarah imagined carloads of stout women with tawny skins and oil-black eyes mapping the wedding, strategizing each detail. She herself longed to dig out her chef's whites and start making a list.

"Tell them to come anytime between ten and four," Sarah said.

"Thank you, Mrs. Hunter." Maria Herrera headed for the door, the red tag in the side pocket of her large leather purse.

"Are you sure you don't have to inspect something? At least look at the roof?" Sarah asked.

"No, *Señora,*" Maria said. "If it is safe for God to live here, it is safe for his children."

After she left, Sarah's leg didn't hurt so much any more. It was clear to her and to Pam what had happened in the town as a result of dedicating the chapel. They couldn't wait to tell Ali how even Tyrone couldn't red tag a church.

"My first wedding was in a church," Sarah said.

"Mine, too," Pam said.

"Did you have any idea what you were doing?" Sarah asked.

"Not then. I was playing through a fantasy," Pam said. "It was all about the dress, and the parties, and feeling special. The honeymoon was a big comedown."

"I thought my first husband was rich," Sarah said. "I remember thinking, 'I'll never have to worry about anything.'" She laughed.

"He was rich, wasn't he?" Pam asked.

"Nobody's that rich," Sarah said. "Didn't matter. My second husband spent everything the first left me. When I married Steven, we had a small ceremony. I wanted it to be very serious, heartfelt," Sarah said, draining her glass of pineapple juice.

"And?" Pam said.

"I wanted it to be my last wedding," Sarah said. "We'd be soul mates, do everything together, know each other's thoughts. His money didn't matter."

"And?"

"Steven got drunk at the wedding and screwed an attractive bartender at the reception," Sarah said. "Nobody's perfect." She smiled. "But he's gone, we're here now and I hardly think about him."

"I didn't think you knew about Steven's—"

"Infidelities?"

"Yes."

"He ever hit on you?"

"Once. I didn't tell you because—" Pam stopped. "I declined the offer and I didn't think telling you would—"

"You thought it might hurt our friendship?" Sarah said.

"No. End it," Pam said.

"Steven was good to me. He paid for everything and mostly we had a good time," Sarah said. "I didn't want to work or to think too hard about much. I accepted his indiscretions as part of the bargain."

Pam started laughing.

"What?"

"Well you sure have changed. Didn't want to work?" Pam said.

"I didn't know what I was doing when I bought this place. I had no idea. I thought we'd paint a few walls, the local ladies would teach me to cook Mexican food, and you and Ali would protect me."

"I bet that's not true," Pam said. "I think you always wanted to work, to create. But when you were young it wasn't easy and then you got scared. Later you got complacent."

"I'm not complacent now," Sarah said. "Speaking of work, I think we're having a wedding here in ten days."

They walked inside the lobby and stood by the wide staircase.

"Shouldn't the bride come down the stairs?" Sarah said.

"Everybody could be in the lobby to watch her—"

"And she can walk through the crowd of her family and friends into the chapel," Sarah overlapped Pam. "They can follow her in—"

"No, they have to see her come down the aisle. She comes down, they go in, then she goes in. They're going to have to stand for the ceremony anyway—"

"Maybe some lawn chairs for the old ones," Sarah said.

"I am not putting plastic chairs in my chapel," Pam said

"Okay, but who's going to tell them to go in once Lupe's at the bottom of the stairs? They'll stand around like confused sheep," Sarah said.

At once they both said, "Ali."

"A theatre director is exactly what we need," Sarah said. "Brilliant move, Pam, getting everybody to come to a Mass."

"Thanks," Pam said. "You've done a few wonders around here yourself."

"Great partnership," Sarah said.

"I better get to work. Kenny's up to his eyeballs in mud.

"Ali should be back by now. Didn't she say she'd be back before dark?" Sarah asked.

They closed and locked the tall chapel doors and went outside. The first stars were appearing, but Ali wasn't. Kenny joined them. He was drinking a cold Corona.

"When this is done, I never want to see wet clay again," he said. Covered in dirt, he looked more like a hog than a ceramicist. "Y'all want a beer?"

"Sarah's worried about Ali," Pam said, taking a beer. "She's late."

"Try her cell phone," Kenny said. He gulped the cold beer.

"I think mine's in the car," Pam said.

"I'll get it," Kenny said, starting for Pam's Miata.

"Her number's programmed in."

Kenny hit Ali's cell number and waited for a response.

Sarah couldn't hear him, but he was talking to someone, probably Ali. He sat behind the wheel in Pam's car and closed the door. Still talking, he fished in his jeans pocket for a key and started the engine.

"Something's wrong," Sarah said. She felt an inexorable dread. Ali was hurt.

Kenny pointed at Pam and signaled her to come quick.

"She's had a little trouble," he said. "She's okay. I'm going to go get her. Maybe you two should stay here, together."

"Where is she?" Pam asked.

"Just outside of town. Got run off the road. She says she's not hurt. We'll be back in twenty minutes max," he said, rolling forward.

Sarah sat down hard in the green Wal-Mart chair in the front courtyard, scarcely able to feel. Pam drained the rest of her beer and started on Kenny's.

"Things get a little better and then they get much worse," Sarah said.

"Maybe she fell asleep. She said she was okay," Pam said, but she didn't sound like she believed it.

"Electricity comes on, red tag goes away," Sarah said. "Then—" She rubbed her knee and around the stump. It felt like sharp fingers were pulling at it. "Did you know that this wedding is my first professional job as a chef? My first job at all."

"No."

"Just once I wanted to come out of the kitchen into the dining room while they're feasting, like they do in Europe."

"To ask them if everything's all right?" Pam asked.

"Oh no. You know everything is all right. You don't send it out of the kitchen if it isn't right. You permit them to tell you what pleased them the most. You thank them and then go back to work. I think that's how it goes."

"What if someone doesn't like a sauce?" Pam asked. "It's made to perfection, but he just doesn't like it."

Sarah knew Pam was trying to distract her, maybe both of them, while they waited for Kenny and Ali. It was sort of working.

"He must be shown the error of his ways." Sarah could hear Madam LeMoyne saying as much.

"So no ketchup?"

"What's that? Ketchup."

"What if he insists it's bad?"

"You throw him out of your restaurant to the applause of the other patrons."

"We're still having the wedding," Pam said. "You're going to cook great Mexican food for Lupe Herrera, come out while they're feasting and take a bow. And you're going to get paid for it."

"Let's see how Ali is first," Sarah said. She felt a piercing guilt that she had somehow forced Ali to stay at the hacienda and in doing so, had endangered her. If Ali was hurt, it was at least half Sarah's fault.

"How much you going to charge?" Pam asked.

A car passed, but it wasn't Ali or Kenny.

"I hadn't thought. How much do you think?"

"Don't hotels get so much per person?"

"I suppose. What if they get drunk and won't go home?" Sarah said. "That happened at Mary Beth Conley's wedding in Natchez. God knows what could happen in the wilds of New Mexico."

"We have a lot of bedrooms," Pam said. "Most even have beds in them." The headlights of two cars split the night.

After an eternity, Ali and Kenny pulled into the parking area in front of the hacienda. It should have been a time for celebration—the hacienda was legal and open for occupation. Kenny helped Ali from the car. Sarah read in his expression that it wasn't good.

Ali didn't remark on the electric light that flooded the entrance and lobby. She looked shell-shocked. Sarah, wordlessly, embraced her. When she pulled back and looked at Ali, an audible sucking sound passed her lips. On the left side, right in front, a thick clump of Ali's hair was missing. The bald patch would be impossible to disguise.

Fighting tears, Ali said, "I'm so tired. I drove all day. I'm just going to go to bed." She scanned the lobby as if for the first time and looked very confused.

Sarah realized Ali didn't know if she had a bed or where it was. When she had left for Texas with Gabriel, the hotel had just been sacked by the DEA.

"We're back in the hotel, honey. Come on up. I'll draw you a bath. The hot spring water will make you feel better," Sarah said.

Late, after Ali was asleep, Kenny told them what Ali had told him. Ortega.

"Why did he butcher her hair like that?" Pam asked. She paced, too upset to sit.

"Like the Indians use to do? A modified scalping?" Sarah asked.

"More like rape," Kenny said. "He invaded her person, marked her or took a piece of her," Kenny said.

"Men do things like that out here?" Pam asked.

"I wouldn't say it's particular to New Mexico, but obviously some men do things like that," Kenny said.

"Ali has such beautiful hair," Sarah said. She watched a roach crawl through the front door and then turn around and leave. Even insects know trouble.

"What did Ortega say to Ali?" Sarah asked. She was afraid to know because she feared it meant the end, the final straw that would drive them from the hacienda.

"Something about getting her to convince you to move," Kenny said. "She said the kid's okay. Go to bed, Sarah. It's late."

Though it felt good to be indoors and in her bed, Sarah couldn't sleep. Bernie stayed close beside her when she checked on Ali several times during the night. There was nothing to be done. When Sarah finally dozed off, she dreamed she was a contestant on a TV game show. She was wearing her chef's toque. A man who looked like Jami Ortega in sunglasses was the other contestant. The grand prize was an all expense paid vacation to Yellowstone National Park. She didn't know any of the answers and time was running out.

29

ALI WOKE LATE, FEELING she had slept the sleep of the dead.

Sarah had insisted that Ali soak in a hot, hot tub. Sarah said a ritual bath in natural hot springs water would cleanse Ortega's violation. Ali winced at the thought of him running his thumb down her face, almost over her lips, looking at her with lust-laced hatred. Her revulsion shot to anger when she thought of him finding Gabriel. Ortega's hands on her were disgusting, but on Gabriel's skinny little shoulders they would be a profane violation so horrible, she would die to prevent it. Her anger loosened the concrete in her head.

In the mirror she saw the result of Ortega's butchery. Leaning close, she traced her fingers over the silver dollar-sized bald patch. Her scalp looked like a stubbled moonscape.

This man knew how to terrorize. How many other women had he intimidated and abused? Had any of them seen their own shamed reflections gazing back in a mirror, wondering how they would hide his mark?

Combating him would be tricky. Ortega shape-shifted, always surprising his victims. Reasonable, even polite one minute, the next he was slicing off trophies and circling for a kill. She ran her fingers up the back of her neck and through her long, thick hair and thought about scarves, turbans, and wigs.

Since childhood, Ali had known that a principal asset to her beauty was her thick, dark hair. Everyone admired it. Sisters wanted to comb it, mothers to pet it, and lovers to bury their faces in it. She had cut it only to trim the ends.

She knew traditional Navajos only cut their hair when a close relative died. Their long, dark hair was shorn as a sign of respect. But hadn't she died in a way? Couldn't she honor the old Ali even as the new one emerged?

The kitchen scissors felt heavy in her hand. Holding out a section, she whacked the blades together. Slowly, the basin filled with the dark tresses. She hardly looked in the mirror as she cut, but when she did her eyes were dry, her mouth determined. As the hair fell on the white porcelain, she tried to imagine that with each clump, she released her pain and fear of Ortega.

"Hello," she said, tracing her hairline on the mirror with her finger. Released from its length, the short hair curled and had the look of a haircut administered by a child. It was a startling contrast from before, but it looked sort of interesting.

She heard women's voices downstairs and wondered how it had happened that they were back living in the hotel. The women were laughing now, Sarah and some others. While scooping the hair into a plastic bag, one heavy lock fell to the floor. For a moment she thought of saving it, but then stuffed it into the sack. She didn't want to get sentimental. She couldn't afford it. She tossed the bag into the trash and got dressed.

Lupe and most of her female relatives were in the chapel when Ali came downstairs. She recognized *Señora* Cantu and Carlotta in the throng. There were also mothers of her dancers.

Standing in the chapel's doorway, Ali watched the women dart about like excited bats. Their hierarchy was evident, as they discussed decorations for Lupe's wedding. Doña Martina, the oldest aunt was top bat, Lupe's mother second and on down to Lupe, whose opinion counted very little.

"My son's band will play for the reception," one aunt said. "Lupe, what is Joaquin's band's name?"

They spoke mostly in English for Sarah's benefit. Ali let the music of their heavy accents wash over her without resistance. The words strained through Spanish, in which i's became e's and e's became a's, composed a comfortable symphony.

"*Lobos Amargos*," Lupe said. Bitter wolves.

"What about for the ceremony?" Sarah asked. "I can play a CD."

Ali smiled wondering which piece from Sarah's limited CD collection she would choose: *South Pacific,* B. B. King, or , maybe, *You've Got the Magic Touch?*

"I'll sing. I know how it should be," Ali said.

Startled by the new voice, they turned to Ali in the huge arched doorway. Gasps escaped.

"I've sung at lots of weddings." Ali strode into the chapel and inspected the new tiles Pam had put up the day before.

Owl-eyed, the women stared at her cropped head.

"*Ella canta muy bien.* A beautiful voice," *Señora* Cantu said, breaking the silence.

"*En Español?*" Lupe's oldest aunt asked.

"*Si, si, claro que si,*" Cantu said. "She sings in Spanish." The focus shifted from Ali's hair back to the wedding. After arguing about appropriate music, they agreed Ali would sing before the ceremony.

One of the women pushed forward to Ali and asked, "Are you going to teach the children to do the native dances?"

Ali wanted to say that she had never stopped teaching, they had stopped coming, permitting their children to come. But then she remembered Ortega's cruel power and knew how he must have frightened them. But why weren't they scared of him now?

"You'll come and bring the children twice a week?" Ali asked.

A few heads nodded.

Obviously, some were nervous about irritating Ortega.

"I won't teach unless you're all in," Ali said. "You tell the others and let me know."

Anxious glances flitted, followed by shrugs. *Doña* Martina pushed forward.

"*Señora*, the little ones have been practicing."

Ali questioned if she should encourage them or the dancing. It could be dangerous for some of them who might be vulnerable to Ortega. He could get them fired or worse, much worse. And she had Gabriel to worry about. But Gabriel had been the one who started it all. Commitment to him meant commitment to their home, to Angustia, and even to these women.

"We could perform at Indian Market, the Albuquerque Cultural Center, maybe even on TV," Ali said. "But I need your word you won't back out."

Maybe they sensed a double meaning in Ali's words. The chapel became very quiet.

"If we work together, stay together, we'll be strong," Ali whispered. The reverberation of her voice in the chapel took on an ethereal quality.

"Like a union," Doña Martina said, lapsing into an explanation in Spanish of how her brother in California got better wages because of his union.

The others were more interested to know if Ali was serious about the children dancing on television. What channel? Could they all go?

Ali left them to plan Lupe's wedding. In the kitchen she phoned Gabriel in Texas. He told her about the new kittens, how Joan had let him name one Ali-cat and he told her how he missed her. She could hardly speak when Joan took the phone. Joan said she hadn't noticed anything suspicious, and Gabriel seemed happy. Because of him, Cheerio and Eisenhower had been adopted.

Kenny came in the kitchen.

"Want to talk to your sister?" Ali asked him.

"No. I'll call her tomorrow," he said.

After she hung up, he told Ali he liked her hair short.

"It's my prisoner of war summer cut," Ali said. She sliced an apple in two with Sarah's French knife. "Thanks for coming for me last night."

"I'm sure you'd do it for me," he said. "You seen any WD-40 in here?

"Matter of fact, I would do it for you," Ali said. She looked directly at Kenny, letting her gaze convey her change of heart.

"You two sure don't have much confidence in Pam's ability to choose friends, do you?"

"None. She's infamous. You may mark a new beginning," Ali said. She washed her breakfast dish.

"You might want to think twice about using a cell phone to call the boy. It's pretty easy to eavesdrop on them."

"What?" Ali's resolve to not be beaten, to be strong, wavered with Kenny's warning. She braced herself as though a tornado were going to smash the kitchen window.

"Last night you told me Ortega was looking for Gabriel, maybe in Texas," he said. "You wouldn't want to help him."

"You're right. I didn't think. I told Gabriel I'd call him every day. What am I going to do?"

Kenny didn't answer. The alternatives were obvious and all were inconvenient.

"I don't think you should drive down there again either. Fly out of Albuquerque," he said.

"I'll kill him if he touches Gabriel," she said.

"I know. But having Ortega dead and Gabriel missing won't make you feel much better."

"Kenny? Where the hell are you?" Pam called from outside.

"The old ball and chain." Kenny smiled. Better get back to work." As he opened the side door, Pam came in.

"Shit," she said, looking at Ali. "I mean, hell Ali are you okay?" Pam ran to her friend and wrapped her arms around her. Tears ran down Pam's cheeks, but not Ali's.

"I'm fine," Ali said. "I'm starting dance class tomorrow. Knowing how you love little children, you might want to go shopping tomorrow morning."

Pam pulled away from Ali and looked at her hard.

"Something's different."

"Like it?" Ali asked, sticking to the hairdo instead of what was inside her head.

"You know, with a little evening up and some mousse, it could be really cute."

"Some spikes on top?"

"I mean it," Pam said. "It's a pixie look. They're back in. Somewhere. Let me shape it up. Why didn't you call me? Let's go to your room."

"How long is this beauty makeover going to take?" Kenny asked.

"About as long as it takes you to load the kiln," Pam said, catching Ali's hand and pulling her out of the kitchen.

"W-D 40's under the sink," Ali called.

Following Pam up the stairs, Ali thought that whatever Pam did to her would make little difference. The makeover of Ali Calderon was already complete.

-⚓- ❈ -⚓-

AT DANCE CLASS THE next morning, Ali was thrilled that all the children showed up, plus a few new ones. The mothers who didn't work came to watch and to pick up the fabric they would turn into dresses and shirts. Pam had sketched pictures of what the costumes should look like. Trying on the donated shoes ate up the first twenty minutes.

"Let's see if you remember any of what I taught you," Ali said. She smartly clapped twice.

Sarah turned on the CD player and the music filled the courtyard. The children were in place before the end of the eight bar intro. Doña Martina had been correct; they had practiced. They danced *El Tapatio* perfectly. The new children had learned the dance from the others. Ali had vowed that Ortega wouldn't make her cry, but she had no defenses against the children. She had to sit down to regain control.

Gabriel's absence was responsible for part of her emotion. He had been the one who first wanted to dance. He was the most skilled performer, but more, he had a natural dramatic flair and a captivating stage presence. She ached, missing him, longing to see his gamine face framed by the straight black hair and the way his nimble feet danced as though he would fly.

Ali had been sure that if the group jelled, she could get it a few gigs, but now she remembered she had promised them performances at the huge August Indian Market in Santa Fe and maybe television. Except for Judy Grace, she didn't know anybody in Santa Fe. Television, however, was another matter.

If they're good, I can get them on TV. It'd be a day Angustia would never forget.

She didn't add that it'd be a day for which the families would be indebted to her and to the hacienda. She didn't say it, but she thought it and drew strength from it. She needed every friend she could get.

The class went over an hour with Ali drilling them on difficult steps that would be used in new dances. No more baby steps.

"Toe, heel, turn, one, and two. Pick up you feet, don't look at them." She could see some of the mothers dancing the steps with their feet as they sat in the shade.

When the children and mothers had gone, Ali wanted to call Gabriel. The pay phone at Jesús' gas station hadn't worked in years and neither *Señora* Cantu nor Carlotta had phones at all. They were the only ones Ali trusted.

"Come with me to the inconvenience store," she said to Pam after *comida*. It was inconvenient because it was fourteen miles away and was always just out of what you needed. "It's Friday. It'll be crowded. Probably we won't be kidnapped."

"Do I need to bring my shotgun?" Pam asked. She and Kenny had bought a gun in Santa Fe when they went in search of stained glass.

"Can you use it?" Ali asked.

"That's the beauty of a shotgun—low training threshold."

From the store's pay phone, Ali called Gabriel and explained three times why it wasn't safe for her to call him every day. She told Joan what Kenny had said about intercepting cell phone calls.

"Make him understand. He'll think I'm abandoning him," Ali said to Joan. "There's a wedding at the hacienda this Sunday, but Monday or Tuesday, I'm flying down there. Can you pick me up at the airport?"

On the ride back to the hacienda, Pam clutched the shotgun. Ali was pretty sure the white pickup following them belonged to Ortega's boys.

⁜

ALI TAUGHT DANCE CLASSES the next Tuesday and Friday. Two of the mothers asked if the children could perform Sunday at Lupe's wedding. They'd all be coming.

"What will the girls wear?" Ali asked.

"The girls' dresses will be ready Sunday if you say they can dance," the mother said. "Maybe a few safety pins, but nobody will know."

My God, the hacienda is becoming the social center of Angustia. Ali smiled. If she ignored the looming threat of Ortega, and that Gabriel was in hiding, not to mention the daunting expense and work of restoring the hacienda, things were looking up.

"And the boys? What will they wear?" Ali asked.

⁜

SATURDAY, THE DAY BEFORE Lupe's wedding, Wanda Begay and Alex Tso visited the hacienda. Wanda had been promising to research the Hacienda Angustia since Pam had met her in Santa Fe. Alex wasn't sure he wanted to see Lorena McCragg again, but Wanda dragged him along.

Pam introduced Sarah and Ali to them.

"Y'all have to excuse me. I have a wedding to prepare for," Sarah said, heading for the kitchen.

Pam told Alex about Lorena breaking the mirror and terrifying the Mexican women. "I saw her once. I feel her presence all the time," Pam said. "Sarah doesn't believe me."

Wanda pawed through her canvas bag decorated with Indian Yeibichi figures.

"There used to be a chapel in the old hotel," Wanda said. She pulled a mess of papers from her bag, searching for one particular photocopy.

"There still is. We restored it. Come see," Pam said.

She flung open the twelve foot high arched doors, flooding the chapel with golden light. The nearly complete mosaic of land and sky glittered.

Inside the chapel, Wanda Begay backed around the curved wall, patting the tiles, stroking the altar and making little sucking noises. "Beautiful, beautiful," she repeated. She complimented the stained glass windows, but reserved her highest praise for Pam's adobes which Wanda recognized were made in the old Spanish way.

Pam told her how she had learned to make adobes from Manny's crew of illegals.

The trio moved to the shade of the *ramada* on the north patio. Sarah had set out a pitcher of iced sweet tea, glasses, and almond cookies.

"I haven't gotten around to doing serious research on this place, but I remembered a story and checked it out," Wanda said.

"I know the story," Alex said. "I'm gonna go look around. That okay?" He took a handful of cookies.

When he was gone, Wanda pulled up her chair. "Lorena McCragg was murdered, and I think I know why," Wanda said. "At the museum I'm in charge of an ongoing oral history project. We interview the old ones before it's too late. I talked to Theresa Montoya who is so old she doesn't know how old she is. She told me a story her mother told her about the white witch that lived here."

"A witch and a ghost?" Ali asked.

"They're the same. Witch in their culture is a little different than in Euro-American cultures. It's a bad translation anyway."

"How did she die?" Pam asked.

"She was strangled. Theresa said one story is that she was murdered because she kept company with an Indian man, probably Apache. He wasn't full-blooded, but back then half-breeds were considered the same or worse than Indians."

Ali thought of Emmett Till, the fourteen year-old black boy who had whistled at a Mississippi white woman. He had been found dead in a muddy river, his face mangled. The south and the west weren't so different after all.

Ali's hand nervously fluttered to her short hair, the site of Ortega's attack. But realizing what she was doing—connecting with her fears—she forced her hand down and her shoulders back.

"And the other story?" Ali asked.

"A treaty gave the Indians water rights. Of course the whites cheated them. The water must have come through some of the hacienda property. A creek maybe. Back then the hacienda covered hundreds of acres. Theresa says the whites were diverting it, stealing it, and Lorena found out," Wanda said.

"And she was going to tell?" Ali asked.

"Theresa says so."

"And they killed her before she had the chance?" Pam said.

"Who could she have told?" Ali asked. "I can't imagine the local law boys weren't in on the deal to steal the water."

"It gets better," Wanda said. "A Federal Marshall from Fort Sumner was due to visit the day before Lorena was murdered. That's in the newspaper. He did visit, but of course her faked suicide hadn't been discovered yet. I think she planned to tell him."

"What about the Indian?" Pam asked.

"Theresa didn't know anything else. She thinks he had worked for Lorena's husband. Maybe it wasn't a love affair. Maybe Lorena McCragg just wanted to help the Indians. There were no casinos back then."

Ali thought about the huge Choctaw gambling casino in Philadelphia, Mississippi. The Silver Star Resort was as luxurious as Las Vegas' best. What irony that Federal laws that herded Indians on to reservations, now made it possible for Indians to open casinos and recoup some of their losses at the expense of the whites.

"Oh, Pam, before I forget," Wanda said, "The clerk at the court house said to tell you the records room is open again. I didn't know it had closed."

Pam smiled and nodded. "So you think water was the real motive?" she asked.

"If she was fooling around with an Indian, the necessity of getting rid of her over the water would become a pleasure," Wanda said. She pulled a cigarette out of her bag and lighted it.

"But there's no creek now," Pam said. "We only have a small spring."

"Water moves, creeks dry up," Wanda said. "And it was a long time ago."

"But Theresa Montoya knows about the ghost?" Ali asked, returning Wanda to the ghost story.

"She does," Wanda said. "But she doesn't think Lorena McCragg's very interesting compared to some others she knows about."

Wanda just started another ghost story when Alex Tso returned. He looked pale and his shoes were wet.

"Oh my God, Alex. You saw her," Wanda said.

"On the back steps." He leaned on the ramada's support post.

"What happened?" Ali asked. She wanted to run to the stairs to see if Lorena was still there.

"What'd you do?" Wanda asked. She stubbed out her half-smoked cigarette.

"It was so weird. I told her I was sorry I hadn't come by sooner. Then I thought maybe ghosts don't have time like we do. Maybe it wasn't so long in her world. I know this sounds crazy—"

"What?" the three said in unison.

Like a practiced story teller, Alex took his time.

"She had on a high-necked white blouse with a cameo at her throat. She just stood for a minute, looking at me, looking through me. There were two of those old galvanized buckets on the landing." He paused. "I didn't see her move, but she made one turn over and then the other. Water came down the steps like waterfall. I swear. Look at my shoes. You can go see it."

"Did she speak?" Ali asked.

"No. She looked real intense. Not sad like before.

"And she just disappeared?" Wanda said.

"After she kicked the buckets down the steps, she faded. Wanda, if you tell anybody at the university I saw a ghost, I'm going to tell some things on you."

"Alex, everybody who matters knows you saw a ghost—"

"When I was a kid. That's different."

"Okay. You didn't see a ghost," Wanda said. "Want a towel to dry the water the non-ghost dumped on your shoes?"

Ali and Pam took off to see the site of the apparition.

The steps, as reported, were drenched and two buckets lay on the bottom step. The ghost, if she were still around, was invisible.

"It's possible he set this up." Ali felt unnerved by the ghost's appearance, but at the same time she thought it might be a positive sign. If the story about Lorena McCragg were true, she wasn't going to be on Ortega's side.

"Maybe he did," Pam said. "But I don't think the Mexican women were making anything up."

"You think we should invite her to the wedding?" Ali said.

30

SARAH FINGERED THE LIST of Mexican dishes Lupe's mother and aunts had recommended. *Chilies en nogada* headed a catalog of traditional fare: *empanadas, enchiladas, flautas, guacamole, rellenos,* and *tamales.* Even as she put on her white apron, Sarah could hear her former teacher, Madame LeMoyne, *"Any fool can make that stuff. Do something creative. They eat that cheese shit all the time. Show them what I taught you."*

"No, it's Lupe and Juan's wedding. It's their day, not mine," Sarah said aloud as though the ruthless chef were present. Sarah could imagine LeMoyne's reply.

"*Merde!* Don't be an imbecile. I remind you that you don't have the opportunity to prepare a feast like this every day."

Sarah weakened, thinking of her *Pissaladière Niçoise,* an onion tart with anchovies and black olives, and her *Terrine de Porc, Veau et Jambon,* a pork and veal pate with strips of veal and ham buried in its slices. A *gordita* couldn't compare.

"I can't disregard their suggestions. I need to win these people, not alienate them," Sarah said to herself.

"Idiot!" The French accent of LeMoyne tore through her head. "Nothing will seduce them like *Timbale D'Epinardes, Fonds d'Artichauts a la Crème* or *Bavarios au Chocolat.*"

"But it's wrong to force them into something they're not comfortable with," Sarah reasoned. She could hear the whiney tone in her voice.

"A fine line exists between forcing and nurturing them past the curve of anxiety to a new and wonderful experience," Sarah suspected LeMoyne would have replied.

Sarah opened a bottle of Bordeaux-Médoc and swirled it, checking its legs.

"But they gave me a menu," Sarah said. She looked on the counter for the list; it had disappeared.

Sarah could almost hear the disgusted noise, somewhere between a glottal stop and a nasal snort, which the arrogant chef would have made. "All right. Go buy twenty cans of refried beans. While you're at it get some Velveeta and Gallo."

"Maybe some Mexican hors d'oeuvres? *Bocadillos,*" Sarah said, her voice now practically a whimper.

"*Sacre bleu!* I blow smoke in the face of your *bocadillos,*" the chef said. "Next you'll want to make catfish burritos."

Sarah knew she had to choose between the unparalleled quality that she could deliver if she followed what her teacher would have recommended or the merely competent fare she'd achieve by following Lupe's wishes.

"Enchiladas Cordon Bleu?" Sarah offered and wished she had kept her mouth shut. "How would I do it?" Sarah wondered.

"*Alors. Très simple.* Cook what you want, but tell them it's what they want." Sarah had a distinct image of the tall, thin LeMoyne with her red lipsticked mouth and impossibly pristine chef's whites.

"They'll notice. *Piece de Boeuf a la Cuillère* doesn't look like *Carne Adovada*."

"Don't be so stupid. A *flauta* is a crepe; avocado soufflé is the rich cousin of guacamole."

"But—" Sarah said. Sarah knew what LeMoyne's second point would have been.

"Next, understand that what you make will be so delicious that after one bite, they won't care," LeMoyne said.

"What if they don't take the first bite?" Sarah asked.

"You'll think of something. You Americans are so clever. Now, I think you should begin with a mousse."

"A mousse?"

"A soufflé is out of the question for so many, *n'est pa? Mousseline de Volaille, oui?*"

Sarah smiled. The molded puree of poultry, chicken liver, stock, vermouth, and crème packed into a decorative bowl had wowed royalty. It might work at the Herrera-Carrasco wedding.

Sarah slipped in a Tony Bennet CD and sorted, sliced and sautéed the chicken livers with shallots. She poured herself another glass of the Bordeaux. The smell of shallots in the hot butter rose and met the vermouth somewhere behind her eyes, reminding her of a bistro in New York where she had let an older man seduce her. She watched the shallots soften and then capitulate to the juices, gelatin, and wine. Before adding the cooked turkey and chicken, she tasted. Strong and authoritative, it needed the tempering of the crème. Sarah wiped her brow and slid everything into the blender. The sound of top speed cut through the kitchen's heat. She tasted again and thought of the man her mother had hired to teach her to ballroom dance. He had never even kissed her, but her underpants were wet after every foxtrot lesson.

Nestling the bowl in a larger one of ice, she whipped the chilled heavy cream until it doubled in volume and possessed an unbelievably tender texture, *moelleux*, the French called it. Slowly she folded the velvet cream into the cold puree, teasing them to embrace one another. Then with her hands she pressed it into the large porcelain bowls with the filigree edges. She licked the mousse from between her fingers and gently sucked her index finger. She wished she smoked.

⚜ ❄ ⚜

Lupe Herrera's wedding date was June 20; the time of day was less specific. Lupe had said about five, but Doña Martina only agreed to late afternoon.

Guests and family began arriving about five. The women were dressed in brightly colored, fancy dresses. Necklines were low and heels were high. It didn't look like a First Baptist wedding on State Street in downtown Jackson, Mississippi. Sarah thought they looked like exquisite, tropical butterflies.

The men, few of whom had attended the Mass in the chapel, looked uncomfortable, but Sarah couldn't tell if it was fear of being caught by Ortega on forbidden territory or merely their tight neckties.

When Doña Martina decided sufficient levels of gaiety and anticipation had been achieved, the wedding began. The costumed dancers, directed by Ali, led guests from prenuptial celebrating in the courtyard into the hotel lobby. Stuffed with flowers from every Angustia garden including the hacienda's, the perfume was more overpowering than the cosmetics department at Macy's. Sarah and Pam stood together by the door at the back of the chapel.

Lupe descended the grand staircase, her satin train rippling down the steps in time with Ali's guitar's music. The children first ushered the bride through the throng toward the waiting groom in the chapel and then herded the guests in. The assembly of nearly a hundred stood packed like asparagus. Ali sang in Spanish, *"Te amo mi corazón, mi vida"* as though her heart would break, her clear voice gliding up and up toward the colored glass windows above. Before Father Gallegos began, most people were dabbing at tears.

The last notes of Ali's guitar faded and Guadalupe Remedio Herrera and Juan Toledo Carrasco promised to love and comfort one another for as long as they should live. They looked deliriously happy. Sarah couldn't understand much of the Spanish, but she knew the language of love.

As the chapel emptied, Sarah started to panic.

Why didn't I just make Mexican food? They'll hate this and I'll never get another job cooking. Sarah headed outside to check the buffet. She asked Pam to check on the ice.

The opulent buffet waited under the ramada. Punch and other drinks weighted down a table beside the fountain; the wedding cake towered on its own ivory skirted table nearby. The guests chatted and milled, but no one except Bernie approached the buffet.

"The vegetables will get soggy. The mousse will turn to cement," Sarah whispered to Pam.

"What the hell are they going to do, order out pizza?" Pam said.

Then Sarah noticed Lupe's aunt, *Doña* Martina, pushing her broad hips through the crowd. If *Doña* Martina's girth meant anything, it meant that she liked to eat.

"*Señora?*" Sarah called, lifting a *Petit Chausson au Roquefort*. "Would you please try this for me? Maybe it's a little dry." Sarah knew that refusing her request would be exceedingly rude. Cultural etiquette required *Doña* Martina to taste and to compliment. Of course it was manipulative. Sarah didn't care. The turnovers were wonderful.

Doña Martina, bracing like an alarmed turkey, realized she was cornered. Reluctantly she plucked a tiny cheese pastry from the tray that Sarah offered.

Sarah watched *Doña* Martina's blocky incisors split the flaky pastry. Then she saw the flicker of smile replaced by a pucker as the Doña rolled the Roquefort filling on her tongue, savoring the blend of cheese, butter, egg, kirsch, onion and cream. She swallowed and reached for a plate.

All at once, like a slow-moving herd, the party moved toward the buffet. They ate like grasshoppers. Some covert, nonverbal code had communicated that the food was acceptable even if it wasn't recognizable. No one so much as asked for a tortilla.

"My grandmother from Oaxaca used to make something like this," Doña Martina said. She served herself a second portion of cold beef and potato salad. "Will you give me the recipe?" she asked Sarah.

Did any higher compliment exist for a cook? Sarah hoped she could remember what Chef LeMoyne had done to the *Salade de boeuf a la Parisienne.*

After the dinner and before the wedding cake, the children danced three dances and received a standing ovation and hundreds of kisses from proud mamas, papas, *tías* and *tíos.* The parents also hugged Ali.

Sarah heard them compliment Ali in Spanish and her reply in kind. She also heard a rumor slip through the crowd that said the children were going to perform on TV.

The wedding cake with white fondant icing brought more applause and the first volley of fireworks. *Lobos Amargos* cranked up about nine and drowned out the coyotes clear over to El Rito. Everyone danced. In Mississippi, the older people fled from popular electronic music, but here they sang along, applauded and participated with every fiber. A huge man, well over six feet tall, asked Sarah to dance. He didn't speak much English, but she knew that's what he wanted.

"I'm sorry. I can't dance," she said, pulling her skirt to show her plastic calf and ankle. "I'm sorry." She rapped on the leg.

In one graceful move, he swept her up and into his arms. Her feet hardly touched the ground as they joined the swirl of couples; he danced for both of them. He smelled like whiskey, wore an impressive moustache and had the light of the devil in his eyes.

The Bitter Wolves Band looked more like sweet puppies, and as the hours passed, their music shifted into *corridos* and Mexican ballads. Sarah heard something about the moon saying one thing, the stars saying another. Looking up at the New Mexico sky, she wondered who to believe.

"We got company," Kenny said when her dance partner finally sat her down. Kenny cocked his head toward the center of the courtyard.

Conversations were dying all around like Texans at the Alamo. The band felt the hush, and one instrument at a time dropped out. Jami Ortega and five men were standing by the fountain. They looked cool and threatening.

"Ali's in the kitchen. Keep her inside," Sarah told Kenny. "She'll come out here with a gun and somebody will get killed."

Kenny slipped away.

Ortega's eyes located Sarah. He walked toward her slowly, his thugs trailing.

Buenas noches, *Señora* Hunter," Ortega said. "I see the whole town is here." His chilly gaze swept the crowd. "My invitation must have been lost in the mail."

It was dead quiet.

Damage control. What can I do? It's not my party. If I say it's Lupe's wedding, that makes it her family's fault. But after what he did to Gabriel and Ali, I can't offer him a drink. Shit. Think. Think.

Sarah saw Lupe and Juan standing by the hotel door. Lupe now looked like the bride of Dracula, pasty white with fear. Juan didn't look much better. Then she noticed a line of men, all the uncles and sons, slowly gathering back by the courtyard wall. They looked scared.

Ortega sauntered to the bride. "*Señora* Carrasco, may I have the pleasure of a dance?"

Lupe looked like she just barely survived a freeway pileup. Ortega took her hand and pulled her to the center of the courtyard. "A waltz," he said to the band as he wrapped his arms tightly around Lupe, who shivered visibly. He lifted her chin with his finger and spoke softly into her face. He looked like he might kiss her. Lupe's expression froze into a grimace. The music started, and Ortega stepped gracefully into the one, two, three rhythm, whirling the robotic Lupe along.

Sarah felt stunned. Ortega had proved he was top ape. If he demanded the right of kings to bed just-married virgins, Sarah thought he wouldn't have been disappointed.

A shotgun blast shattered the night. On its heels came a deafening explosion. The cache of fireworks detonated all at once sending a riot of bangs and sparks into the yard.

Sarah looked around wildly in time to see the puff of gun smoke dissipate beside the upstairs window. Ali stood framed by the red drapes.

Ortega's bridal dance gave way to putting out a small fire, and Sarah knew she'd have one chance before Ortega struck again.

As calm returned, Sarah pushed herself to the edge of her chair and willed herself to stand upright without stumbling. She walked straight to the bandstand. Stepping up, she grabbed the microphone from the band's bewildered singer.

I can't protect all of these people. They have to stand or to run, and they have to choose now.

All she could do was give them an example.

"I want to thank you all for coming to the Hacienda Angustia. For many of you, the hacienda is part of your past. *Abuela* Carmen Ramon told me she used to come to church here as a little girl. Some of your grandfathers worked this ranch. It's my home now, but I welcome you. *Mi casa es su casa.* Father Gallegos offered to bless the hacienda and because you are all here, I think this would be the perfect time."

Nervous applause sputtered.

The priest, who couldn't have missed that something was wrong, put his glass of whiskey on the table, came forward and called on the Heavenly Father. Sarah hoped He was listening.

When the blessing finished, Sarah said, "I'm making cherries jubilee, I mean, *crepas con cerises del fuego,* in the kitchen. Come by and have some." Then she poked the lead singer and hissed, "Play something lively, now."

The band blasted. Sarah grabbed Lupe's hand and escorted her to the kitchen. The throng of men by the wall had grown and its power lay in its size. Unless Ortega was up for machine gunning everybody, there wasn't much he could do. Nobody was leaving. Nobody except Ortega and his five *guarda espaldas.*

In one glance Ortega sized up the situation. The fear he had generated with his arrival had dissipated. His moment had passed. He strode toward the gate, pausing only to knock a cup of punch out of the hand of one of his men.

THE BAND QUIT AT midnight because the boys had to go to school the next day, but no one was in a hurry for the celebration to end. Whatever fears Ortega had stimulated, they were waiting until *mañana* to respond.

Ali rubbed her feet, Pam ate another piece of wedding cake and Sarah drank a brandy someone had put in her hand. Punchy and nearly drunk, they had collapsed on the old mission leather settee.

"Things could be worse," Sarah said, putting her feet up on the leather topped coffee table.

Pam licked the icing off her fingers. "Piece of cake."

"I knew it'd be okay," Sarah said.

"You liar," Ali said. "You looked as terrified as a carjacking victim."

"Hell and damnation, what if you had missed the fireworks and killed somebody?" Sarah asked.

"A chance I had to take. No point worrying about it now," Ali said. "I'll kill that motherfucker if I can."

Sarah was glad when Kenny slid in beside Pam on the bench and changed the subject.

"Did anybody invite the ghost to the wedding?" Kenny asked. The last time Sarah had seen Kenny, he had been sitting on the tailgate of a pickup talking to a bunch of Lupe's relatives, passing a bottle of tequila.

"I'm afraid I don't know ghost etiquette," Sarah said. "I assume they attend whatever they want."

"You didn't see Lorena McCragg, did you?" Pam asked Kenny.

"No. I just think Alex's story is—wasn't his name Alex?"

"Alex Tso," Pam said. "T S O; the T is silent."

"Assuming he really saw the ghost, look what he said."

"She turned over two buckets?" Pam said.

"No, no. He said she kicked the buckets of water," Kenny said. "If you were a ghost and wanted to communicate something about your predicament, but you couldn't talk, what would you do?"

"Write a note," Ali said. "On the wall, like in the Bible."

"In the movie Matilda, she wrote a warning on the blackboard," Pam said.

"Charades," Sarah said.

"Email," Ali said.

" 'Kicked the bucket' isn't a phrase that means anything to you?" Kenny asked.

"Oh my God," Pam said. "You die when you kick the bucket. Her death is something about water. This corroborates what Wanda said the old Indian woman said—that Lorena McCragg was going to tell the sheriff about the whites stealing the Indians' water."

"What I want to know," Sarah said, "is why all of you believe in ghosts."

"What I want to know is, where's the Indians' water now?" Pam said.

※ ❈ ※

A FEW GUESTS STILL lingered in the courtyard when Sarah went to bed. She liked hearing voices in the hotel. It was alive. A vitality flowed in its veins. The trees seemed to stretch, shaking off a spell-induced sleep. The embers in the courtyard beehive fireplace pulsed like a fiery heart. Sarah perceived a new energy running through the walls, floors, ceilings. And she felt it hum inside herself.

She silently ran through her spiel to Pam on why having a little bed and breakfast would be good for them. Pam's studio would be off-limits to guests. Sarah wouldn't let it grow into a monster. She fell asleep exhausted, but gratified in spite of the terror Ortega had stirred. In her dream that night she had to spin a gigantic *Wheel of Fortune* game show wheel. The wheel, however, was frozen with rust.

At seven the next morning, Sarah ambled into the kitchen to face the mounds of garbage, sticky dishes and empty bottles. Ali, Pam and Kenny were arguing.

Pam and Kenny thought it was important to look at the records in Santa Fe, the ones Pam had been prevented from examining by the surprise visitor and blackout. Wanda had told Pam the records room had reopened. They wanted to leave as soon as the wedding mess was cleaned up.

"I have to see Gabriel," Ali said. "He called me at five AM crying. I'm afraid he might try to come here on his own."

"Okay, okay," Pam said. She sounded exasperated. "But we need to go to Santa Fe. This is important too."

"We shouldn't leave Sarah here alone," Ali said.

"Sarah can stay here one day alone," Sarah said, breaking in on the debate. "Leave early tomorrow, drop Ali at the airport in Albuquerque, do your research at the court house and come back at night. Simple."

That's what they did, all driving off on Tuesday morning, leaving her at the hacienda. So they weren't there that afternoon to see a neat Hispanic woman in a light blue suit drive her small gray car up to the hacienda.

"I'm looking for Sarah Hunter," she said.

"I'm Sarah Hunter." She felt wary about this businesswoman. Strangers usually didn't bring good news.

The woman produced a packet of papers from a slim leather case Sarah hadn't noticed. "Mrs. Hunter, I'm serving you these papers regarding the ownership of this property."

"What?" The woman seemed to be talking, her mouth moved, but Sarah couldn't understand her. She noticed the woman's feet swelled out of her tight shoes that matched exactly the blue of her suit.

"Your lawyer can explain. I'm not supposed to—"

Sarah heard disconnected words: old properties, boundaries, problems, historic, Mr. Ortega, not clear.

"Mr. Ortega is challenging your purchase of the hacienda," the strange woman said. "He believes the title is not clear."

"The title?" Sarah said.

"It's all in here," the woman said. "I'm not supposed to—"

Sarah took the papers. Her head started to throb.

When the woman and her gray car were gone, Sarah stumbled back into the kitchen and carefully made an omelet for herself and another one without onion for Bernie. Then she drank a fifth of leftover wedding champagne.

31

SARAH CALLED THREE LAWYERS. One called back. She fought off discouragement by attacking the weeds in the garden. It didn't work very well. She tried to contain her fears, but inside felt like a mother who had just been told her child had a rare disease.

Dennis Robb, the attorney recommended by Judy Grace, found time to see them a week later. Ali came back from Texas for the meeting. She said Gabriel was fine, but it was clear she was scared Ortega would find him.

Sarah, Ali, and Pam sat in identical uncomfortable chairs in Robb's Santa Fe office. Kenny had stayed at the hacienda, although they agreed Ortega's new battlefield was the court, not the courtyard.

Robb, heavyset with a good suit but a bad comb-over, looked harried. "I can't say yet how strong Mr. Ortega's case is, but to be honest, it appears to have merit. At least precedents exist. Anyway, you never know what a judge is going to do."

"But we paid for the hacienda," Ali said. "It was on the market for over a year before—"

Sarah interrupted Ali, "Are you saying the sale wasn't valid?"

"The title isn't clear," the lawyer said. "Old properties in New Mexico, many like this one, were bought and sold, mortgaged, used as collateral, every kind of damn thing."

"Weren't records kept?" Sarah asked.

"Whole ranches were won and lost in card games. People took them over, but didn't necessarily file the proper papers." Robb's tone was sympathetic, but his gaze flitted behind them to a series of framed prints of Anasazi petroglyphs.

"I've made a photocopy of every public record that pertains to the hacienda," Pam said.

"And did you find anything pertinent?" Robb asked.

"Not yet. I don't even know what some of the papers are," Pam said.

"I can believe that," Robb said. "You said no one's lived out there for seventy years?"

"That's right, Ali said. "Except for the hotel and a few outbuildings, it's a hundred and sixty acres of nothing."

"They can't just take our home," Sarah said. "We acted in good faith."

Robb flexed his tongue over his front teeth in a practiced routine. "Ortega claims his father traded some land for part of the present hacienda acreage which Ortega says his father lost when divisions later occurred. One hundred sixty acres didn't matter when nobody wanted them. The boundaries have to be researched, surveyed and marked."

"Why didn't he bring this up before?" Pam asked. She twisted the horsehair bracelet on her left wrist.

"Maybe he didn't know until he hired somebody to do some poking around," Robb said. "Maybe if he did know, he thought it'd be easier and cheaper to just buy the place."

"But we had a title search done. Why wasn't it found then?" Sarah asked.

Robb looked at his watch. "It may not have shown up or there may have been nothing to find," he said. "And don't assume Mr. Ortega's right. He might have made all this up."

"So it's not hopeless, is it?" Pam asked. A red welt spread under the bracelet.

"Anything is possible," Robb said, "but the sure thing is that it will take a long time and cost you a lot. All those records you've been researching? For starters, I'd have to hire a trained aid to go through every one. I wouldn't even begin without a fifteen thousand retainer. That may be what this fellow, Ortega, is counting on."

Sarah felt dizzy at hearing the cost of defending her home. She looked at Ali and Pam. They looked shell-shocked.

"Why does he want it so bad?" Robb asked. He leaned back in his leather chair.

"We're not sure. He owns adjoining property; says he wants it for a horse farm," Sarah said.

"He owns land next to us?" Pam asked.

"He said he did," Sarah said.

"I don't remember that." Pam twisted in her chair toward Sarah. "When?"

"When he was trying to buy it from us," Sarah said.

"No, it was the first time he came out," Ali said. "He knew about the electricity problem, said there were two different suppliers. Then he mentioned his land."

"Excuse me, ladies," Robb interrupted, "I didn't mean to imply that why he wants it is that important. No matter what's there or not there, it's your home and you want to keep it. Look, I have another appointment in fifteen minutes. I think you three ought to think about your options and the costs of each and call me tomorrow. I'd be pleased to represent you."

He opened the heavy wood door. They rose in unison.

"Remember, it's going to cost him a lot too, even if he wins," Robb said. "Try to not let your emotions sway you. You might make a deal and come out just fine. There are a lot of ranches for sale in New Mexico." Robb tried to smile pleasantly; they didn't.

It was a long ride home. Ali dozed in the back seat while Pam drove Sarah's Toyota over the narrow curving roads.

Sarah thought about Robb's comment that why Ortega wanted the property wasn't important. Robb was correct. Regardless of why Ortega wanted it, she wanted to keep her home. If it had some unknown value, a gold mine maybe, she'd be delighted, but she knew she couldn't want it any more than she did now.

And yet, some question snaked through her mind: if she knew what Ortega wanted, could she somehow use it to keep him from getting it?

"Why'd you ask about Ortega owning land next to us?" Sarah asked.

"Something Kenny said about oil." Pam said. "Sometimes oil is on one piece of land, but they drill horizontally from the best location which could be on somebody else's land. Maybe something on his land is on ours too, and he wants all of it."

"You think it's oil?" Sarah asked.

"No." Pam said. "I think it's water—what everybody in the west fights over."

"I think it's Ortega's colossal ego," Sarah said. "Getting beat out by three *gringas*."

Pam swerved to avoid a busted bag of cement that had been dropped in the road. The car fishtailed.

"Why not water?" Pam asked, yanking the car back into its lane.

"Because we went over every acre and found nothing," Sarah said. She felt exasperated with Pam's wild notion that some aquifer lay hidden beneath the hacienda.

Sarah looked back at Ali sleeping. She looked different than when they first arrived in New Mexico, and it wasn't just her tanned skin and cropped hair. She had become a mother, infused and overtaken with the instinct to protect.

"Ali thinks Ortega knows the Feds want it, and he wants to be the one to sell it to them," Sarah said.

"All Ali thinks about is Gabriel," Pam said, slowing down as they approached Angustia.

⊹ ✳ ⊹

THAT NIGHT, AROUND THE heavy oak kitchen table, Sarah laid out the expenses. They listened as if she were reading a list of war dead. They drank *Te de Manzanilla* and didn't take long to realize that they couldn't afford a prolonged legal battle and that immediate negotiation with Ortega was their strongest position. Ortega might make a deal if he hadn't spent too much on his lawyers and if he could save face with a clean victory.

In the silence that followed, Sarah studied her friends and reflected on how each had become captivated by the hacienda in the past months. Pam couldn't bear to leave her chapel or her studio, and Ali needed a place to raise Gabriel and teach dance to the rag tag group that adored her. For Sarah, the defeat was like losing her other leg or worse, her heart. Here she was a chef, in charge of her life. Here they were all artists, creating art that recreated them. And no one really had a past to return to in the south.

Sarah felt dizzy. She couldn't give up the hacienda. It had become her life, and without Pam and Ali, her goose was cooked. She had a vague image of a retirement village where cripples like her used wheelchairs and weren't allowed even to cook for themselves.

"There's gotta be something else we can do," Ali said. She laced her fingers until the knuckles turned white. "What are we going to do?"

"It doesn't matter," Pam said. She had tears in her eyes. "We don't have the money to fight." She picked up a handful of documents that had come in the mail—a cesspool of legalese.

Throwing the papers hard on the table, Pam walked out of the kitchen.

Kenny drank his tea in the troubling stillness. Ali looked grim, Sarah frightened.

"I walked it all again today," he said. "Me and Bernie. Every acre. I didn't see anything. Hell, most of it's just parched scrub."

"Maybe that's because there isn't anything to see," Sarah said. "It's about power." She sounded like she might just have enough energy to step off a cliff, but not any more. "I've known men like Ortega before." She thought of Randall Crane. "Winning is always more important than the prize. And for Ortega, losing to three white women, is intolerably humiliating. If he loses to us, he won't be who he thinks he is."

"I better go see about Pam," Kenny said. He left Sarah and Ali staring into space.

Sarah felt like a mourner at a wake. The Hacienda Angustia was laid out and quiet, and in the morning they would have to see about putting a little makeup on and burying her.

A scratching at the screen door brought them around.

"Bernie," Sarah said. Since Bernie's scrape with death by poison, the dog had kept close to Sarah. She had left him with Kenny for the trip to the lawyer and hadn't seen him since.

Ali opened the door, and Bernie clamored into the kitchen and headed for his bowl.

"Bernie!" Sarah and Ali said together. Bernie was soaking wet with mud caked on his chest and legs. When Sarah examined him, she saw that his front paws were scratched and his toenails frayed.

She yelled for Kenny, who came running with Pam close behind.

"He's hurt. Look at his paws. Somebody did something to him," she said. "Goddamnit Kenny, you said you'd watch him." She frantically examined the dog for other signs of injury.

"He hung out with me all day," Kenny said. "When I saw y'all drive up the road, I hiked back and he stayed out."

"He looks okay, Sarah," Pam said. "He smells like rotten eggs, but he's not hurt."

"He doesn't look okay; he looks like hell," Sarah said.

"Let me clean him up," Kenny said. "I'll hose him off right now and wash him good tomorrow."

It was too late to argue. Bernie snapped up the remains of his morning kibble.

Kenny led the dog outside and the three women went to their rooms to divine a way to outsmart Jami Ortega.

-ᛟ- ᛞᛟᛒ -ᛟ-

SARAH WAS AT THE kitchen table early the next morning, trying to figure out how to borrow enough money to fight Ortega when Pam came in from outside. A wet Bernie tagged behind.

"Did you wash him?" she asked.

"Kenny did last night."

"Why's he still wet?"

"I just hosed him down again."

"Thanks. Sorry I got so mad," Sarah said. "I'm afraid they'll try to kill him again. That bastard, Ortega, knows just what will make us crazy. He doesn't even have to threaten us if he threatens the things we love."

Beyond the kitchen window in the early light, the desert landscape looked like a sepia print of dwarfed fir and pinon dotting acres of sand that crawled to the distant mountains.

"You think you could take a walk with me?" Pam asked.

"A walk? Me?" Sarah said. Pam's energy was way too high for Sarah, especially so early.

"We can drive part way."

"Where?"

"There's something I want to show you," Pam said.

"Pam, I'm not dressed to go out." Irritated by Pam's persistence, Sarah turned back to the balance sheet on the table in front of her.

"We won't leave our land." Pam stood over her, waiting.

"What is it?"

"I can't tell you. You have to see it. Please."

Pam drove Sarah's Toyota as fast as the dirt road permitted. Bernie sat on the back seat, poking his head between the front seats. Sarah, feeling Pam's excitement, became uneasy, imagining Pam had something unpleasant to show her, maybe a horse's head impaled on a spike, a gruesome Hollywood warning from Ortega.

Pam helped her out of the car and rousted Bernie. "We have to go up there to those rocks," she said, pointing. She held Sarah's arm, almost pulling her up the slope.

Bernie ran ahead and disappeared into the cluster of boulders. After ten minutes of hard walking Sarah said, "I have to rest." She plopped on a granite wedge that had broken away from the outcrop in a time when Indians still freely roamed the land.

"We're almost there," Pam said.

"We're almost where? Where's Bernie?"

At the sound of his name, the dog emerged from a crevice Sarah had not observed and bounded down the hill. Two feet from her, he shook himself, drenching her.

"He's wet."

"Yes, he is," Pam shouted.

"What is it?" Sarah asked.

"Water," Pam said. "It's what Ortega wants, what Lorena McCragg died for. Water." Pam clapped her hands.

"A well?"

"Wells don't have hot water," Pam said. "There are springs under all these rocks, and we aren't the first to find them." Pam practically danced, leaping from one rock to another.

"It was here all the time," Sarah said. "Just as you said." She pulled herself to her feet. "I can't even think what this means, what it changes, if anything."

Then Sarah felt her heart sink at the recognition of the true resource of the hacienda. She felt stupid. Evidence had been everywhere.

"How could I have been so blind?" Sarah said.

"Don't beat yourself up. Kenny and I looked at the geologic surveys and didn't realize they'd been changed," Pam said.

"What?"

"The records from Santa Fe—somebody must have switched them. I didn't even notice until after Bernie found the springs."

"Bernie found them?" Sarah said. It was too much to grasp.

"Remember the smell of that mud on him last night? Rotten eggs?"

"Like they put in natural gas."

"Yes." Pam scratched Bernie's neck. "It's also the smell of sulfur, sulfur springs. I woke up at about three and I just knew."

"Bernie led you here?" Sarah asked.

"I let him out and followed. He peed on your car's tire, checked out the barn and headed here. He likes the mud." Pam stooped in front of Bernie and hugged him.

"I'm sorry I didn't listen to you," Sarah said.

Pam shrugged. "They've been underground for a century. Nobody knew."

"How did Ortega know? Him and not anybody else?" Sarah said.

"Maybe you can ask him someday."

Sarah tried to understand how to use this new information. Did it matter that Ortega wanted the land because of the water?

"Are we going to have enough money for the lawyer?" Pam asked.

"I can get him started, but—"

They stood, watching the sun breach the eastern horizon, teasing the landscape to life. The bones of the earth had shrugged out of the loose soil eons ago. No softness disguised the unforgiving, incredible space. Twenty yards away a rattlesnake draped himself on a ledge.

"If my house in Jackson sells, I can pay off my debts and still have something—" Sarah stopped. It was clear that using the money from the sale of the Mississippi house to defend her claim to the one in New Mexico would be a gamble with bad odds.

"I want to see the spring," Sarah said, changing the subject.

"Sure."

"Leave me out here a little while. I need to think."

"Want some help getting to it?" Pam asked.

Sarah shook her head. "Come back in an hour. And Pam, I'm sorry I didn't respect your instincts about the water. I should have. I don't know how to say this but, I'm impressed with your strength."

"Strength? Are you serious?"

"The art you've done here. How you cope. Hell, you found what we were all too blind to see."

"Thanks, Sarah," Pam said. "I don't feel strong, but I do feel good when you say I am."

When Pam had driven away, Sarah slowly climbed up to the opening in the rocks. Camouflaged by brush and the mottled rocks, the narrow slit was impossible to see even a few feet away. A pile of slag indicated that until fairly recently, the cave had been completely sealed. Following Bernie, she slipped between the two flat boulders into the cave.

Water bubbled. Even in the half light, she could see the pool and feel vapor rising off its surface. It was bigger than she expected, covering maybe 200 square feet. The rocks arched high above creating a cathedral-grotto. At the peak, a cleft formed a natural diamond-shaped sky light.

This must be where they dumped Lorena McCragg's body. Maybe she met her Indian lover here too.

Sarah started to cry, and Bernie moved close, pushing her with his big head. Crawling on all fours across the soft, pungent mud, she approached the hot pool and pulled off her prosthesis. Easing herself into the steam, she let the waters take her tears. The warmth raced to her aching leg, anesthetizing the phantom pain. Air bubbles sprang from the bottom and broke against her skin. An intense, low groan rumbled out of her and ricocheted on the rocks. Bernie matched it with a high keening.

A mist rose, condensed and fell from the grotto's ceiling, playing a melancholy song. Sarah could envision the spring revitalized as the centerpiece of her bed and breakfast. Close by, in Ojo Caliente, the multiple pools of hot mineral water were the single reason for the town's place on the map. People drove miles and miles to soak at Ojo. Angustia wasn't any more isolated. Sarah imagined the combination of her food, the New Mexico air and the healing waters. It would be good for the whole town. She lay back in the water, letting it cover her face and fill her ears. The sound of blood coursing toward her heart was all she could hear.

Bernie's sharp warning bark brought her to the surface fast. His raised lips quivered and a slow trill pulsed from him.

"What? Bernie what?" Sarah asked. Anxiety edged her voice. Alone and without her leg, she was completely vulnerable. She thought she heard pebbles sliding outside.

Bernie leapt for the cave's entrance and disappeared.

"Bernie, no."

Sarah struggled out of the pool and jammed her right knee into the prosthesis.

Shit. How could I be so stupid?

She scrambled out of the cave, tearing her knees and her clothes. Both Bernie and whatever had alerted him had vanished.

Sarah leaned on the rough rocks, catching her breath and scanning for trouble. Would Ortega or his men come on her land in daylight? Had someone taken Bernie? Was she totally paranoid and crazy?

Sarah limped down the hill, her fear subsiding. Nobody was around. She sat to wait for Pam and noticed the snake. It lay coiled on its rock ledge a safe distance away, absorbing the sun's warmth. It could have been the same rattler that visited her patio.

"Hey," she asked. "You see anybody out here?" She moved closer, unafraid. When Pam drove up, Sarah was still interrogating the snake.

Pam looked her over. "You went in the water?"

Sarah nodded and then held out a broken gourd, shaped into a dipper and scored with wavy lines.

"It was inside," she said.

Pam nodded without comment.

"I want Wanda to look at it," Sarah said. "It's Indian, but I don't know what tribe. Must be old."

"Where's Bernie?" Pam asked.

Sarah started to explain Bernie's alarm, but then held back. Fear had a way of leaching and spreading. "He's probably back at the hacienda by now."

They were quiet on the ride back to the house. In the dusty hotel parking lot, Sarah got out of the car and stepped back too quickly, a move that sent her crashing to the ground.

Pam ran to her. "Are you okay?"

As Sarah fought tears, whatever fragment of hope that had germinated at the spring wilted. "Why did I ever think I could do this? I can't even walk." Her scraped fist closed around sand and pebbles and she hurled them. The pebbles skittered across the drive, but an inopportune breeze tossed the sand back into her eyes.

"I'm crippled, broke and blinded. I'm a heartbeat away from having no home. Could things get any worse?" She felt cheated. Although she had wanted the hacienda no matter what, now she wanted its water. Perhaps the water was the connection to the power of the place. She could feel her energy leaking, flowing out, and leaving her. It was as though Ortega had hooked into her aura with a sharp tentacle that slowly drained her.

32

THAT NIGHT SARAH SAT alone by the kiva fire in the courtyard, staring past the flames into the open doors of the hacienda. She had delayed calling Dennis Robb. There was no rush to surrender. Ortega had won. They didn't have enough money; he could outlast them.

She worked her fingers into Bernie's ginger fur. He squinted and raised his chin.

Ortega had not only won, or soon would win, but he had been so clever. Certainly he, and it appeared he alone, had known about the hot springs. And he must have realized from the start that the title had problems he could turn to his advantage.

"That was his ace," she said to the dog, "but he wanted to torment us first because we made him look bad." She thought about Ali's hair, Gabriel's capture and Ortega's intimidation of most of Angustia.

Bernie growled and rolled on his side.

"You were the one who found the springs, weren't you?" she baby-talked. "Hidden all those years, and you sniffed them out. You tried to tell me. That's why they poisoned you," she said, appalled by the truth.

Kenny, who thought the underground springs were extensive, had explained how hot springs have to be developed. Most stay underground, Kenny had said. Springs form when ground water hits an underlayment of hot rock, maybe magma. When it boils, it's forced up through fissures and runs off or collects in pools.

Now they'd be Ortega's springs, his pools.

When Ali and Kenny found out, they had gone to see the springs, but Sarah couldn't bear to return. She could still smell the minerals on her skin and feel the heat that had embraced her.

She stood beside the fire and wished she had the guts to burn it all down. The two feet thick vigas that they had lovingly scrubbed and polished would burn for days. The rustic old southwest furniture and Navajo rugs they had salvaged would explode like tinder, the smoke rising over the hacienda like ghost riders in the sky. Pam's beautiful tiles wouldn't burn, but the fire would scorch, leaving them greasy black. When the blaze had exhausted itself, crumbling adobes would outline the Hacienda Angustia like the ancient Indian ruins at Chaco Canyon.

A log rolled out of the pit, offering itself, but Sarah poked it back. It was impossible to kill what she had brought to life even if a man like Ortega would unfairly take it from her. She wanted to howl like the coyotes; she only managed a sigh.

Pam was asleep but not with Kenny. Sarah thought that Kenny scared Pam. He was turning out to be a great guy and Pam was more comfortable with not-so-great. He might want some commitment from her. And if Kenny turned out to be a prince, Pam wouldn't feel like she deserved him. She'd find a way piss him off and send him back to his sister's cat ranch. At least that's what Sarah thought.

She also thought Ali looked older each day. Along with Gabriel's absence, the cessation of the dance group had depressed her. Folklorico was probably the poorer children's only chance, but without Ali, there'd be no more dancing.

Sarah felt sure that the hot springs and B & B could have revitalized Angustia. There would have been jobs and the opportunity for the people to open their own small businesses for tourists. Did Ortega hate the town or only that it might prosper without him?

She went inside, Bernie trailing.

A toilet flushed somewhere, and she remembered all the petty fights over flushing water. Pam had been the water Nazi, and Ali couldn't bear clutter, awry rugs or dog fur dust. Sarah wondered what she had done to drive them crazy and make things harder.

In the chapel she lighted a candle. The flame crouched and sprung across the tile mosaic. The dark Apostle's windows stared blankly down at her. She could hear again Father Gallegos's Latin Mass, *In nomine Patris et Filii et Spiritus Sancti.* She looked up at the carved angel placed above the altar by Lupe Herrera's family. The gift had almost touched off a war of icons, as other families not wanting to be left out, delivered all manner of religious imagery: a shell-encrusted Virgin, a paint-by-numbers portrait of St. Francis of Assisi, and an image of St. Jude, Patron of Lost Causes made of corn husks and raffia.

Sarah didn't believe in any religion, but she had unwittingly become the owner of a Catholic chapel where virgins, saints, and angels held sway, so she prayed to them.

"Beautiful, bright angels, help us. I know I've made mistakes and been selfish. I pushed my best friends to come out here because of what I needed, not for their good."

The angle was mute; not even a nod. Sarah looked at the statue of the Virgin of Guadalupe from her blue mantle to the bar code on her sandal.

"Please help me, *Señora*. I'm not asking for money. And it's not just to save my home." The candle light flared. Mary showed zero emotion. "I can do good things here. Don't show me I have a purpose in life then take away the means to—" Her eyes filled.

Lit only from below, the Madonna's face looked faintly ghoulish. She wasn't talking either.

"Go to hell then. All of you." Tears gushed and slid down her face. She slumped to the floor, kicking away a padded kneeler that Father Gallegos had donated.

"It was just a tiny dream. You're so fucking stingy," she sobbed.

Bernie licked her hand.

"Go ahead and strike me dead," she said. "You took my leg. Finish me off."

A high pitched noise startled her. Bernie leapt to his feet, a ridge of fur lifting along his spine.

Christ Almighty. What if it's God?

It was her cell phone.

"Hello." She held her breath.

"*Señora*, it's Hay-soos."

Hay-soos. *Jesus.* It was Jesus.

"From the gas station?" he said. "Jesús Dominguez."

Jesús Christ.

Sarah remembered the man who ran the gas station in Angustia. He gave terrible directions and would never admit he didn't know an address.

"Yes, Jesús."

"There's a mini-bus of tourists here. They're broke down."

"There is?" Sarah said.

"They got no place to sleep except the bus." Jesús sneezed and wiped the phone with something rough.

Sarah wasn't quite sure what he meant.

"And?"

"I told them you had a hotel. I know it ain't open, but—"

Sarah looked at the statues. For an instant she thought she saw the virgin lift her eyebrows and shrug one shoulder.

Shit.

"How many people?"

-◈- ✣ -◈-

MICHAEL LA GUARDIA, THE tour guide from Roswell, New Mexico, paid Jesús and his friends to ferry the group of eighteen out to the hacienda. They arrived stuffed into assorted vehicles including Carlos Herrera's low-rider. Sarah threw her gray serape over her shoulders, turned on the lights and met them at the main gate. Before she could explain that the hacienda wasn't exactly ready for guests, the guide grabbed Sarah's hand and pumped hard.

"Thank you so much for taking us in. There are nine couples plus me. I don't know what you have, but it's better than sleeping in the bus." He sucked a quick breath. "It'd be morning before the other bus in Roswell could get here to rescue us. Been on the road all day. Scenic byways are exhausting."

She thought he might have overdosed on NoDoz. He jangled on fast and without pause as people climbed out of the bus and gathered behind him.

"How do you do?" Sarah managed. She looked back toward the chapel. Who had sent this alien busload?

"This is the Hacienda Angustia?" he asked.

"Yes."

311

Desperation edged the guide's features. He took her aside, away from his charges. "Look, I'm in trouble. We're a little company. Bad word of mouth will ruin us. These folks are worn out. I'll pay you extra if you take care of us." He took a breath.

"Mister...what'd you say your name was?"

"Michael La Guardia." He spelled his last name.

"Mr. La Guardia, did Jesús tell you this hasn't been a hotel for seventy years?" Sarah asked.

"I know you're not open, but Jesús says there's a chance—"

He looked like a taller Danny DeVito, pacing in the gravel, stirring dust. "I told them it was rustic, so they don't expect Holiday Inn."

Sarah looked at him, thinking. He took her pause as an opportunity for him to download more information. "They're really nice people. It's a club of space alien trackers. There's a festival in Roswell."

She vaguely remembered something about Roswell, New Mexico making a tourist industry out of a crashed flying saucer.

"If you lend me a car, I could go buy groceries for breakfast," La Guardia hurried on. "We'll keep it simple. These people are galactic citizens who believe space aliens landed in Roswell. They're flexible." He licked his lips.

The words breakfast and groceries kindled a spark in the synapses of Sarah's brain. She had planned to let them camp at the hacienda, but perhaps more was possible. Had she ironed her white chef's jacket since the wedding?

"Let me talk to my partners," Sarah said.

"Can my people use the restroom?" he asked.

"In the lobby and go right," she said moving fast, almost dancing toward Pam's studio.

33

"I CAN'T BELIEVE YOU TOLD them to come here," Pam said. The four of them whispered in the kitchen.

"They're stranded," Sarah said. She had rousted them from sleep and assembled a meeting.

"Tell them to go to Santa Fe. Lots of rooms there," Pam said.

"Aren't you listening?" Sarah said. "Their bus is broken down. They can't go anywhere."

"Do we have that many rooms with beds in them?" Ali asked.

"I think so," Sarah said. "Yes, if Pam will let them borrow the futon from her studio."

"They just showed up out of nowhere?" Pam asked.

"Almost. It's a club that believes extra-terrestrials visit earth. They're going to a UFO festival in Roswell."

"I don't believe this," Pam said.

"Oh, yeah," Kenny said. "July 1947. Flying saucer crashed near Roswell."

"Not that," Pam said. "I don't believe—never mind."

"I'll do all the work, but I need you to agree," Sarah said.

"Are you crazy?" Pam said. She pulled her terrycloth robe tightly around her. "Nineteen people are out there."

"We can't turn them away," Ali said.

Ali was a sucker for anyone in need.

"Do you have sheets and toilet paper, like that?" Kenny asked. "They gotta have pillows, don't they?"

When they had first moved in, many of the rooms still had beds, armoires and chests. Sarah had persuaded Manny and his crew to haul in all the old furniture they could find stored in the outbuildings. Even with the added pieces, the big, high-ceilinged rooms looked Spartan, but they also looked like many hotels in Mexico. In lamp or candlelight, they would look quaint, even romantic.

"We can make do," Sarah said. "They believe they were guided here by extraterrestrial forces. They won't be persnickety," Sarah said.

In the silence, only the refrigerator's purr and the clock's tick could be heard.

"Hell fire," Ali said, breaking the quiet, "who's to say how any of us got here?"

Kenny shook his head. "Okay, tell me what to do."

"Pam?"

Pam made an exasperated gasp that sounded like a cross between *arrrgh* and *yeugh*. "How much are they paying?"

It took over an hour to prepare the rooms. Michael La Guardia took off in Sarah's car to buy groceries. Sarah set out wine and thawed *Galettes au Fromage*, cheese wafers left over from the wedding. The guests seemed delighted to be allowed to stay and pitched in to make beds.

Sarah paused at the top of the stairs, watching the group. Except possibly for the copper pyramid hats worn by two of the travelers, the lobby looked as she had always imagined it.

Guests pointed to the huge old vigas holding up the roof, to the niches, the chapel windows. Fingers trailed appreciatively over the old adobes and Navajo rugs. None had escaped the enchantment of the hacienda.

-╬- ☆ -╬-

In the quiet, well after midnight as she lay in bed, Sarah's head buzzed. They still had most of the borrowed tables, chairs, dishes and such from Lupe's wedding. Ali could arrange fresh flowers, Pam would help serve, Kenny would set up everything. Even with the looming loss of the hacienda, Sarah felt elated.

Then reason returned.

Oh God. I can't do this. I had over a week to do Lupe's wedding. I had help. Shit. I hardly charged them anything. It was a lark. This is different.

Her brain double-tracked through terror and planning: *Eighteen guests plus Michael means fifty eggs. I have a stove made in the last century. I'm not ready for this.*

Sarah fell asleep dreaming of taking a tenth grade chemistry exam. She woke five hours later from a sci-fi nightmare in which she was abducted by aliens and forced to operate an anti-gravitational egg beater. Dune-sized mounds of egg whites the consistency of Gillette Foamy buried the hacienda and rolled on, spreading in all directions.

-╬- ☆ -╬-

At six am, Sarah turned on the light in the kitchen and began sorting through the food Michael had bought. Then she put on her stiff white apron and washed her hands. Four dozen eggs stared up at her.

"I can do things with you," she told them. "I know how you came into the world, but your fate is with me now." She began cracking eggs into her large stainless bowl. "In a couple of hours everybody is going to be oohing and ahing over you," she coached. "You, the onions, peppers, and cheese, will be like exhibition ballroom dancers—forceful, but deft, complicated, but smooth and utterly sensuous." The growing mass of innocent yellow yoke-eyes looked back at her, uncertain but hopeful.

She switched on a tape of opera greatest hits, keeping the volume low.

Slowly, Sarah's nervousness dissipated into the beaten eggs, the sizzling sausage and the sautéing veggies. She felt her rigid focus transmute into pure creation. She was Georgia O'Keefe slapping sensual flowers on canvas and Maria Benitez stomping through the flamenco. It felt so good.

She turned up the volume and sang along with Pavarotti's spicy tenor, wondering if saints high on religious fervor had felt any better or surer that what they were doing was right.

Sliding the egg concoction into casseroles, Sarah moved on to the ripe strawberries. She hatched each large berry five times, careful not to slice through the stem and leaves.

Gently she fanned the juicy sections, opening the rosy, lush, private flesh.

Then she thought about Chef LeMoyne. Sarah remembered hearing the arrogant teacher say, "Haute cuisine is not about stuffing food down gullets. American tourists are nothing more than food processors. Their mantra is all you can eat. You could serve canned cat food and they'd never know *le* difference."

Sarah wished she'd defended her kinsmen, but back then under LeMoyne's tutelage, she'd been too scared. She still felt insecure doing things her way instead of LeMoyne's way. Sarah looked at her reflection in the window pane. *"Alors! Adieu, Madame* LeMoyne. *Merci beaucoup et adieu."*

━╬━ �֎ ━╬━

WHEN PAM WANDERED IN at 7:30, fresh bread was coming out of the courtyard *horno.*

"God, that smells good," Pam said, yawning.

Ali followed, in search of coffee. "You're going to wake them all up with that smell."

Efficiently, Sarah smacked another measure of coffee beans into the grinder. Things were okay at the moment, but conditions in a kitchen could change as fast as a soufflé could sag.

"The strawberries look good," Pam said. She set down a heavy canvas bag and poured herself a cup of coffee.

"What's in the bag?" Ali asked, arranging tiny wildflower bouquets for the tables.

"Leftover tiles," Pam said. "They'd make good coasters."

Sarah put aside the ground coffee and peered into the oven at the rapidly browning frittata.

When she didn't move from her bent position, Ali asked, "Sarah, what's the matter?"

"I never cooked fifty eggs before," Sarah said, transfixed by the dish in the oven. "It's a big responsibility." The longer she watched the eggs the less secure she felt. *Merde. Why did I tell LeMoyne to kiss off?*

"We're here," Ali said. "It's just like old times."

"The problem is that opera crap you're playing," Pam said, searching through the CDs.

Voices of the approaching guests echoed in the hall.

"Ready or not, it's showtime," Pam said. She stuck a hot pink zinnia behind her ear.

The alien trackers tumbled into the patio dining courtyard, chattering excitedly about a two AM sighting from the rooftop patio. They asked to stay another night even though it meant they'd miss the outdoor theatre performance of *Roswell, the Musical.* Some claimed they saw the hotel ghost. They were only distressed that Lorena McCragg seemed so unhappy. One, a retired psychologist, passed along the name of a ghost therapist.

For Sarah, it felt like they were cooking together as they had done for years in Mississippi when they called themselves the Chefs de la Lune. Sarah heard laughter and was startled to realize it was their laughter. She saw that Pam and Ali noticed it too. Pam ejected Pavarotti and popped an oldies CD in to the boom box. Like syrup on hotcakes, the Searchers poured out *Love Potion Number Nine.* Sarah felt that they could probably make up a batch right there in the sink.

✛ ❉ ✛

PAM SET THE LEFT over chapel tiles in a basket on the main counter in the lobby. A card read: TILES, $5. When she swept through the patio with a coffee pot, a couple, Veronica and Tom Holt, beckoned her to their table.

"You make these here?" Tom asked. He held up a blue tile to the light.

"I do," Pam said, pouring coffee refills. "Did you see the chapel?"

"Yes. It's stunning," Veronica said. "Where do you sell your work?" She unclipped her mass of red hair and corralled it again under the tortoise shell barrette that looked like a tarantula.

"New Orleans," Pam said. It was not completely a lie. She had shown her work there. "But not the tiles. These are new for me."

"Are you interested in a custom order?" Tom asked.

"I don't know. I'm not sure if we're—if I'm staying here," Pam said. She tried to reconcile the images of this couple as business people and alien trackers. Last night Veronica had told her that one of the couples on the tour was, in fact, alien.

"We're interested in the work, not your work place," Veronica said. She dug in her black leather bag for a business card.

Pam remembered the movie, *Cocoon*, and how the aliens took on human skins when, in fact, they were pure light.

"We have a contract for an upscale hotel in Newport Beach," Tom said. "I want something really special for the foyer. Shimmery. Very light, pure light."

"How big?" Pam said, sitting down with them. She eyed them carefully. Maybe Tom and Veronica were the couple from outer space.

"Probably thirty feet high and a hundred wide," Tom said. "I'd have to check the specs. It's partly glass, but it's big." He waved his hands, and Pam saw the tips of two of his fingers were missing.

"We could talk this afternoon, if you're free," Veronica said. She placed a strawberry between her lips and sucked it hard.

Thinking about the Starship *Enterprise*, Pam agreed and returned to refilling coffee.

-¦- ⁂ -¦-

WHEN IT BECAME CLEAR that the guests weren't leaving for another day, Ali arranged an after-dinner dance performance. She told the children that maybe they weren't going on television, but a performance was a performance. She neglected to add that the audience believed space aliens had crash landed less than 200 miles away.

For lunch, Sarah prepared a picnic of gazpacho, sliced beef, boursin cheese in fresh focaccia bread, and chocolate caramel cookies. She listened as her guests debated support groups for alien abductees and alien assisted clinics in which ET doctors, usually invisible to the patients, performed medical treatments.

For dinner the second night, platters of chicken and sweet sausage with olive and anchovy sauce were served under the stars. Oil lamps gleamed from each table and tiny white Christmas lights winked from the trees. They finished with a layered dessert of lady fingers, ice cream and fresh berries topped with whipped cream and Kahlua. Feeling more and more at home, the group members vociferously discussed the personal psycho interactive responses with aliens that had prompted their world view shift in consciousness. They asked Sarah if they could sleep out on the roof top in case another UFO happened by.

The dance performance went off without a hitch, but Pam became the star of post-performance conversation when she revealed she had watched every episode of the TV show, *Roswell*. The program that ran about three years examined the lives of teenaged extra-terrestrials who attended Roswell High School and wanted to get home.

But the visit by the accidental tourists gratified Sarah the most. The food, its presentation, the sounds of contented people at her table. She had done it. Just like a professional chef, she had done it. Then she remembered her prayers in the chapel just before Jesús' phone call. Was the Virgin Mary interested in gourmet cooking?

Thank you, thank you, Señora.

Watching the banquet as if it were a movie, Sarah sipped a glass of Châteauneuf-du-Pape provided by one of the guests, who insisted Sarah reopen the hotel. When she walked out to greet them, everyone rose and applauded. She'd been standing for about five hours, working hard, but her leg didn't hurt. It was too good to be true. She thought she might levitate.

-⊹-   ✸   -⊹-

SARAH WATCHED THE GROUP board the bus the next morning. Invitations to join them in Roswell were pressed on Pam, Ali, and Sarah.

"Thanks," Michael La Guardia said. "If you decide to open up, you let me know. I'll put you on the regular tour. You'd be surprised at the connections the people on that bus have." He cut a quick glance at the cloudless blue above.

Then he handed her a check that he explained in his jumbled fast talk, and then he asked her if it were enough.

"It'll be fine," she said, looking for something to sit down on. She couldn't believe the amount.

The money changed something Sarah couldn't exactly put her finger on. Money was energy; it opened doors. With enough money, you could fight.

When the Roswell Tours bus departed, Sarah, Ali, Pam and Kenny sat in the improvised patio restaurant and toasted their success with a bottle of champagne Michael La Guardia had given them.

Ali alphabetized the business cards they had been handed; Pam faced and stacked her cash. All the tiles had sold.

"I'm going to make some tiles for a hotel in California," she said. She held out her glass for a refill and told them about the Holts' offer.

"You sure they're for real?" Kenny asked.

"You mean do I think they're legit or do I think they're space aliens?" Pam said.

"Either," Kenny said.

Pam extracted a check from her shirt pocket. "Let's see if this is real." She set the check on the table beside Sarah's.

"I have an announcement too," Sarah said. "I'm putting every dime I can get toward keeping this place. I'm calling Dennis Robb. I'm going to fight."

"Good for you," Kenny said.

Sarah could see the gears in Pam's head meshing.

"You're flushed with success and a fat check," Pam said. "What about in a month?"

"There's more," Sarah said. "I want to open the hotel to make some money."

"Have you thought about how much work it is?" Ali asked. "We haven't even washed the sheets from the space cadets."

"It's our best bet to make some money. Judy Grace said she would help me get a business license and insurance. Some of the B & B's in Santa Fe charge over $300 a day and only provide breakfast. There's no other restaurant out here." Mentally she was doing the arithmetic: maybe eight people an average of five nights a week, was how many thousand dollars?

"How are you going to advertise?" Pam asked.

"Internet," Sarah said. "Unless you say no and have another plan, the Hacienda Angustia Hotel and Spa is in business."

"What about all the washing and, well, laundry you have to do for a hotel?" Pam said. "We have one Kenmore. You can't cook all day and scrub all night."

"Lupe Carrasco is coming to work for me, for us. There are others too. We'll have plenty of help," Sarah said.

"When did you do all this?" Ali said.

"An hour ago," Sarah said. "It just took a few phone calls." Kenny gave her one of his slow lazy smiles. "Providing jobs for the locals won't hurt."

"Look, I'm committed to keeping this place if we can," Pam said. "Hiring the lawyer is fine with me. But the reason I want the place is that it's isolated, quiet and unmolested. Regular tourists will change that."

"I need you, Pam. Just until we beat Ortega or we don't." Sarah said. "You have what you want here: Kenny, peace and quiet, tile orders. But I need people to feed. I'm a chef. Even if we didn't need the money to pay Dennis Robb, I'd need to cook. I'm asking you to compromise." There, she had said it.

Pam finished her champagne and put the Holt's check in her pocket.

Sarah watched Pam glance at Kenny and saw him look away. Maybe things weren't so sweet between the two of them.

"I know you," Pam said. "If we beat Ortega, you aren't going to close up."

"I didn't know I needed to work, to cook, when we drove out here," Sarah said. "But I found that out about myself." She wanted to tell them how cooking had given her the energy to fight. Preparing meals for the Roswell tourists had been so engaging, so deeply satisfying. It was what she was born to do, and she had waited her whole life to do it. Sniffing seasonings and tasting sauces had reshaped her attitude like molding jelly into aspic. Most important, it had crushed her self doubt.

"You can cajole me and make me say okay, but I don't want to run or live in a hotel," Pam said.

"Not a hotel," Sarah said. "A bed and breakfast."

"You're not being fair, Sarah," Pam said. "You're not listening to me." Pam tossed the limp pink zinnia on the table and walked away.

Kenny sat quietly for a minute and then followed Pam. Sarah turned to Ali and asked, "Am I being unfair?"

"Probably, but I understand," Ali said. "You finally found something you want to do and you can't just let it go."

Sarah knew Ali's all-encompassing devotion to Gabriel had changed her. Ali never whined about her philandering ex-husband or the downfall of her professional life. Like the UFO group, her world view had shifted.

"If you want to be a chef, it's fine with me," Ali said. "If we get to keep this place, I want to do more than just raise Gabriel."

"Like what?" Sarah asked.

"I don't know yet," Ali said. You found your calling. Maybe I will too."

"We're going to keep this place. We're going to beat that son of a bitch Ortega. I feel it," Sarah said.

34

HE NEXT DAY, PAM threw herself into filling the California hotel tile order. There were six basic styles, six shades of shimmering deep ocean. The heavy work distracted her. Somehow, she knew she'd have to face something about herself if they lost the place. Constantly up to her elbows in clay, she was too busy to worry about Ortega or her own demons. And she was too busy to notice the apparent success of Sarah's Web site. Guest bookings poured in.

Business at the hacienda didn't creep slowly like ivy, it exploded like ragweed. Sarah hired Kenny to build a hot mineral pool outside the cave. She hired Lupe and her cousin, Consuelo as housekeepers. Guests wrote in the guest book that they loved everything, especially the food.

Pam had reluctantly agreed to Sarah's opening the hotel if she limited the number of guests. Sarah had agreed that after their case was heard in court, the issue of hotel guests would be reexamined. Assuming they won. Pam automatically started making escape plans just in case. She hated herself for doing so.

The three women tried not to concentrate on what would happen if they lost in court, but the potential disaster colored everything. No one slept well, tempers flared easily, and a great deal of energy was expended in keeping depression at bay. The lawyer filed the proper papers, but a court date hadn't been set yet. The hacienda held its breath.

-⧈- ⚜ -⧈-

In spite of the tension over the hacienda's ownership—or perhaps because of it, Pam and Kenny's sex life flourished. They had made love on the futon in Pam's studio. In the afterglow, they'd stared at the Milky Way through the huge window that took up most of the studio's north wall. Their easy conversation drifted to why Cat Stevens had become a Muslim and had given up a huge career in pop music. Pam thought that he gave up fame and money to find himself. Kenny agreed but wondered if Cat could find himself in any organized religion.

"I think he traded one madness for another," Kenny said.

"Maybe changing his name three times was responsible," Pam said. "He went from Steve-something-Greek to Cat and now he's Yusuf Islam. Purely from a numerology perspective, that's gotta be troubling."

"What was your favorite song?" Kenny asked.

"*Morning Has Broken.* Yours?"

"*Looking for a Hard-Headed Woman,*" Kenny said and sang the first line of the song.

"I love to talk to you," Pam said. She felt closer to him than ever, touched by his vulnerability. "Do you talk to everybody like this?" She stretched, the contours of her naked body merging into his.

"You mean lovers, girlfriends?"

"Yes."

"Depends on the lover," he said. "It takes two."

Pam looked at the whorls of dark hair on his chest and belly and thought he was just as he had been the first time they made love. Kenny was himself. There was no bullshit.

He curled himself around her and took her hand. "I love you, Pam. I need to tell you that. I love you."

Pam froze, trying not to let him sense her stiffness. She knew her line, "I love you, too," but it stuck in her throat like dry corn bread. Alarms of all tenors and types blared.

Mayday. Incoming.

Then the censor voice she had hoped was dead or anesthetized rose as from a refreshing nap and said with a laugh, *"Three little words—the beginning of the end."*

"What's wrong?" Kenny asked.

"Kenny, I can't explain it. Can we not say those words? I do feel a lot for you, but—"

She fumbled, her words sounding lame even to her. She expected him to get up. She expected that in the morning he'd tell her he was sorry but he had to leave.

"No. You have to tell me why," he said. "You can't hogtie the most important thing in life and paste conditions on it."

"It'll go bad if we do," Pam said. "If I do."

"Explain."

"When things go good for me it's because I've paid for them somehow. Like after eight months of total shit, I got a real good job in New Orleans. If too many good things come along, then I know some real bad stuff is on the way."

"Is this related in any way to karma?" he asked.

She didn't think he was poking fun at her.

"I don't know, but I know my life. All the good guys, good jobs, good opportunities eventually go bad unless I can do something to buy some more good. See?"

Pam had never gotten so far into an explanation of this particular neurosis before. She expected Kenny to laugh. She would have if he had been doing the talking.

"Let me get this straight. If you say you love me, saying so will screw everything up because you'll have announced your happiness to some destiny deity."

"Unless—"

"Unless you've already suffered to earn this state of bliss."

"I know it sounds crazy, but—"

He sat up in the bed. "Pretty crazy." He paused, untangling the sheet. "But not much crazier than lots of things people invent to protect themselves."

Pam sat up and looked at Kenny. He radiated sexuality tinged with openness. Any woman would want him. She did. But would he really want her if he knew what a fuck up she was when it came to loving? She had failed to take care of her own baby brother. Her parents hadn't loved her. Somewhere deep inside her a small, sealed vault popped open and she began to cry uncontrollably. Like a cresting river, the flood of hurt and guilt raced across the breached levee, threatening to drown her. Her body convulsed.

He took her in his arms. When she quieted a little he said, "I see a couple of ways out of this. First, you've already paid in full for your whole life. You're paid up in suffering by what your parents did to you and your brother. Your internal banker is fucking with you. She's lying to you. Based on what I see, you've bought the rest of your life's worth of pure happiness."

Pam's sobs turned to soft hiccups. She so much wanted to believe him.

"Or maybe none of that's true and you're just scared to love because your parents couldn't love you," Kenny said.

"Don't tell me I have to learn to love myself," she snuffled. "By the time that happens, it'll be too late."

"I love you regardless of what you do."

Pam's head was spiraling. She saw herself coming down the aisle flanked by grinning girls in pastel J.C. Penney formals. A band played. Rice fell. But at the bottom of the fantasy came excruciating pain. She knew that in addition to her psychological explanation there was more. She had never opened up to anybody, and with Kenny she had no good reason for not doing so. He loved her; he was a good man. If she rejected him, she'd have to admit that she was the problem, not all the men she had bedded and blamed. Love terrified her.

"Why do you think it'll be okay?" she asked.

"Because I've lived it too," he said. "You're going to figure this out, Pam. It's going to be okay."

"Easy for you to say."

Kenny hummerd the Cat Stevens song about hard-headed women. "I miss The Cat," he said.

Relieved that Kenny had drifted away from the specific to the general topic of love, Pam laid down beside him.

They settled together, exhausted, as a billion stars delivered the energy they had released a million light years ago. As soon as Pam heard Kenny's breathing steady with sleep, she rose and crept out of the room.

-╪- ✳ -╪-

ON JULY TWENTIETH, WANDA Begay and Louis, an anthropology graduate student, drove up from Albuquerque. Sarah served grilled salmon with garlic and parsley butter for lunch to six hacienda guests. Wanda joined them while the student searched the springs area for artifacts.

Pam had immediately liked Wanda when they first met in Santa Fe. Wanda Begay was Navajo, Dine' as she called it, but she was really of the world and fascinated by all of its problems. Her long hair was pulled back in a yarn-wrapped bun and her arms were laden with Indian silver and turquoise, but her summer suit was smart and her shoes, expensive. She didn't seem to take anything too seriously. Pam thought her deep, resonant laugh probably came from this philosophy. The day they had found the springs, Pam had called Wanda to tell her about them.

When the hotel guests left and the dishes were cleared, Pam, Ali, and Sarah sat with Wanda in the shade of a huge Navajo willow.

"I've been talking to the Apache tribal council and our lawyer and I might have a solution to your problem here," Wanda said. She pulled out a cigarette but didn't light it. "I'm quitting, but I still like to hold them."

"Which problem?" Ali asked.

Pam guessed that Ali was more worried about Gabriel than about losing the hacienda, even though the two were linked. It was getting harder for her to see Gabriel regularly.

"We're starting to make some money," Sarah said. "I hired a lawyer. We're going to fight to the last."

"That's what worries me," Wanda said. "Look, I don't mean to be negative, but it doesn't take a genius to see that if this place is going to work, you're going to have to invest thousands." Wanda's gaze raked the hacienda as though with x-ray vision she could see through the walls to the dozens of impending maintenance problems. She shook her head slowly.

There, somebody else had said it, Pam thought. She had tried to, but Sarah didn't want to listen. Living in the hotel was one thing, but making it suitable for public use was quite another.

"Ortega will win because you three will die of exhaustion working to pay your lawyer in a prolonged legal battle," Wanda said. "You need to get rid of the lawyers."

"What do you suggest?" Ali asked. She ran her hands through her hair which had grown considerably since she whacked it off. It framed her tanned face like a salt and pepper cloud. Pam wondered if Ali would ever dye it again. Nobody in Jackson would recognize her.

"You can keep it by giving it away," Wanda said.

"Give it away?" Sarah repeated.

"To whom?" Pam asked.

"The Apaches," Wanda said.

"The Indian Apaches?" Pam asked.

"There aren't any Apaches who aren't Indians," Ali said.

"It's the one sure way you can keep Ortega from getting it," Wanda said. She put the cigarette back in its pack and opened her briefcase. Among the files and loose papers, she selected one bundle.

"I didn't want to do all the research until I was sure you'd agree, but what I'm suggesting is that you set up a trust: land, hotel, the springs, especially the water, in which you give it to the Apache Tribe."

Sarah started to interrupt, but Wanda charged on.

"It's well-documented that Apaches used the springs around here as a healing place. Your springs have been lost for a long time, but the gourd dipper shows the Apaches were here. But this is the important thing. Although the government never made good on it, the Indians have historical claims on the waters."

"How come Ortega knew about the hot springs?" Sarah asked.

Wanda shrugged. "Ask him."

Pam's mind was racing to catch up and pass Wanda. The Federal Government had promised water to the Indians. If she, Sarah, and Ali gave the hacienda to them, the old water score would be settled—the one Lorena McCragg had died for. And even if Ortega's claim turned out to be valid, the Indians' claim would supercede his. It might work. Or it might scare Ortega. Pam couldn't guess what would happen then.

"The tribe will have to apply to the Federal Bureau of Indian Affairs to acquire the land and take it into trust," Wanda said. "If the BIA approves it, the land will become part of the reservation and protected by sovereignty rights." She adjusted the tangle of silver and turquoise bracelets that encircled each wrist.

"And if the BIA doesn't approve it?" Sarah asked.

The lawyer says that if the BIA can't or won't cooperate, you could put the land in a trust to benefit the Indians. They'd get any income produced. There's also the possibility of giving it to one Apache who would then give it to the tribe. I never said it would be easy." Wanda took out another cigarette and stuck it between her lips.

"I want to live here, to die here," Sarah said. "Keeping it from Ortega and honoring disrespected Indians is fine, but—"

"You would live here," Wanda interrupted. "The Apaches would get it after you three die," Wanda said.

"I don't understand. Would we will it?" Pam asked.

"No," Wanda said. "Wills can be changed. It would have to be put in a trust you couldn't revoke. You'd have it for your lifetimes."

"If the BIA says okay," Pam said. She felt afraid to even get her hopes up that this plan would work. She was accustomed to failure. What if she could actually keep her studio and more importantly, keep Sarah, Ali and Kenny?

"That's right," Wanda said. She stuffed her papers back in her briefcase. "But you have some allies." She smiled. "Think about it, but not too long. If it's going to help your case, we need to get cracking."

Pam nodded. "You want to see the springs?" she asked.

"Of course," Wanda said.

"It's just a cave in a pile of rocks now, but give us a year," Sarah said.

They all squeezed into Wanda's old Range Rover and bumped over the dusty road that was hardly a road at all to the springs. The anthropology student said that from what he could tell, the ancient Indians had at least one pool outside the cave.

"I can send you some material on the Indians that used to live near here," he said. "If you understand how they lived, how they thought, you'll be able to create the right kind of baths."

In a flash Pam saw how the baths would look with native rock and her tiles. Since she and Bernie had first found the springs, she sensed they were a healing place. Maybe they'd heal her.

-◈- ⋇ -◈-

It took two weeks for Jami Ortega to find out what Pam, Sarah, and Ali were up to. His first response was to inform them through his lawyer that they couldn't give away what they didn't own. Dennis Robb, who was turning out to be a very satisfactory advocate, told Ortega that he didn't own it either and the ladies were just trying to see that some of the original owners got a piece of it someday.

"I think he wanted to offer more money," Robb said on the telephone, "but if he does that now, and you refuse, it hurts his position. He can't buy something from someone who doesn't own it. An offer implies he thinks you do."

Ortega's next response was more direct. Through *Señora* Cantu, he sent a cryptic message: he knew where Gabriel was hiding.

35

OR DAYS THE INTENSITY of Gabriel's homesickness grew. Joan and her ranch for orphaned animals had been fun in June and offered work he enjoyed in July, but now it was the middle of August. He wanted Mama-Ali; he wanted to go home. Ali said she loved him, but she hardly called him anymore and that frightened him. She was the only person he could remember who cared about him.

Before he had been sent to Texas, Ali sang songs she made up just for him. She fixed him mayonnaise and tomato sandwiches like they ate in someplace she called the South. She told him stories about magic beds that flew, coyotes that played tricks and bears that stole honey. He had caught her looking at him when he was dancing or simply waking up in the morning, and he recognized the love in her eyes. He had to get back to her.

Gabriel knew why he was hiding at Joan's cat ranch. But that trouble had happened a long time ago. If he was careful, nobody would catch him. Storm, the big dog, could go with him to protect him. Ali would be glad when she saw him.

He knew that when kids on TV shows ran away they got together supplies like food and flashlights. Gabriel made sure that Joan saw him go to bed. While she was in the shower, he stuffed an old Boy Scout pack with crackers, two apples, peanut butter, Fig Newtons, water, and dog biscuits. He took no clothes, but dressed in his newest shorts and shirt and wore his sturdiest running shoes.

"Come, Storm," he whispered when he was sure Joan was asleep. Quietly he let Storm out onto the back porch and then followed, keeping to the shadows.

Gabriel heard the whine of the distant highway. He knew about rest stops and that truckers frequently pulled into them for the night. He planned to hitch a ride, he and Storm. They'd travel north toward the Hacienda Angustia, toward home, to Mama-Ali. All he had to do was walk until he found a trucker willing to pick him up.

THE AUGUST HEAT BORE down on Ali as she drove south on New Mexico Highway 285. She kept the windows down so that she could stay completely alert. Ortega's cryptic message had said that if they wouldn't give up their claim to the hacienda, they'd never see Gabriel again.

Immediately she had called Joan in San Antonio but there had been no answer. Something was wrong, and it didn't take a genius to figure out that the boy was in danger. She had run through the various scenarios: Ortega had him and was hurting and terrifying him; Joan had been beaten and tied up or maybe killed trying to protect the boy; Gabriel had escaped and was trying to get to her. What chance did an eight-year-old boy have alone on the open road? It was also possible that Joan wasn't answering the phone because she had the boy with her shopping, at the doctor's or at the Dairy Queen. No matter what, Gabriel wasn't safe anymore. Ali had told Sarah,

Pam and Kenny she was going to Texas. "If that monster calls, you call me on my cell phone."

Nobody tried to stop her.

Ali had to force herself not to think about what Ortega or his men might do to Gabriel. Instead she thought about Gabriel's father and how he'd think the boy had been better off before Ali meddled with his life. She was near tears.

I'm going to find him. Screaming and crying gets me nothing.

She slowed the car to the speed limit and called Sarah to see if Joan or Ortega had phoned.

⊹ ✳ ⊹

Gabriel's pack cut into his shoulders forcing him to dump the heavier items: peanut butter, apples, and flashlight. He cut back to the dirt road; the rocky terrain was too tough. He had nearly fallen into an arroyo. As dangerous as the exposed road was, it seemed safer. From the top of a rise, he could see I-10. Cars and trucks inched along like lighted ants. Then he felt headlights on his back. There was no place to hide. What if it was Ortega?

A dusty black truck pulled alongside him and slowed. An older man, Hispanic, rolled down the window. "*Buenas noches, amigo.* Where you going so late?" His Tex-Mex accent sounded friendly.

Gabriel put out a hand to stop Storm's growling. He knew Ortega and it wasn't Ortega.

The man was wearing a white shirt and a bolo tie. The dash light reflected off the white, casting ghostly shadows up his face, hollowing his eyes.

"I was spending the night at my *Tía's* house, but I decided I wanted to go home," he said. "It's not far." Although he had planned this lie, he struggled to keep his voice even.

"Well, if you want, I'll give you a ride," the man said. He sounded tired, unconcerned.

"No. I have my dog. We'll walk. *Gracias*."

"Okay." He shrugged. "Be careful," he said, accelerating and shifting into gear. The truck disappeared around a curve into the dark.

Heart pounding, Gabriel stopped and drank from his water bottle. There was no moon, and only a few ragged stars managed to shine. He moved on, stumbled, and spilled most of his water. The interstate loomed in the distance. Ahead at a juncture in the road he could make out a group of sagging mailboxes. He'd keep straight toward the Interstate.

Ten yards past the boxes, he felt a heavy hand on his shoulder and then he was hoisted into the air. Storm went crazy barking. Gabriel kicked and twisted, but he was no match for the big man. He felt himself being carried, then shoved into the truck's cab and cuffed across the face. The blow sent his head smashing against the door. As Storm lunged for the man, he kicked, landing his boot in the dog's face. Storm fell back, whimpering, as the truck door slammed.

"I'll tie and gag you and put you in a bag if you want me to," the man told Gabriel.

Gabriel pressed his hand over his bruised cheek and said nothing. He knew lots of bad men like this one. Don't antagonize them was the first rule. Show respect, but not weakness. Weakness made them meaner. Gabriel nodded silently but looked the man straight in the eyes.

✦ �֎ ✦

SARAH COULD FEEL THE hairs all over her body rise at the sound of Ortega's voice on the phone. When it rang, she had known it would be Ortega, but now she could hardly speak.

"*Señora* Hunter, I hope I didn't wake you," Ortega said. When Sarah said nothing, he continued. "I believe I have something you want."

Sarah felt sick. He could only mean that he had Gabriel. "You think you can get away with kidnapping?" she said. Her pulse raced, her anger was way out in front of control.

"Kidnapping? We found him," Ortega said. "A child alone on the road at night. This is how you take care of him?"

Pam and Kenny pressed close to Sarah, trying to hear.

"Where is he?" Sarah asked. She bluffed sounding hard when all she wanted to do was snivel and beg for the boy's release.

"In good time," Ortega said. "Since I have something you want and you have something I want, I see no problem in making a trade. Do you?"

Sarah's eyes ran over the familiar colors and shapes of the hacienda kitchen. The hanging old wooden spoons that looked like a musical instrument, the antique dry sink, the cupboard doors wrought of cactus ribs and burled pine. Out the huge window the early sun shot through the firs and cottonwoods. Paradise gained and now to be lost.

"Bring him here."

"*Sí, Señora,* but first there is the matter of the deed."

"You slimy bastard," Sarah screamed. "I'm not trusting you. I'm not signing anything until I see the boy." Her voice was wet and ragged in contrast to Ortega's smooth satin purr.

"You have no choice, *Señora.* I'll let you think about this a little longer. You tell Ali what's going on. *Sí?*" He hung up.

"They've got him," Sarah said to Kenny and Pam. "If we want him, we have to give up the hacienda."

GABRIEL SAT BESIDE THE bad man as the black truck drove west on I-10 until it turned onto Highway 285 that would take them north into New Mexico: Carlsbad, Artesia, and Roswell. The man said nothing, but surveyed the boy with frequent rapid glances. Once he stopped at a deserted roadside pullout and urinated, allowing the boy to do the same. Back on the road, Gabriel saw the bad man's eyes close and jerk open. Gabriel knew the bad man was falling asleep. Beyond the New Mexico state line, he pulled off onto a deserted farm road.

Gabriel didn't resist when the bad man pulled him from the truck and wound layers of duct tape around his wrists and ankles. He choked when a cotton sock was stuffed in his mouth and bound tight with a cord. Then the bad man hoisted him up and tossed him like a sack of oranges into the bed of the truck.

"I'll be in the cab," the man said without emotion. "Don't wake me up."

Gabriel held his fear in check as he felt an oily tarp cover his body. In minutes he heard snoring.

Slowly, Gabriel twisted himself so that he could sit up and peek out from under the cover. There were other things in the truck bed, maybe some kind of pump, empty oil cans, and a wad of dirty rags. He tried to force his arms and leg apart to tear the tape, but it held fast.

As the sun rose and tracked upward, the bed of the truck heated up. Sweat poured down the boy's face, into his eyes and over the new bruise on his cheek. He had drunk no water in many hours and he thought he might die of the heat. Then an idea started.

Once when Lukey had been drunk and was beating his wife, Amelia, she had eluded his grasp simply because she had baby oil on her body. Lukey was twisting her arm behind her back one second and the next she was free and out the door.

Gabriel pressed his face to the hot metal of the truck and worked his jaw up and down. As sweat ran down his face, lubricating it, the rope across his mouth slipped a fraction. But he could tell the process would take too long. The bad man would wake up before he got the gag loose. Frantically, he searched the truck. Would the sharp edge of the pump thing cut the tape if he could scoot to it? He wiggled sideways, careful not to rock the truck. Two minutes of sawing against the sharp flange told him he would run out of time. "What else? What else?"

Then he saw on the other side of the pump an empty can of Valvoline 10W-30. Sticky oil had run down its side and pooled. Struggling like a moth trapped in its cocoon, he inched toward the spill and laid his face in it. Some oil worked into his eye and stung, but it also soaked the cord holding his gag. Working his mouth and raking at the cord with his shoulder, gradually the rope slipped from his greased face, past his lips and chin. He spat out the sock and with his teeth, went to work on the layers of tape around his wrists.

After his hands freed his feet, light as rain, he slipped from the truck bed.

In the dirt road, he saw old tire tracks and even older hoof marks. Silently, he ran down the dusty road, embossing clear footprints. When he reached a fenced meadow, he ducked under the slats and doubled back toward the highway.

It took only thirty minutes to reach the road, but he figured that even if the bad man followed the false tracks, he'd be back on the highway searching for him soon. Gabriel looked up at the sun and guessed it was noon.

He waited on a curve for the first vehicle and when he saw the huge City Market semi approach, he stepped out in the road and madly waved his arms. The low screech of the air brakes deafened him. The truck shimmied to a stop and Gabriel jumped onto the running board and beat hard on the door.

A black man swung open the truck door, and Gabriel heard a torrent of swearing. But when the driver looked at the bruised child with shreds of duct tape dangling from his wrists and ankles, he held out his hand and hauled him into the seat.

"Goddamn nearly ran over you," the driver said, easing the truck into gear.

Gabriel caught his breath and sitting low in the seat, tore at the remaining tape that left glowing welts on his thin arms and wrists.

"What the hell am I going to do with you?" the driver said. "I know you're in some kind of trouble and if you in trouble I'm in trouble." The truck picked up speed.

Gabriel didn't say anything.

"I'm taking you to the police station in Carlsbad. I ain't getting arrested for what all I don't know. In fact, I'm calling them right now." The driver lifted a cell phone from the console.

In an instant Gabriel realized that it was no longer an issue if Ortega traced a cell phone call and found the hiding place. No hiding place existed.

"Wait," Gabriel said. "Call my Mama-Ali. Please." He gave the driver the expression he had used to get a free hot dog or a winter night's lodging in Jesús' gas station.

"What's the number?" the driver asked. Now up to fifty miles per hour, the driver steered with one hand and pressed the tiny buttons with his other.

Ali answered on the first ring. Exhausted, she had pulled over at a state rest area and fallen asleep in the car.

"What, what?" she said. "Did you hear anything else?"

"Who's this?" the driver asked.

"Who the fuck is this?" Ali yelled back.

Gabriel shouted, "Ali, Mama-Ali help me."

"If you touch that child, I'll kill you," Ali said.

"Touch him, shit, I almost ran over him. Where the hell are you? Why ain't his Mama watching out for him is what I want to know."

"Let me talk, please," Gabriel said.

"I'm putting the kid on, but I expect you to come to me to get him. I ain't driving out to Bumfuck, New Mexico to deliver him. And I ain't getting in the middle of no domestical dispute." He handed the phone to Gabriel.

Gabriel described what had happened and what he imagined would happen when the bad man woke up. He understood that Otega's man had lost him and would be in big trouble with Ortega. The man would be desperate and stop at nothing to reclaim him. He listened as Ali tried to calm him.

"I'm sorry," Gabriel said for the tenth time.

"None of this is your fault," Ali said. "It's going to be okay. Put the truck driver back on the phone."

"I'm going to find a safe place in Roswell and call you back," Ali said. "If you get him to me safe, I'll pay you well for your time. What's your number?"

Ali tried to call Sarah, but the line was busy. Then she called Michael La Guardia in Roswell. La Guardia questioned nothing and directed her to a private landing strip just outside of Roswell.

✦ ✶ ✦

SARAH'S LINE HAD BEEN busy because she was talking to Jami Ortega. They had struck a deal. She'd relinquish claim to the hacienda, and he'd give her the boy. But he wanted a face to face meeting at the hacienda. He had said he'd be there in an hour.

They arrived in two black SUVs. Sarah thought of the Mafia and almost laughed when Ortega's seven men emerged, all dressed in shades of black with identical panzas protruding over cinched belts. In their pointed toe boots, they swaggered into the lobby.

"*Buenas tardes,*" Ortega said, removing his cowboy hat, a crisp, off-white straw.

Sarah, with Pam and Kenny beside her, stood in the kitchen door. "We can do business in here," Sarah said.

"You won't mind if I take a short tour," Ortega said. "Naturally, I want to see what I'm getting." In the kitchen, he turned on the tap, letting the water splash over his hand, and smiled. He admired the restored fountain in the small courtyard and traced his fingers over Pam's tiles in the chapel.

Ortega's men leaned casually on the restored adobe walls; one rested on the leather sofa, his foot square on the painted coffee table. Another ground out a cigarette on the tile floor. Sarah recognized one of the men from Ortega's raid on the hacienda. He wore the same tight collar and bolo. As she watched, Sarah felt as though she were being gang-raped.

The arrangement was simple. Ortega would get the hacienda for the price he had originally offered Judy Grace

344

months ago. Their financial loss would be substantial, but nothing compared to the emotional one.

"If you will just sign this, I'll have my attorney take care of everything," Ortega said, pointing to a document one of his men exhumed from a briefcase. "I'll give you until September first to be out." He sounded accommodating, even kind, like a kindergarten teacher. "The boy is on his way here."

"I want to read it," Pam said.

While Pam read the two-page document, Sarah walked to the side door to breathe. The hot August dust stuck inside her lungs. Part of her was angry. Why should she give up what she most loved? She hadn't decided to adopt the boy. It wasn't fair. But another part knew that without Gabriel, Ali wouldn't stay at the hacienda. Without both Ali and Pam, Sarah wouldn't last long there. Her anger turned to shame. She had a house to lose; Gabriel could lose his life.

Her phone rang. She pulled it from her pocket, knowing it was Ali, dreading telling her what they were doing.

"I've got him. I found him," Ali said. "I've been trying to call you. A friend of Michael La Guardia's is flying us to Durango, Colorado."

Sarah was too stunned to make a sound. She silently clutched the phone, listening to Ali, but not hearing much beyond, "Gabriel was safe and with Ali." Sarah could see that Pam had finished reading Ortega's agreement.

"Call me when you get there," she told Ali and hung up.

One of Ortega's men fingered a silver framed photograph of the three women in front of the hacienda. "Don't touch that," she ordered. Before Ortega could look up, Sarah had snatched the shotgun from its place beside the horno. "Get out," she said quietly.

Amazed, Pam dropped Ortega's document. Kenny stood up, closing in behind Pam. "We're not signing anything," Sarah said.

Ortega looked like a boy whose classmates had pulled down his pants at recess. His men looked at the floor.

Sarah waved the gun recklessly. "You're a liar and a cheat, Ortega. "You got no *cojones*. You couldn't beat three women, so you used an eight year-old boy. Nobody respects you. Fear is all you have. When you're dead, there'll be a *fiesta* in Angustia. Ding dong, e*l brujo esta muerto*." She brandished the shotgun again, and Ortega's men headed for the door. He, more slowly, also retreated, forgetting his hat.

"You will regret this," he said through clenched teeth.

"You filthy son of a whore. Get out before I shoot your black heart and cut off your ears." Sarah tried hard to think of cuss words in Spanish.

Backing toward his car whose motor was now nervously revving, he said, "You'll never see the boy again."

"I'll see you in jail," she yelled to his departing back, searching for some final insult, some gesture that the men would remember and describe when Ortega wasn't around. Something symbolic of his impotence that could linger and poison their faith in him.

Then with one hand, she pulled her skirt up above her knees and shook it. "Cowards, *cobardes*," she yelled. "A one-legged woman is kicking your ass."

36

SARAH FELT WARM AND muzzy from the long healing soak in the hot pool. She turned out the bedside light and nudged Bernie with her good leg to his side of the bed. In two weeks Kenny had channeled the water, dug the pool, and inlaid a sandstone platform around it. For Sarah, building the mineral pool signaled a turning point, a change in fortune. They were doing the right thing by the land and would be granted the opportunity to be its stewards.

Lying back on the fat pillows, she imagined the Indians who soaked their wounds and cares a hundred years ago. Since she had started daily baths, her phantom pain had almost disappeared. She felt confident that the Hacienda Angustia Land Trust would prevent Jami Ortega from stealing the hacienda and all her dreams.

Heat lightning flashed in the distance. Bernie thumped his tail against Sarah's prosthesis.

But her tenuous confidence faded the longer Ortega stayed in her thoughts. Since the day two weeks ago when Sarah had humiliated him in front of his compadres, he hadn't been seen by anyone including his own lawyer. Maybe his absence had something to do with Sarah's reporting to the authorities that

Ortega was guilty of kidnapping, extortion, blackmail, and assault. She had no proof, but the FBI started an investigation after Gabriel turned over the package of cocaine Ortega had given him to hide in the hacienda. But Ortega's absence might also mean he was formulating a new offensive.

Unable to sleep, Sarah rose, lurching like Frankenstein until she felt stable.

Nobody can imagine what it feels like to be missing half a leg.

The irony of standing on your own two feet when you had only one foot did not elude her. Yet standing strong with her new family, fighting for what she wanted without a man stepping in and rescuing her was the most important thing she had ever done.

Bernie following, slowly she toured the hall past Pam's studio, the kitchen and the lobby, finally ending up in the chapel. Ali and Gabriel slept upstairs. After a week in Durango, Ali had brought Gabriel back to the hacienda because he refused to leave her and because hiding him hadn't worked well. They could protect him just as well at the hacienda. They had to be vigilant until September ninth. The judge had finally set a date for a hearing. They'd be ready.

Again, lightning flashed through the chapel windows, this time followed by thunder. The air, humid for New Mexico, pressed heavily on her skin. No guests visited the hacienda that night. It was dead quiet.

Sarah knelt on the padded kneeler and lighted two candles.

"*Señora,*" she said, bowing her head before the statue of the Virgin Mary. "I'm sorry for those bad things I said. You sent a busload of tourists, and I've tried to make the most of your gift. Thank you. You sent Wanda who showed us how to keep the place by giving it to the Indians. *Gracias.* Most of all, thank you for Gabriel's safe return. Don't forget our court date, September ninth; we need you to be there. Protect us and give us grace—"

Bernie scrambled to his feet and began a high pitched keening.

"Shhhhhh, Bernie."

When Sarah turned to calm the dog, she saw her. Lorena McCragg hovered in mid-air just over the altar. The translucent apparition appeared to be cloaked in a long, burgundy velvet cape. The cape was soaked.

The hair stood up on Sarah's neck as a ridge of fur rose on Bernie's back. One candle flared high and went out. Lorena looked at Sarah.

"What?" Sarah said, barely able to breathe. "What is it?"

The ghost's choice of time and place: midnight in a chapel, seemed significant. The specter faded like evaporating steam and reappeared beside the chapel door. Closer to her now, Sarah saw purple marks on Lorena McCragg's neck. The second candle flared, making wild shadows on the high walls. It went out, shooting a plume of white smoke straight up. Lorena disappeared again.

"Bernie, hush," Sarah said. The dog quieted, but stayed pressed to her side.

Lorena was trying to make Sarah connect the dots—from the altar to the door to where? Grabbing for support, Sarah stumbled through the dark hacienda, looking for fire, intruders, Ortega. But nothing seemed amiss.

"What? Tell me?" Then she remembered the trail of water in the ghost's wake. "Water."

The hot springs.

She returned to the lobby. At the front door, she looked out through the darkness toward the parked cars. Lightning flared again, closer now; thunder growled in its wake.

"Shit."

Lorena McCragg's ghost, or part of it, seemed to sit in the Toyota.

Sarah didn't bother to change out of her nightgown, but she did grab the shotgun. The car cranked and without headlights, she and Bernie headed down the gravel road toward the springs. She stopped at the base of the hill and got out.

Nobody, not even Ortega, argues with a loaded shotgun.

Sarah walked quietly on the road and then took the path that wound around the back of the hill to the springs. When the incline became too steep, she crawled, nudging the gun ahead of her, tearing her nightgown in the rough and the cholla. She froze. Voices.

"No, no, pendejo, póngale aquí," a man's voice said.

"No, aquí esta más seguro," another answered.

"Más fácil, no más seguro."

What was better here rather than there, she wondered? What were two men doing in her cave in the middle of the night?

She was close enough to hear them moving about. One threw something to the other that skidded in the dirt.

"You're trespassing," she shouted. "Leave now or I'll shoot." She pulled the gun up to her shoulder; her index finger found the trigger.

The two men walked toward her, and even in the dark she could read their cocky gaits.

"Sí, Señora," we were just leaving."

"Just having a little bath," the other said in a sing-song, mocking tone. "For rheumatism."

They spoke in Spanish; *bruja,* witch was one of the words she understood.

Then she saw the dynamite. One held fistfuls of dull red sticks; the other cradled a reel of fuse. A shotgun blast would send them all up in little pieces.

"If you blow up the spring, it'll be dead for a thousand years," Sarah pleaded. "The town can prosper from these waters. We're building a spa. There'll be jobs. Don't you see?"

A wind came up and she could sense the men's nervousness on the breeze.

She fingered the shotgun. "He's using you. Ortega. He lost and he wants to ruin it for everyone. Not just me. The hot springs are Angustia's only asset, only chance."

Before their indecision could ripen, Ortega's unmistakable, overly-polite, *"Buenas noches, Señora,"* sounded behind her. She heard the solid click of a gun cocking. *"Andele,"* he said to the two men, who turned and disappeared into the darkness.

Bernie growled softly.

"I am sorry, but it is your fault entirely," Ortega said. "You would not give up." He tsked once. "Giving this land and its water to stinking Indians. It's mine. Put the gun down, *por favor.*"

She lowered the muzzle, her finger still on the trigger, and turned to face him.

"How did you know about the water?" she asked.

"My great-uncle's wife gave me a map." He laughed. "She was half Jicarilla. She had been protecting the secret of the springs since she was a girl, but she didn't want to die with it. She told me to give the map to the Indians."

"And you just kept it until now?" Sarah asked.

"I know the value of water. Telling anyone would only mean I'd have to share it."

Sarah gripped the shotgun.

"Set the gun on the ground and move away," Ortega sounded serene, like a funeral director instructing mourners.

Her anxiety welled but then transformed into a furious calm. If she gave up the gun, he'd blow up the springs and her with it. She could join Lorena McCragg's frustrating haunting. If the game was over, why not play out the hand?

"You bastard. You won't get away with this," she said, digging a firm stance on the rocky hillside. The storm, close now, drove a cord of electricity across the sky, backlighting Ortega.

"You've got nothing on me," he said. "You're a desperate woman."

"People will testify now who were too scared before. Lukey's wife," Sarah said. Even as she talked, she felt he was right. He'd beat the drug charge somehow. He'd never go away. But then neither would she. Was it possible she was the stronger?

"Put the gun down, *Señora*," False politeness left his voice.

A voice echoed from the cave, one of the men. As Ortega turned toward it, Sarah raised the shotgun and fired. She lurched backward but regained her balance.

An earsplitting noise cut past her. Ortega's bullet hit the rock next to her and ricocheted. Her left thigh stung. She fell backward over the rise, tumbling over rocks and cactus, landing hard against a boulder.

When she looked up, Ortega stood over her. Blood soaked his thigh. In his right hand he held a gun; in his left he held her right leg.

She squirmed to sit up. Bernie was nowhere.

"You won't get far, *Señora*, I don't think," he said. He tossed the prosthesis into the air and fired. It fell with a thud beside her, the artificial foot shredded.

"Go ahead, shoot me. You son of a bitch."

He ignored her. "Do you know what this is?" He held something metal in front of her face. "A blasting cap. I don't have to waste a bullet on you." He looked at his men.

"Fernando, *lista?*

"Ready," he answered.

The first drops of rain spattered, kicking the sand.

"All of this is going to blow sky high and you along with it. My men believe you're a witch. Well, *Señora Bruja,* this will be the ride of your life." He laughed. "The last one. Up and up over your precious hacienda."

Blood saturated half her nightgown. She could hardly breathe from the pain, but she forced out the words, "You're a coward, Ortega."

Ortega stepped close and kicked her twice in the ribs.

"The coyotes won't find enough of you for a meal," he said slowly, biting his words.

Gasping, she tried to crawl away, pulling herself over the rocks, and then pausing to suck in air. She heard him laugh at her and then she heard a humming. Looking up, she saw Ortega against a glow on the horizon.

I'm hallucinating and dying.

The sound grew louder. Ortega heard it too.

Simultaneously, they saw it. Still miles away on the main road out of Angustia, a convoy of cars and trucks moved toward them. It approached like a mirage posse, coming to help, but coming too late.

Ortega shouted commands and snatched the end of the fuse, violently trying to couple it to the blasting cap.

Lightning zapped the sky.

Sarah watched wild-eyed. She had to do something. If she could slow him down, he'd have to run. People were coming.

Her hand closed over the half-shattered prosthesis; splinters of plastic dug into her palm. When Ortega stepped in range, she swung the leg at his wounded thigh. He screamed, turning toward her, but lost his footing and toppled. As in slow motion, she saw him fall, his hand reach out and then a blast shook the desert.

She heard Ortega's men scampering away, simultaneously blaspheming and praying to the Holy Mother for protection from the witch as the storm bore down.

What had happened? Something exploded, but not the dynamite. What?

The wind howled, pouring sand into her eyes.

Mysteriously alone now, Sarah's attention returned to her injuries. Holding her sides and sipping tiny breaths, she wondered if her ribs had perforated her lungs. Huge rain drops pelted her, but she hardly felt them. Then there were voices. Sounds of Pam, Ali, and Kenny drifted up the hill toward her. When she tried to move, her leg felt as though it had been shoved into a wood chipper.

My God, I'm going to lose my other leg.

The nightmare wheelchair rolled into her head. Dying might be better.

She felt something wet on her cheek and then she felt the fur. Bernie. Sharp barks followed. In the blur over the nearest rise she saw the cars again, thirty or more, coming fast, a stampede riding on a cloud. Horns honked. Every car in Angustia was coming to her rescue.

How had they known?

As Sarah felt herself slipping into a fog, the pinion trees turned into dark magnolias. Wisteria with blooms like fat clusters of grapes perfumed the moist summer night. Moon flowers, camellias, and gardenias popped open like tiny umbrellas. Then the new moon rocked over and a perfect rattlesnake coiled around it. The Virgin of Guadalupe stepped onto the shiny crescent. She had only one leg and a bar code stamped on the bottom of her sandal. She smiled at Sarah.

37

ARAH LAY IN ST. Vincent's Hospital in Santa Fe. Her broken ribs hurt the most, but infection from the rock shrapnel in her leg worried the doctors the most. In and out of consciousness for days, she was aware that the people around her thought she was dying. She perceived time through Pam and Ali's alternating vigils.

"Jami Ortega's dead," Ali told her. "The blasting cap exploded in his face." She sat bedside, leaning close to Sarah.

Ali said the authorities said the cap had been an old, non-electrical fuse cap. They had found a tin of them in the cave. It may have been defective and maybe lightning was a factor. Sarah wondered if Lorena McCragg had ignited it.

Sarah struggled to speak. She felt like Lady Usher, trapped in a tomb, unable to reach anybody.

"You won't believe Pam and Kenny." Ali sounded urgently over-cheerful like a door-to-door vacuum cleaner salesperson. Sarah didn't understand what Ali said about Pam and Kenny.

When Pam's shift came up, Sarah heard that it looked like Ali would be able to adopt Gabriel.

"Wanda Begay helped her through state social services," Pam said. "Ali's his foster mother now."

Pam lifted the light blanket to check the drainage tube in Sarah's leg.

Sarah thought she remembered Ali saying that it had been Gabriel who had followed Sarah to the springs and then, seeing Ortega, had run back for help.

Like Ali, Pam's anxiousness was overlaid with cheer, and also like Ali, she ended her visit in tears, begging Sarah to awake and come back to them.

Images melded in Sarah's head, confusing her. When she could understand the voices again, Ali was by her side.

"After the ambulance took you away, it was so crazy," Ali said. "Ortega's entire face was blown away. The whole damn town was out there, dynamite everywhere, pouring rain." And as though reading Sarah's mind, Ali said, "I took Bernie to the vet—just a gash—he's going to be fine."

Sarah faded out, and when consciousness returned Pam was in the middle of a story.

"I had decided I was going to go to sleep in my studio and not wake up. Ever. Suddenly we'd won the hacienda, and I had to face up to Kenny. I panicked."

Sarah tried to move her fingers, to move anything. She felt like a carved marble image on a tomb. Had Pam succeeded in killing herself and was Sarah now with her in some afterlife waiting room?

"But then I decided I could kill myself just as easily by doing what I feared would kill me," Pam's voice came back. "I could risk trusting. I could fall in love and let the fall kill me."

Sarah could feel Pam's quiet sobs. The two of them weren't dead after all. Sarah wondered if Lorena McCragg had told Pam that suicide might not be deliverance at all. Pam could end up replacing Lorena as the hotel ghost. The next voice she heard was Ali's.

"Kenny's trying to buy Ortega's land, the acres next to us."

"If his house in Texas sells," Pam said.

They were both at her side.

"Please come back to us," Pam said.

"Sarah, you can open a restaurant," Ali said. "We'll be there for you. Please wake up."

"Open the whole damn hotel if you want," Pam said.

Sarah detected panic in their voices. Had the doctor told them she was dying? How long had it been? It felt like a few days. But her ribs didn't hurt quite so much. Could ribs heal in only a few days?

✦ ✳ ✦

SARAH WAS LYING QUIETLY in the dim hospital room when she became aware that Wanda Begay stood beside her. Someone else stood beside Wanda.

"Sarah, Clara Bitsui is with me," Wanda said. "The people in Angustia think Jami Ortega's ghost is holding you on account of you killing him, and he's trying to suck you over to his side."

An unidentifiable darkness like a gritty fog had hung in a corner of her room. Sarah had thought the drugs produced it.

That bastard doesn't give up.

"Clara wants to sing and give you a protection," Wanda said.

Clara Bitsui chanted quietly over Sarah for what seemed to Sarah a long time. Sarah felt like she was floating peacefully through a film of the last four months of her life.

A naked Randall Crane asked her to dance, but she smiled and told him to put on his clothes. The *Penitentes* invited her to join them, but Father Gallegos told them to leave and asked Sarah to help him say Mass. Chef LeMoyne, wearing a red Coco Channel suit, handed her a bag of groceries and ran to catch a train that was already pulling out of the station. Children danced the flamenco as Manny Sanchez, Jesús Dominguez, and

Michael La Guardia sang and clapped. Bernie dog-paddled by, steam rising off his fur, and *Señora* Cantu pushed a wheelchair down a staircase. Jami Ortega sat in the chair.

Hours later, Sarah opened her eyes and pressed the call button. When the surprised nurse on duty arrived, Sarah asked if there might be a little pate or crostini in the house.

-+- ❋ -+-

SIX WEEKS LATER, WHEN Sarah was nearly healed, Father Gallegos said Mass in the hacienda chapel. A huge crowd spilled out into the lobby and the courtyard. After the biggest potluck Angustia had ever seen, the priest dedicated the hot springs, naming it *Aguas de las Esperanzas,* waters of hope. Sarah announced that it was their wish that after their deaths, the hacienda and the waters return to the Apaches. The arrangements with the BIA were almost complete.

That night, after the last guest had gone home, Pam, Ali and Sarah drove out to the springs. Bernie sat on the back seat with Sarah. He stayed by her side as Pam helped Sarah out of the car and over to the pool. Ali lighted a small fire.

The harvest moon's golden film glazed the rocks and played with the bonfire light.

"How come we never did a ritual before?" Ali asked.

"I remember we were going to cast a spell to freeze your ex-husband's balls," Sarah said.

"And I remember we were going to dance under the stars like wild women," Pam said.

Ali laughed. "Wardo needs his balls. They're all he's got."

They slipped out of their clothes and into the hot pool.

"Is it time for the ritual yet?" Sarah asked.

"Don't ask me," Ali said. "I'm the dance company director, not the ritual director."

"Would you two shut up?" Pam said.

"Have we started?" Sarah asked.

"Shhhhh. First we have to soak and meditate. Purification," Pam said. An hour later they sat naked beside the fire ready for the next phase of the ritual, the release. Pam explained what they had to do. A tape of Carlos Naki's Indian flute and drums wound among them.

"I'll go first," Ali said. She pulled her wedding photograph from her bag. "I'm releasing Eduardo and forgiving him." She gently laid the picture on the flames. "He was a lesson on the path to where I am now." The photograph bubbled and melted in on itself.

Pam had difficulty talking because she was crying. "I forgive my mother and father for—" Her words unintelligible, she set afire a snapshot of her parents. When she regained control she said, "I release this burden of guilt." As she rambled on about her brother, the photo turned to ash and gently broke apart. "I'm grateful to be alive and to have two such friends as you."

While Sarah didn't have photos to burn, she did have things to release. She tossed dried rosemary for remembrance into the flames. "I forgive myself for being weak." Next she laid on the fire a bundle of sage for her new home and one of mint for her old one. "I forgive myself for being afraid. I ask you, my family, to forgive me for all my trespasses." Then into the fire she gently threw the dry, molted skin of a rattlesnake.

Sarah imagined that someday they might repeat the ritual and forgive Jami Ortega. Someday.

The music lulled them into a trance as they watched what had been released rising up with the smoke into the glassy night.

"I brought something for Lorena," Pam said. "She needs to be released now." Pam stood by the fire and wrapped a long white shawl around her naked body. "Lorena McCragg, justice has been done. These waters will flow to the Indians you tried to protect. We're the protectors now, and we won't let you down. Thank you. Bless you." Pam held the white fabric over the dying fire, releasing it as the flames approached her fingers.

The sound of the fire's crackle blended with the coyote's barks in the distance. Bernie lifted his chin.

After a minute, Sarah said, "That was nice, Pam. All of this was very nice. I thought it'd be sappy, and I was going to feel really silly." After another minute, she said, "When we reopen the hacienda after Christmas, I think we should name something after Lorena McCragg. I don't think we're going to see her anymore."

"Like what, your restaurant?" asked Pam.

"Widow McCragg's Café," Ali suggested.

"Maybe," Sarah said.

"What about Chef LeMoyne, the terrifying teacher?" Pam asked.

"Terrifying, but terrific, too," Ali said.

"I don't think she's going to be around anymore either," Sarah said.

Ali reached for her guitar as the Indian flute finished. Her fingers played the rich melodies of the Southwest, hymns, Mexican songs and their favorite pop tunes of the sixties. Passing a very good bottle of Cote du Rhone, their second, they sang together *Vaya con Dios*, Go with God. Ali, who had chosen the song of letting go, sang the verses that started with a story about a sleeping hacienda. Sarah and Pam joined her on the chorus, *"Vaya con Dios..."*

THE END

ABOUT THE
Author

DINAH LEAVITT SWAN, A native of the Gulf Coast of Mississippi, is the author of *Cana Rising* and *Now Playing in Cana*, the first two books in the Mary Alice Tate Southern Mystery Series.

She's also written eighteen plays—all produced, five national award winners—and the women's lit novels, Romantic Fever and Hacienda Blues. She lives in Colorado with her husband and dog.

You can write Dinah at dswanstory@yahoo.com .

PHOTOGRAPHY BY JUDITH REYNOLDS

If you enjoyed this book, please consider letting others know about it by leaving a review at your favorite online bookstore, blog, or book discussion site. Readers and reader reviews are the best friends and resources an author can have!

A Sample Chapter from Dinah Swan's novel
ROMANTIC FEVER

CHAPTER 1

INTERSTATE 10 ROLLED OUT before her like the run in her nylon hose: curving and continuous. Ann accelerated, the speed fortifying her for the weekly family meeting ahead.

Red and blue flashing lights yanked her from reverie back to reality. The Lexus' speedometer said seventy something. Her adrenaline raced. Like a dentist's drill, a siren pierced the humid spring air. The Mississippi Highway Patrol.

Ann Chandler had never had a ticket in her life. She pulled over and quietly panicked. The only highway patrol officer she knew was the one she had created for her third novel, Destiny's Highway. The fiery Felina Beauchamp of the Beauchamp's of Boudreaux Parish had seduced her Officer Randy Kockrel. Felina was an excellent shot, had sailed solo around South

America and always did exactly what she wanted. Felina had sex, lots of it, lots of ways. Once she decided she wanted the handsome lawman, he never had a chance.

Dazed, Ann fumbled for her license and registration as beads of perspiration purled along her hairline.

I'll be late for lunch. Stella will kill me.

The officer took his time adjusting his sunglasses. His upper body rigid, he strode toward the Lexus.

What am I going to do? Oh my God.

The uniformed figure loomed, filling the open car window. The distorted reflection of her face swam in his official aviator sunglasses, but when she focused on her captor's face, her jaw slackened. If he had been ten years younger, he would have been the spitting image of her own Randy Kockrel.

What am I going to say?

"Good morning, Ma'am. May I see your license, registration and proof of insurance?" he asked. His voice was Nazi crisp, barely even Southern.

What would Felina Beauchamp say?

Tears eased down Ann's cheeks as she wordlessly handed him the rectangular scraps of paper.

"Do you realize you were speeding?" he asked.

"Was I?"

She let her head fall back on the headrest and tried to look brave in the face of doom. Touching her throat and sighing, her right hand slid to her bosom. The top button popped loose.

"Are you okay, Ma'am?" he asked.

"Yes. No," Ann said, fleeing into the world of erotic fiction. She turned her dazzling jewel eyes on him full force: fire opals ringed in cerulean. Ann knew she looked ten years younger than her fifty-five years. "I wasn't paying very close attention.

I'm so sorry." She dabbed her eyes with a scented, lace-edged handkerchief she had found in the glove box when she extracted her auto registration. She thought she remembered the hanky from a research trip over a year ago, but on the spot, couldn't recall why this prop had been necessary.

He hesitated before turning away.

In the side mirror, she watched the tight uniform disappear into the patrol car.

What if Stella finds out?

Felina Beauchamp had found it enjoyable getting out of a ticket. She had flirted with Officer Kockrel, starting with tears, segueing into sliding up her skirt and finishing with an appeal for help.

Ann fluffed her hair and thanked God she didn't need to use hairspray. Felina never would have worn a lacquered helmet. Looking at herself in the visor mirror, Ann rehearsed, first, haughty-pouty-Scarlet-O'Hara expressions, then sultry-seductive-Marilyn-Monroe ones. The fear of a ticket and its discovery by her straight-laced family ebbed, giving way to the kind of excitement a chase generates. She wavered because the officer and the violation were quite real and yet everybody knew pretty women got out of speeding tickets. At least they did in Germaine LaForce novels.

The officer was still in his car.

She tugged on her bra, wedging her breasts up to maximize cleavage. Another button was set free.

I created Felina.

When the patrolman returned from running Ann's plates, he almost caught her rehearsing lines.

A semi whooshed past.

When he gave her back her papers, her fingernails lightly grazed the back of his wrist, just as Felina's had done. He did not miss the gesture.

"I don't know what got into me. I've never had a ticket in my life," said Ann, positioning her hands on her thighs and then inching up her skirt—a move Felina would have approved of.

"You were nine over the limit," he said. No smile.

Is he still going to give me a ticket? Ann searched her memory. Felina had been several books ago. What else had the willful temptress done?

Ann twisted in her seat to face the officer, the neckline of her dress gaping to reveal the rounded tops of her breasts. She inhaled deeply, her chest heaving.

The officer took off his glasses. His eyes rhythmically darted: chest, legs, chest, legs, chest, legs.

"I'm going to give you a warning today, Ms. Chandler. You slow down now, you hear?" he said, stroking the chrome trim around the window.

"Thank you, officer. I will. I promise," she said.

He ducked his head and touched his belt, but didn't move away. She was free. She and Felina had done it. Elated, Ann was about to crank the engine when she felt Felina look at her accusingly from the rearview mirror with an expression that said, *"That's it? That's all you're going to do?"*

Again Ann felt the ancient dual pulls of good—evil, passive; active and dry—juicy. She couldn't vacillate for long because the Randy Kockrel look-alike was turning away.

"You know, you look awfully familiar to me. Have we ever met?" asked Ann. She ratcheted up her Southern accent. Words like "me" and "met" now had two syllables each.

He was back like a shot.

"I don't think so. I just transferred down from Jackson last month."

Ann arched her back slightly and tipped her chin up. She had to get him to do something for her. Anything.

"Officer, do you know which exit I use to get to downtown New Orleans?"

He flew across the asphalt to his prowler for a Louisiana map.

"Here it is," he said holding the map and leaning inside her car. "Go right, then under the freeway, then right again at the first light." Together they traced the route, her finger chasing his.

He smelled of Obsession aftershave braided with perspiration. Ann fluttered her lashes and looked helpless as though he had asked her to navigate the Magellan Straits in a leaky frigate.

He looked at her. He looked at his watch.

Is he going to offer to escort me to New Orleans?

The novelist and researcher in Ann said, *"Don't stop now,"* but the mother, grandmother, and figurehead of *Family Practice* Magazine said, *"Stop while you're ahead."*

Felina had taken her Officer Kockrel to bed and had sex with him in every way Ann could think of. Unable to wait for the bed, they had done it standing in the foyer, Felina hanging onto a heavy brass sconce, her tawny thighs wrapped around the handsome lawman.

"I'd better go if I'm going to be in New Orleans by noon," she said.

"Noon?" he said, mesmerized.

"That's why I was driving so fast. I have an audition at the Royal Orleans," she said. She wasn't sure if the pricey French Quarter hotel had a nightclub, but she bet that the officer newly down from Jackson didn't know either.

"You're a singer?" he asked.

"Yes. Are you a music lover?"

"Yes, I am."

Ann turned the key in the ignition, but the officer didn't move. He struggled, words nearly forming an invitation. One heavy second more and he had waited too long.

"Uh, well. Don't be late to that audition. You hurry on now, ya hear? But no speeding," he said.

"You are a savior. Thank you so much," Ann said. She held him in her gaze while the tinted window crawled up. As in a silent movie, she saw him mouth, "Good luck."

If you were Randy Kockrel, you'd be following me.

Exhilarated, Ann drove to her daughter Stella's house. The encounter with the officer had lifted her spirits, readying her for the Sunday family business brunch. No matter how dour they might be, for the time being, she felt sexy and attractive. She felt like Felina.

She forgot about the writing problems with *Longhorns and Lingerie* that she needed to finish. She needed the money. Singing along with The Beatles on the radio, she wished she did have an audition at a New Orleans nightspot.

As she approached the house that looked like Tara with a fresh coat of Sherwin Williams' best, Ann noticed a new black Lincoln in the port cochere. Stella had not said anyone but the family was coming for the weekly council. No sooner had she cut the engine than Bradley Ramsey jigged down the steps off the veranda to open her car door.

"Hello, Annie. Church out a little late today?" Bradley boomed, probably the most imaginative remark he would make all day. Only Bradley called her Annie.

Why was he here? Business with Marcus, Stella's husband?

"Why Bradley Ramsey, what a genuine pleasure to see you. You have been such a stranger," said Ann, sounding like the beautiful-but-insincere Lettie in Ann's seventh novel, *The Colonel's Stepdaughter*. Her reply also avoided his question about being late. She toyed with the notion of saying, *"no, I was pulled over by a hunky highway patrolman I nearly seduced."*

Bradley steered her on to the huge screened porch with its bowling alley polished floor. Rum punch, gin fizzes, and Ann's family waited.

"Mama has not been well, Annie. But I am glad to hear I was missed," he said, beaming.

Except for the thinning brown hair, Bradley looked a lot like he had in the tenth grade. Hundreds of freckles shifted around white blocky teeth that flashed and disappeared in smiles that came and went without reason. Bradley was fifty-six and had taken care of his ancient mother who had been poorly since his father died some thirty years ago. Even if he was an unmarried mama's boy, Bradley was decent and kind, and Ann hated herself for deviling him.

"Mother, so glad to see you," said Marcus, placing a drink in Ann's hand.

Ann, pretending not to see the chair Bradley was edging toward her, reclined on the pink floral chintz chaise. The overhead fan whirred, conversation resumed, and Ann crossed her ankles and let the sweet gin drink slide down her throat.

I wish Marcus wouldn't call me Mother, Ann thought. That wish was the only genuine thought she allowed herself. Here on the veranda she played the character that she played whenever she was with her family: maternal, agreeable, and pliable. With Bradley in attendance, she added a gauze of Southern coquetry.

Ann observed Stella's eyes clicking like a Nikon with a motor drive. Mother in a designer dress, neck open, knees almost showing, Mother holding Bradley Ramsey's arm, Mother picking up a second gin fizz.

"Marcus swears this is the original St. Charles Hotel recipe for Ramos Gin Fizzes, but I don't believe it," said Ann, her voice a tad shy of a slur. She swirled the icy drink.

Marcus, who had the unfortunate habit of taking everything seriously, began a long-winded defense. "I said the Fountainblue. Last week you said it was the Monteleon."

Foot by foot, Bradley scooted his chair closer and closer to Ann's chaise.

"Say that again, Annie. I couldn't hear you." Scoot. He was like the relentless kudzu vine, resolute and impossible to deter. Bradley was not hard of hearing, but he was a poor actor.

Before things could get worse, Stella announced that brunch was served in the dining room. But when Ann ducked into the powder room, Stella followed, closing the door and leaning back on it.

"Mama, are you feeling all right?" Stella sounded like the head nurse on a psychiatric ward.

Ann was accustomed to Stella's tone, but dismayed by her proximity in the bathroom. The fact that prim Stella was in a bathroom with anybody signaled to Ann the something was afoot.

"Why is Bradley Ramsey dining with us?" Ann asked as she pulled down her pantyhose. "You think anybody would mind if I just took these off?" said Ann stretching the elastic waistband. "I snagged them in church on my diamond and have a run wide as a dime."

"I'll be back in a second with a new pair. You just, just sit." Stella scuttled away.

Ann peeled off the injured hose and tried to remember the last time she had worn a garter belt and nylon stockings and what they had felt like. Garter belts seemed to be popular again; satiny and sexy. They bore little resemblance to the ones Ann had worn as a teen. She often used the Victoria's Secret Catalog to inspire a boudoir costume for a heroine or her rival. Ann found it hard not to plagiarize the descriptive texts that all but promised orgasm with proper use.

Stella returned moments later with the correct shade of size mediums, Control Top.

"Brad's mother went into a nursing home, and they don't expect her to last the summer," Stella said as Ann pumped the new hose over her hips.

Maybe Diane could be wearing pantyhose instead of Wranglers. Or better nylons with a garter belt and some tiny thong panties. Ann had struggled for days over a chapter in *Longhorns and Lingerie* in which Diane and a handsome cowboy named Larry were supposed to be getting it on. Larry had managed to remove Diane's jeans, but the scene still wasn't working.

"She's in Sunshine Gardens," said Stella with an expression that said what everybody knew: The Gardens was the end of the line. The quiver in Stella's voice said that Bradley's mama's end might be their beginning.

"It was nice of you and Marcus to invite him," said Ann avoiding her daughter's intimation that Bradley might soon be an heir. The pantyhose felt like a wetsuit, and Ann gained new insight into the control of Control Tops. She knew better than to complain.

Stella flicked her nail in and out of successive grooves of the heavy frame of the vanity mirror. Each stroke harvested tiny particles of dust.

"He's a very nice man, Mama. Well-off now and when his Mama goes, Marcus says Bradley may be the richest man on the Gulf Coast except for Mr. Formby, old man Pearlman, and one or two others."

Ann had drunk two gin fizzes and only eaten a Pop Tart for breakfast, but she was on to Stella.

"He may not have a lot of chemistry, but he has charm, don't you think? And he's a real Southern gentleman," pushed Stella.

"Good heavens, Stella. Are you trying to fix me up with Sadly-Bradley?" Ann rinsed her hands and patted them on the petite-point towel that she rated high for style but low for absorbency.

"It wouldn't hurt you to have a date," said Stella. She wiped down the hand painted Italian porcelain basin with a Clorox Wipe.

"Your father was the last man I will love. Your meddling has probably injured my friendship with Bradley. Damn it, Stella, I went to high school with him. You have put me in the position of rejecting him."

"Then don't. Give him a chance. Mama, it's been years since Daddy died."

Ann knew exactly how long it had been since Harry had been killed. The thought of sleeping with Bradley Ramsey made her want to wash her hands again. She brushed past Stella into the large, over-decorated guest bedroom with its huge tester bed.

```
     Larry   pushed  Diane   back   onto   the
 enormous  tester  bed.  Grabbing  her  jeans,
 he  expertly  snatched  them  off  in  one
 swift  movement.  Her  legs  were—
```

"Daddy would want you to go on with your life," said Stella.

Ann smiled and, for the second time that morning, wondered how Stella could be her flesh and blood. Was she imagining it or was Stella more pushy than usual? If so, what did she want? Ann couldn't imagine, and though it seemed to include a new husband for her, she was sure that wasn't Stella's only objective.

"You think my life hasn't gone on?"

"You know what I mean," answered Stella.

"Life can't really go on until you have a man?" asked Ann.

"That's not what I said or meant." Stella still held the used Clorox Wipe, hesitating to toss it in the clean carved wood trashcan.

Ann clicked through her memory reviewing her inability to communicate with Stella. Things fell apart before Stella married Marcus and even before Stella's professional years with an Atlanta advertising firm. Mother and daughter had not communicated well while Stella was at SMU. Maybe they never had. Since Harry's death, however, every issue was contentious as though Stella held some pent-up rage she could neither express nor quell.

"Where are my grandchildren?" Ann asked, changing the subject.

"Late. They went to First Presbyterian with Flossie's boys. I forgot that first Pres is Evangelical. They can go on forever."

"I brought something for them," Ann said. Ann wanted to tease Stella, reminding her that the family business, *Family Practice* Magazine, was popular with Evangelicals and that disparaging remarks were in conflict with her bread and butter. The gentle jibe would become a fight, Ann knew.

"Think about it, Mama."

Ann opened the bedroom door and inhaled the rich odors of the brunch that waited, a cholesterol nightmare of bacon, eggs, sausage, pancakes, cheese grits, and biscuits slathered with butter. Bending her knees as though she were warming up for ballet class, she stretched in the unyielding pantyhose and continued on like an impaired heron. "Are you sure these hose are mediums?" she asked.

END OF *ROMANTIC FEVER* SAMPLE

You can find more of Dinah Swan's books at any major online bookseller.

Made in the USA
Charleston, SC
07 October 2013